ALSO BY

SANTIAGO GAMBOA

Return to the Dark Valley
Night Prayers
Necropolis

THE NIGHT
WILL BE LONG

Santiago Gamboa

THE NIGHT WILL BE LONG

*Translated from the Spanish
by Andrea Rosenberg*

Europa
editions

Europa Editions
1 Penn Plaza, Suite 6282
New York, N.Y. 10019
www.europaeditions.com
info@europaeditions.com

Translation by Andrea Rosenberg
Original title: *Será larga la noche*
Translation copyright © 2021 by Europa Editions

Library of Congress Cataloging in Publication Data is available
ISBN 978-1-60945-711-2

Gamboa, Santiago
The Night Will Be Long

Book design by Emanuele Ragnisco
www.mekkanografici.com

Cover illlustration by Ginevra Rapisardi

Prepress by Grafica Punto Print – Rome

Printed in Italy

CONTENTS

Provoni raged and roamed the outskirts of the galaxy, searching, in his wrath, for something vague, something even metaphysical. An answer, to so speak. A response. Thors Provoni yelled into the emptiness, dinning out his noise in hope of a response.
—PHILIP K. DICK, Our Friends from *Frolix*

Close the door tight, brother;
the night will be long.
—JOSÉ ÁNGEL VALENTE, *Punto cero*

THE NIGHT
WILL BE LONG

PART I

THE BEGINNING

According to the boy's account, at around six in the evening three SUVs came around the curve and into the hollow to cross the Ullucos River. The bodyguards were riding in the first and third vehicles, two Land Rover Discoverys, both silvery gray, or at least that's what it looked like with the last rays of sunlight smacking him right in the eyes. The one in the middle, the biggest one, was an unmistakable black Hummer with level-six armor—a fact that would be established later—and windows tinted so dark that it seemed impossible for anyone inside to actually see out. The attackers were waiting in three different spots, arranged in a triangle. They'd planned to dynamite the little bridge, but something changed and they decided against it. Instead, they blocked the convoy's path by laying the desiccated trunk of an old eucalyptus across the road, which proved effective, since when the SUVs found themselves in the middle of the hail of bullets, they were unable to retreat.

The drivers had good military training. When the first shots rang out and they realized they weren't going to be able to escape around the next curve, they spread out in a V shape, protecting the Hummer and illuminating the area with their headlights, which worked for a while, since the tracer bullets just hit the chassis, shattered the lights, and pierced the tires. Even hemmed in, the men organized to repel the attack. Their first move was to get out of the vehicles and figure out where the enemy was located, but they soon realized they were surrounded. The heaviest fire seemed to be coming from the road itself, as if a nest of machine gunners were lurking a few meters ahead.

And the worst was still to come.

The boy watched two attackers pass close by the tree (a mango) he was perched in and felt a mix of fear and vertigo. They climbed up from the stream bank and positioned themselves on the rise, less than a hundred meters from the armored Hummer. They had a bazooka. They lay down in the grass, gesticulated, and moved their arms, as if they were using complicated calculations to work out the shot, but without making a sound. At last they decided. One of them got on his knees and rested the barrel on his shoulder. The other one, behind him, calculated the trajectory, paused a few seconds that the boy thought would never end, and fired. The Hummer flew backward, wiping out one of the men. It crashed back to earth and burst into flames. The artillerymen had time to calmly reload the bazooka and retake their position. The second shot blew up the righthand Landrover, proving its armor to be inferior. A second bodyguard was crushed, and flames took over part of his body.

The gunfire intensified.

From where the boy was hiding, the air was a fabric woven of sparks and flashes.

One bullet sailed through the night and entered the base of the skull of another of the men, possibly the youngest and most aggressive, who had grabbed a fire extinguisher. It was later learned that his name was Enciso Yepes. He was of average height with a powerful build, and he had close-cropped hair with a longer patch on top like a soccer player. On the left side of his chest was a tattoo that said, "God is my buddy, my homie, my key," and on his right arm was one that said, "Estéphanny is Love and she is God and I♡Her." The bullet pierced his brain and, from within, shattered the frontal bone at the level of his right eye. After killing him, it reemerged into the open air, which was saturated with smoke and gunfire, grazed a mudflap, and, changing trajectory, plunged into the trunk of a cedar tree fifty meters from the road.

If he had survived, Enciso Yepes would have been an invalid and unable to talk. He was thirty-five years old and had three young children with two different women. His bank account contained 1,087,000 pesos, but he had debts totaling 7,923,460. Life had not been stingy with him, but it was tremendously lopsided, since at the same moment that his soul was heading toward (we assume) purgatory, his beloved second wife, Estéphanny Gómez, thirty-one years old, born in the village of Dosquebradas, Risaralda, was sprawled naked on a heart-shaped bed at the Panorama Motel in Pereira, in the position known as doggy-style, with her hips hoisted up in a pyramid and her face buried in a flowery pillowcase, suffocating in rapturous grunts of pleasure. It would soon be discovered that Estéphanny was the shouty type, and among the things the people in the room next door heard that afternoon, the most memorable were phrases of the sort "Pound me, honey, whip me good!" or "Harder, Papi, give it to me!" or "It's so good to fuck stoned, baby." All of this in the company of a man who, to the best of my knowledge, was her brother-in-law, Anselmo Yepes.

Far from there, by the Ullucos River, the fighting grew even fiercer, and the men, sweaty and firelit, no longer looked like heroes. But they were holding out. From that keep of fuel and twisted metal, an intrepid group was still defending, and it appeared they had a lot of ammunition. They were well trained. They barely needed to look at each other to implement a strategy. The Hummer was on its side, but as the flames abated it was clear that the chassis remained intact. It was impossible to imagine that the occupants were alive, given the impact and the heat.

But alive they were.

A helicopter's sudden arrival caught everyone off guard. It was a Hurricane 9.2, but that was learned afterward. From the air, via radar, the aircraft identified the origin points of the attack and destroyed them with its .52 caliber machine guns. The attackers, who'd been on the verge of victory, were stunned, unable to process what was happening. Then all hell broke loose. The guys with the bazooka raced toward the slope, heading down to the riverbank, but then realized that they could attack the helicopter and maybe bring it down. Those seconds of indecision were fatal. The one carrying the bazooka hoisted it to his shoulder and kneeled down, but as the helicopter's spotlight swept toward him, he leaped to one side and almost ended up shooting in the opposite direction. Then the machine guns took the men down from above. First one, then two. The crisscrossing bullets, like in the third secret of Fátima, came out of the darkest night. One man dove into the water and hit his head on a rock. The machine guns must have found all the nests of attackers, because the gunfire suddenly ceased. Any survivors managed to flee; everything happened really fast.

Then the helicopter alighted next to the SUVs. The doors of the battered Hummer opened and the boy, from the tree, saw a man dressed all in black climb out along with two young women, one of them wearing just a swimsuit and inadequately covered with a towel. The three boarded the helicopter, which immediately lifted back into the air and disappeared into the night.

Then the bodyguards loaded the bodies into the ruined vehicles, collected the weapons, and headed toward San Andrés de Pisimbalá. A little while later a second group arrived in two huge utility trucks. They cleared away the eucalyptus trunk and meticulously gathered up the remnants of the battle until there was no sign remaining on the hillsides or roadway.

The boy waited another hour. He climbed down from the tree and walked along the shoulder, searching the ground, but they'd taken everything, from the ruined SUV chassis to every last shotgun cartridge. He didn't find a single spent casing.

THE PROTAGONISTS

The person who told me this story is an old friend. Her name is Julieta Lezama, a seasoned freelance reporter who sells her stories to press outlets in Spain, the United States, and Latin America. She's young—on the brink of forty—and has two sons plus a divorce from another journalist whose beat is politics and finance, topics far removed from the things that make Julieta's soul thrum. What interests her is harsh reality, public order, crime, and the blood that flows out of bodies and gives a tragic hue to the contours of this beautiful country, whether it's splashed on asphalt or grass or plush pillows in affluent homes.

What Julieta is passionate about is the violent death that certain human beings, one fine day, decide to inflict on others for whatever reason: venting old animosities, love, resentment, self-interest, or, of course, money and the endless variations on that theme: commercial benefit, extortion, competition, envy, embezzlement and pilfering, inheritance, identity theft, fraud—how many justifications are there for crime? According to Julieta, they are as varied and inventive as humanity itself. No two people kill the same; there's something uniquely personal in the act that defines us, just like there is in art. And in the moment, it gives us away.

Julieta has a small office in the same building where she lives with her two teenage boys, in the Chapinero Alto district of eastern Bogotá. The only luxury she enjoys (and only for the last eleven months, as her work with the Sunday magazine of

the Mexican newspaper *El Sol* has stabilized) is a full-time secretary and all-around collaborator named Johana Triviño, who
organizes her files and keeps her deadline calendar up to date.
In addition—and this is her favorite part—Johana's in charge of
arranging meetings with people involved in the cases, and
sometimes goes with her, especially when Julieta wants a witness around. Johana has a virtue that's rarely found in female
communication studies graduates: she knows how to use (and
identify) all kinds of weapons, from handguns to less conven-
tional arms, since she spent twelve years as a member of the
FARC's Western Bloc. At first it was a bit of a lark for Julieta:
working with someone who came from a world so different
from her own, from the shadowy Colombia that, incredibly, had
existed apart from the rest of the country for more than fifty
years and now, with the arrival of peace and then the ultraright's
rise to power, was in a very delicate position, on a tightrope.

Johana, protagonist number two in this story (though not
necessarily in hierarchical order), is a Cali native, from a family that moved in the eighties from Cajibío, in Cauca Department, to the Aguablanca district. It's the toughest area of Cali,
that stunning city known as heaven's branch office. There she
grew up among migrants from Tumaco, Cauca, and Buenaventura. Among gangs of criminals, members of the FARC and
ELN, paramilitaries, and drug dealers. Her father was a jeep
driver, informal taxi driver, and finally the personal chauffeur
to a wealthy family, the Arzalluzes, who lived in a fancy house
in the Santa Mónica neighborhood.

The Arzalluzes, as it happened, had a little girl, Costanza,
who'd been born on November 9, 1990, the exact same day
and year as Johana. The family (the Arzalluzes) took this to
heart, and on the shared birthday, they would give Johana suitcases of barely used clothing, shoes, books, and toys that their
daughter no longer wanted. The ritual played out every year:

bright and early that day, Johana's father would take her to Connie's (as Costanza was called) house to visit and accept the gifts. They would share a slice of cake with the servants, have a glass of soda, and that was it. After that Connie would start getting ready for her other birthday party with her cousins, friends from the club, and schoolmates, and Johana would be sent back to Aguablanca. That's how things always went until the year they turned fifteen.

Naturally, the Arzalluz daughter was having a huge bash at Club Colombia that year, and she was so busy getting ready that she couldn't take part in the traditional celebration with Johana. Starting early that morning, Johana's father the chauffeur had to make a million trips between the club and Santa Mónica. The caterers' van wasn't big enough, and since the food had to stay chilled, he was stuck ferrying the trays of appetizers, spring rolls, finger sandwiches, octopus carpaccio, and, most especially, the six pyramids of king shrimp that were to preside over the central tables. Added to that was an endless stream of baskets of dishware, three sizes of wineglasses, water glasses, and cutlery. He had to transport the decorations that the mother wanted brought from home to the club ballroom to enhance the elegant atmosphere, which changed with the hour according to her whims and anxiety levels: a two-seater Chesterfield for the birthday girl's grandparents to sit on; several bronze sculptures of Mercury and young Bacchus, his hair made of clusters of grapes; a Louis XV–style gilt-framed mirror; and an old painting from the English romantic period, a hunting scene that, the family claimed, could be from the Turner school. He helped supervise the lights and sound checks for the band, which started setting up its equipment at four in the afternoon, and to top it all off, he had to make three trips to the airport to pick up relatives flying in from Bogotá and Medellín. He got off of work at eleven that night, dead tired, and was finally able to go home for his daughter's fifteenth birthday party.

In Aguablanca, Johana and her family were celebrating in the church's community hall, with speakers and a good sound system. Her father loved old-school salsa and they were playing compilations of Héctor Lavoe, La Fania, Ismael Rivera, Richie Ray and Bobby Cruz, La Pesada de Cali, musicians who dominated the scene in this city that loved rhythm, the sound of trumpet, bass, and percussion.

Carlos Duván, her older brother, helped hang banners and decorate the room with posters and balloons. Her friends wrote phrases about life, enthusiastic ideas, and "aspirations" for the future. Her father bought twelve boxes of Blanco del Valle aguardiente, Viejo de Caldas rum, and a few bottles of Something Special whisky for the family's nearest and dearest.

And the food!

Balls of unripe plantain stuffed with pork rind, plantain fritters stuffed with cheese, slices of fried plantain with tomato onion salsa and guacamole, three massive pots of sancocho stew, white rice, and several kinds of meat. When the father arrived, people were dancing already, but out of respect for him they played the waltz again so he could take his daughter out on the dance floor, to the applause of friends and family.

The call came after midnight. It was Mrs. Arzalluz; she was so embarrassed to do this, but Connie needed to ask him a favor. What was it? In all the commotion, the girl had left her makeup bag in the car the chauffeur had used to pick up the grandparents from the airport and then driven home. When she'd gone to touch up her makeup for the first dances, she discovered—a tragedy!—that the bag was still in the car the chauffeur had headed home in. Connie had left it there and then forgotten to ask him to take it out with everything else. She wanted to know if it would be too much of an imposition to ask him to bring it to her; her party was going to go on all night and the bag had the makeup a cousin had bought for her in Miami that matched her dress perfectly.

The driver explained that he was at his daughter's party and had already had a few drinks, so it wasn't a good idea for him to drive, but then Connie came on and begged him to bring it to her. What was she going to do without her makeup? She'd need to touch it up during the party! The father had no choice but to agree. He put on his jacket and told Johana he had to go back to Club Colombia, just for a minute. Seeing everybody's disappointment, he added: what can you do, it's work.

Our guess, or really what the police told us, is that as he was pulling up to the club he didn't spot a cyclist coming until he was right on top of the guy, and swerved so violently he skidded over the median and overturned the car into the river. He died of a skull fracture. The Arzalluzes came to the wake, but not the funeral. They gave us big hugs and I realized something: poor people are important only when we die, that's it. Connie didn't come to either the wake or the funeral, since she was hungover from her party. The cunt who killed my father for a fucking bag of makeup, my little rich friend, didn't even come to offer her condolences.

From that day on, I was filled with hate.

I said to myself: We can't leave Colombia in those bastards' hands. This country is perverse, diseased, and it has to change, even if it's by dubious methods. I refuse to just sit down and cry.

The neighborhood had these urban militias roaming around, and paramilitary groups too, and from time to time you'd hear gunfire. I liked the FARC guys; they had a certain mystique and were tough as nails. No soft talk—they knew what was needed. A cousin of mine, Toby, was with them. I talked to him and he gave me pamphlets about the guerrilla groups and their cause. Even a well-thumbed book. How the Steel Was Tempered, *by Nikolai Ostrovsky. It had been so thoroughly and sweatily manhandled that I thought I might get mange from turning its pages. I didn't understand a thing, but I liked it. It convinced me that a person needs to study and understand History, with a capital H. That's what I did, on my own, all throughout my time in the guerrilla. Fight and study. Often the two activities were one and the same. By the time I turned sixteen, Carlos Duván and I had traveled to Toribío. We managed to make contact with the FARC and asked to join. They accepted us. We completed the politics and training courses, and then our military training. After a few months, hearing my comrades' stories, my anger began to dissipate. What had happened to my brother and me was nothing compared to the horrors other people had experienced.*

I remember thinking, this fucking country where I had the bad luck to be born is an execution yard, a torture chamber, a machine for disemboweling peasants, Indians, mestizos, and blacks. Which is to say, the poor. Whereas the rich are gods just because. They inherit fortunes and last names, and they don't give a shit about the country—they look down on it. What's behind those fancy last names? A thieving great-grandfather, a murdering great-great-grandfather. Men who stole land and resources. So I decided: I'm going to fill those fucking bastards with lead—it's the only thing they fear or respect. The only thing they listen to. That way they'll learn.

That's how I started, first helping around the camp and later wielding a gun.

It was through Johana that Julieta met her primary associate, a prosecutor of indigenous descent who worked in the criminal affairs unit, with whom she would exchange information and theories about the cases under investigation, and who, over time, had become her friend.

His name was Edilson Javier Jutsiñamuy, known to his colleagues as Wildcat. His family was from the Nipode Witoto community in Araracuara, Caquetá, and his last name meant, almost prophetically, "insatiable fighter." A man well into his fifties, unhurried and weedy, who had left behind family life and a childless marriage to devote himself entirely to justice. He had sought out Johana early on in the peace process to corroborate certain facts and have someone trustworthy who could provide him with information. They gradually got to know each other and over time developed a cordial friendship that was later expanded to include Julieta, since the prosecutor was interested in her journalistic investigations, and particularly in her ability to access milieus that were off limits to him and uncover useful information. He is the third protagonist.

And there will be more as we go along.

Action!

The story begins in the Office of the Prosecutor General in Bogotá on an ordinary Thursday in July, when prosecutor Edilson Jutsiñamuy received a call from one of his most trusted men, Agent René Nicolás Laiseca, notifying him of an incident that had taken place near Tierradentro, in southern Colombia. Early that morning, somebody had called in to the police station in San Andrés de Pisimbalá to (anonymously) report combat with heavy weaponry that had occurred on a rural road the previous evening and night. Though the area was small and very remote, the possible use of "heavy weaponry" and its implications set off alarm bells, and the information was sent up the chain to the national office in Bogotá.

Jutsiñamuy was used to getting this kind of news all the time, so he was somewhat distracted as he listened to the report. Combat with heavy weaponry? Jesus, what now? "Dissidents" again? Who had they been fighting? Had the army gotten involved? How many were dead? A little later, around eleven, he was informed that agents had spoken to a few people who lived nearby and were conducting their initial investigations. In the afternoon, Laiseca gave him an update based on the information coming in, but some of it was contradictory: "There was a violent skirmish with several vehicles and a helicopter," the anonymous caller had said. "We didn't hear anything unusual. It was the rainstorm—there was thunder," said local residents.

Who was right?

Wary now, the prosecutor kept an impatient eye on the telephone, but there were no more calls. Nor any the next day, nor the day after that, which was Saturday. Agents in Inzá—the region's municipal seat—told Laiseca that it would be best to drop the matter until something more concrete was found. At this strange silence, the prosecutor's doubts grew. What was in that area? A bit of everything. Cauca Department, with its indigenous communities and humid alpine tundra, had been and still was one of the country's primary hotbeds of violence.

The weekend passed without further news, but on Monday there was a development: another call in to the Inzá police station, seemingly from the same anonymous person. And once again the same report: there had been fierce combat with large-caliber weapons and several people killed last Wednesday night. The caller even mentioned a bazooka. A military scenario. Laiseca called the prosecutor to let him know.

"So our informant called back in, huh?" Edilson Jutsiñamuy asked, stroking his chin. "All right, well, what's the caller's voice like? What did they say?"

"According to the secretary who answered the phone, it may have been a man," Laiseca said, "or possibly a woman."

Jutsiñamuy gripped the handset tighter. *All hail Captain Obvious,* he thought.

"Great observation, Laiseca," he said sarcastically. "That'll help us narrow things down. Is there any other sort of living being that would be capable of calling the police?"

There was an uncomfortable silence on the line. After a long while, Laiseca ventured a response. "Of course," he said.

"Oh, wow, you don't say. And what sort would that be?"

"A child, boss," Laiseca said.

That afternoon, Jutsiñamuy decided to follow his wildcat nose. There was something in this, something big. Even if there wasn't much evidence so far. He decided to call Julieta and

Johana to discuss the situation. If they were interested, they could help him figure out what the hell had happened in those chilly mountains and whether it truly required Bogotá's attention, which would help him avoid butting in from afar, since his colleagues in Popayán were sure to accuse him of snatching local cases from them.

He hunted in his pocket for his cell phone and dialed.

"Well, this is a surprise!" Julieta said when she picked up. "How's my favorite prosecutor?"

Through the handset she heard a quiet but protracted giggle that reminded her of Bugs Bunny.

"I've got a bit of a weird situation, Julieta, very delicate," Jutsiñamuy said. "There was a gunfight on a backroad near Tierradentro. It could be something big."

"Soldiers? The ELN? Dissidents? Criminals?"

"Not clear yet," Jutsiñamuy said, "but I think it's a matter to be discussed in person."

They agreed to meet up in their usual spot, and half an hour later they were sitting at a table at the Juan Valdez café on 53rd Street and 7th Avenue. Jutsiñamuy, in keeping with indigenous culture, didn't drink coffee, not even at eleven A.M. He was a tea drinker.

"It was on the road that goes to San Andrés de Pisimbalá," he explained, "a narrow mountain road that crosses the Páez River and then, after a lot of twists and turns, ends up in Tierradentro. Have you heard of the place? Decorated tombs, hypogea—you must have seen them on TV. It's Páez, or Nasa, territory. An anonymous witness says there was gunfire and explosions from a number of cars. Even a helicopter, which is really weird since the army didn't report engaging in any combat that day. But then something happened and everything suddenly went quiet. Some of the locals claimed the noise was thunder and rain."

"How did you hear about it?" Julieta asked.

"The police station in San Andrés de Pisimbalá reported the first anonymous call to the headquarters in Inzá, and since they mentioned 'heavy weaponry,' it got sent to the Office of the Prosecutor General's internal network. One of my men saw the report and called to ask about it, but when the officers went to the scene, they said there was nothing there. As if somebody was trying to cover up what happened."

"Did anybody die?" Johana asked, glancing at her boss for permission to speak.

"Not clear yet because nobody can confirm it," Jutsiñamuy said, "but the caller said several did. It would be weird if nobody went down in a dustup like that. If it's what I'm guessing, it could be serious. And if somebody's trying to cover it up, even worse."

"Tell me what your guess is, Edilson," Julieta prodded him. "It's true sometimes people hear thunder and start concocting conspiracies, but if you're sitting here in Bogotá worrying about a gunfight in a town in Cauca, it's because there's something going on."

"I'm not positive, though, and that's why I want you to poke around before I get involved, shall we say, officially. It could be a good story, right? The people in that area are all from the Nasa community and lived through the war. Combat and local color. Remember, it was FARC territory for decades. Johanita can confirm that for us, right?"

She nodded.

"It's just a matter of finding out what happened," the prosecutor continued, "if in fact anything did happen. But I think it did—I can smell it from here. Something juicy."

The roar of a minibus accelerating on 7th Avenue drowned out his last words. Three drops fell on the terrace awning, announcing rain. A sparrow landed on one of the arms of a streetlight.

"I know you wouldn't have called me otherwise," Julieta said. "And I appreciate it."

Jutsiñamuy scratched his chin and peered up at the storm clouds. A plane lurched out from behind Guadalupe Hill. Which city was it coming from? He took a long, slow sip of tea, aware that Julieta and Johana were waiting for him.

"It's definitely not people from the area," he said. "If it had been locals fighting, there'd be more information."

"We'll have to start by finding the person who made the call," Johana said. "And look for traces of the combat on the road to confirm it took place."

"The one thing we never see is God, and we still believe in him," the prosecutor said. "Everybody else always leaves something behind, even it's just a bit of thread or a hair. And then the police find it."

"Is this story worth the trouble?" Julieta asked.

"I called you because I know you, and I know you like getting in on the ground floor," Jutsiñamuy said. "Let's work together on this."

They got up from the table, and the drizzle intensified a bit.

Before they parted ways, out on the sidewalk on 7th Avenue, Jutsiñamuy said, "One last thing, I almost forgot."

"What?"

"The anonymous caller was a kid."

"A kid?"

"It could have been a Nasa kid—there are a lot of them in the area. We'd have to look. But it's odd. The Nasa are shy and don't put much stock in police authority; they rely on the indigenous warlord instead. Anyway, I wanted to give you that tidbit."

They returned to the office and Julieta checked her date-book. She didn't have any important appointments that week, and the truth was she was low on pieces. It was an intriguing story, and she made the decision without much deliberation.

"We'll head to Tierradentro tomorrow," she told Johana, "to find out what happened. Something interesting might come out of it. Go ahead and set up the trip."

She went home and packed a small suitcase. They'd only be gone a couple of days. Then she took the two boys to her ex-husband Joaquín's apartment, since she didn't dare leave them alone. They were teenagers, and though she couldn't stand seeing Joaquín, she had no choice. She hated his stupid smirk. It made her want to slap him.

"If they're going to go out at night, please tell them not to get a girl pregnant, OK?" she said.

"Don't be paranoid, Juli," Joaquín objected. "You're such a nag about this. There's a sex ed class at their school—or do you think they're animals or something?"

She hated it when he called her that, by the shortened form of her name. She detested everything about him.

"Just talk to them," she said. "For your information, the Anglo has an alarmingly high teen pregnancy rate. Just because they're preppies doesn't mean they're not idiots."

"You can't be serious," Joaquín said.

"Look it up on the internet if you don't believe me. Bye. And lock up the liquor or at least mark the level of booze in the bottles."

"You want me to institute the Third Reich in my apartment! I don't like it when you call our boys preppies, you hear? They have names: Jerónimo and Samuel."

"I do remember that," Julieta retorted. "And while we're on the subject, if you call me Juli one more time, I'll open that goddamn window and jump."

"You'd land on the Escobars' balcony and look like an ass," Joaquín said. "At most you might break a leg or flatten their grill. They do a mean barbecue."

"Fine," Julieta said. "Buy them thin condoms, the ultrasensitive ones, because otherwise they won't wear them. Ask at the drugstore for condoms for preppy boys. They're the most expensive ones."

Joaquín shrugged and gave her a haughty look, as if to say, "My sons are the young kings of the castle, just like their dad. Stop being such a pain."

On her way back to her car, Julieta thought, *I was so stupid and blind to get involved with an asshole like that.* In her mind she'd made a list of adjectives that described him: *opportunistic, unsophisticated, arrogant, ambitious, self-important, stupid, aggressive, idiotic, selfish, deceitful, boastful, lazy, unscrupulous, intense, dull, ordinary, thoughtless, crude, big-headed, prickish, insolent, spoiled, obtuse, cruel, rat-bastard, dumb as a post . . .*

Life was a game of Russian roulette.

As she'd read once, "A person should live *a posteriori.*" How had she ended up with Joaquín? After three years with a bohemian painter, a drug addict and boozehound, she'd desperately needed something grounding. And then Joaquín had appeared: a lawyer from the University of El Rosario who specialized in suing the capital district of Bogotá, a partner at Los Lagartos, bilingual, knew his way around a wine menu, a good cook ("the kind of guy who knows how to use arugula in salads," she used to say, back when she still loved him), and to top it off he knew a dozen Bob Dylan songs by heart ("it's impossible to love somebody who doesn't know who Bob Dylan is," she also used to say). They got engaged when she started becoming obsessed with having children, that biological urge that some women feel deep inside, which torments them and blackens their sight. The marriage started off all right, fully dedicated to the reproductive endeavor. But the lengthy pregnancies and the bell jar that descends over every woman newly transformed into a mother contaminated the air: decaffeinated VIP clubbing; trysts on farms in Anapoima; weekends in Aruba or Punta Cana, or worse, in the beach-fringed shopping mall commonly known as Panama; Iranian music concerts at the Teatro Mayor; trips to the Hay Festival in Cartagena; Zacapa rum and cocaine. Gradually poisoned by the Bogotá aristocracy, she swiftly became bored. From then on, everything was contradiction. She hated the Iranian music concerts, the transplanted Sundance Film Festival showings, the visits to world museums at the movie theater on Saturdays. Whereas Joaquín loved the aseptic, *important*, and buttoned-up literature of AA, she secretly preferred the unruly, cruel, and nocturnal novels of BB.

And that's how it was with everything.

AA versus BB in movies, in music, in restaurants and bars.

She stopped feeling desire. Maybe it was because of the kids, as one therapist told her. Whatever the case, sex ceased to give her pleasure. What she found most exciting, besides smoking joints in Villa de Leyva and occasionally eating mushrooms, was a heteroflexible group sex experience. Even today, ten years later, she still conjured it up in bed.

It was the best thing she had.

The end came after an epic fight over something that was, oddly, completely trivial (how spicy a dip that they would be serving to friends should be). It was the point of no return, and Joaquín moved out at last. Now free, Julieta threw herself body and soul into rituals. One Saturday she stripped the sheets off her king-size bed and, even though new they'd cost 1,650,000 pesos at Zara Home, burned them at a cousin's farm near Tabio. An act of purification. Seeing that high-thread-count fabric lapped by flames, fabric in which she'd spent the last seven years, where she'd made her children, and that, even though they were washed regularly, must still contain particles of their bodies—pubic hairs, faint traces of discharge or semen—anyway, as she watched that intimacy go up in smoke, being erased from reality, she took swigs from a box of unsweetened Néctar aguardiente, which Joaquín always viewed as a sign of moral degeneracy.

She felt happy, laughing and pouring shots into the fire in a sort of *auto-da-fé*.

AA versus BB.

Still not satisfied, she decided to change the entire apartment. She rolled up and gave away the old rugs, got rid of paintings, took down picture frames. Her two sons, Samuel and Jerónimo, watched her go back and forth carrying boxes, unable to believe what they were seeing, saying, "Look, Mom, stop, if this is what you want, we should just move to another place, don't you think?" She redid the living room with ethnic-inspired decor and changed the vibe with indirect lighting (Joaquín couldn't stand pseudo-hippie dimness). She bought handicrafts and ordered Indonesian fabrics, started using incense, even bought a menorah in the Jewish section at Pricesmart, not because she was Jewish but to have somewhere to put more candles. Then her transformation obsession shifted to music: no more Bob Dylan or Leonard Cohen, but instead her beloved Cuban ballads, which Joaquín deemed lame and outmoded.

Discovering that she was lonely, she started hanging out with her colleagues more, and after a cookout at the home of a Chilean correspondent she ended up kissing and then going to bed with another legal reporter, Víctor Silanpa, and kept seeing him from time to time.

Better a fuck buddy—or several—than another husband.

She put it like this: "I'm bored by the idea of another steady man. You spend all that time getting to know what he likes, meeting his friends, his family, learning his allergies, the things he hates—in politics, religion, soccer—knowing what excites him or pisses him off, not to mention meeting his parents and attempting to get along with them, or having to put up with a spoiled brat sister or niece . . . What a joke. And if he has kids, nightmare territory."

Silanpa was the one who introduced me to her, which is

how I got to know some of her stories in detail—I'm talking files, journals, photos, all the elements that would enable me to tell those stories persuasively and effectively.

But let's get back to this one.

T he trip to Tierradentro was long and uncomfortable. It started very early, with a dawn departure on a flight to Popayán. From there Johana had rented a Hyundai SUV, but when they arrived the rental agency said it only had compact cars available, so they had to settle for a little toaster on wheels that inspired no confidence in Julieta. But Johana was the one driving anyway. "I've looked, and the road isn't bad," she told her boss. "Don't worry, we'll make it." They left Popayán around nine, and past the junction to Silvia headed toward Inzá, the largest town in the area, in the foothills of the mountain range.

The road went up and up into the highlands. Fields of frailejón plants. Ferns. A dark, vegetal green and water on mossy stone. The road was good in stretches, but it was full of detours because of construction. Yellow bulldozers, dump trucks, and steamrollers were arrayed on either side. Every once in a while they had to get over into the left lane and drive slowly, amid a sea of trucks and buses. At other times the road was unpaved, full of rain-puddled potholes. And mud. What time was it? It freaked Julieta out that they kept losing the cell signal. "I can't stand being incommunicado!" she said. "Look at the gorgeous ferns, boss, focus on the landscape instead," Johana suggested.

Suddenly the road started heading steeply up, and when they got to the top, the asphalt abruptly ended. To the right, Johana saw a worker, his head covered with rags and scraps of plastic, pointing to the route across a massive expanse of mud. "Through here, go on," he seemed to be saying, waving his hands. Seeing that strange, gesticulating creature, Julieta felt like she was in a still from *Star Wars*. Off to the left, they spotted a bus sunk into the mud. The passengers were pushing while the driver made the wheels spin without succeeding in extracting it from the mire. Johana hesitated, but eventually obeyed the hominid. As she accelerated, she felt herself floating, the little Hyundai bucking like an eggshell on a swift river current, but they made it to the other side. From there they continued down a stony track and managed to negotiate the quagmire. Half a kilometer later, the asphalt returned and they were able to keep going.

Three hours of driving through one of the most beautiful landscapes in Colombia—rather draining.

At last they reached Inzá, descended a couple of kilometers, and after passing the Tierradentro archeological park, turned onto the road leading to San Andrés de Pisimbalá. A small hamlet. Johana stopped outside something that could have been a store, a warehouse, or a restaurant. They ordered two lunch platters. The owner was a Páez woman of about fifty. Julieta asked her about the weather, the plants, the flowers. She knew how to carry on this kind of conversation. The fact that they were all women helped create an atmosphere of trust. When Johana felt the moment was right, she ventured a question.

"What happened the other day at the bridge over the Ullucos River, ma'am?"

The woman glanced around for a second and then back at them. "When?"

"Last Wednesday," Julieta clarified. "We heard there was a shoot-out."

She looked at the road again. Three kids were splashing around in a stream of water pouring out of a tank. The sun was only a light bulb.

"I haven't heard anything about that," the woman said.

"Maybe with the rain you couldn't hear it," Johana said, "but some people heard gunshots."

The woman pondered a moment.

"It didn't rain here on Wednesday. I don't remember."

She added something in the Nasa language that they couldn't understand, as if talking to herself, and retreated to the kitchen.

They went back to the car and returned to the archeological park. It wasn't going to be easy to communicate with the indigenous people—they were always so laconic. To break that silence, they'd have to stay for several days. They checked in to a room at El Refugio, the only hotel in the village. At reception, Johana asked a young woman what things were like.

"Around here?" the Nasa woman asked. "It's all pretty calm, thank goodness."

"Nothing unusual's been happening?"

The young woman looked down and said, as if to herself, "Nothing, ma'am. Mercifully."

They dropped off their belongings in a room with two beds. The bathroom wasn't anything special, but it had running water and seemingly even a water heater. The mirror had a yellow tint to it and chipped edges. Julieta looked at herself and grimaced. In the reflection she looked like an old photo. A vintage image of herself. Then they got back in the car to look for the road where the alleged shoot-out had taken place. Before they headed out, Julieta decided to call Jutsiñamuy.

"It isn't easy to build trust with people here. They're saying nothing happened. They're wary. Did you find out anything else?"

"The latest is that the incident simply disappeared."

"What do you mean?" Julieta exclaimed.

"Just what I said: without a trace. Hang on a sec."

Julieta heard the scrape of a chair, then a door opening and, in the background, city noise. She realized that the prosecutor had gone out onto the balcony.

"Now I can talk," he said. "The report from the San Andrés de Pisimbalá police station disappeared from the system, and several agents from Inzá who'd gone down there to investigate were sent home. I'll have to find out who issued that order."

Julieta lit a dried-out cigarette from an old packet of Luckies she found in her jacket. She'd quit smoking eleven days ago, but these situations got her worked up.

"Who would want to hide something like that? And why?"

Jutsiñamuy was silent a moment, then said, "People who are involved. Two groups shooting at each other and then a helicopter comes in—it was serious business."

"I'm going to go inspect the road," Julieta said. "Do you remember how far it was from San Andrés?"

"Seven kilometers," Jutsiñamuy said. "Actually, the report said *about* seven kilometers. Be careful. Be discreet if you talk to the police. At least until we find out what happened to that report."

Julieta took a drag on the cigarette and closed her eyes. She blew the smoke out through her nose and took a deep breath. "This is all really weird. I'll call you later."

They went up the road toward a grove of trees and saw the immense mountains around them, dark green masses that gave the region its name and were full of hypogea with geometric drawings. A roadside sign mentioned a few names: El Tablón, La Chaquira, Aguacate. They drove through town and passed by a church with whitewashed walls and a thatch roof. Pure white and apparently under construction, with fencing and plastic sheeting cloaking its sides.

"OK then," Johana said, "let's calculate seven kilometers from here."

"The Ullucos bridge isn't on the map," Julieta said, "but we'll find it."

They drove slowly down the road.

Any detail might be important. Eucalyptuses, willows, and poplars. The occasional guayacán. Bamboo on either side. Mango trees. They kept going. Behind the barbed-wire fences they saw fields of coffee and corn. Stony dirt paths climbing up into the mountains. And many streams of water, little creeks passing under small bridges in the road. Which of them was the one? There weren't any signs. Just endless twists and turns.

Suddenly Johana said, "It's got to be around here. And this is 'about seven kilometers.'" She pointed at the odometer.

Julieta studied her curiously. "Did you see something?"

"There's a straight bit and a bridge. If I needed to ambush somebody, I'd do it right here. I would put shooters there and there."

They parked the Hyundai in the scrub and walked slowly along the shoulder of the road, scrutinizing everything. Johana looked for signs of fire, ashes, burned rubber, traces of fuel. But there was nothing. They went up and down the roadside a number of times, looking at every bush. Then Johana moved off into the scrub. In three areas she saw that it had been cut to the ground or uprooted. Somebody could have done it to get rid of signs of burning. Julieta went to the riverbank and walked down under the little bridge. The only odd thing was the circles of cropped vegetation, but it wasn't much. Johana went a little farther. Julieta saw her pull out her knife and dig something out of the trunk of a cedar.

"Come here!" Johana yelled.

When Julieta reached the spot, Johana opened her hand and showed it to her: a bullet. She peered at it against the light, feeling the heft of it, and said, "It weighs at least eight grams. It's a 7.62 mm cartridge."

"And what does that mean?" Julieta asked.

Johana tossed it up in the air and caught it, as if she were throwing heads or tails. "Assault rifle, AK-47. It was fired from over there. I was calculating what direction it came from."

She showed Julieta the bullet and pointed to the dents. "This at the tip is where it hit the tree trunk, but this other one is different. It hit something and bounced off. Changed direction. These guns fire multiple rounds at a time. There have got to be more out here. But it was definitely fired from an equivalent distance on the other side of the road. It came from the attackers. It may have struck a car and then landed here. That's just a theory. We'd have to examine it in a lab to see if there's any human tissue on it."

They went to look at the other area, among the poplars. There was a small incline.

"They must have lain in wait here," Johana continued. "It's the perfect spot."

She scraped in the dirt with her knife, drawing several circles. The pebbles seemed loose. They must have been disturbed recently. The two women walked around the grove of trees and Johana climbed a small hill. The attackers could have fired from there. She scrabbled in the soil with her knife.

"If this was one of the attack positions, there must have been another one over there," she said, pointing to a slope a hundred meters away.

They went to look, but they didn't find anything. The vegetation was intact. Julieta studied the bark on the trees, looking for bullet holes. "Or maybe on the other side of the road," she said, indicating a spot with her finger. "Over there." A little higher up was a cliff with a position that seemed good. She pointed it out to her colleague. "Let's look there too."

Johana wagged her finger. "No, nobody lies in ambush that far away," she said. "Your goal is to surprise your enemy and leap on him suddenly. A quick attack that forces a swift collapse. Too far away and you lose your advantage. These guys carried out their ambush in the evening, when it was still light, which means they thought they might have to pursue their enemy. They knew the enemy was strong and might fight them off. They had respect for them."

Julieta looked at her. "Very good, professor. Do all guerrilla fighters know these things? It's a wonder you didn't win the war! Let's go over to the other side."

Johana pointed to a steep slope. A grove of trees. The same distance from the highway, ideal in an exchange of gunfire or for a second ambush in case the enemy scattered along the riverbank.

A few meters farther along, Julieta found a shell casing. Seeing it, Johana said, "Yep, AK-47. It was a major assault."

Julieta lit another cigarette. A cloud shrouded the sun and a sudden cool gust of wind announced that the afternoon was coming to an end. She rubbed her forearms and an inexplicable sense of unease made her look up high above the road. What was that? Concealed behind a tree trunk, she saw a shadow.

"We're being watched," she said.

It was a man in a black helmet, on a motorcycle. But as soon as they started walking toward him, he took off in the opposite direction. The two women stood expectantly. Was it just a coincidence?

"That's enough for today," Julieta said. "We'll come back. Tomorrow we can go talk to the San Andrés police."

It had grown dark, and it seemed like the night would bring rain again. They ate in the dining room at the hotel, which was empty at first, but halfway through their meal, a group of Russians arrived, four couples, filling the silence with their racket. They had two bottles of whisky and were spinning them on the table.

"That guy on the motorcycle was spying on us," Johana said.

Julieta cut into a somewhat dry chicken breast. Before lifting a piece to her mouth, she said, "It could have been a coincidence. Somebody who was driving by and saw us. It's unusual to see two city women in the middle of a country road."

Johana took a sip of her guava juice. "I prefer to be paranoid, boss. Safer that way. They heard we were there and sent someone over. That's why the guy arrived with his engine off."

"Who?" Julieta asked, not expecting an answer.

"We definitely know there was a gunfight, a big one," Johana said. "Ordinary bandits don't use assault rifles."

The air, still damp with rain, was getting cooler. Night loomed heavy. Julieta thought about calling Jutsiñamuy, but the group at the next table had started singing and clapping.

"Drunk Russians. I hope they don't stay here drinking all night," Julieta said.

"They're not Russian, boss. They're Ukrainian," Johana said.

"How do you know?"

"They're all wearing T-shirts that say *I love Kiev*, which is the capital of Ukraine."

Julieta looked at her in surprise. "OK, OK. Sorry, then. Ukrainians . . . I'm going to bed."

The hotel room was big. Julieta sat down at the small desk and started making notes. She wrote out a brief account of the day's findings and the most precise description of the road she could. As they turned out the light, rain started pouring down. The torrential racket on the roof brought back memories of her childhood and a vague sense of being orphaned. It was on nights like this that she most wished she had a partner, someone to cling to and seek comfort in. The rain falling on everyone's memories and obsessions. But she managed to sleep.

She opened her eyes and found that it was still raining, but more lightly now. What time was it? Maybe three in the morning. *The hour when the ailing go into their death throes*, she thought. She had awakened for a strange reason: the unsettling sensation that something had come into the room, and was still there. So close that if she reached out her hand she could touch it—and worse, the idea that that *thing* was drawing closer, like a sniffing animal. A shadow in the darkest night. Or maybe she was still dreaming? No. Somebody was there; something that could see her, even though there wasn't a bit of light. Not daring to move, she felt her muscles tense.

Though it was pitch-black, she sensed that part of the darkness was moving. Worse still, something seemed to writhe or gesticulate in front of her face. Her childhood terrors surged forth. She closed her eyes and opened them again. The blackness was unchanged. It wasn't a dream, she was awake, but she didn't dare rub her eyes for fear the *thing* would notice. Her only protection was to pretend she was sleeping. She pricked up her ears, and amid the pattering of the rain she thought she could hear Johana's regular breathing.

A few seconds passed, and the torrent increased again, as if the entire sky were pouring onto the earth. Somewhere out there a roll of thunder echoed in the mountains, and then another. Suddenly, inexplicably, Julieta got the feeling that the air was moving; something in the dense darkness had shifted again. She thought her pounding heart might burst, and under the covers she managed to move her hand and reach her cell phone. But she didn't know what to do with it. Another series of thunderclaps boomed out. Suddenly there was a rush of cool air and, amid the rumbling of the thunder, the unmistakable sound of a click.

The visitor had left and closed the door.

She touched the screen and her cell phone lit up. When she pulled it out from under the covers, she dimly saw the empty room.

"What's going on?" Johana asked, waking.

Julieta got up and turned on the light. "Somebody came in."

"Came in where? Into this room?" Johana exclaimed in disbelief.

"Yes. They just left."

"Well, I didn't hear anything."

"Clearly not," Julieta said. She went to the door and found that it was unlocked. "Look, they forgot to press the lock. They left it open. I locked it last night."

"It's a cinch to open one of these doors—you can do it with a credit card," Johana said.

They examined their belongings. Everything was in order. They stepped out into the breezeway, which led to a swimming pool, but nobody was around. They headed to the hotel office. Everything was deserted. Of course, it was three thirty in the morning. They rang the bell and a young Nasa man wearing a traditional poncho and socks emerged from a side room, rubbing his eyes.

"Yes?" he said.

Julieta asked if anyone had come into the hotel recently. The young man said no. She asked who else was staying there, apart from the Russians.

"Ukrainians," Johana murmured.

"Nobody else, ma'am," the Nasa man said.

Julieta grew impatient. She hadn't dreamed it all up! "And is this the only entrance?" she asked.

The young man said yes, though you could also come in from the gorge or hop the parking-lot fence. But had that been the case, the dogs would have barked. "Sometimes the dogs get scared of storms," he added, "but sometimes they don't."

Julieta looked at him curiously and Johana whispered in her ear, "It's OK, they're not easy to understand." They went back to the room. The rain was horizontal, blown by the wind and spraying the breezeway they had to walk down. At the door it occurred to them that the visitor must have left footprints, but the mat was dry.

"I didn't dream it," she told Johana.

"I believe you, boss. Let's go back to bed."

When they left the room at first light, fed up with trying to get back to sleep after the strange incident, they saw a fine layer of mist rising from the grass. The sun was gradually drying the damp. In the distance a rooster crowed. Up from the valley came a rustic smell, a mix of woodsmoke, brewed coffee, and humid earth.

They had breakfast on the terrace next to a rudimentary swimming pool filled with river water that made Julieta shudder just looking at it. Three horses that were wandering around came over to their table to beg for food. One of them ambled up the steps and placed its front hoofs on the terrace. The Nasa waiter came out of the kitchen and shooed it back to the field.

"I swear somebody came in last night," Julieta said.

"I believe you, boss," Johana said. "But what would somebody be looking for in our room? Let's discard the obvious: a rapist, a thief, a psychopath. They wouldn't have left without trying something."

Julieta cut a piece of papaya. It was delicious, sprinkled with lemon juice. "He must have sensed that I woke up, the same way I sensed him. He took advantage of the thunder to get away."

"Why didn't you turn on the light?" Johana said.

"I was too scared to move," she said. "I couldn't."

They sat watching a hummingbird drinking sugar water from a cylindrical feeder that hung from a roofbeam. In the distance, in the cluster of trees along the river, a woodpecker was tapping.

"Do you think it was the guy with the motorcycle?" Julieta wondered.

"Could be," Johana said. "Somebody's clearly either curious or annoyed that we're poking around asking questions."

"Somebody from the village?"

"They're the only ones who've seen us," Johana said, "unless one of Jutsiñamuy's agents has been keeping somebody informed."

"Do you think we're in danger?" Julieta said.

Johana pondered for a moment. "Not in the way you're thinking, boss. If they wanted to scare us, they would have done something already. For now they're just keeping an eye on us."

Julieta downed the rest of her coffee and got up from the table. "All right, well, let's keep digging, so they get even more pissed off and show their faces and we can see who they are."

All at once she stopped short and, staring at Johana, said, "The car."

They raced to the hotel parking lot. The Hyundai was there, and at first glance they saw nothing unusual. It was locked. Everything normal inside, no sign of an intruder. They searched under the seats and down between the cushions. Julieta turned the key to check the fuel level, and it was unchanged from the night before. They opened the trunk and then the hood, but everything was in order. Johana crouched down and peered underneath.

"No bombs," she said.

"No need to be melodramatic," Julieta retorted.

They walked toward the breezeway, lost in thought, but just as they were about to head to the room, Julieta stopped. Something had surfaced in her recollection. A small triangle of paper poking out of the glove compartment. The image persisted in her memory, unnoticed in the search, and now returning as if to say: there's something else, there's something else.

They went back to the parking lot.

It was the rental agreement for the Hyundai. Somebody had taken it out of the plastic envelope and then carelessly shoved it back in. This was real evidence. She was sorry she'd left it there, since now they knew everything about her: her name and address, phone number, ID number, and license number. What was going on? Who was spying on them?

"Let's go talk to the police," Julieta said.

They drove to San Andrés de Pisimbalá and parked across from the church. The police station was around the corner. A new building. Julieta mused how during the war they would have needed a sturdier building, and one farther from the center of town.

The door was open and led into an office with an old wooden desk and a number of posters that boasted of the pride and courage of the national police force. A young officer in uniform was dozing on a sofa, lying face up with his cell phone on his chest. He started when Julieta came in, and the phone slid to the floor. They introduced themselves as journalists and asked to speak to the sergeant. Was there a sergeant? The officer told them to wait. Five minutes later another man appeared; as he walked toward them, he raised his right leg a little and let out a thunderous fart that echoed off the walls. He seemed more surprised than anyone.

"Excuse me, ladies. I've got terrible colon trouble, and you start to forget your manners in a place like this. How can I help you?"

He had a name embroidered on his right pocket: Bocanegra. Sergeant Bocanegra.

Julieta got straight to the point. "I'm a journalist and I'm looking into the gunfight on the bridge over the Ullucos River. What information do you have?"

The man looked them up and down without saying anything. He would have been about forty, forty-five at most. He looked surprised. He wasn't indigenous. He had a Pasto accent.

"What gunfight are you referring to, ma'am?"

"Your office submitted a report to the Inzá police last week."

The sergeant went and sat at the desk. The young officer moved off to one side and went back to looking at his cell phone.

"What organization are you with?"

"I work on investigations for a number of papers in the States." Mentioning that country in this context could give her some authority.

"You must know that these things are confidential," he said. "I have to get the OK from on high before I talk to the press. I'm afraid I can't help you right now."

Johana got impatient. "Somebody's been watching us," she said. "They broke into our hotel room."

The sergeant scratched his cleanshaven cheek. "Which hotel are you staying in? Did they steal anything? Did they attack you?"

"No," Julieta said, "but they came in. And they broke into my car."

"Did they steal anything from the car?"

"No."

"Well, that's pretty weird," he said, looking at the younger officer. "Isn't that right, corporal? To break in and not steal anything. This country is definitely changing. Are you at El Refugio?"

They both nodded.

"All right, I'll keep my eyes peeled. How long are you staying?"

Julieta felt a rush of renewed strength. "Until we find somebody who can tell us what happened on that road."

The sergeant smiled back at them, the first one that seemed

genuine. "Well, if you learn anything, please make sure I'm the first to know."

"But if you won't help me out, why should I help you?"

"Because I'm the authority here, ma'am," he said. "When the bandits come to take over the town, it's me they'll shoot at, not you or the hotel guests. Don't forget which side you're on."

"We're on the same side," Julieta said. "Don't you forget it either."

They left.

It was starting to drizzle. They walked across to the church. It was surrounded by bamboo scaffolding with sheets of green plastic, as if from unfinished restorations. A sign at the entrance explained that it was an "indoctrinating church"; besides being a house of worship, it served as a classroom for teaching religion to the indigenous population, but it had been burned down years back during a conflict between Nasas and peasants.

They went inside.

An altar boy was sprinkling the wooden pews with something that looked like oil. When he saw them, a strange expression crossed his face, as if he'd been expecting them. Julieta asked for the priest, and the boy, a Nasa who looked about fourteen, replied that the church was closed.

"It got burned down a long time ago," he said, looking at them curiously. "You're from Bogotá, right?"

"Yes," Julieta said. "Is it that obvious?"

The boy's face twisted vaguely into something resembling a smile.

"I saw you yesterday at the restaurant."

"So you already knew who we were," Julieta said. "These villages have a thousand eyes. But tell me, so there's no priest at the moment?"

"Not here. You have to go to Inzá." The boy continued to scrutinize them. "What did you want with the priest?" he asked. "What do you need?"

Julieta moved closer.

"To find out about something."

The boy put down the rag and dried his hand on his pants. "About what?"

"A gunfight," Julieta said. "On the road down to the Páez River, in the Ullucos gorge."

The boy's expression changed. He took two steps toward the door and peered outside, as if reassuring himself of something. A local on a bike rode by on the sidewalk across the street, carrying an umbrella. The clouds looked dark, rain gathering in their bellies. The boy looked back at them.

"That's what you came to ask about?" he said. "The priest might be back later."

They walked to the altar and then back to the entrance. Johana jingled the car keys in her hand.

"If he comes, tell him we're looking for him," Julieta said.

The boy nodded. He picked up the rag and brush he'd been using to clean. The two women went out into the street. In the distance, maybe coming from the restaurant, they could hear faint music. They climbed into the Hyundai and headed toward the hotel, but before turning the corner Johana hit the brakes. In the rearview mirror she saw the boy from the church waving at her. She backed the car down the street and Julieta lowered the window.

"What is it?"

He looked off toward the mountains, nervous. His pupils looked like two spheres dancing in the air.

"I saw everything," the boy said.

The two women looked at each other.

"You mean what happened on the Ullucos River?" Julieta asked.

"Yes."

"Come with us. We'll go somewhere quiet and you can tell us."

He got into the car and they went to the hotel restaurant. The boy ordered a soda and two empanadas. Chicken-flavored French fries. Julieta asked if she could record the conversation, and the boy looked at her uncomprehending. She waggled her cell phone at him, and he said, yeah, that's OK.

After hearing the full story of the battle, Julieta asked about the people he'd seen. "Who would you say they were?"

The boy stared at the floor, at some spot between his shoe and the table leg.

"I don't know, ma'am. They didn't look like soldiers."

"Have you seen fighting like that before?" Julieta asked. "Have you seen troops of guerrilla fighters or paramilitaries?"

He scratched his head and twined a few jet-black hairs around his finger. "I've seen people shooting at each other in the mountains a few times, ma'am. I've seen armed men in uniform climbing Aguacate Hill. Soldiers too."

"And these looked like them?"

"They were different. No uniforms."

"During the attack, did they say anything?" Julieta asked. "Did you hear their accents? Were they from this area?"

"I could barely hear them, ma'am. They didn't talk—they knew what to do without saying anything, just by looking at each other. They made signals with their hand."

"Did you see how many died?"

"At least five. I saw them go down. They got shot. There was a lot of gunfire and a car caught on fire. They put it out."

"What did they look like?"

"Tall, in city clothes. They weren't farmers or Nasas. They were from somewhere else. The leader of the ones being attacked was dressed in black. He got out of the SUV with some women. They tried to kill them, but they couldn't because of the helicopter."

"And the man in black and the women, what did they look like?"

"They got out and climbed into the helicopter. The man was tall and thin. I think. I didn't see him very well. And a woman with no clothes on, almost. Almost naked. They got out of the biggest vehicle, the black one. A Hummer. And another woman, also different."

"Different?"

"She had clothes, pants."

"And why do you say the other woman was naked?" Johana asked.

"She had really short shorts. Almost no clothes."

"And which direction did the helicopter go?"

"It rose up and went off that way . . ."

Toward the west, Johana wrote.

"They took everything away in trucks," the boy said. "They were there all night with flashlights."

"Were they wearing uniforms?"

"They weren't soldiers. They had jackets, but a different kind. Dark-colored, I think. I got scared and stopped looking as much. I thought they might spot me, and I held on close to the tree trunk. If they saw me they'd shoot. I was scared."

"Did you see anyone from the village?" Johana asked. "Did anyone besides you see what happened?"

"I don't know," the boy said. "I was alone. I didn't see anybody else."

"Do you think it's possible that the people in San Andrés didn't hear anything?"

The boy smiled.

"People here are trained not to hear."

Julieta held up the cell phone and said, "I need to ask you a favor. Close your eyes for a second, concentrate, and tell me again what you saw, from the beginning, every detail."

The boy complied.

He closed his eyes and began to talk.

When he'd finished his account, he looked at the kitchen door. "Can I order another soda?"

"Of course," Julieta said. "Same kind?"

"A Fanta, please."

Johana got up and went off to order it.

"After what you've told me about, has anybody gone there to look at what happened?" Julieta asked.

"I don't know," the boy said hesitantly. "What do you mean? Anybody who?"

"Somebody on a motorcycle, for example. With a black helmet. Did you see him?"

"Everybody here's got a motorcycle. The farmers and the Nasa. There are lots of motorcycles. Especially Suzuki 350s. And Kawasaki 250s, the old ones."

"But they don't wear helmets," Johana said.

"Depends," the boy said.

"You know a lot about cars and motorcycles," Julieta said.

"I like them. I look at them on the internet."

"What's your favorite car?"

"The Chevrolet Camaro and the Toyota Fortuner," the boy said, then added shyly, "Do you guys work with the law too?"

"More or less," Julieta said. "We're journalists."

"Oh!" the boy exclaimed, opening his eyes wide.

Figuring they had enough, they asked if they should take him back to the church.

"No," the boy said. "I'd better go on my own."

"Can I call you if we have any questions?" Julieta asked. "Where can I find you?"

"At the church or at the store. Ask for me. My name's Franklin. They know me there. Franklin Vanegas."

As he was leaving the dining room, Julieta called him back over. "Just one more thing, Franklin. Was it raining that night?"

The boy gazed up at the ceiling, then lowered his eyes to look at them.

"At first yes, later I don't remember. Maybe not. I was scared."

"Did you call the police to sound the alarm?"

The boy hung his head, ashamed.

He didn't say anything.

Julieta took notes for close to an hour. Then they packed everything into the Hyundai and headed to Inzá. After the events of last night, they had no desire to stay in Tierradentro. They could return the next day. Even if they'd already been spotted.

"He was easy to find," Johana said.

"It must have been him who called the police," Julieta noted. "Now we have to find out who the man in black who got out of the Hummer is. Then we can work out the rest of it: who attacked him and why. Who has armed men like that these days? What did they do with the bodies? How did they get rid of them? Do those people not have families?"

Johana was driving. "That's easy, boss. Or at least it used to be. Nowadays I don't know. They would toss them into a river or bury them in a ditch. The paramilitaries had cremation ovens. These guys must be ex-paramilitary. They're the only ones who could have that kind of weaponry. The man in black must be a drug capo—who else would have a Hummer, soldiers, and a helicopter?"

"Remind me to call Víctor. He might know about that."

"Silanpa?"

"Yes."

They drove through the dark mountains. Occasionally the clouds came down to cloak the road: grayish masses made opaque by the deep green hills. The road sloping and leveling out. Streams of water flowing down from above at every curve. A hawk circling.

Suddenly Johana, looking in the rearview mirror, said, "There he is again."

"Who?"

"The motorcycle . . ."

Julieta turned and saw it some three hundred meters back. It was the one from yesterday, no question. "What do we do?" she wondered aloud.

"We speed up or we stop and confront him," Johana said. Tracking his movement, Julieta saw that he wasn't gaining on them. "Slow down a little, and let's see if he catches up."

They slowed, but so did the motorcycle. He was just following them. Or making sure they knew he was there.

"Let's stop—park there," she said, pointing to a pull-off near a curve.

The motorcycle stopped too, and the man in the helmet watched them calmly from afar. Julieta got out of the Hyundai and stared at him defiantly. Would he come closer? Was he the same person who'd entered their hotel room? He sat there, a figure in a helmet and black jacket, motionless as in a game of freeze tag.

"Turn around," she told Johana, "let's go after him. Let's find out who the hell he is!"

Johana made the tires spin. They needed to move nimbly, but the motorcycle wheeled around and accelerated. A little farther along, it turned off onto a dirt road that climbed up the mountain and disappeared from view.

"Well," said Julieta, "at least we don't have to be afraid of him."

"He just wanted to make sure we were leaving," Johana said.

Inzá sits at 1,800 meters above sea level. Like most of the cities in this country, it is noisy and its outskirts are somewhat shabby and neglected. From a distance, from the Tierradentro road, it looks like a line of houses clinging to the mountain's mane. If we'd had a Middle Ages in Colombia, Inzá would have a castle, the city looming over the neighboring slopes, tablelands and canyons. The conflict hit Inzá hard, as it did the entire region. People still remember the FARC attack that killed nine. Soldiers, police officers, and civilians. They fired tubes stuffed with ammo and explosives from a pickup truck transporting bales of onions. It destroyed the police station. That was in 2013.

The mayor received them in jeans and short sleeves. He had a laborer's hands—short, thick fingers, rectangular nails. A well-preserved forty-five, certainly no older than fifty. Black mustache, dark skin, and a small body, deformed by an unexpected hump on his right side.

He introduced himself: Horacio Barona.

He offered them coffee and a seat by the large window in the second-floor office overlooking the park.

"What's that lovely tree with the yellow flowers?"

"We call that one guayacán," Barona said. "And that one over there, the little red one, is an acacia. This town is certainly blessed by Mother Nature."

They gazed out; it was very beautiful.

The mayor's lyrical, even sappy, tone seemed to suggest that this blanket of foliage was somehow a representation of the eternal innocence of the human soul, of any living being under its stylized shade. That was clearly far from the reality. Julieta wasn't sure how to broach the subject that, through all the twists and smokescreen, had become a mystery in itself, and even a little embarrassing. She took a breath and tried to organize her thoughts. Ultimately, it was just one more violent incident of the thousands that occurred in this cruel, irascible country that paradoxically claimed, when asked, to be the happiest nation on Earth.

"As I mentioned, Mr. Mayor, I'm a journalist," Julieta began, "so you can guess what I want to talk about."

The man nodded.

"Of course," he said, "and you know what I say? Ask anything you like. I just want to make it clear from the start that I am explicitly neutral. I know the parish priest is upset; I've been hearing about it. Have you talked to him?"

Julieta and Johana looked at each other in bewilderment.

"The priest?"

The mayor didn't even hear her. He was still talking: "The vicariate is very powerful and has a long tradition here in Inzá, but Don Tomás needs to accept that the Alliance represents a lot of good people too. And how can I forbid them to use the park? The Alliance people have every right to be there, even if they're evangelicals. Besides, their gathering this weekend drew people from all over the world and was a national event. Our little town was in all the papers! How can I stand in the way of that? I abide by what the Constitution says: we have freedom of religion in this country."

"Maybe there's been a misunderstanding, Mr. Mayor," Julieta said. "I don't know what you're talking about. We came to ask about a shoot-out that took place on the San Andrés de Pisimbalá road last week."

Now it was the mayor's turn to look bewildered.

"Oh dear. You aren't here about the Alliance gatherings? It's all the local radio stations are talking about." The mayor took a moment to pull himself together, downed the last of his coffee, and said, "I did hear the police lieutenant talking, he said there were rumors, but he didn't give me any details or mention it again. Did you talk to him already? I'm sure it's just idle talk. With these gatherings taking place in town, I admit, I've been completely swamped all weekend . . . He gave me a report yesterday, but he didn't mention that. Strange." The mayor twisted his mustache and tapped his thumb on the edge of the table.

Julieta glared at him. She recognized this situation a mile off: because they were women, he wasn't taking the matter seriously.

"There was a gunfight with AK-47s, heavy weaponry, and a helicopter gunship. All in your little town, and you didn't know about it because you were at an evangelical celebration?" Julieta asked, her eyes spitting fire. "That sounds interesting. Shall I write it up that way?"

The mayor stood nervously and went over to the phone. Holding the handset to his ear, he gestured to them: *wait, wait.*

"Hello, lieutenant," they heard him say. "Yes, this is Mayor Barona, how's it going? Well, great, listen, I've got these two journalists here from Bogotá who are asking about a shoot-out on . . . Where was it, miss?"

"In the Ullucos gorge," Julieta said.

"Near San Andrés," the mayor continued. "Have you heard anything about that? Oh, OK, yes, yes. All right, all right. Understood. Two people? Oh, all right, last Wednesday? Sure, sure. Of course, great. Write me a report including that detail. Thanks so much."

He sat down again.

"Well, you were quite right, ladies," the mayor said. "My apologies. The lieutenant tells me there was gunfire on that road on Wednesday night. A drunk guy in a pickup truck tried to pass an SUV and apparently they grazed or bumped each other, and there was an argument and gunshots, but he tells me the shots went wide and no one was injured. The culprits have been arrested and just this morning were sent to Popayán. A shopkeeper from La Plata and a truck driver from Silvia."

He tapped his fingers on the edge of the table three times, as if playing along to a song. "I'm glad I was able to help," he added, "but I do find it curious that you've come about an incident like this, all the way to Cauca! Is Bogotá really so quiet these days?"

The two women stood, and Julieta said, "The story I got is quite different, Mr. Mayor, but I appreciate your time. You've helped me understand some things."

They walked out into the reception area. A woman with dyed hair and long fingernails was talking loudly on her cell phone. Another was peering at an Excel spreadsheet through a pair of glasses perched halfway down her nose. They both looked up.

"Do you need something, sir?"

"These young ladies are leaving," the mayor said. "I'll see them downstairs and be right back."

Out on the street, it was drizzling again.

"That's the problem with this time of year," the man said. "Are you parked far away?"

"We're quite close, Mr. Mayor. Thank you."

They said goodbye. He watched them until they reached the corner of the park and then went back inside.

"What do you think?" Julieta asked.

Johana pulled out the parking slip and they paid. "Everybody seems to be hiding something," she said, "but why? We have to find out who this person is who was targeted in the attack. The man in black. He's clearly powerful—everybody is shielding him."

"Yes," Julieta said, "and the guys from the other side too."

"I thought you were going to tell the mayor about the guy on the motorcycle," Johana said.

"I'd rather keep that to ourselves for now. I suspect we'll be speaking to him again further down the road."

They pulled out of the parking lot.

"Where to now, boss? Are we staying here?" Johana asked.

"No, let's head to Popayán to see if we can let things cool down and change cars. I'll call Jutsiñamuy later to find out if he's learned anything. He's going to like the story the kid told us."

They drove out of Inzá.

Julieta watched the houses speed past, keeping an eye on the road in case their spy returned, but everything seemed quiet. Relaxing, she started thinking about a nice hotel in

Popayán where she could take a long shower, write some notes to organize her ideas, and eat a good meal. What should their next step be? Maybe talking with the boy from the church again.

She stopped looking at the road and closed her eyes for a minute. But as soon as she did, an image stood out in her mind. She sat bolt upright. "Stop," she said. "Go back."

"Go back? To the mayor's office?"

"No," Julieta said. "Just a little ways. A hundred meters or so."

Johana pulled off onto the side of the road and made a U-turn.

"Slow down a little . . . Look, there. Stop here."

From the side of the road, deeper into the valley and through a gap between two houses, they could see a three-story building with a steeple and a neon cross. Below it was a lighted sign: "Christian and Missionary Alliance Church of Inzá."

"Those must be the people from the religious gatherings the mayor was talking about," Johana said. "He called them 'the Alliance.'"

In front of the church, on the street, were a number of pickup trucks and SUVs. A few men were smoking, waiting. They looked like bodyguards.

Suddenly, a side door opened and they saw a group of people come out. The security guys got out of their vehicles and went over to them. It looked like a warm goodbye among evangelical pastors, the ones who'd come from all over the world, as the mayor claimed, thought Julieta. They embraced, clasped hands, and triumphantly punched their fists from shoulder height toward the sky, like athletes after a win. The pastors were all dressed in black from head to toe. The other men must be their assistants. Just then more Toyota trucks arrived and parked near the door. The SUVs started their engines and the group climbed into their vehicles.

"There are the men in black," Julieta said, snapping photos with her cell phone. "Our guy could be one of them. An evangelical pastor."

A little nervous, she asked Johana to move the Hyundai over to some parched shrubs for a better view and so they were out of sight. She got out of the car and held up her phone to film the end of the scene: the pastors climbing into their trucks, the security vehicles on the move; each group filing out in order. They tried to spot a name or logo on the doors, but they were too far away. They didn't catch the license plates either. The vehicles headed toward Inzá. The women watched them disappear down the road and over a hill behind the first houses.

"All right, let's get moving to Popayán now, quickly," Julieta said.

They made another U-turn and accelerated onto the road.

"One of those guys could be the survivor," Julieta mused. "Early tomorrow we'll come back to San Andrés and show the kid the photos. He's the only one who could recognize him."

Popayán's Hotel Camino Real didn't have anything to do with the famous Mexican network of inns, but it was actually pretty nice, comfortable and affordably priced, and only twenty meters from Caldas Park, which was always swarming with tourists gawking at the colonial architecture. The Cathedral Basilica of Our Lady of the Assumption sat at the edge of the square, with its gleaming white walls and aseptic air. It had been reconstructed just two decades earlier, after the earthquake.

The best thing about the hotel, in Julieta's view, was one of the dishes its restaurant offered: *Pacific shellfish soup with cream of peach palm fruit.* The dish had won first place in a gastronomy contest at the 2010 Forum on UNESCO Heritages, held in Hondarribia, in Spain's Basque Country, a place that knows something about good eating.

They settled into their room and then headed down for dinner. Julieta ordered the soup without a second thought. Johana went for a basket of roast chicken. And meat empanadas to start. A delicious meal that should help them put their notes in order. Julieta reviewed the low-quality video on her phone. Everything was far away: the moving vehicles, the sound of the wind. She tried to zoom in on the men in black and was only somewhat successful.

"Anyway, it would be a little weird," Julieta said, "for somebody who was almost killed less than a week ago to be still driving around on the same roads."

Johana took a sip of her Club Colombia beer. "Well, they're clearly still jumpy," she said. "Look at all those bodyguards. If our survivor is one of those men, it's only because the attackers failed to take him out. They're probably licking their wounds right now. When you go after someone that hard, boss, you don't come back the next day."

They finished the empanadas, which were nice and crisp. Julieta ordered another glass of wine and said, "Let's see who took part in the Alliance gathering." She pulled out her phone, put in the date and the details, and swiftly found what she was looking for. Focusing on the Christian Alliance, she noted that one of its tenets was that Jesus's return is imminent. *Our King who is coming. Acts 1:11. "The crown represents the blessed expectation of Christ's imminent return."*

On their phones, they each reviewed the guests at the event. There were pastors from thirty-seven "Christ-centered" churches across Latin America, the full gamut of the evangelical community.

"Wow," Julieta said, "this event was huge. A sort of missionary OAS. In Inzá? It's weird they didn't hold it in Popayán or Cali."

"Well, it says here that the theme was solidarity with the rural community," Johana said. "They see Cauca as sacred territory because of the way it's been resurrected after the war."

They kept scrolling through pages until they came across the guests' bios. They started going through them.

Rubén Electorat Andrade, Chile. Christian and Missionary Alliance, Ñuñoa, Santiago. Seventy-six years old. Carlos Perdomo Montt, Chile. Pentecostal Church of Valparaíso. Fifty-four years old. Mario Andrade Paulista, Brazil. New Christ Church, São Paulo. Forty-seven years old . . .

"I don't think our guy was a foreigner," Johana said. "It would be odd for someone who isn't from around here to have that kind of security force. On a rural road in Cauca!"

"I've got an idea," Julieta said. "Let's call my friend Doris Helena. Copy the pastors' names and nationalities and I'll send them to her to see what she says."

Doris Helena worked in the immigration office at El Dorado Airport in Bogotá, but her database allowed her to see all arrivals and departures at every international airport in the country. Julieta knew she worked late because of night flights, so she called and explained that she was investigating an evangelical gathering in Cauca and needed to know the arrival airports and dates for a number of people. She emailed the list of the twenty-eight foreign pastors.

"Give me the names of the Colombians too, and I'll tell you what airports they used and when," Doris Helena said.

"Oh, absolutely," Julieta exclaimed. "Thank you."

While they waited, they started looking at the Colombians: two from Barranquilla, one from Cúcuta, two from Medellín, two from Bogotá, one from Cali, and one from Pasto. Which of them might it be?

After half an hour, Doris Helena called back and told them that all of the pastors, except the ones from Cali and Pasto, had entered the country or flown to Popayán on Thursday—*in other words*, Julieta thought, *twenty-four hours after the attack*. In addition, the foreigners had left on Monday, and the Colombians were returning home tonight and tomorrow.

"The last two names aren't on any passenger lists," Doris Helena said. "It makes sense, since they're from Cali and Pasto. They probably drove."

"Thank you so much, Doris," Julieta said. "I owe you."

"So the process of elimination leaves us with the guy from Cali and the one from Pasto," Johana said. "Let's see who they are. 'Edwin Moncayo, Christ of the Border Church, Pasto. Seventy-nine years old. Fritz Almayer, New Jerusalem Church, Cali. Fifty-three years old.'"

Because of his age, both women thought the latter man seemed more likely. The kid hadn't said he was elderly.

"Look, this could be the guy," Johana said, pointing to a photo of Pastor Fritz Almayer.

The pastor was a slim, muscular man with gray hair. He was wearing sunglasses and a black hat. It was a group photo, but he was hanging back, as if he was trying to hide or avoid attention. They looked for him in other photos and finally came across another one with his name in the caption: "Pastor Fritz Almayer of the New Jerusalem congregation . . ."

"What an odd name," Julieta said. "It must be an alias. Maybe he's one of those Canadian evangelicals lost in the tropics."

They looked up the church and discovered that it had a headquarters in Cali, plus other smaller branches in Florencia, Mocoa, Pasto, Barbacoas, and Tunja. The page didn't seem very up to date. There was no mention of peace-related projects, which was what most of the country's evangelical churches were involved in, lured by post-conflict resources. "Money provided by the very same peace process they so vilely opposed during the referendum," Julieta thought angrily.

Their food arrived.

The aroma of the shellfish soup brought memories flooding back for Julieta. What was it? Something seemed to be moving toward her from very far away, at the end of her childhood. The steam from the broth rose to her nostrils. The faint smell of shellfish. For a moment she daydreamed, adrift.

She hated talking on the phone while eating, but she was impatient to make some more progress. She searched for Silanpa's number among her contacts.

"Hi there, what a surprise," he said. "Are you in Bogotá?"

"No, no, I'm in Popayán looking into a weird situation. You doing OK?"

Julieta's tone was different from usual. When she talked to

Silanpa her voice regained a certain youthfulness, a vibrancy it didn't have when she was dealing with everyday affairs. "Look, Víctor," she said, "I want to ask you a favor. Do you have something to write with? Jot down this name and see what you can tell me about the guy: Fritz Almayer. He's an evangelical pastor. He's got a church called New Jerusalem. Does that ring any bells?"

Silanpa was silent a few seconds. "Not off the top of my head. What's up?"

"There was a shoot-out near Tierradentro and I think this pastor was involved. It seems like he was attacked with heavy weaponry but he fought back. I thought maybe you'd heard of him."

"Who attacked him?" Silanpa asked.

"I don't know yet, I'm starting my investigation with the target."

"Let me see what I can find out and I'll get back to you, OK?"

"All right, thanks. Kisses."

She ate another spoonful of soup, still holding her cell phone. She dialed Jutsiñamuy's number.

"You must have something good to be calling at this hour," the prosecutor said. "What's up?"

"Oh, I'm sorry. Is it really late?" Julieta said.

"I only just ate, don't worry. Tell me how things went down there. Are you back?"

Julieta described her discoveries in detail. From the shell casings on the road to the motorcycle that had been following them, the mayor's obfuscation, and the Alliance event in Inzá. But especially the story of the men in black and the boy who saw them.

"Excellent," Jutsiñamuy said, slamming his hand down on the table. "So there was fighting! And the boy confirmed he was the one who called it in?"

"When I asked him, he went quiet and hung his head," Julieta said, "but he didn't deny it."

She gave him the name of the pastor they thought might be the survivor, Fritz Almayer, to see if he had a criminal record. Excited, Jutsiñamuy promised to get back to them soon.

"You two should work here in the prosecutor general's office," he said.

They said goodbye—it was late.

Julieta decided to stay in the bar, have a little more wine, and go over her notes. She sent a message to one of her editors in Mexico, updating him on the investigation and promising a good article. By her fifth glass of wine, she was in high spirits and considered calling Víctor again, but she refrained.

When she went up to the room, she saw that Johana had lain down in the bed nearest the door and was already asleep. Trying not to make noise, she got undressed and slipped under the covers. As she settled onto the pillows, she heard her assistant get up to go to the bathroom, and saw her walk by not in pajamas but in a cropped T-shirt and underwear. She had muscular legs and a nice butt. Julieta felt a strange curiosity and waited for her to come out, pretending to be asleep. When Johana returned, Julieta stared at her taut belly and saw in the backlight that the skin there was covered with a fuzz that made her tremble. What was going on? She'd never felt this before.

It must be the wine, she thought.

Eight in the morning, back on the road under a cloudy sky. A few scattered drops heralded rain. This time at the rental agency she chose another Hyundai, a 4x4 with tinted windows. Though in her eyes the vehicle was ugly and incredibly tacky, it also made her feel safer and more protected. They skirted Inzá, spotting the Alliance church in the distance. They arrived in Tierradentro at about noon. If Franklin recognized Pastor

Almayer, they could focus the investigation on him and move forward.

They went straight to the church, but the boy wasn't there. They stopped a woman walking by with a basket to ask about him. The kid Franklin? Have you seen him?

"No, miss, I haven't seen him."

"Do you know him?" Johana asked.

"I don't know, miss."

"He's the kid who cleans the church pews," Johana said.

"Oh, yes, the Vanegas boy."

"Do you know where he lives?"

"He's not from the village," the woman said, setting the basket on the ground. "That boy comes down from the hills, but I don't know where. I haven't seen where he comes from."

"Who's in charge of the church?"

"I don't know, miss. Ask at the store—they'll tell you."

The woman lifted the basket again and continued on her way, slowly occupying her place in the harsh landscape. Looking at her, Julieta pondered that strange Nasa silence, that *not being there*, as if they were cloaked by the weather or the shadow of the mountains.

The store was on the north corner of the main square.

"Yes, his name is Franklin, right?" said the woman behind the counter. "He lives near El Tablazo. A little further on, I think. Ask around up there—do you know the way up?"

They were glad they'd chosen a 4x4, since the road was nothing but rocks, tree roots, and potholes. At a certain point, it was no longer drivable and became a stony trail. Johana parked the Hyundai off to the side as best she could, and they continued on foot. They ran into a man on his way down with two mules.

"The Vanegas family?" Julieta asked.

"Yes, miss, just over there," the man said, pointing vaguely to a spot between the mountain peak and the heavens.

Johana climbed quickly and energetically. She was used to long walks in the mountains. Julieta was panting, and cursed whenever she saw that each dip was merely a prelude to the next steep incline. Where the hell was the kid's house? At last they reached the summit and a track etched in the grass, which fortunately spread out level before them.

The view was incredible, but Julieta wasn't in the mood for landscapes. Johana took a couple of photos. They spotted a clump of trees with a hut under it surrounded by an expanse of corn.

"Hello!" Johana called.

A scabby mutt started barking, and a hen hurried across the dirt path, followed by a dozen chicks. Eventually an old woman peeked out from behind a door.

"Good afternoon," she said.

"Does the Vanegas family live here?"

The woman looked anxious, but came closer. "Who wants to know?"

Julieta held out her hand to shake, and the woman barely touched it before letting go.

"We're journalists from Bogotá," Julieta said. "We met Franklin at the church and wanted to talk to him."

The woman looked behind her, hoping for someone to come out and back her up. An elderly Nasa man emerged from the field and came over, tucking his machete into its sheath.

"Mr. Vanegas?"

The man lowered his head and placed his hand on his chest. "Yes, ma'am, but the boy isn't here. They came for him yesterday."

"Who?"

"I don't know, miss. He'd just gotten back from town and said he needed to go back because of something to do with the church, so I didn't ask any more. He didn't come home last night."

"Can we talk for a minute?"

The man hesitated, but finally made a gesture with his forearm that indicated to follow him. They sat down in front of the house, which looked out not on the mountain view but on the flat field and grove of trees. From the kitchen, the woman offered them a hot drink made from hardened sugar cane.

Julieta told them what the boy had seen on the road by the Ullucos River. "Did you know about that?"

"No, miss, the boy didn't tell us anything," the man said.

"And you didn't notice anything unusual about him at the time?" Johana asked.

The man wasn't expressing any concern, but Julieta had already learned not to prejudge the Nasa.

"No, miss."

The woman came out with two steaming mugs and deposited them on the table.

"Are you the boy's parents?" Julieta asked.

"Grandparents," the man said.

"What about his parents? Do they live around here?"

"The father's dead. He died young."

Julieta sat waiting for another statement that didn't come, so she ventured to ask: "And the mother?"

"The boy doesn't have a mother."

She took a sip from her mug and burned her tongue, but the sweet flavor lingered behind the pain.

"Everybody has a mother, don't they?" Julieta said, placing a hand on the old woman's arm.

The woman smiled briefly, but she didn't say anything. She stared at the ground as rivulets of water began to run across it, pushing small twigs. It was raining again.

"His mother left when he was very little, that's why we say he doesn't have one. We didn't know her."

"Oh," Julieta said. "That's different."

The drizzle intensified to a steady downpour. Deep in the

mountains, thunder rumbled, and when they looked up at the sky they saw a dense raincloud, dark and menacing. The air was no longer transparent, the other mountains no longer visible. A thunderclap boomed. And then another that made the ground shake. The old couple invited them inside.

Julieta said, "And what happened to Franklin's dad?"

The man shifted in his chair and said, "I'll tell you, just until the rain stops." And he began to talk:

The boy's father was named Justino, and he was our only child. We didn't have any others, who knows why. That's how our family turned out, very small. You can't do anything about it, it's decided up there and down here we just have to accept it. Justino was born big and strong and with good arms for working. So I raised him. I taught him about us, our traditions, our old stories.

Everything.

When he was five years old, a teacher from San Andrés came and told us the boy had to go to school. I told him no, the boy didn't need that school because we were teaching him what he needed to know right here, but they insisted he had to go, it was a child's right, imagine that, miss, as if his parents didn't know how to educate him; I didn't want him to, but they kept coming and talking to his mother, you know? Of course, she always told them, it's up to his father, he makes the decisions in this household, and so I asked Justino if he wanted to go, and he told me, whatever you say, Father. But do you want to go or not? He said, yes I do want to, if you give me permission, yes, but if not, no, the boy said, so well-mannered, and they pushed so hard about San Andrés that one day I said, well, just for a year to see how it goes. But your work here at home has to get finished the same as always, all right? So he did. The boy went up and down every day, he went to school when it was still dark out and came back in the early afternoon and worked hard in the field, and then the next year I let him keep going because he'd kept his word, and that's how Justino got an education, he learned the textbooks, and when he finished high school they said he was a good student, that he had good grades and should go to university, but there I did put my foot down, no, I said, he's our only son, he can't leave us, I need him working here at home, and then he was the one who told me one day, look, Dad, if I go to college I'll be able to get a better job, and then I can hire laborers for you so you can rest because I'll be making good money, and I'm going to fix up your house, and maybe we'll even buy a couple of cows and the large field out back, so we can plant more crops, beans and potatoes and cassava and even bananas and coffee, and so I said to him, well, where's the university? and he said, I have to take an exam and then if I pass it's in Inzá, at the University of Cauca, that's what he told me, and I thought about it for a few days, and I asked the committee and they told me it was a good idea, said the community needed educated people who could help defend our rights, so I said, go ahead and study, and so he left, and we saw less and less of him, he would leave for the whole week and come back on Friday night, on Saturdays he'd work with me farming cassava and bananas, working twice as hard now because he had to make up for his time away, and so I said to him, take it easy, mijo, now that you're gone there's one less mouth to feed so we don't need as much, don't worry, go on and rest, you must be tired, and we saw him deep in those books, studying, what was it that he was studying? I don't even remember the name, some university subject, and that's how things were for two or three years, he would always come bringing gifts, sweets, candy, once he brought some fabrics for his mother, a new radio, until eventually he stopped coming, first one Friday and then another, and when he showed up the next he explained that he'd been too busy, he had a lot of studying, it was finals, and we told him, don't worry; we stopped asking after that because we got used to it, whether he came or not, I would hear the dog barking like crazy and I'd know Justino was on his way up, and so another year passed, I think, or more, until one day he didn't come back, two, three weeks, a month, and he didn't return; at first I didn't say anything, but after a while, when I went down with the harvest, I asked, and they told me, we'll ask around in Inzá to see what happened, find out why Justino hasn't been coming, he must be busy, and so another couple of weeks went by until they gave me a letter from him, I have it right over there, but I didn't know how to read, miss, you know? But anyway I brought it here to the house, and his mother and I studied the piece of paper even though we didn't understand a thing, but it made us happy because it was a message from Justino, he was the one who had written it; about three days later a neighbor's son read us the letter and it said that after his studies Justino had decided to join the guerrillas to change the country and defend the people, that's what it said, and his mother wept, of course, and I didn't say anything, but I went out with the machete and chopped at a eucalyptus tree because I felt like it was my fault for allowing him to go to school. And so we ended up without our son, waiting to see what would happen, and well, one day they showed up with some money that was supposedly from him, a group of those guys who were in the area left it here, and they gave us some news of him, said he was fine, not to worry, he was still working for our sakes and would return soon, and so another year went by and we gradually got used to not hearing from him, to being alone, until one day someone brought us the boy Franklin, about a year old, saying he was Justino's son, that Justino couldn't take care of him and his mother couldn't either, and we took him in gladly, of course, and we raised him, and I was reassured because I figured that since we had the boy here Justino would have to come back, nobody abandons their son, but as time passed and we didn't hear anything, I started wondering, what about the mother? They'd said she was a fighter too, but that's it. Every three or four months

*we'd receive a message or a little money, for the boy, that's what
the guy who brought it always said, and I'd send word to Justino
asking for him to come visit, to bring the mother so we could
meet her, but they said it was too dangerous, that Justino was in
leadership and couldn't, that the region was sealed off, and so
time passed, and then right before those damn peace agreements
were signed, just a little before, they informed us he'd been
injured in combat, that he was alive but wounded, and I said, ah,
that's how evil arrives, the devil brings his winds and his brews,
and I could already see that devil's tail in the sky, and the next
time they came it was to say he'd died, they brought a box with
the ashes and a bag with his things, and they said I had given a
son to the people's struggle, which was a just cause, and they
gave me some money and said they were going to help me, but I
said thank you, there's no need, and I asked after the boy's
mother, whether she was ever going to come, and they said she
was in another region, fighting, that's what they said. I didn't
even know her name, so I asked them so I could tell the boy
when he grows up, but they wouldn't tell me, they left and here
we are, until today's sunrise, ladies, or rather, until today's rain,
which is clearing, and now we're waiting for the boy instead; this
time the people who came looking for him said they were from
the church, and he didn't seem worried as he left, they often call
him and he's gone two, even three days, we don't ask anymore,
we're old, and eventually you learn they always leave anyway.*

It was hard going on the way down, since the path was now
full of puddles and mud and wet, slippery rocks. Johana was
quiet. Julieta figured she'd been deeply moved by the boy's
story. Did she know something? Had she met the boy's father?
Seeing her colleague so subdued, she decided not to ask, but
they'd talk about it later. Johana must have seen a lot of female
fighters give birth, and know a lot of stories. The soldier who
hands her baby over and goes back to the fight. Had she

known Franklin's mother? Did she have a kid herself, or several, growing up in a shabby farmer's hut somewhere? The image of Johana's taut belly rose in her mind: abs like that haven't ever been pregnant.

When they reached the car, she thought Johana's eyes looked a bit red. Maybe some of what she'd imagined was true.

"You OK?" she asked.

"That kid's story hit me hard," Johana said. "We have to find him."

"Do you know anything? Does the dad's name sound familiar?" Julieta asked.

"I didn't know many people's real names, and I wasn't in this area at the end of the conflict. Comrades were dying all the time."

They went down to the church in San Andrés de Pisimbalá, which was still closed, with nobody working on the roof repairs, so they headed over to the archeological museum. Julieta asked to speak to the director.

They were shown into an office that looked out on the San Andrés gorge. A colonial-style house with wide corridors and windows with frames made of orange-hued wood. The director, Jacinto Duque, an anthropologist from Popayán, greeted them. They sat down and were offered coffee.

Julieta explained that they were looking into an armed confrontation that had taken place a few kilometers away. The director knew nothing about it.

"I was in Popayán for a lecture at the University of Cauca last week," he said apologetically. "Nobody here told me anything. Combat? Where?"

They recounted the boy's tale. The museum director, surprised, kept repeating that nobody had said anything to him about it.

Next they asked who was in charge of the church.

"It's a long story," Duque said. "Because of the delicate

situation in keeping public order, they made this an apostolic vicariate. In 1989 Don Germán García Isaza was named prefect, but in 2002 the FARC threatened his life and he had to flee. So because of the problems with the guerrillas, it was given to the Apostolic Missionaries of Yarumal, and Bishop Edgar Tirado was named prefect, but he never comes here. A priest comes on the weekends, but everything else is managed from Inzá. And then there was the church fire—do you know about that?"

"More or less," Julieta said.

"There was a conflict between the reservation indigenous community and farmers over some issue about education and land, which isn't at all clear. Honestly, it's best to leave it alone. The church is being repaired now, even if it's slow going. It's an eighteenth-century church! It was constructed by members of the indigenous population. Using their materials, but following the Spanish tradition. Cultural synthesis. Did the boy you're looking for work there?"

"Yes," said Julieta. "We talked to him yesterday. He was cleaning the pews with some sort of wax. Today we went up to El Tablazo to look for him at his house, but his grandparents said people came for him yesterday. From the church."

"They must have been from the church in Inzá," the anthropologist said. "Definitely, they're the ones who manage the repairs. You should go and ask there. The parish priest is Father Tomás."

"When will the restoration be finished?" Johana asked.

"It's been years, but there's no money. It's getting done a little at a time. Like everything good in this country. Did you go to see the hypogea? Do you know about them?"

"Yes," Julieta said. "I'd love to see them, but we've got this other issue to deal with. We need to talk to the boy again."

"I suggest you go to Inzá, they'll tell you what's up. Maybe they took him somewhere else to do some kind of job."

"It's strange they didn't tell his grandparents though," Julieta said, "don't you think?"

"People move at a different pace here. Remember, they're Nasas. At twelve, a boy is already a man."

"Well," Julieta said, "I'm sure you're right. We'll head to Inzá."

As they left the museum, Julieta looked around. The image of the motorcyclist was still at the front of her mind, but she didn't see anything. Everything seemed calm, so they pulled onto the road. Johana kept her eye on the rearview mirror and they stopped a couple of times.

But there was nothing.

Inzá's parochial church stood on the north end of town, on a leafy square shaded by oaks, palms, and shrubs. A neatly tended garden. The women were impressed by the majestic architecture. The central tower was topped by a cupola of arches. Inside, a nave ran down each side. At the far end they saw a large statue of Christ on the cross, known locally as Our Lord of Guanacas.

The priest, Father Tomás, greeted them with a big smile.

"It's wonderful that journalists from Bogotá are taking an interest in us," he said. "What brings you here?"

Julieta cleared her throat and looked at Johana. "We're here about a boy from Tierradentro, Franklin Vanegas. Do you know him? He works in the church in San Andrés de Pisimbalá."

"Of course! That's a lovely church, isn't it? And it's looking fantastic too. We're slowly getting there. Did something happen with Franklin? He works for Francisco, the missionary priest who's there on weekends."

"He hasn't been heard from since yesterday, Father," Julieta said. "That's why we're looking for him. His grandparents say people from the church came by to pick him up, but he didn't come back today, and nobody knows where he is."

"From the church? That's not possible—Francisco was in Popayán yesterday. The grandparents must have misunderstood."

Julieta and Johana glanced at each other anxiously. Had he been taken because he'd talked to them? They hadn't been prepared for that, but it was possible. It was also clear that the priest didn't know a thing.

Julieta started getting impatient. "Forgive me for changing the subject, Father. What do you think of the Christian and Missionary Alliance?" she asked.

The priest shifted around in his chair and for a moment she thought he was going to laugh, but his face took on a grimace.

"Well, that question is . . ." He moved his thick neck against the too-tight collar of his cassock. "You see. They're our competition, and of course with the resources they have they've already got the mayor in their pocket. There's no point in pussyfooting around it—it's a fact. They monetize faith, and we frown on that. But I'm saying this in confidence, between us; I'd rather not have them as an enemy."

"Do you think they could be dangerous?"

"I don't know that they'd be dangerous the way things are usually dangerous in this country," the priest said. "Or so I'd like to believe."

"We need to speak with Father Francisco urgently. Do you have his phone number?"

"Of course, hang on."

He pulled out his cell phone and scrolled through it. "Here it is, copy this down."

It was getting dark as they left.

On the way back to Popayán, Julieta called Father Francisco. Once, twice, nothing. "Why does nobody answer the phone in this fucking country?" she fumed.

Johana looked over at her with a mixture of mirth and

seriousness. "And it's no good leaving messages either—nobody listens to them or responds."

Just then her cell phone rang. "It's a miracle!" Julieta exclaimed—the priest was calling her back.

"Somebody called from this number?" the voice said.

Julieta introduced herself, gave a brief recap of events, and asked about the boy, but the priest didn't know anything.

"Nobody from the church sent for him at his home yesterday?"

"No, miss. That's what I mean. I was in Popayán, so why would I send for him?"

"And you're the only one who would?"

"Nobody can enter the construction site without my say-so. For starters. Franklin helps out with the cleaning during the week."

"You know the kid," Julieta said. "Where do you think he could be?"

The priest reflected a moment. "He loves the internet. Maybe he went to Inzá—there's a good signal there. But it's odd he didn't go home last night. Maybe he stayed with a friend from school."

"His grandparents said he left because he got a call from the church."

"He could have made it up so they'd let him go," the missionary said. "You know kids these days, especially with the internet. They'll do anything!"

"I'm on my way to Popayán," Julieta said. Her next question came out more like an order: "Could we meet up when I get there?"

"Of course, absolutely."

They met in a café cattycorner to Caldas Park. Pochi's. Fresh-squeezed fruit juices, chilled oat drink, organic orange juice, meat empanadas, gluten-free cassava cheese bread.

Julieta and Johana ordered coffees.

Francisco was an odd-looking man. A scraggly mustache strove, without much success, to disguise a cleft lip that had been sewn up, probably when he was a teenager, which created a strange tension in his mouth and twisted when he spoke. He was skinny and anxious. Instead of coffee, he ordered a glass of the cinnamon oat drink. Julieta guessed that his nerves had destroyed his digestion. Coffee is a powerful irritant. He might have hemorrhoids or reflux. She studied the way he was sitting and noted that in fact he was favoring one side. He couldn't be older than forty. The clerical collar under a gray zip-up jacket, dark pants, and thick-soled black loafers completed the stereotypical image of a priest on his day off.

"Franklin spends a lot of time in Inzá so he can connect online," he said. "He has friends from school there. He probably stayed with them. But I don't know who they are, I've never met them."

"And the people who came for him—could they have been from the Pastoral Alliance?" Julieta asked.

"Well, they do organize a lot of things for kids," Francisco said, "a way of getting them young and drawing in the parents."

The coffee cups were empty. Julieta signaled to the barista to bring her another.

"What about you, Father? How did you end up in San Andrés?" Julieta asked.

A very elderly shoeshine man, skinny and hunched from the weight of his box, crossed the street diagonally and came toward the priest, pointing at his shoes, but Francisco wagged his finger no. The last light of evening turned the sky purple behind the lush trees in the plaza: Castille guava, mora, mango, charichuela. The twilight scene, with the beds of hydrangeas and ornamental hedges, evoked the colors in an old engraving.

Let's see, where do I start? I'm from Madrid, outside of Bogotá. At sixteen I was ordained as a Franciscan. No, actually that was my first vows and investiture. Ordainment came later, when I was eighteen. I joined the order to study—I was determined to get an education one way or another. It would have been dumb not to. If I didn't join the church I was going to have to work in the fields, on someone else's land, because my parents didn't have much. And being poor is tough and miserable, especially in this country, which is so unjust and hard on the poor. You dream and dream, only to get nowhere, and poverty is a tombstone you carry on your back that just gets cold in the night. I don't want to lie to you, miss.

And I did study, of course. I didn't manage to travel the world, but I saw Colombia. Ultimately, that's my world. They sent me to Virrey Solís, the Franciscan school in Bogotá. I was so thrilled to go! I taught Christology, my favorite subject, the life of our Lord. I taught the kids his ideas, but I mixed mine in too, and after a while I started getting warnings from the administration. I was in the doghouse! Don't say this, and don't say that, it's forbidden . . . To avoid conflict I shifted to ministry with the Yarumal Society for the Foreign Missions. I've been strong in my life. You have to look out for yourself.

I was there for a while and later was sent to Caquetá, far from the trouble I'd had with the Franciscans. The people there are good, reliable people, strong. The children of poor country folk, indigenous communities, displaced or forgotten people—the dark and invisible people of Colombia. They started coming to listen to me, and I would tell them that I wept with those who wept and felt the pain of those who were in pain; I talked to them about the cross and painted it on their foreheads and in their minds: the cross, †, †, over and over, †, †, and I was a wounded man with the wounded children of war, and an orphan with the orphans, and I wept with the widowed and the mutilated, and if someone was missing a leg, I would draw a cross there, †, and if they were missing an arm, I would draw a cross there, †, and if someone lacked good eyes and a good heart and a good soul, I tried to draw a thousand crosses, †, †, †, †, †, and so I became a distributor of crosses, the cross thrower, because that's what missionary priests are: they throw crosses. The cross is the pencil with which we sketch on the heavens or on the souls of the wretched.

Forgive me, ladies, I got carried away with my own musings. It happens sometimes. Where was I? Oh, right, in Florencia, Caquetá, in the lost villages, all those gray children and men and women, gray like trees or stones scattered in a field—they're just there, in their silence, and one day they're gone, but others arrive, that's the law of life and of silence in those lonely places; places that may be insignificant to the nation but not to the Lord, and that's why I was there, struggling in those difficult places, where—forgive me—buttoned-up city priests who freak out when their cassock gets muddy don't go. The Church has its assholes too, ladies, if you'll excuse my French. Whereas I am imbued with the sinew of Christ. I am passionate about the word, enamored of the word. I know you want to know about the boy and how I ended up in San Andrés. Well, one day I was in Caquetá when I got a call from the diocese: you've got to travel to Medellín immediately, pack up all your things, and I wondered, what have they been hearing about me now? I was resigned, but when I got to Medellín, to my surprise they wanted to transfer me to San Andrés de Pisimbalá, and why me? I asked, and they said the previous priest had been threatened by the guerrillas, and since I was coming from Caquetá, the FARC probably already knew me.

So that's how I came there, and of course there were problems, but I've stuck it out. The Nasa boy started coming to help, Franklin, or Frankitón, as I call him. He was looking for work after school, said his parents were poor and couldn't afford to give him an allowance—the kid's obsessed with the internet—and, well, I've always thought that work is a way to learn too, so I started paying him a small wage to maintain the church, because since the construction's going so slow, the floor gets filthy and the pews get infested with beetles; I give him a bit of money and he keeps it all spick-and-span, and when I go there, sometimes on Saturday or sometimes starting on Thursdays, he has everything ready for me. So he's disappeared? They came for him from the church? To be honest, he uses that excuse to get away from his grandparents. My bet is he's at the cybercafé in Inzá or staying at a friend's house. I've been in Popayán, so how would the church be sending for him? The people at the missionary inn can vouch for me. He's a good kid, but I'm only just starting to teach him. He does like to fib sometimes. I work with him, talk to him about the Creator and the mountains and the sky and the graves of his ancestors, but he looks at me like he's listening to the rain.

It was dark when they returned to the hotel. They had something to eat in the restaurant and Johana went up to the room. Julieta stayed downstairs with her notes and ordered a double gin and tonic. She was nervous, anxious about the boy's fate. Something from their talk with the priest kept nagging at her: what was the gossip that hounded him? Her first thought was the most obvious: sexual abuse. She called Jutsiñamuy's cell phone.

"Hi, friend," the prosecutor said, "I'm all ears."

Julieta told him what they'd found out.

"OK, I'm writing this down. Francisco Berrocal? All right, we'll see what we've got," Jutsiñamuy said. "We didn't have anything on that other guy, Fritz Almayer."

"He doesn't have a record?"

"He's cleaner than a porcelain Christ. Not one complaint, not even a ticket for running a red light."

"Well," Julieta said, "it's not for sure it was him anyway. It was just a guess because of the black clothing. We need the boy to confirm."

"Remember, all priests wear black."

"Let's wait a little longer," Julieta said. "And . . . speaking of tickets, can you find out whether he's got a car registered to him? Or to his church? Is there a Hummer or some SUVs?"

"That's good," the prosecutor said. "I mean the Hummer. Everybody's got SUVs, you don't have to be mobbed up for that. But Hummers are a different story."

"And did you learn anything about why they're hiding what happened?"

"No, I haven't looked into that yet—I need a little more meat on the grill first. But I'll dig around soon."

They said goodbye.

As she sipped her gin and tonic, her mind started to make strange associations. The missing boy, the man in black, the biker in the tinted helmet, the chatty priest. She doodled several circles and drew some lines. A possible trail emerged:

The man on the motorcycle kidnapped the boy because he saw him talking to us.

The biker works for New Jerusalem. They want to know what exactly the boy saw and what he might have said that would implicate . . . the priest?

Always back to Fritz.

She thought: *Thanks to the car rental agreement, they know who I am and what I do, and why I'm here. They know I'm investigating. They have my documents, my address in Bogotá. They've been spying on me since the day we went to inspect the road.* "Maybe they're watching me," she wrote at the bottom of the page. She tapped the table with her index and ring fingers to help herself think. *Fritz, Fritz.* She drew a larger circle in the center of her page and wrote: "Mr. F. Who is this mysterious person?" From the *F* she drew an arrow to another bubble, in which she wrote, "Attack on the road to San Andrés." And from there another arrow to an empty circle where she wrote, "Mr. F's attacker."

Another circle was still floating on the page. In it she wrote, "Father Francisco." *Another F! And the kid Franklin too! Everybody's an F in this story. Aren't there any other letters they could use?* Wanting a smoke, she went out into the street, still holding her drink. It was a cool night, and groups of teenagers were walking past toward the park, talking over-loudly. She asked the doorman for a cigarette.

"I don't smoke, but I'll get you one." He went out and intercepted the group. "Would one of you be so kind as to offer the lady a cigarette?"

They gave her a Belmont, the brand she hated most, but she was in no position to be choosy. She thanked them and smoked, watching the crowds congregating toward the square, as if the ground were sloped so that everybody would inevitably end up there. Suddenly, amid the tide of people, she saw a different group approaching. Men in suits and ties, with a preening, tropical sort of foppishness, at least from afar; elegant women in swaying skirts and heels. They were all wearing lanyards with their names and a logo around their necks— what was it? They were headed straight for her, and she moved aside to let them pass. *ACOPI*, she read, the acronym for the Colombian Association for Small and Medium Industries. Black, gray, blue clothing. Each with their own idea of sophistication. Not just in their attire but also in their gestures and expressions, waving one another through at the door, exaggerating like bullfighters: "Please, go ahead," "Oh, no, you go," "Absolutely not, you first," their interactions an implicit display of hierarchies, salary differences, seniority, and career paths.

Off to one side, Julieta observed the ritual. The complex shorthand of the Colombian middle classes. She recognized in it something that had always disturbed her: the national obsession with respectability.

She suddenly wished to be very far away.

She wanted to do something shameful.

She felt an irrational urge to abandon her gin and tonic and go to the park to drink cheap aguardiente in the crowd. To sing reggaeton, smoke a joint, and do a line of coke or dance barefoot on the sidewalk. A strange beast was breathing inside her and telling her, *run, get out of here, scram*. A wild animal huffing and stamping and furiously beating the bars of its cage, wanting to be free. She imagined herself very drunk, with dirty hands groping her; the smell of sweat, dirt, rank old age. She conjured up a fantasy of a disgusting piss shower and several of those young men pulling off her pants and licking her buttocks and groin with their disgusting mouths.

She downed the rest of her drink and was about to flee to the plaza when she spotted someone familiar in the ACOPI group. Who was he? He was dressed differently. Instead of a dark suit, he was wearing a tan jacket, white linen shirt, dark jeans, and tennis shoes. He was talking to two older executives, but it was obvious from a mile off that he wasn't from that world. Julieta studied him closely. Shit, she was already a little drunk. As the man approached the door, her disorderly mind returned the search results. She couldn't stop herself saying it out loud, practically shouting: "I know you! You're a journalist . . . Which outlet are you with?"

The man looked at her amicably but didn't answer. Julieta grabbed his arm and said, "I've read some of your work." Not knowing how to respond, he murmured a few polite words.

Then Julieta said, "What are you doing with these people?" She was clearly drunk.

"Working on a story. How about you?"

"Another story," Julieta said. "Let's go get a drink, yeah?"

The next day, her merry-go-round memory would recall that they went to a bar on a dark street, then another, and then a third and possibly a fourth, and that they drank an endless succession of gin and tonics that were delicious merely because she needed them to be, on a fevered path that bore them aimlessly but relentlessly into the depths of the night.

She awoke after ten the next morning. Johana wasn't in the room, and when she got up to pee and drink some water from the sink, her head felt like a block of concrete. Vaguely, she saw disconnected images of her nocturnal adventure: dancing in a crowded space that was suddenly empty. An exhausting walk. Lots of gin and aguardiente. A stop in the main square and, she wasn't quite sure, maybe a kiss . . . She didn't remember. Then, back in the hotel, a room that wasn't hers. A man's body at her hips. A rather cinematic blowjob and, when she touched herself and smelled her fingers, the memory of an exuberant entanglement that came to her in fragments, through a fog.

Exactly what she'd wanted.

But Christ, the headache now!

In a fit of lucidity she saw herself clutching a pillow, biting something and twisting the sheets with her fists. The smell of alcohol, cigarettes, and sweat. It was too bad the memory was so fuzzy, since she was alone now and her head was killing her. In the bathroom she splashed water on her face and, though she felt ill, managed to swallow a cocktail of two ibuprofens, a Dórex painkiller, two lemon-flavored effervescent aspirins, and three glasses of water with Alka-Seltzer. Then into the shower, which luckily was large enough for her to sit on the tile floor and let the stream of purifying water wash away the remains of the night.

"Everything OK, boss?"

Downstairs, Johana was at a table in the courtyard. She saw a jug of coffee, now cold, scraps of egg, and a piece of croissant.

"Are you still serving breakfast?" she asked a waiter.

"Of course, ma'am. Eggs, coffee or hot chocolate, toast, cassava cheese bread. Orange juice? Just tell me what tickles your fancy."

The huge black glasses hid her eyes and made her feel protected, as if she were looking out from inside an armored car. A Hummer? From a reality that was far from her harsh, insistent memory. She felt the blood surging and ebbing in her veins.

"I'm not going to ask what you got up to last night, boss, but I was getting worried."

"What time did I come in? I don't even remember."

"Like after six. It was already light out."

"Did I wake you? Sorry."

The waiter appeared with coffee, juice, toast, and scrambled eggs with onion and tomato. Julieta looked it all doubtfully. She speared a bit of egg with her fork, waved it in front of her face, and put it back on her plate. She drank a sip of juice and felt it slide sharply down into her stomach, like a cat slipping and digging in its claws to keep from falling. She nibbled the croissant, but the flavor that hit her palate was not at all what she'd expected. It was a crescent-shaped sweet bread, not a croissant. Never in her life, she thought, had she felt so far removed from the concept of a croissant as she did biting into that awful bread. She pushed it aside. A sip of coffee— that was good. The toast would be best, with a bit of jam, but there was another problem. Her taste buds bristled at the sugar that overwhelmed the flavor of the bread. She decided to leave it.

"I've got the worst hangover," she said. "I'm dying."

Johana laughed. "Hangovers are a symptom of withdrawal, boss. Have a beer—that'll fix it. Hair of the dog and all that."

Julieta glared at her through her glasses.

"No one's going to serve beer for breakfast!"

"Then have a Gatorade to rehydrate. It'll help your headache."

"I'd rather be in pain that drink that crap, it tastes like toilet cleaner."

"At least try to finish your eggs," Johana said. "The cysteine will help your liver process the ethanol."

Julieta lifted her glasses and stared at her. "Are you a biologist too? These fucking eggs are disgusting."

"I was a nurse, boss. I know what I'm talking about."

She grasped the fork again, pushed the skewered bit aside, and retrieved another. A curl of steam rose from the bowl.

"It's too hot."

"Blow on it."

"It doesn't taste like anything when it's this hot," Julieta said.

"Chew slowly. Pretend it's medicine. For you it is."

Just then Julieta's cell phone rang.

It was Silanpa.

"How are you?" she said.

She set the fork down on her plate again, nodding at Johana's insistence, yes, yes. Into the phone she said, "I'm still here, in Popayán, with a massive hangover. I had the brilliant idea of getting wasted last night, in the middle of this investigation. I hate myself."

Silanpa recommended that she eat some protein. What people on the coast call a basic breakfast. Bone broth, eggs, arepas with cheese. "And drink lots of water."

Julieta nodded again. She was getting fed up with people telling her what she needed to do. "Everybody in this country is an expert in curing hangovers. Fantastic. Did you find out anything about that guy?"

Silanpa answered not much. Pastor Fritz Almayer was clean, no record, but there was something odd.

"What?"

"It's like he appeared on Earth just over fifteen years ago," Silanpa said. "There's absolutely nothing from his previous life; apart from his ID, there are no other documents of any kind, no registration at any school or university or even library, no recorded travel out of the country. So basically, he was born at thirty-eight. Either he's an alien or he's a textbook example of someone who changed his name to start a new life."

"Sounds intriguing."

Julieta pulled out her notebook and in the empty bubble next to "Mr. F's attacker" and a question mark, she added "Possible enemy from previous life."

"What's weird is he's got an official ID with that name," Silanpa continued. "I managed to get a copy. Fritz Almayer, born in Florencia, Caquetá, on December 30, 1965. According to the records, he first applied for that ID at the civil registry office in Florencia on January 18, 1984. Even though he didn't exist until 2003. He renewed it twice and requested a replacement for a stolen card eleven years ago. That's all we've got."

The three bodies appeared in the ditch beside the road from Santander de Quilichao to Popayán, at kilometer 46.7, but a number of indicators suggested that they'd been shot much earlier and somewhere else. The closest town was seven hundred meters away. The person who sounded the alarm was a motorcyclist who'd stopped to piss and gotten the scare of his life.

"It's evident they were dumped here early in the morning," Jutsiñamuy said.

The medical examiner nodded. "So it would seem."

The prosecutor had arrived by police helicopter with part of the specialized team. They'd been sent from Bogotá when it was learned that the corpses could have been dead for up to a week. Before taking off he called Julieta and gave her the information, but also a warning: "Most likely, these guys are a completely separate case, but you never know. Best to go see for myself."

"You've got a good nose for this stuff," Julieta told him. "See you there."

The two women hopped into their Hyundai to drive over a hundred kilometers of perilous road to the crime scene. It was like an existential curse: being hungover and having to race down a road that resembled a water slide—and to top things off, it was just two lanes, which meant braking and accelerating again with every truck or bus they encountered. Three times she had to stick her head out the window, convinced she was going to throw up, but eventually she started feeling better. "No better hangover cure than a bit of momentum and some adrenaline," Johana said, to which Julieta replied, "Enough about the stupid hangover, focus on getting there quickly!"

They were still a ways off when they spotted the Volkswagen police van, with its green and orange stripes and the words "Mobile Crime Lab" emblazoned on the side. "It's way worse than a hearse," Julieta would say later. "When you see that van, brace yourself for something grisly." Yet more evidence of the ingenious and infinite ability of humans to hurt other humans.

When they reached the police tape, Julieta texted the prosecutor and he came out to retrieve them.

"This way," he said.

The bodies were lying on the ground, covered with sheets and waiting to be placed in plastic body bags, after which they'd be transported to the morgue. A forensics expert was collecting traces of blood and tissue. Others were taking photos of the scene and the positioning of the corpses. Julieta was used to this precise, incisive way of dealing with the material world. Latex gloves, tweezers, evidence bags. Nobody liked it, of course, but it had to be done. They all carried out their work in silence. *No matter how often it happens, this is what death is like in a country of murderers,* Julieta thought, *always inopportune, ugly, uncomfortable.*

"Any idea who they are?" she asked.

"We're in the process of identifying them," Jutsiñamuy said. "Naturally, they didn't have any ID."

Johana went over to the bodies and studied them from various angles, trying to process their wounds. Julieta took Jutsiñamuy aside and spoke to him quietly. "The fact that you came here and had me come too means you think these guys might be from the battle in Tierradentro."

The prosecutor scratched his chin.

"That is what I thought, yeah. I figured they'd started dumping the bodies, but now I'm not sure."

"Go on."

"The forensic team tells me time of death wasn't a week ago, it was in the last seventy-two hours. Of course it's their initial assessment, but if that holds, the timing doesn't fit."

"Oh," Julieta said, "that seems irrefutable. Unless they were wounded and took a long time to die."

"That's a possibility," the prosecutor said, "but they could also be from a hundred other places. We'll have to wait for the results."

Julieta lit a cigarette. "The Ullucos people cleaned up and erased their tracks. It would be odd now to just toss bodies in a ditch. Why go to all that trouble before, then? These guys will have families, people who will recognize them. They may be dead, but they still talk."

Jutsiñamuy looked at them again. "They could be low-level hitmen the bosses don't care about. The most people will say is 'we knew they were involved in something unusual.' Generally in these cases, the dead man's background becomes invisible. It's part of the criminal mind-set."

"Unless they were left here for us to find," Julieta said. "It's not like it's hard to bury three bodies. The person who dumped them here wants somebody to see them."

Before they left, Jutsiñamuy sent his two agents to ask around at the morgues and police stations in the area. Any death registered in the past week from a 7.62 caliber rifle or .52 caliber machine gun could be useful. Upon receiving their boss's instructions, agents José Cancino and René Laiseca headed to their vehicle, a silver-colored Subaru 4x4 SUV, rather dirty and with battered mud flaps. They'd driven in from Cali. As they left, Julieta gave Cancino her card and said, "If you learn anything, call me any time." Cancino was a young man, nearing forty. He looked at Laiseca, who was older, and Laiseca looked at Jutsiñamuy, as if their eyes, too, had to follow the chain of command. Jutsiñamuy nodded the OK. At that, Cancino relaxed. "Of course, ma'am, I'll be happy to let you know if anything develops."

Laiseca climbed behind the wheel, backed up somewhat clumsily, and drove off down the road, heading south. Everybody else remained standing next to the black bags containing the bodies.

"What caliber are the wounds?" Julieta asked.

"We'll know that soon," Jutsiñamuy said, looking at the forensic technician for confirmation, "Right? They're only just getting them ready to move. Don't rush me."

"My ballistics expert here can tell you the caliber in less than a second," Julieta said, nodding at Johana.

"Don't exaggerate, boss. From what I saw, they don't look like they're from the same battle," Johana said. "The one guy's gunshots are close range. The other two are a possible match. One is missing three fingers on his right hand and has a cut on his left palm—in other words, he died firing his gun. Typical combat corpse. He was shot from far away, downward trajectory. That one could be one of our guys. Shot from a helicopter, maybe."

Jutsiñamuy listened with interest. He signaled to the team to leave the bodies where they were.

"Hang on a minute, if you don't mind. I'm going to take a look at what Johana's talking about." He turned to one of the team members. "Open them up."

The sound of the zipper set their teeth on edge. Three bodies: their faces pale, parched, swollen masks. Johana bent down and pointed out the gunshot wounds. Indeed, one guy's wounds were different. Four impacts that exited through his back.

The forensic pathologist put his mask back on and leaned

closer. The body had sunken eyelids, as if the eye sockets were empty. Focusing, he reviewed the wounds one by one. Suddenly a pointing finger intruded on his gaze. It was Johana, gesturing to the mustache. Several of the hairs were clumped together.

"Look, sir. Melted frost."

Everybody peered at it.

"They took this guy out of a refrigerator," Johana said. "That's why his eyes are sunken. He's been dead longer than the other two."

There was an awkward silence. The photographer came over and took several closeup shots. Jutsiñamuy got impatient. "What do you think of the lady's theory?" he asked the forensic pathologist.

The man stood up, removing his mask. "She's right. They kept him cold—he's different."

They zipped up the bags again.

"I'd better take them to Bogotá to take a proper look at them," said the prosecutor.

PART II

Not-so-human Beings

Jutsiñamuy's office looked like an artist's studio. But then, he wasn't like other prosecutors, or even like your everyday citizen. Widowed and childless at fifty-nine, he spent more time at the office than in his gloomy Niza home full of memories and nightmares. If he was going to be alone, he preferred his office. It was a mezzanine, full of files, battered books, and art-history magazines that he bought at the used bookstores downtown. As well as outdated encyclopedias, like the *Ariel Juvenil* and several from the Salvat publishing house: the *Encyclopedia of Colombian Art* and the *History of Colombia*. And of course an array of seemingly useless objects: a small basket of rusty keys, three plastic Kodak cameras, a damaged music box with a circus horse, ashtrays from European hotels, padlocks, buttons—where did he get it all? He liked flea markets. His office was unusually large, even if it wasn't the most comfortable or easiest to access in the building. He had a bathroom with a shower, a triangular nook with a wicker sofa and two more armchairs, plus a work table with a computer and printer, telephone, and ancient fax machine, barely used. The table stood in front of a huge picture window with a view of Avenue of the Americas, Guadalupe Hill, and, in the distance, the clustered lights of Usme and Ciudad Bolívar, the impoverished areas to the south, a Lumpenproletariat landscape and the unfortunate source of most of the city's cases of violence, robberies, murders, stabbings, and shootings. Petty theft and drug dealing.

Sometimes the prosecutor would stare out at those lights and, overwhelmed by reality, would imagine heartrending scenes: children begging their mothers not to do drugs and feed them instead, fathers beating those same children, men punching pregnant women, drunk men raping their wives in front of young children. It wasn't all like that, of course. Most of those households were just struggling to get by, honest people trying to make it in back-breaking, ill-paid jobs, but his experience insisted on showing him the other side: the savage face of the ferocious, indifferent city, the scarred and wounded skin of this wretched metropolis that swallowed up its most vulnerable children alive.

When he left his office and walked to the end of the hall to get some hot water for tea from the communal urn next to the elevator, he could see the lights of northern Bogotá. The opulent, wealthy end of the city. That sight evoked other crimes, more compatible with the view, since in Bogotá crime, too, is stratified by social class. Those hills housed the corruption of congressmen and civil servants, illegal commissions obtained for prominent families, the pilfering of public funds validated through contracts, influence peddling, tax evasion, the misappropriation of resources, breach of public duties, fraud, and every possible and conceivable form of theft, but at high—astronomically high—rates. The difference was that the northern thieves stole millions of dollars, so they were arrogant, lazy, and depressed: the domestic factory for social contempt and violence. Of course in the north there were also rapes and beatings, drug addicts and psychopaths, murder and femicide, abuse of minors and exploitation and assault, Jutsiñamuy would remind himself. *They're not as desperate, but they're the same species.*

Musing on the crimes inflicted on Colombia's citizens by day-to-day life, he decided to take a look at the news bulletin from the Office of the Prosecutor General itself. He switched on his computer and opened the page. What's on the menu today? What have we got?

He read:

April 27, 201– / 8:47 P.M. /
Seven families received psychological, psychosocial, and legal support from the Office of the Prosecutor General, in collabora-tion with the Unit for Holistic Aid and Redress to Victims (UARIV), to assist them in preparing to receive the remains of their family members, who were victims of the Colombian con-flict.

The interagency support team of forensic pathologists and odontologists, psychologists, social workers, and other profes-sionals worked for three days with the thirty-five relatives of the victims, whose bodies were exhumed between 2011 and 2016 in Florencia (Caquetá) and in the departments of Tolima and Meta. The homicides were committed by participants in the country's armed conflict.

Seventeen years after she was disappeared, Yolima Orozco Arango's family received her remains. She vanished from a rural area outside Palo Cabildo (Tolima) while working as a physi-cian's assistant. On March 10, 2017, the incident was attributed to the arm of the Self-Defense Forces of the Magdalena Medio led by Omar Isaza.

Javier Castellanos was last seen in the year 2007. He was killed in combat in 2008 in Puerto Rico (Meta). His exhumation was carried out in accordance with Agreement #62, signed in Havana, Cuba.

Also exhumed under this agreement was the body of Luis Emiro Mejía Carvajal, whose family never heard from him again after Holy Week in the year 2000.

On April 8, 2000, José Abel Tafur was taken along with sev-eral family members by an unlawful armed group in Morelia (Caquetá). After three days his family was freed. His body was recovered in the rural settlement of Palmarito outside Florencia, the capital of Caquetá.

The victims also include Edison Varón Alarcón, who left his farm along with his brother and another man. Following a tip received by Justice and Peace in 2009, the criminology team exhumed the body in 2014.

At the Office of the Prosecutor General's request, the body of Daniel Sanabria was also exhumed in 2011, but the crime against him was committed on August 16, 2000.

Additionally, Sergio Guarnizo Rodríguez, twenty-three years old, disappeared in 2003, when he was loaded into an SUV. His whereabouts thereafter were unknown. Along with his body, three other bodies were also recovered.

The judicial proceedings took place in the Hotel Lusitania in the city of Ibagué (Tolima) through the Search Unit for Disappeared Persons run by the National Office of Transitional Justice of the Prosecutor General.

The menu presented some appealing options, but when he reread the entries, he saw that they were all incidents from the past. The vast wave of war, now subsided, was still tossing bodies up onto the sand. The country was still uprooting its beautiful blanket of vegetation to exhume the thousands of lonely bones so that each one could reclaim its name and tell its story. "Colombia: a box of bones," he said aloud.

The ring of his cell phone startled him from his musings. He patted the pockets of his pants and shirt—where the hell had he put it? With the echoing acoustics in the office, the sound seemed to come from everywhere. The pocket of his jacket, hanging from the coat rack. He jumped toward it. If there was one thing he hated, it was failing to pick up the phone. He considered it a minor defeat. He calculated one more ring just as he spotted his phone, on a bookcase across the office. He lunged for it, but missed, and his hand knocked it skidding over several large binders and onto the floor. When he finally snatched it up and hit the button to answer, it had gone silent.

"Damn it!"

He saw Laiseca's number on the screen.

"I didn't reach it in time," he said. "What's up? Did you find something?"

"Nothing, boss," Laiseca said. "Not in Cali or Popayán, and not at any of the smaller police offices either. The problem is there aren't killings like this anymore. These days it's all small-ball stuff: crimes against social activists, scandals, sicarios with two-for-one deals, revenge beatings by local thugs and wannabe mobsters. Stabbings. There's a lot of that stuff."

"Keep looking," Jutsiñamuy said. "Ask for the reports from the provincial police stations. Maybe bodies have been dumped in remote areas. Remember: we're looking for gunshots from a 7.62 rifle or a .52 machine gun."

"At your orders, boss. Over and out."

After hanging up, Jutsiñamuy called the forensic pathologist. "All right, Piedrahíta," he said, "what did you find inside those stiffs?"

The pathologist was speaking from the autopsy theater at the coroner's office, where he was still working.

They'd known each other more than twenty-five years.

"Well, they are in fact from two different incidents. One's been dead about two weeks, and the other two are from within the last five days. I may be off, but not by much. The caliber of bullet is different too. The one who's been dead longer is the young guy, thirty-five. Four through-and-throughs. A nine-millimeter, something homemade. The other two, on the other hand, suffered much more serious injuries: one, destruction of the right lung with a lot of bleeding, the heart perforated at the mitral and tricuspid valves. The other, shattering of the skull, wounds at the clavicle and neck."

"What caliber?"

"Point five-two. Machine gun. Pretty heavy weaponry for peace time."

There was a silence. The pathologist spoke again. "Tell me if I need to pack a suitcase and leave the country."

"What are you talking about, man? You didn't leave even when things were totally fucked. It's weird, though. I hope the old conflict isn't surfacing again."

"I was thinking that," Piedrahíta said. "I've been getting nothing but stab wounds and small bullet holes for a while now. These ones scared me."

"How far away were the shooters?"

"I'd guess about fifty meters."

"From above?" Jutsiñamuy asked.

"Yes, exactly," Piedrahíta said. "Wow, you're learning!"

"The young woman who was at the crime scene said it."

"Oh, I remember," Piedrahíta said. "I met her last year during that case with the guy where they amputated everything and cut off his balls. She's sort of Indian-looking?"

"Jesus, Piedrahíta, remember I'm the Indian here."

"All right, sorry. Don't be so touchy. You told me about her. The guerrilla girl."

"Yeah, her. Ex-guerrilla."

"Well, she knows her stuff, because seeing all that without opening the bodies up isn't easy."

"Anything else worth noting?" Jutsiñamuy asked.

"The young man's stomach was empty, which is weird. And he was in cold storage for a few days. I sent off for blood and tissue analysis. If anything pops up, I'll call you."

"Were you able to identify him?"

"His fingerprints are worn off, but they're working on it. The other two we got."

"Who are they?" Jutsiñamuy asked.

"Their names are—or, rather, were—Óscar Luis Pedraza

and Nadio Becerro, both from Bugalagrande, thirty-eight and thirty-two years old, respectively. We've even got their social security numbers. They worked for a security firm, SecuNorte, based in Cali. What's strange is that in addition to the injuries I've already described, they were both finished off execution-style in the base of the skull."

"Really?" the prosecutor said, surprised. "People say it doesn't hurt that way."

"Come on down and ask them if you like," Piedrahíta said. "They look pretty relaxed here on the trays."

"According to the word on the street."

"Well, unfortunately I've never been shot in the back of the head. So I can't confirm."

"Do they look like drug dealers?"

"Haha, don't make me laugh. In this country anyone who gets shot and dumped on the side of the road looks like a drug dealer. Especially if nobody reports him missing. But those who die are victims. Don't forget that. They have their own dignity and tragedy about them."

"You're awfully philosophical today, Piedrahíta. Why is that?"

"You need some erudition to understand this shitshow, don't you think?"

"All right, Prof," Jutsiñamuy said, "I'll let you get back to work. Send me the reports when they're ready."

He hung up and sat thinking a while: *So yes, the caliber suggests that two of the bodies could be from the shoot-out at San Andrés de Pisimbalá. But why put bodies from different incidents together? Were they trying to disguise the other one? And who's stupid enough to think we wouldn't realize? Or the opposite: did they leave him there precisely so we would realize?* The exciting thing about this work, he thought, was that it always took him to the far reaches of human existence: of its idiocy or its cynicism.

Feeling agitated, he tried to settle his thoughts before pursuing his theories any further. He removed his shoes, lay down on the wicker sofa, and stretched his legs up against the wall. This would send the blood to his brain, but he didn't have to do it for long. Just seven minutes. After that he put on a CD of jungle sounds: wind in the trees, a gentle waterfall, water flowing over rocks, a bird taking flight . . .

At about ten that night, with something he couldn't pinpoint niggling at him, he decided to call Piedrahíta again. The forensic pathologist had just arrived home.

"What's going on? Having a hard time sleeping tonight?"

"I'm still at the office, turning this over in my head," Jutsiñamuy said.

"As soon as we get the results of the blood and tissue analyses," Piedrahíta said, "I'll finish up my report and send it over to your office. Ten tomorrow, max. So relax. Have a beer or a drink and put on a movie. There are some great series on Netflix."

Jutsiñamuy tapped his finger on his desk twice and said, "Tell me something. Was there anything else about the bodies that caught your attention?"

"Anything else? Like what?"

"Tattoos, for example."

"They do have tattoos, a lot of them. But everybody has that stuff these days. You can see them in the photos."

"All three men?"

"I think so."

Jutsiñamuy took a deep breath before he spoke. "You're going to have to forgive me, Piedrahíta, but I'm coming by to pick you up in thirty minutes. I have to see those bodies tonight."

The pathologist cleared his throat and was silent a moment. "Well, law and justice before health. I will ask that when you come you get out of the car so my wife can see you from the window and won't get suspicious."

"Absolutely. I'm on my way. Still in Torres del Parque?"

"They're never getting me out of here alive."

Despite the late hour, the traffic was still heavy in Bogotá. The falling drizzle was only a respite between downpours. The entire country was enduring severe rains and melting like a cube of sugar. The earth had become too saturated to absorb any more water.

Arriving at Torres del Parque, he got out of the car while his driver went over to talk to the guard. Before leaving he'd stuck a bottle of wine in his briefcase to give to Piedrahíta. It was the forensic pathologist's job to handle cases at any hour of day or night, but he believed in personal gestures. Plus he didn't drink. He couldn't remember who had given him that bottle or why. It had been in his office for more than six months.

The forensic pathologist didn't smile when he saw him; he only shook Jutsiñamuy's hand, a worried look on his face. He was wearing his pajamas under his suit. Jutsiñamuy looked up at the sixth floor and saw that the curtain was being drawn back. He raised his hand and waved.

"That'll be enough to reassure her," Piedrahíta said. "At this time of night, the only reason to go out is usually that somebody's died."

"Just think," Jutsiñamuy said, "we've got three."

"That's what I told her."

They drove through the Egipto neighborhood, which was populated with beggars, crack smokers, and hurrying pedestrians. They headed down 7th Street to Third Millennium Park—it was a strange name, futuristic and hopeful in a city that seemed on the brink of self-destruction. Watching the "dregs" of society preparing their doses so they would sleep easy, Piedrahíta mused, "I imagine the corpses of all of these people while they're still alive; they still move and talk and have their memories, but they're already dead. Humans are nothing, really, aren't we?"

"Nothing at all," Jutsiñamuy interrupted, bringing him back down to earth. "But don't start getting philosophical. We're going to see our guys."

The three bodies were on metal trays stored in a refrigerated cabinet.

"More light, more light," Jutsiñamuy said, bending over to study their tattoos.

He peered eagerly at the images imprinted on the bodies, studying them through a magnifying glass. What was he looking for? The two more recent bodies had a lot of symbols: suns with rays of light, gothic letters, images of Jesus on the cross, naked women with the name "Yeni." The prosecutor scrutinized them again and again. He took photos with his cell phone.

"Can we turn them over?"

"Yes, yes, of course."

A nurse, possibly an intern, turned the bodies over. They saw more tattoos: falcons, names, ribbons, daggers, harps, horses, tigers. The prosecutor eagerly studied them until finally pausing on one.

"There it is!" Jutsiñamuy said exultantly. "Look at this one!" He pointed to the ribs of the man named Óscar Luis Pedraza: the tattoo of an open hand, in shades of black and gray, with the words "We are healed." Nadio Becerra had the same image on his right shoulder, and the John Doe under his left nipple.

"'We are healed,'" Piedrahíta read. "What the hell does that mean?"

"Maybe it means the three of them are from the same team," Jutsiñamuy concluded. "Just because they didn't die on the same day doesn't mean they weren't part of the same clan, or cartel."

"Or one of those weird churches," Piedrahíta said. "The phrase sounds more like evangelicals than it does drug dealers."

"I was just about to say that. You took the words out of my mouth."

"How did you know they had those tattoos?"

"I didn't," the prosecutor said. "But a few days back I saw a TV show about Salvadoran gang members. Their tattoos identified which group they were with. I remembered that and thought we might get somewhere if these three had any that match."

They took photos and looked to see whether the bodies shared any other features, but they didn't find anything. They left the lab sometime after two. Jutsiñamuy thought of Julieta and sent her a message: "Call me when you wake up. I've got something good." Then, stretching his arms, he asked his companion, "Should I take you home, or shall we get some food?"

Piedrahíta looked at his watch and said, "Food. At this hour of night, it's definitely chow time."

Back in Popayán, Julieta thought again about the missing boy and called Father Francisco. "Please tell me he's showed up," she entreated after saying hello.

"Unfortunately not. I've been making calls everywhere, but no dice. I even talked with the people from the internet café in Inzá where Franklin hangs out, but they said he hadn't been in. Weird, right?"

"Really weird," she said. "Please keep looking, and if he shows up, let me know. I hope you understand that the situation is rather serious."

"Of course, Julieta," Francisco said. "Just think, a kid that young gone missing. It's unacceptable."

Reviewing her notes, Julieta decided she should go to Cali to check out Pastor Fritz Almayer's New Jerusalem Church. But she was worried about the kid. There were matters in Tierradentro that remained unresolved, like the man on the motorcycle and their nighttime visitor.

Now she was certain of it: the incident by the Ullucos River had been a battle that nobody wanted to leave evidence of. Between two groups powerful and well connected enough that the police had pulled their report. She decided to stay in Popayán one more night. It was five in the afternoon and her head and bones still ached, but she felt calm. A healthy meal, some solid sleep, and she'd be set. The next day, bright and early, they'd go back to Inzá to search for the kid and make a visit to the pastor of the Christian and Missionary Alliance Church.

"Johana, find out who's the pastor there. I'll need his name and where he's from, his educational background, if he's married and to whom—anything you can find. And get us an appointment for tomorrow."

"Sure, boss."

Julieta pulled out her cell phone and called her elder son. As usual, he didn't pick up, so she called his younger brother instead. Three rings and it went to voicemail. Anger began to rise in her. She didn't have the number for her ex's landline, so if she wanted to know how the boys were, she'd have to call him directly. She tried her sons two more times, with no success. She had no choice.

"Hi, Juli, how's the trip going?" Joaquín answered.

The hangover, which she'd had under control, returned in a wave of nausea.

"Good, are you with the boys?"

"Yeah, babe, we're at the Corral Gourmet on 85th, we just ordered some burgers. Which one do you want?"

"Please don't call me babe in front of them, or anybody else. Pass me to Jerónimo."

She heard some noises and Joaquín's voice. She imagined him telling the boy, "Watch out, she's in a mood." She could kill him.

"Hi, Mom."

"Why don't you answer your damn cell phone, huh? I called you a hundred times."

"It died. I left the charger at school. It wasn't my fault, I swear. It died, literally. The battery was at zero."

"Don't eat French fries—that's not food, it's garbage, and you'll get pimples. And go to bed early. I'll call you again tomorrow. Bye."

She sat in the restaurant and, in an attempt to calm down, pulled out her notebook. She wrote, "Three bodies tossed in the ditch by the side of the road between Santander de Quilichao and Popayán, kilometer 46. One with four gunshot wounds. The other two shot from above. Could they be ours? We'll have to see what the techs at the forensic lab find."

Suddenly she remembered Daniel Zamarripa, her editor at *El Sol*, the Mexican newspaper that was funding her investigation. She sent him a message: "Daniel, the story's going really well. Three corpses have shown up by the side of a highway. There are evangelical churches involved, and pastors. I'm on top of it, and I've acquired information nobody else has."

Instantly, as usual, Zamarripa responded: "Keep going, it sounds dark and interesting. Try to focus on the evangelical churches, that's a bombshell. But be careful. Ciao."

Johana came over and sat down next to her with a notebook.

"All right, boss," she said. "The guy's name is Ferdinando Cuadras; people call him Pastor Cuadras. We've got an appointment at ten in the morning. He's forty-two years old, from Pereira. He did seven semesters of systems engineering at the Technological University of Bolívar. He dropped out and enrolled in the National Training Service to do a computer course. He was a novice with the Jesuits, and while he was in the National Training Service he joined the Franciscans. He was there less than two years and left to start an ice-cream shop in Pereira, called Pipo's. It went under, according to the web page."

"How did you get the appointment?"

"I said we wanted to talk about the Alliance gatherings and their pastoral significance. He doesn't seem too bright. He's only been with the church for five years. From what I saw, most of the congregants are indigenous."

"Well, he must have good friends if he got that set up so quickly," Julieta observed. "Do you have a photo of him?"

Johana showed her one on her phone. "Here."

She zoomed in on the photo until the face went blurry. Then she wrote the name in her notebook. He looked familiar, but she knew that happened if you stared at somebody enough. Everybody reminds you of somebody. *All right, Mr. Ferdinando Cuadras, tomorrow we'll meet face to face.* Another damn *F* name, for a change.

"Thanks, Johana," she said.

Johana gathered up her things and got up. "If you don't need anything else, I'm going to watch TV in the room."

"OK, I'm going to stay and work a while longer."

Julieta watched her skirt the courtyard and go upstairs, gripping the handrail. She was a good assistant.

Now that she was alone, she really wanted to order a gin and tonic, but she resisted. *Away from me, Satan.* Better have a really strong green tea, with two teabags, instead. She called the waiter over.

"What'll you have, ma'am?"

"Do me a favor and bring me a strong green tea, with two teabags."

"Unfortunately, we don't have green tea, ma'am."

She looked at the menu again. "Then an Earl Grey, two teabags."

"Oh no, I'm so sorry, ma'am, we've just run out," the waiter said, bowing slightly. "We'll be getting it in tomorrow, God willing."

Julieta stared at him. "What do you mean, 'God willing'? Why wouldn't he be willing?"

"Of course, ma'am. It's just an expression. Sorry."

"Bring me a chamomile tea. Really strong. Two teabags."

The man bowed again and disappeared behind a door. After a short while he returned.

"I'm sorry, ma'am, but unfortunately we're out of chamomile too."

Julieta banged her fist on the table. "Then bring me a goddamn gin and tonic!" She took a deep breath. "I'm sorry. As you can see, I'm a little anxious."

"No worries, ma'am. Should I make it a double?"

"Yes."

The young man swung his arms, as if reciting a poem for his teacher.

"We can offer you Bombay Sapphire, Tanqueray, Gordon's, Beefeater, Hendrick's, Larios, Gilbey's, Bols . . ."

"Jesus," Julieta said. "You have all those brands of gin and you don't have chamomile tea? Even a nightclub wouldn't have that selection."

"No, ma'am, this isn't a nightclub, but there's one we recommend nearby, right on the plaza. It's called El Cauca-No."

"Thanks. Gordon's is good."

"Right away, ma'am."

She hated herself, but she kept working.

First a description of the battle on the bridge based on the kid's account and then the incident that night in the archeological park hotel. As she wrote them out, one after the other, something occurred to her. A possibility she hadn't considered and that, at first glance, seemed unlikely: what if it had been the kid who came into their room? Maybe he wanted to tell them something. They'd spoken to him the day after the nighttime visit, when they went to the church, but Julieta recalled having noticed something odd in the way he said hello. As if the kid knew they'd be coming and was waiting for them. But if that was the case, why had he stayed silent in the darkness? There were a thousand possible answers. "Franklin: likely nighttime visitor at the hotel." She remembered that the rental car had been broken into that same night. Was it a coincidence?

The gin and tonic produced a notable improvement in her general well-being. Draining the last of the drink, she started to feel really good. *I think I cured my hangover a little too well,* she thought.

She signaled to the waiter again. "Bring me another."

"Coming right up, ma'am."

Writing, like reading, is a socially aggressive behavior. A person writing is alone and oblivious to the things happening around her. As a result, Julieta didn't see the group of executives from ACOPI come into the restaurant. When she noticed them, they waved and invited her to join them. But she finished her second gin and tonic and went up to the room, bored by the prospect of bantering with the group. Johana had turned on the TV to watch the news and was lying in the bed by the window, on top of the comforter. She'd taken off her pants. She had nice legs and skimpy underwear.

Julieta couldn't resist teasing her. "Jesus, the guerrillas let you wear thongs? They can't be very comfortable during a gun battle."

Johana sat up with a start, embarrassed. "Oh, boss. You don't spend the whole day fighting. Obviously."

Julieta went into the bathroom with her pajamas and toiletry bag. She'd decided to take a long, restorative shower. Standing in the tub with the steam billowing around her, she was finally able to empty her mind.

When she came out, Johana was asleep.

*

Though he'd slept little and badly, at seven in the morning the prosecutor was already in his office. The events of the previous night in the autopsy room at the coroner's office kept replaying in his mind. They unsettled him. *Are the churches really tied up with this business?* he wondered. If so, Julieta's guess about the "man in black" was correct. He'd refused to believe it until now, but this was looking like evidence. He pulled out his notepad and read again: "We are healed." And his quickly sketched rendering of the hand tattoos. He studied the photos on his cell phone, zooming in on them as close as he could. He turned on the computer and searched for references to the phrase and the image. He kept mulling on it and finally called one of his colleagues.

"Wendy, can you come to my office for a minute?"

A little while later he heard two knocks on the door. Wendy was thirty years old, athletic and somewhat sinister-looking, with black lipstick and eyeshadow. Large tattoos peeked out from under her shirtsleeves. She seemed like the perfect person to ask.

"Wendy, honey, do me a favor and look into what the hell this means."

He showed her the photos of the tattoos and the phrase.

"It seems like it might be something religious. I'll take a look and let you know."

When she left, Jutsiñamuy stared after her. He didn't know anything about Wendy's life except what could be gleaned from her appearance: She was a goth, which could suggest a tormented person with social problems, but Wendy was one of the most well-liked workers in his unit. She never forgot a birthday, she was the first to give out gifts on Secretaries' Day, and she was always looking out for the cafeteria workers and the woman who came around with the coffee cart. Everybody thought she was an angel. "A Colombian-born angel," as he

called her. Did she have a boyfriend, husband, steady partner?
It was a mystery. Was she a lesbian? Not a clue.

He was lost in these thoughts when his cell phone rang. The
screen showed Julieta.

"Good morning, my dear friend."

"I just read your message. What's up?" she said.

He explained what Piedrahíta had discovered. The evangelical church theory was picking up steam.

"I have an appointment with the pastor of the Alliance
Church in Inzá in a little bit," she said, "the one who organized
the Pentecostal Woodstock over the weekend. I'll look into the
hand and that phrase. Send me the image."

After they hung up, Jutsiñamuy sent her one of the photos
of the tattoo, and as he pressed Send he felt a twinge of vertigo.
Was he overstepping in collaborating with the journalist?
There was no going back now, but he deleted the message
exchange anyway, pointless though it would be in the event of
a serious accusation.

With that done, he continued his research. He needed to
address another issue, one that, to be honest, he'd somewhat neglected: who had blocked the information on the attack from
within the police network, and why? He'd have to look into that
himself. He couldn't entrust it to anyone else until he knew more.

He decided to do an analysis, as objectively as possible, of
the facts:

1. Alert issued by a police sergeant in San Andrés de
   Pisimbalá, who calls the police headquarters in Inzá.
2. In Inzá, a corporal on duty receives the call and sends a cable
   informing of and reiterating the alert. He mentions the
   attack, the use of war weaponry, and the involvement of two
   well-armed groups.
3. An agent from the prosecutor general's office sees the cable
   and sends it on to his office.

4. He requests a more detailed report from the headquarters in Inzá, which in turn requests the same from the post in San Andrés.
5. The station in San Andrés replies: "That's all we know. Over. Huge shoot-out. Danger. Attacks in the area. Determine who they were."
6. But a few hours later everything was different.
7. The corporal in Inzá didn't say anything more, and headquarters changed its story: an argument between drivers that devolved into them shooting into the air. The station in San Andrés, after an additional inquiry, said it had been a minor incident.

Which means, he thought, *someone intervened in the middle of the chain of events, after the info was posted to the network.* First obvious conclusion: someone in law enforcement saw it and sounded the alarm (organization, group, church?). Meaning they stepped in and communicated with the Inzá headquarters. Who was the police chief there? He searched online: Genaro Cotes Arosemena. *Shit,* he said to himself. *From the coast? Let's see.* He pulled up the guy's file. Lieutenant, born in Planeta Rica, Córdoba. Fifty-seven years old. Served in law enforcement in Catatumbo, Antioquia, and La Guajira. Head of Inzá police since 2013. Theory: someone called him and asked him to change the report. He'd have to find out who'd contacted the lieutenant that day.

He called the technical investigation unit and requested a report on calls to and from the lieutenant's cell phone. Confidential information. Top secret. Then he went back to the three bodies in the morgue. He flipped to a new page in his notepad and wrote the three names again: John Doe, Óscar Luis Pedraza, and Nadio Becerra, from Bugalagrande, thirty-eight and thirty-two years old. He also put the name SecuNorte, the Cali-based security firm.

He called Agent Laiseca. What time was it? Nine already.

"Good morning, Laiseca. How's the search coming along?"

"Well, boss, it's slow going. We haven't been able to find any more cases."

Jutsiñamuy was silent a moment. "In the meantime, go ahead and look into the other two, the ones we've identified. Óscar Luis Pedraza and Nadio Becerra. Look into them at SecuNorte. They worked there. That's in Cali."

"All right, boss. I'll call as soon as we learn anything."

He hung up. He needed a boost.

He went out into the hall and walked to the urn. He'd been holding on to the information about Pastor Fritz Almayer. Once he knew more and the inquiry was headed down a solid path, he wanted to investigate it more thoroughly. Julieta's report on the other pastor, the one from Inzá, would be interesting.

At the coffee station he ran into a colleague with his shirt-sleeves rolled up to his elbows.

"How's it going, prosecutor? Want to take a stab at who wins tomorrow's Tour de France stage? We're taking bets."

The secretary of the archive was writing down the bets on a notepad. Up to ten thousand pesos.

"Put me down for Nairo in third but keeping his leader jersey."

"But that's not possible. If he comes in third, he'll lose several seconds for each rider and lose the lead. It's really tight."

"Write it down. I've got solid intel."

"Wow, OK. If you say so . . ."

"And fix that shirt and tie, man," he said. "We're supposed to represent order."

On his way back to his office, he saw his secretary coming toward him down the hall. "Sir, you have an internal call."

He raced to his office, closed the door, and picked up.

"Boss, I've got something good for you." It was Laiseca.

"I'm calling on this line for security, plus I'm out of minutes. I talked to SecuNorte and we learned something unbelievable. Pedraza and Becerra haven't reported in for a year, but the last job they did was providing security to some people who came in from Brazil and a Brazilian man named Fabinho Henriquez. I just sent you the name so you'll have it."

"Henríquez with an accent?" Jutsiñamuy asked.

"No, sir. It's Portuguese. The accents are different."

"Oh, OK," the prosecutor said. "Go on."

"I looked into him and found out he lives in French Guiana. He has a legal gold-mining company based in Cayenne, but I found some other articles. They're in French and Portuguese, but as far as I can understand, he has links to mining companies in other parts of the Amazon, and of course in Colombia."

The prosecutor listened impatiently, guessing the best was yet to come, and Laiseca said, "But here's the juiciest bit, boss. Hope you're sitting down. He's the founder of several evangelical churches that are part of the Assembly of God, in Belém do Pará! Huh? What do you think of that? According to what I read, he founded them himself in rural areas and in jungle villages."

"Hot damn. That is interesting. What kind of church is it?"

"International evangelical, sir, with a footprint in northeastern Brazil. They're Pentecostals, boss."

"What the hell does that mean?"

"It's a long story, but it's based on some verses from Mark that describe the power of God and the way it is transmitted to humans. They believe that God acts through the pastor's hand, so pastors have supernatural powers."

"Supernatural?"

"Yes. Bringing the dead back to life, curing the sick, speaking foreign languages without ever learning them, healing wounds, immunity to poisons. What do you think?"

"Amazing stuff. I should become Pentecostal."

"I saw it on YouTube," Laiseca continued. "There was this one pastor who used to do a show from the pulpit. He'd arrange to be bitten in front of the congregation by this super deadly kind of snake they've got down there, the lancehead. Its venom causes gangrene and heart attacks. I don't know what the trick was, but the video shows the fang marks in his forearm. And nothing happens to him!"

"A fake snake?" Jutsiñamuy said, joking.

"There's no such thing, boss. I was thinking maybe it didn't have any venom. That happens with snakes that are—"

"All right, tell me about the guy," Jutsiñamuy broke in.

"Well, that's all we've got for now."

Jutsiñamuy drew two lines under the information in his notepad, and in a fit of meticulousness looked at the time and jotted it down.

"Very good, Laiseca. Is Cancino with you?"

"Right next to me, sir. Do you want to talk to him?"

"No thanks, I believe you. All right, go out and get more info on the two guards, and I need you to find out who the third guy might be, the John Doe, OK?"

"At your orders, boss. Over and out."

When he hung up, Jutsiñamuy scanned the list of foreign pastors from the Inzá gathering that Julieta had sent, to see if one of the Brazilians was Henriquez. But the name didn't appear. *This is getting good*, he thought.

Julieta scoped out the building again from the side of the road. It was about three hundred meters away. A three-story structure with a steeple and a neon cross. Underneath, a lighted sign: "Christian and Missionary Alliance Church of Inzá." They turned right and drove through what had to be the furthest-out houses on the south side of town, went along the road, and parked in front. Her cell phone said it was a quarter to ten. She liked being punctual, but this often happened: she would arrive way early, when people were still getting ready.

They were greeted by a young woman in a skirt and a white shirt with the church's logo embroidered on the left pocket. "Pastor Cuadras will see you in just a moment. Would you like coffee?"

They thanked her and declined.

From the foyer a lateral arch led into the nave of the church. Julieta glanced inside. A massive stage or pulpit with an iron table on marble legs. Curtains to either side. Speakers concealed amid the fabric.

In the back, partially recessed into a wall made of something made to look like alabaster (or was it genuine?), a modern statue of Christ. Julieta imagined that during worship the figure, made of a strange red glass with purple streaks, must light up. Don Ferdinando's finances clearly weren't suffering, since unlike the plastic chairs she'd seen in other places, he had pews of cedrela or comino wood. Everything seemed very pleasant, but instead of an air of tranquility, the place set her teeth on edge. What was it? Maybe a foul whiff of air freshener that didn't go with the wood or the fake alabaster. A lavender scent, like a locker room or a motel bathroom. The fragrance was coming from the dark expanse of the floor. It had been mopped recently. *Gross*, she thought.

She turned to mention it to Johana and came face to face with Pastor Ferdinando Cuadras—he was practically on top of her. She recognized the man from the photo, though Photoshop had helped him out there. Whereas on the screen he looked young and energetic, in reality he was a pudgy guy with visibly unwashed hair dyed a mahogany color with gray roots showing. All of Julieta's revulsion for the lavender was transferred to this humble servant of Christ, who, to top it all off, almost bowled her over with the reek of his breath as he gave a beatific smile and said, "Welcome to our church." *Just what I needed*, Julieta thought. It was the thing that disgusted her most in a person.

"Come into my office," Pastor Cuadras continued. "I'm delighted to have you visit."

Julieta tried to avoid being directly in front of him and moved off to the side, but it was no use. Sensing that she was the boss, he pursued her, speaking even louder. In accordance with (unwritten) provincial protocols, he needed to put on a show for her, the well-educated urban woman.

"Besides my religious readings," he said, "I love reading investigative journalism. We have some great journalists here! What's that book about the life of Saint Laura? Oh, yeah. A-ma-zing. A fantastic study. And I still listen to the radio too: the W, Blu Radio, Caracol . . . I always say that here in Colombia we've got the best journalists, don't you think?"

Julieta sat down on the far side of the table and, still suffocating from the smell of his rotting teeth, managed to say, "Thank you for seeing us, Pastor."

"Always in the Lord's grace," he said. "This house belongs to everyone and to the Father of the world."

She longed for a cigarette, to shield herself with a curtain of smoke.

"All right then, how can I help you?"

Julieta glanced at Johana. "Well, my colleague and I wanted to talk to you and learn about the Alliance event you held last weekend."

"Oh, of course. Hang on a second, honey, did we offer you anything to drink? Esther, come here!"

The same employee, this time sour-faced, appeared in the doorway.

"I did offer but they said they didn't want anything, sir."

"Oh, OK, well, bring me a Coca-Cola Light, would you?"

He turned back to his visitors. "That was a huge event, you know. We prepared for more than a year, and I'll tell you some-

thing, it could be—I don't know, it could be the largest gathering of Christian churches ever in Colombia . . . Do you know
how many came? Thirty-seven! What do you say to that? And
not some dinky congregation that meets in a garage, no sir, none
of that. Thirty-seven of the biggest Christ-centered churches.
The theme was, of course, solidarity with the rural world in post-
conflict Colombia. I wanted to focus the discussion on declaring
those long-suffering territories a sacred zone, one of resurrection
after war, because that's the basis of Christian thought and evangelical action: forgiveness and reconciliation. Over the weekend
we gave twenty-three seminars and indigenous people came
from all over to tell us their experiences."

"But . . . are the indigenous people Christian?" Johana
asked.

"Some are, some are, honey. We're working hard on that.
The important thing is to look for topics where we're in agreement."

"And what topics are those?" Julieta asked.

"There are plenty, really deep stuff. For example, the thing
that worries every decent Colombian: the ideology of gender
and the creation of a homosexual state. We can't allow it. It's
an affront to God, and we've got to band together to fight it.
Fortunately we've been able to block it. The guerrillas keep
demanding it, of course, and since the government used to give
them everything they asked for, well . . . But luckily that's over
now."

"Tell me something, Pastor Cuadras," Julieta said. "You
pastors are allowed to marry, right?"

"Of course. We understand that human love is not an
impediment to loving God."

"And are you married?"

The pastor was silent. He cupped his hand over his mouth
and coughed gently. "No, miss, not yet, by the grace of Jesus
Christ and the apostles."

"May I ask why?" she asked. "You're older, experienced. You could start a family."

"Up to this point, it's been God's will to have me working exclusively for his glory rather than devoting myself to one person. We pastors are devoted only to the Lord and the Bible."

Julieta pretended to take notes, but she was only scribbling random words and doodling. She hadn't gotten to what she was really interested in: his relationship with Pastor Fritz Almayer.

"And which Christian church do you have the closest ties with? The Christian and Missionary Alliance is huge, right?"

The pastor shifted in his chair. "Absolutely. We're associated with congregations from lots of countries. People of faith seek us out and love us and above all support us practically all over the world."

Julieta didn't like for interviewees to notice her eagerness to learn something specific, but this guy was driving her crazy.

"Is that so? In what ways do you influence and improve the life of the community?"

The man raised his index finger in the air, as if he were pointing. "Well, miss, as I said, we're working for the people on a number of issues that are our church's main areas of focus in the world. For starters, providing relief and spiritual counsel. In these postwar times, you can't imagine the wounds people harbor in their souls! Here in the church we listen, organize prayer chains to help victims overcome their suffering . . ."

Julieta was getting ahead of herself, but she couldn't resist. "Have you received any government funding for your programs?"

The man hesitated. "Well, we have projects that require financing. But that's not the important part. What really matters is what helps people find the path to Christ—that's the key."

"And how's your relationship with the other churches in the country?"

"We have an assembly and there are meetings at least every three months. We're organized because the different institutions are all engaged in the same activity: our objective and our purpose is the word of Christ. We all agree on that, and because we're united we can express our opinion with strength on certain domestic issues. We are the voice of many people who have never been heard."

Julieta was about to give up on the interview, but Johana, noting her irritation, decided to jump in. "Pastor, I'm from Cali, and my mother goes to a church called New Jerusalem. Is that one of your churches?"

The pastor smiled broadly. His foul breath spread through the room and Julieta almost passed out.

"They're not part of the Alliance, but they're close collaborators. Pastor Fritz, who leads that church, was with us this past weekend. We work in the remote village areas and are good friends. He's a disciplined man and his expression of the message is exemplary. Tell your mom she's in good hands. I've been to some of his sermons and he's a wonderful speaker."

"How long have you known him?" Julieta asked.

"At least five years, shortly after he opened his church. He's from the plains region, from Caquetá I think. So he's sensitive to the country's problems, like us. He offers people consolation. We agree on that: you can't talk about the word of Christ without having your feet on the ground. I always wonder: if Jesus Christ were here, what would he do about this or that?"

Julieta's bile rose again. "Do you think that if Christ were here, he would have voted against the peace process the way you did?"

The man smiled nastily and looked at Julieta with a strange gleam, as if something had lit up in his mind. He was silent a moment, making a gesture of suspense that might have come out of a manual such as *How to Speak in Public*, the spine of which was visible in the bookcase behind the desk.

"If Christ were among us, honey, none of this would have happened, believe me. We would be in his glory. And now, if you'll excuse me, I have to prepare my noon sermon."

Julieta knew she'd lost an opportunity, and she hadn't managed to find out anything about the image of the hand or the phrase "We are healed." At any rate, she hadn't spotted them anywhere.

"One last thing, pastor. Do you know a boy named Franklin Vanegas?"

The man was already getting up. He was startled by the question.

"Of course. I know him well. Why?"

"He disappeared two days ago."

"Disappeared? Are you sure?" he said, reengaging in the conversation. "That boy is always off somewhere. He's young, but he gets around like an adult. He goes all over the place."

"Sorry, pastor," Julieta said, "one last thing. I'm curious how you met him."

"Oh, everybody knows Franklin," he said. "He's well liked. He comes to do odd jobs for a little money. Whenever he shows up I hire him for something, even if I don't need him. He loves poking around on the internet. Franklin's a good kid, besides that. God knows what he's up to on there."

"When did you last see him?"

"Just at the Alliance gathering. He was helping out with the delegations from other churches. He was assisting Pastor Fritz, actually, now that you mention it. He was with that group, if I recall correctly."

"Group?" Julieta asked.

"Well, the pastor didn't come alone, of course. He brought people with him."

"Women?"

"He performs his services with two women. He's almost always with them."

Seeming suddenly wary, Pastor Cuadras stood up and stared at them oddly, even icily. "Did you really want to talk about the Alliance gathering, or are you after something else?"

Julieta looked him in the eye. "We're interested in the relationship between the Catholic Church and the evangelical churches in the region. We were just in Tierradentro and San Andrés."

"Oh, I figured. So Father Tomás sent you here. All right, now I understand the point of these questions. You can tell him I said hi."

The goodbyes were somewhat rushed. Julieta couldn't wait to get out of there.

When they got into the car, she turned to Johana. "Are you thinking what I'm thinking?"

Johana eyed her cautiously. "It looks more and more certain that Pastor Fritz was the one who survived the attack. This pastor's story matches up with the kid's. The women who got out of the Hummer and climbed into the helicopter!"

"Exactly," Julieta said. "But there's something I don't understand."

"Franklin," said Johana.

"Yes, the kid. Or young man? I don't even know what to call him. If he was with Pastor Fritz during the festival, he must have recognized him, so why didn't he tell us? And another thing: how is this Cuadras asshole bound up in all of this? Did he send the motorcycle spy? Did he give the order to delete the report about the attack?"

They were full of questions, which was what Julieta most enjoyed. The twists and inconsistencies of a story made her eyes shine. She felt like she was deep into it now. It warranted a cigarette.

"We didn't find out anything about the tattoo," Johana noted.

"Well, one thing at a time."

They drove back to Popayán, where they retrieved their belongings from the hotel, returned the Hyundai, and hired a taxi driver to take them to Cali.

On the road, Julieta tried to organize her thoughts again. What was she looking for now? She had a hunch that she couldn't put into words. She considered calling her sons again, but just the thought of talking to her ex made her feel exhausted. She scanned the day's news on her cell phone and found an article about the bodies on the side of the road.

"The police found three bullet-riddled bodies in a ditch along the road between Popayán and Cali, near the village of El Bordo. The victims' identities remain unknown, police say, as does the motive for the crime. The three men were shot to death. The preliminary theory of the prosecutor general is that the murders are linked to local drug-trafficking mafias."

Julieta looked for additional news on the incident in other papers, but all she found was the same brief article from the Colprensa news agency. In Cali's *El País* she found a photo of the road and the bodies in plastic bags.

She called Jutsiñamuy and recounted her conversation with Pastor Cuadras. She told him she was on her way to Cali. "Did you see the news in the press?"

"Of course. *El Espacio* has pretty detailed photos of the corpses. In two of them you can see the tattoo I told you about."

As Julieta listened, an idea occurred to her. "Hey, tell me something. Are the tattoos recent? I mean, could they have been done after the men were dead?"

Jutsiñamuy froze. He hadn't considered that possibility. "I'll call Piedrahíta right this minute."

They hung up. Julieta closed her eyes. The heat and the winding road were making her sick.

"I'm heading your way, my dear," Jutsiñamuy said, calling Piedrahíta from the car. "Get the highway stiffs ready for me again."

"What for? We were just about to start processing them for release."

"I'll explain when I get there."

He got to the coroner's office as quickly as he could. He didn't have his driver, so he left the car double parked in the parking lot and raced up the stairs two at a time. Piedrahíta was at his desk. They said hello and went down to the morgue. The prosecutor was so worked up that he didn't want to waste time explaining what he was thinking.

The three bodies were still on the metal trays.

"The religious tattoos, Piedrahíta, that's what I want to see."

The assistants turned the corpses over. Once more they saw the open hand, black and gray, and the words "We are healed." Jutsiñamuy bent down as close as he could.

"Do you have a magnifying glass?" he asked.

Piedrahíta handed it to him and Jutsiñamuy took a careful look.

"All right," the forensic pathologist said, "tell me what you're thinking, would you?"

"I want to see how new these tattoos are."

The pathologist studied them and said, "To the naked eye they don't look very old, but we can analyze the ink."

"That's perfect. I need to know if the tattoos were done after death or if the men had them already."

"We'll need proper tests for that. Leave it to me. As soon as I find anything, I'll call you. I understand your urgency—it's an interesting idea."

They parted ways and Jutsiñamuy returned to his car. As he drove back to the office, he got a call from the technical investigation unit.

"We have the information on the calls you asked for. But it's highly confidential. Shall I bring it by your office?"

"Yes, leave it with my secretary."

"This has to be delivered to you directly, sir. You know how it is. These are delicate matters."

"I'll let you know as soon as I arrive. I'm on 26th now."

In the office, he weighed the various theories. If the tattoos were recent, as Julieta suggested, maybe one side was trying to send a message, a warning, to the other. Or just to pin the blame on them and bring them to law enforcement's attention, figuring the authorities would notice the tattoos and follow that lead in the investigation. A way of getting rid of the enemy—but which side?

Best to keep the tattoo lead under wraps for now. The case was starting to draw media attention, though they were completely in the dark as to the facts. The prosecutor was happy to avoid that pressure. He called Laiseca.

"What have you got for me today?"

"Nothing yet, boss, apart from it's boiling here in La Sultana. We still haven't finished digesting yesterday's sancocho stew."

"Don't you know it's against the rules to eat sancocho on duty?" Jutsiñamuy scolded him. "The dish violates the Geneva Conventions."

They laughed.

"I knew about the bandeja paisa, but not sancocho!" Laiseca quipped. "Over."

"Seriously, now," the prosecutor said, "go talk to the families of the two men we identified. They were informed last night. We told them that once the analyses in Bogotá were completed, the remains would be brought to Cali. All right? And tread lightly. We need to find out who the men were and why they were killed. That's it."

"Oh, is that all? It's easy to ask," Laiseca said. "The hard part is getting people to answer."

"If you pull it off, I'll recommend you for a promotion," Jutsiñamuy said, "so get moving. Is Cancino with you?"

"Yes, boss, right beside me. Do you want to talk to him?"

"No need, I believe you. Look, Laiseca, one more thing. As soon as you talk to the families, call me and tell me what they're like, OK?"

He hung up just as another call came in from the technical investigation unit. Half an hour later, they delivered a printed list of calls for Chief Genaro Cotes Arosemena and the station in Inzá. Organized in several columns were times, dates, durations, and phone numbers. The surveillance guys had written in the name for each number.

He went down the list.

Cotes had made and received thirty-two calls. *Damn,* Jutsiñamuy thought, *this guy's a social butterfly.* He checked the names: three from the wife, one from the mother, six to police officers, a mysterious Yuliana had called him four times and gotten six calls from him, nine to police numbers. He also found two long conversations with a private cell phone, no name. The first, incoming, lasted thirty-seven minutes; the second was an hour later and a bit shorter, eleven minutes. He called the electronic surveillance people and mentioned the two calls to a private number—could they find out anything more?

"That one's got added security shielding it," the technician said. "We were able to identify the number, but not the name associated with it."

"What level of security?" the prosecutor asked.

"Similar to what we use here. Should we keep trying? We may need to get authorization."

"Leave it for now."

Jutsiñamuy drew a line in his notebook to apply what he called the "jealous husband technique," in which he worked to come up with a sequence of events that best fit his suspicions.

The first call (received by Cotes) could have been somebody asking the police chief to drop the Tierradentro investigation and offering a bribe. That call, with all the discussion and negotiations, could have lasted thirty-seven minutes. Then, an hour and fifteen minutes later, Cotes called that number back and said, *Yes, I'm in, I'll do it.*

The theory fit, but there was nothing to show it had to be true. Maybe Cotes had talked to a colleague or relative who worked in security and then called them back to confirm something. There was only one way to find out: dial the number. A bit tricky. From his office? His telephone line was hidden from cell phones.

Before he could change his mind, he lifted the handset and dialed.

One ring, two, three.

Hardly anybody answers the phone these days, especially if they don't know the number. He figured this time wouldn't be any different.

"Hello?"

Jutsiñamuy almost fell over at the voice. He'd been so sure nobody would answer, he hadn't planned what to say. "I'm calling from the Office of the Prosecutor General. With whom do I have the pleasure of speaking?"

There was a silence . . . the clearing of a throat.

"The Prosecutor General? What is this about, if I may ask?"

Jutsiñamuy decided to show his cards. "I'm Prosecutor Edilson Jutsiñamuy from the criminal affairs unit. Please identify yourself and don't hang up; we are recording this call and have pinpointed the number."

"Lieutenant Argemiro Cotes, from the Bogotá police. What can I do for you, sir? What's going on?"

Jutsiñamuy was even more startled to hear this. He thought quickly. "Lieutenant Cotes, it's a pleasure to speak with you. I'm sorry to take up your time, but we need to confirm some details for an investigation."

"Happy to help, sir. Tell me what this is about—I'm getting concerned."

He had the same last name as the Inzá police chief. A relative? Even better.

"It's nothing serious, Lieutenant. We're looking into some bodies that turned up by the road from Cali to Popayán, and I was given your number to follow up on some information, but I see there's been a misunderstanding. Are you by chance related to the police chief in Inzá?"

The man laughed. "Of course. Genaro's my cousin."

"That explains it," Jutsiñamuy said. "You'll have to forgive me."

"No problem, sir, this has happened before. If I can be of any use for the investigation, you can count on me. Do you have my cousin's number?"

"I'll track it down, Lieutenant, don't worry about it. Have a good day."

He hung up and raised an eyebrow. A cousin?

He'd have to look into it. Argemiro Cotes. Police lieutenant. Cousin of the Inzá police chief. Excellent.

T he two women arrived in Cali mid-afternoon and got a room at the El Peñón Hotel, near the Dann Carlton. Two single rooms on the fifth floor, right next to each other. Julieta liked this neighborhood, midway between south and north, with lots of great restaurants and bars. New Jerusalem Church was north, in Menga, by the turnoff to Yumbo. They planned to attend the noon service the next day to hear the sermon and see what the church was like.

"Find out what you can about this man," Julieta said. "I'll see you in a couple of hours for dinner."

"No problem, boss," Johana said.

Julieta went to her room and got in the shower. She'd been hot all day, but now that she was naked in front of the deluge of water, she couldn't face a cold shower. The water felt freezing; she had to make it warmer. She sat back in the tub and plugged the drain. She couldn't stop thinking about the kid. Franklin. Had he really been kidnapped for talking to them? It was just a theory, she knew—if he'd actually been working with Father Fritz and his people at the Alliance event, what did he have to fear? She should disregard Pastor Cuadras's claims and keep looking.

Suddenly something lit up in her head.

She got up and, dripping, went to rummage in the room fridge. There were two small bottles of Blanco del Valle aguardiente, unsweetened. A bottle of Viejo de Caldas rum, the famous "twat loosener" of her youth, and two of gin. Among the sodas she spotted a Sprite. She grabbed a large glass, poured in the bottles of gin, and topped it up with Sprite. A Colombian gin and tonic, she thought. Clutching her drink, she headed back to the tub, but then she remembered her cigarettes. "Shit," she said, spotting the no-smoking symbol. She called down to reception and asked if there was a smoking room available.

"Go ahead and smoke in that one," the receptionist said. "I'll make a note."

The tub was full, so she got in and, shaking, closed her eyes to hold onto the moment of pleasure. Then she lit a cigarette and took a long sip of her drink.

Such restfulness, such peace.

A gray cloud passed over her mind when she remembered she hadn't called her boys, but her inner adolescent immediately snapped at her: *Leave them alone, they're with their dad! Enjoy this.* She took another sip. The flavor of the gin was a wash of cool water, something intrinsically and morally good. She felt primitive. An animal on a rock beside a lake.

The kid—was he really a kid? Yes, he was. He must be around thirteen or fourteen. Say what you like, you're a kid up till fifteen. A FARC commander had said that in the guerrilla forces, as in the rural tradition, boys are considered men at fourteen. At that age they go to live with their brides, who could be thirteen, and children come along at fifteen.

But just because it's normal in the countryside doesn't mean it isn't completely uncivilized, she thought. *They also confine women to the house to cook, clean, grow vegetables, and procreate. It may be tradition, but that doesn't mean it should be respected.*

The kid, the young man. Had he been the one who came into their room? What was that strange familiarity she'd sensed from him when she first saw him? She couldn't get that idea out of her head. The kid's face smiling in the church, the way he cocked his head as if to say, what took you so long?

He'd been waiting for them. He spent his afternoons on the internet, so he obviously wouldn't be able to tolerate rural life. He'd seen other worlds. Maybe he'd run away from his impoverished mountain life. Julieta repeated the notion to herself, but she wasn't persuaded, and her worry swelled again, inflamed because of her own children. Johana didn't feel like this. She got sad when she associated the kid with her past life in the guerrilla, but then promptly forgot about it. Julieta was a mother, so it bothered her more, calling up her own fears. It terrified her to picture him as one of her sons.

Suddenly something strange happened (time, her thoughts), and her glass was empty of the delicious gin. *I finished it already?* she wondered, with a rising panic and a guilty grimace. She got out of the bath and went to the fridge. She stared at the Blanco aguardiente for a while, but refrained. She poured some Sprite into the glass and lit a cigarette.

She returned to the tub, but the sweet taste was cloying. She stretched out her arm and picked up the bathroom phone to dial reception. "Could you bring me some little bottles of gin, the ones from the fridge?"

"Absolutely, how many would you like?"

She pondered a moment. "How much are they?"

"Seven thousand pesos."

"Send up six, thanks. And two Sprite Zeros."

A little while later she had a delicious drink in her hand once more. She took a big sip and felt its protective embrace. She could sink back into the blind zeppelin of her fantasies and fears, her musings and endeavors.

She was jolted by the ringing telephone. It was Johana.

"Did I wake you, boss? Sorry. But I found something good."

"Go on."

"I started reading the forums for the church people, and I see there are a few women who talk about Pastor Fritz, but not as a religious leader, as a man. Saying things like he's strong, he's athletic, he has nice legs. There are comments in several chat rooms and even on Facebook. One young woman says, "Getting involved with Pastor Fritz is playing with fire. I did it and got burned. Watch out, ladies."

"That's fantastic," Julieta said, energized by the drinks. "Try to find out more and line up some appointments. Hey, another thing: you should order room service. I'm tired, so I'm going to stay here. Or if you'd rather go out and meet a friend, that's fine. I'll see you tomorrow at breakfast."

"Thanks, boss, but after seventeen years in the guerrilla I'd best not be seen around here. If I show up in the neighborhood, the gossip mill cranks into gear. I'll just keep working. See you tomorrow."

"All right. If you find anything big, call me back."

"Of course. Good night."

Julieta closed her eyes and heard the snorting of that animal as it awoke inside her, pounding the cage with its hoofs.

She filled the glass again and lit another cigarette. She remembered the fuzz on Johana's belly and shivered. She reached down and touched her own. There were the extra kilos and the stretch marks from two pregnancies, plus a horizontal scar where no hair grew. When she hadn't waxed it looked like a crater, a balding skull.

She poured another two bottles and remained in the water, her mind wandering, conscious of the soundtrack of the animal huffing inside her. She still had two bottles of gin left, so she figured she could control it. She closed her eyes but was swamped by a jumble of images: the kid in a dark basement, shaking with fear, scared and alone. Who? It could be the evangelicals. She recalled Pastor Cuadras's halitosis and retched, but rinsed her mouth with a sip of gin and pulled herself together. Gross. Her mind turned to the common assumption made of a pastor or priest: that he's a pedophile. Was he keeping Franklin tied up in a room to abuse him? That seemed even more awful, but it was only an idle thought. She went back to the previous images. She imagined the pain of torture and, via a strange crossover, felt a craving for pleasure. She would have liked for a man to walk in just then, maybe a guest who'd gotten the wrong room. And end up rolling around in bed. Even if her body was no longer attractive, she still felt the same desire she'd felt as a teenager, when she'd had dozens of idiots after her. What she wouldn't give for one of those! She picked up her cell phone and typed into Google, "male escorts Cali." The ads appeared. "Afro-Colombian student. I can help you confirm certain anthropomorphic stereotypes."

She laughed and nearly dialed the number, but she imagined the scandal: an assault and the hotel staff rushing to save her; or even worse, the young man secretly filming her and then blackmailing her. *No*, she said to herself, *that can only happen in Bogotá, with the ones I can trust.* She was pretty drunk when she finished her glass, but still wide awake. She didn't feel like calling down to reception for more gin, so she opened the aguardiente and mixed it with Sprite. At least it was unsweetened. To make things worse, on the other side of the wall a couple was enjoying some foreplay. Though they were speaking quietly, she was able to catch a sentence or two. "Go slow, it's my first time this way," a woman's voice said.

That was the last thing she remembered.

When she opened her eyes she saw cigarette butts floating in the tub. The water was black and foul-smelling. The ashtray had slid off the edge, as had the glass. The water was very cold. An unbearable shrieking assaulted her until she realized someone was calling on the bathroom phone.

She answered. "Yes?"

"Jesus, boss, I was getting worried. There's only half an

hour left for breakfast—they stop serving at ten. I'm down in the restaurant."

It was Johana.

"Oh, shit, what time is it?"

"Nine thirty."

"I overslept. I'll be right there. Tell them to wait for me."

Full of self-loathing, she gathered the cigarette butts and stood up. Her head was pounding, but nothing that couldn't be fixed. At least she hadn't left the hotel. Somehow she'd managed to control the wild beast.

When she looked at her cell phone, she saw lots of messages. Several old friends were texting her. They were replies. She was terrified to read what she'd written them the night before while drunk. Three were from Silanpa. "I'm pouring myself a gin along with you," the last one said. Reluctantly, she scrolled back in the conversation to see what she'd sent. "I'd like to have you here in the tub with me." She erased the conversation without reading the rest. And the others? She deleted them without looking at them. One of the chats provoked a particularly acute wave of shame: a guy she'd slept with once last year. What had she said to him?

Best to forget. Or not to know.

Menga, just north of Cali, is famous for its nightclubs and motels. By law, Cali's bars had to close early on the weekends, so Menga, which was in a different district, was full of bars that could be open all night. People would go there to keep partying till dawn or to recover, now paired up, in one of its imaginative motels: Motel California, Kamasutra, Eros, or the famous Geisha, a Japanese-style place. All in a sea of gas stations, parking lots for semis, and fake-rustic restaurants. It's at the northern edge of the city, on the way to Yumbo, the industrial park, and the new developments in Dapa, heading up into the hills, where some Cali residents flee in search of cooler temperatures and respite from the clamor of the city.

Between two giant gas stations, a red warehouse with a corrugated metal roof announced the church: New Jerusalem.

Julieta and Johana got out of the taxi and found that even at that time of day, eleven thirty in the morning, there was an impressive crowd lined up. Ordinary people from the lower and middle classes. With a few exceptions, the church staff came from the populations hardest hit by economic crisis, unemployment, and violence: single mothers, internal refugees, parents of drug addicts, recovering alcoholics, domestic workers, battered women, and also regular people, of course, people who lead repetitive, arid lives, but who are there, smiling and eager, full of aspirations, seeing the future not as a protracted sentence of forced labor, even if in practice that's precisely what it is, but as a blank page on which, with a bit of luck, great things could still be achieved. The old dream of being seen by someone up on high, and receiving their mercy; of having a hand appear and pluck us from the mud. Being discovered, being saved. The obstinate human hope that insists on believing that the best is yet to come, and allows us to bear our heavy burdens.

They saw people of all ages and races. Women in flip-flops with stretchy shorts, miniskirts, blue jeans; young people in athletic clothing, Colombian soccer team jerseys with 'James,' the nation's idol, emblazoned across the back; older men aided by a nephew; elderly women; children dodging in and out through the line; workers, laborers, policemen, security guards. And countless impoverished Venezuelan immigrants, the ones that have been selling whatever they can at the stoplights of Colombian cities ever since their country fell into ruin. An expectant crowd chattering endlessly or talking on cell phones that, even if they weren't high-end models, still connected them to other people. Johana saw a familiar reflection and recognized herself in them. Whereas Julieta, bourgeois and from Bogotá, found herself in an environment that clashed with her own. Just the idea of wearing those flip-flops was inconceivable to her, much less a sweatsuit or tank top. But she was adaptable.

The worst aspect of life in the provinces and among the lower classes was their obsession with listening to music constantly. It drove her nuts! A characteristic of those who live below two thousand meters above sea level: an indelible conviction that silence is sad and dull; for most of the population, silence produces discomfort, unease, or annoyance, and so must be suppressed at all cost. A metaphysical terror of silence! One young man was listening on his telephone, not with earbuds but through tiny speakers that distorted the music. She was forced to endure this demented invasion, to allow herself to be irritated by it. Even with a faint hangover still lingering in her system.

At any rate, it was a tricky situation. Julieta hated evangelical churches, but she felt compassion for their believers, whom she viewed as hostages. Most of them had little education and, thanks to circumstances or ignorance, were easy prey for the nonsense, slogans, and quackery that these calculating, smooth-talking gurus put in their heads. She knew that tithing was obligatory and strictly monitored; followers had to present paystubs to calculate their contributions. Ten percent that was supposed to be for the Lord, but that instead remained in the pastor's pocket, funding his luxuries and comforts.

And all of it untaxed.

She wasn't a fan of normal religion either, the kind with priests and missals, but at least it didn't extort its flock.

The line advanced slowly. Security guards were searching each person. The women had to open their purses, backpacks, and bags as well as their water bottles and lunchboxes. Even the children were scanned with the metal detector.

Julieta and Johana were behind a family carrying a couple of babies and pushing a stroller. The grandmother was talking to the mother. The father, in a sweatshirt and red América de Cali jersey, was on the phone, talking loudly to somebody who was supposed to have come and hadn't shown. All were in flip-flops. It was hot, and Julieta was starting to relive the drinks from the night before. Up to this point she'd been submerged in a soothing wash of Alka-Seltzer, aspirin, and ibuprofen. With the heat, the vapors were rising once more to her brain.

Then she saw him.

On the other side of the chain-link fence, at the top of an exterior staircase that led into the warehouse.

"Franklin!"

She raced toward the entrance, jumping the line, but when she got there three guards blocked her path.

"Where are you going, ma'am?" One of the men, an Afro-Colombian who seemed to be higher ranking than the others, removed his mirrored Ray-Bans and looked at her sternly. A white cable snaked out of his ear.

"Do you have a problem standing in line or something? Everybody has to wait their turn or they don't get in."

"I just saw a missing boy! Let me through, it's important!" She didn't know how to explain.

"Wait your turn, wait your turn!" The crowd, once calm and happy, turned in a moment to angry shouts.

She tried to explain. She pulled out her press pass but then realized that showing it would be a dumb move if she wanted to go unnoticed.

When she turned around, she found the agitated mob glaring at her.

"Line jumper!"

"Respect the line, bitch!"

Realizing she was on the verge of ruining the plan, she quietly apologized and returned to her place in line.

"I saw Franklin, I swear. He was at the top of those steps."
She pointed. He was gone.

"The kid? You're sure?"

"Yes, damn it, I don't know. I think so. And I think he saw
me too."

"What was he wearing?"

Julieta concentrated. The crowd kept moving toward the
entrance like a school of fish pulled by the tide. The sun was
getting hotter.

"Blue T-shirt, gray shorts. Sneakers. But I'm not sure, I was
looking straight into his eyes."

"All right, relax, boss. We'll look for him inside. For now
we just need to avoid calling attention to ourselves, all right?"

"Yeah," Julieta said. "It was stupid for me to bolt off like
that, running and yelling. I don't know what the hell came over
me."

The secretary called in over the internal line: "Prosecutor
Jutsiñamuy, Wendy's here. Shall I send her in?"

"Send her in, yes."

Wendy was holding several sheets of paper. Jutsiñamuy
invited her to sit down.

"All right, Wendicita," he said, "tell me what you've got."

The young woman spread some papers out on the table.
"The image is from an evangelical church in Denver, in the
United States. It's called the Church of Saints and Sinners.
They work with the Lutheran idea of healing. As long as they
have the power of God in the body, nothing can harm them.
They see a relationship between 'being healthy internally' and
'being healed,' which of course has spiritual connotations. It's
related to a concept of good and evil. Being *healed* is being virtuous in goodness and purity, whereas the opposite is pain and
sin, impurity. The idea of evil is closely associated with illness."

"And the hand?" the prosecutor asked.

"A visual synthesis," Wendy said. "The open hand means stop. It's a vigorous, healthy hand that stops illness. The good that blocks evil's path. Honestly, boss, it's nothing complicated. There are communities that practice religious tattooing and demand it of their followers. You're saved by getting Jesus tattooed on you. There's a tradition of images in which good overcomes evil. This is the same thing, but with a really simple principle."

"Where is this church?"

"Denver."

"That's pretty far north, right?"

"Yes, boss. Sort of northwest."

"OK, and tell me, is there an evangelical church in Brazil that's associated with it?"

Wendy touched her nose, a sort of nervous tic. "I don't know, sir, I didn't find that out."

"Go look into it, Wendicita. And one more thing: would you be up for an undercover operation? It's nothing too dangerous."

The young woman looked at Jutsiñamuy, her eyes fierce. "Of course, I'd love to. And if it's dangerous, all the better. Ever since I started working here I've imagined getting to be part of a *Carlito's Way* operation."

The black eyelids gave the young woman a toughness and surety that she might not actually possess. It occurred to Jutsiñamuy that she might use her getup to mask her fear. Her enormous fear. Like those animals whose only defense is to bamboozle their predators.

Fear, the great theme of human life on Earth.

Could be.

"It has to do with evangelical churches, Wendicita. Are you religious? Not that it's any of my business, but I'm asking because you'd have to pretend to be devout."

The young woman again looked at him, her expression

hard. "You tell me what you need, and I'll do it, don't worry about me. I can take care of myself."

"The thing is, if you're a believer, you might not have the distance . . ."

"I can do it, sir. Tell me where I need to go."

"Cali. The church is called New Jerusalem. I need a full report on the pastor who runs it: who he is, where he came from, what he does, how much money he has, what he likes to eat, if he has girlfriends, if he smokes, what diseases he has, what his favorite drink is. Everything. His past too. How he got where he is and where he's headed. OK?"

Wendy jotted it down and stood up from the table.

"I'll do some preliminary research and get back to you to tell you what I'll need, sir."

"Perfect, I love it."

"Are you going to tell me what you're after with this guy?"

Jutsiñamuy scratched his chin. He trusted her, but it was too soon.

"Not yet, Wendy, I don't want to distract you. For now I'm after everything. I'll tell you more later."

The young woman didn't even blink. "Understood, boss, and thanks."

In the doorway, she spoke again: "By the way, sir, I don't believe in anything, nothing at all, so don't worry."

"So how do you explain human life on Earth?"

Wendy looked him in the eye, her expression mocking. "The only thing that's for sure is that we reproduce by fucking, boss, just like all the other animals. Pardon my French. Good afternoon."

"Bye then."

Jutsiñamuy called administration and gave them Wendy's details and the task she would be completing to kickstart securing resources and filing the necessary paperwork. Two hours later, Wendy was back in his office.

"Here's the mission, sir," Wendy said. "The form for you to authorize my expenses."

Jutsiñamuy signed four different documents, each one in triplicate. "When are you leaving?"

"At six this evening. I'm starting first thing tomorrow."

"Report only to me, Wendy, please. I don't want anybody else's nose in this business. Got it?"

"Absolutely, sir."

When the agent left, Jutsiñamuy lay back on the sofa, shoes off, and lifted his feet against the wall. Seven minutes for the blood to feed his brain. It was good for the mind and for balding pates.

He picked up the list of Chief Cotes Arosemena's calls and continued analyzing them.

He was struck by the man's persistence with Yuli; Cotes had spoken to her repeatedly throughout the day but to his wife only a couple of times. *Married men's secrets*, he thought. He called the technical investigation unit and asked to speak to Guillermina Mora, who'd been his secretary for more than twenty years and was the person he trusted most in the department.

"Wow, boss, what miracle is this?" she said.

"How's it going, Guillermina?"

"All good here. I'd love to stop by your office to say hi."

"Otoniel and the boys—are they doing OK?"

"Yes, boss, mercifully. Ricardo graduated in business administration from Tadeo University, and Alfonsito is finishing up his pilot training in the air force. You know he's always been obsessed with flying. And Otoniel retired with his pension from Catastro; he keeps himself busy getting on my nerves and watching Netflix. Everyone's great."

"Guillermina, I need something extremely confidential, and I don't dare request it through official channels to avoid unwanted eyes and ears. Understood?"

"Of course, boss. Go on. What is it?"

"There's this police lieutenant. Argemiro Cotes."

"Bogotá?" she asked.

"Yes."

"Am I looking for anything in particular?"

"Relationships with Cauca politicians or Christian churches. And any priors related to corruption."

"All right, boss. I'll get on it and call you later. Or even better: I'll go by your office, and we can have coffee."

"Perfect. Thanks so much."

He raised his legs back up against the wall. He had a custom-made seven-minute hourglass, and he watched the grains of sand fall through the funnel. He'd done it so many times he almost recognized each one. When he stood up, he went to the window and stared out at the city. A front of clouds, unusually dark, was arriving from behind Monserrate. Soon the drizzle would turn into a furious downpour, with lightning and everything.

The telephone roused him from his thoughts.

It was Piedrahíta.

"I'm calling about the tattoos on those stiffs."

"Oh, yes, what's up?"

"One of the experts here says that, in fact, they could have been done after death. It's not for sure, just a possibility. Here's the deal. The skin obviously becomes less elastic in death, but it can be treated with chemicals to make it absorb the ink. But the molecular density of the ink is hard to measure because it gets compromised by the embalming fluid, you know? Nothing you can do about it. According to the expert, it's getting more common. He says there are postmortem tattooists who call themselves 'dermatological artists.' The technique of tattooing on a cold, stiff surface is booming. People like the idea of the body being marked for the wake. The loved ones choose motifs or phrases that evoke the deceased's life. There's a real religious valence to it."

"Wow, interesting," Jutsiñamuy said. "Excellent work, Piedrahíta. Anything on the John Doe?"

"Not for now. Identifying him is taking longer than we thought. But don't worry, we'll figure it out in the end."

"When do you hand the bodies over to the families?"

"We planned to transfer them to the Cali morgue this afternoon."

Jutsiñamuy pulled on his mustache. "Wow, seems like everybody's going to Cali today."

"What's that?"

"No, nothing, just thinking out loud. Thanks a lot. I'll await an update on Mr. Doe."

"As soon as I find anything I'll let you know."

By the time he hung up, the downpour looked like it was made of thick cords of rain. It wasn't even two in the afternoon yet, and already it was as dark as six o'clock.

Jutsiñamuy went to his road map, studied it, and murmured, "Laiseca, Laiseca." He pulled out his cell phone and dialed the number.

"What's up, boss? Laiseca here. Over."

"How's it going questioning the family members?"

"I'm actually with Nadio Becerra's widow and son right now. They're telling me about him. There's a sister here too."

Feeling too far removed from the action, Jutsiñamuy made a decision. "I'm on my way there. Keep them busy for a while. And tell Cancino to come pick me up at the airport. Is he there with you?"

"Right next to me, boss. Do you want to talk to him?"

"No, send him to wait for me."

"Aye aye, boss."

ORPHANS

When she walked in and saw the warehouse's interior, Julieta was reminded of Bogotá's indoor coliseum, beside the soccer stadium, where she'd once attended a Joaquín Sabina concert. Long benches made of plexiglass screwed to metal bases, fifty rows in a hexagonal shape. Concrete floor. The vaulted ceiling was at least fifteen meters tall, and industrial fans were deployed to combat the heat. There were also a dozen air conditioning units in the corners.

It was jam-packed.

Kids were running up and down the stairs through the crowd. At the front was a minimalistic stage, with just a lectern and microphone stands. Vivaldi music. *The Four Seasons. Spring.* They found seats in the back, and as soon as they were settled, Julieta went off to look for the kid. She was absolutely certain of it: she'd seen him. For a second their eyes had met—and the more she thought about it, the more it seemed to her there'd been a strange glitter in his eyes.

It was him, no question.

She made her way through the crowd toward the dais, but it wasn't easy. She was constantly being stopped by security guards and asked where she was going. The surging tides of humans prevented them from maintaining strict control, and they seemed nervous. As she fought her way through, Julieta decided she needed to revise her theory: if the kid was with Pastor Fritz, that changed everything. It was even possible that

Fritz wasn't the man in black from the attack, since the kid would have recognized him. The fact that he'd run away to the pastor added a new twist to the story, if he had actually run away voluntarily and hadn't ended up there some other way. Some kind of coercion. But she couldn't deny it. The kid she'd seen a moment ago on the steps hadn't seemed to be looking for help. He wasn't being held against his will.

According to her mental map, the steps where Franklin had been should connect up to the rear part of the dais. Maybe he was in a special room right now, or in the pastor's dressing rooms. It wouldn't be easy to gain access, so she made her way back to where Johana was sitting, other people's sweat and odors swirling around her body.

"See anything, boss?" Johana asked.

"Nothing. The kid must be in the dressing rooms. Maybe the pastor brought him as an assistant. We'll see if he comes out during the . . . What's this thing called? Mass? Homily?"

"Not a clue," Johana said. "Some were calling it a lecture and others a talk."

"It looks like the studio set for that old variety show, *Sábados Felices*."

A little while later a voice came on the loudspeakers and announced that the doors had been closed. The event would start in five minutes.

What took place after that was something that neither had ever seen before, and something they'd never forget: a cross between a rock concert, a popular mass, and a TV show. Before Pastor Fritz came out onto the stage, the lights went low and music that sounded like an airline ad started playing, the volume increasing until it suddenly transformed into Strauss's *Also sprach Zarathustra*. At its climax, a door that looked more like a trapdoor opened, and the stage filled with white smoke with blue and red spotlights playing on it.

And he appeared.

Given the staging, the person emerging from the darkness could have been a pop star, but no: it was Pastor Fritz Almayer. A man of about fifty-three, muscular, with a black shirt clinging to his abs, black polyester pants, and a black Nehru-style jacket.

And despite the heat, a black hat.

From the stage, he greeted his audience. He started by going down a list of names. "Where are the Marías?" Throughout the hall, women raised their hands, shouting, "Here! Here!" He blessed them. "I greet you in Christ." Then he walked to the other end of the dais and said, "And the Helenas?" Other women raised their hands and he repeated the blessing, and so he went through the most common names, until suddenly he said, "And the Johanas?" Julieta was startled to see her companion spring up from the bench with her hand raised, and shout, "Here!" caught up in the charisma of the man. The final name he called was Rafael. "Where are the Rafaels?" When several men stood, the spotlights sought them out and the pastor said, "Today's talk is going to be dedicated to you. To the closeness between Jesus and Rafael."

The build-up over, he began to speak.

(From Julieta's rapid notes . . .)

"Moses finds himself in a tricky spot, between the desert and the sea, and instead of complaining, he prays. That's what we should all do. When we're in pain, we should pray. God responded to Moses and showed him a piece of wood. Moses threw it into the sea, and in an instant the saltwater turned to fresh. And Moses was able to slake his thirst. And why? Because he believed!"

"Because he believed!" the crowd chorused in reply.

"Then God said to us, 'If you hear my voice and do what I consider to be right, and if you obey my laws and commandments, I will not bring down upon you any of the plagues I brought upon the Egyptians. I am the Lord, who restores you to health.' There the Lord revealed himself as Jehovah-Rapha!"

"Rapha, Rapha, Rapha . . . !" the people cried.

"Amid bitterness and pain, God was his doctor, his healer. The word *rapha* appears sixty times in the Old Testament. It means 'he who restores, heals, and cures.' And how?"

He walked to the center of the stage, slowly raised his eyes to the projection of a cross on the ceiling, and said, "Some of us are living through difficult times, trying to process pain and despondency. Because of the cruelty of others or the wounds inflicted on us. Or because of those we inflicted on others. Deep wounds. That's why we have to ask Rapha, Old Man Rapha, to do his healing work.

"That's why, in the Gospels, we see Jesus healing people.

"Spiritual healing is the most important of the three realms of healing. We are spiritually sick, and the Lord offers us healing and wholeness through the blood Jesus spilled on the cross. Our diagnosis is bad, and the prognosis is terminal: cancer, leukemia, AIDS, Alzheimer's, typhus, leprosy, cirrhosis, diabetes. How many fatal diseases are there? Gonorrhea, syphilis, chancroid.

"And the incurable disease of the human heart.

"Jesus stood up in the synagogue and quoted the book of the prophet Isaiah: 'He has sent me to bind up the brokenhearted, to proclaim freedom for the captives and release from darkness for the prisoners.'

"Not all diseases are related to sin, but all are *the result* of Adam and Eve's sin.

"We must be careful with these things. Are you going to be careful?!"

"Yes!!!" A thunderous reply.

"Better go to the Great Doctor first. God can heal with a single word. Asa in the Old Testament is a warning. When he was sick he did not pray to God first; he went straight to the doctor: 'Though his disease was severe, even in his illness he did not seek help from the Lord, but only from the physicians.'

"And he died alone.

"We also need the community of faith; call on the church elders and ask them to join in prayer. Second, confess your sins in public. Third, pray for one another. This is only possible here, at New Jerusalem Church. Isn't that the truth?!"

"It's the truth!!!!!" the crowd roared.

"Christ's cross is the source of healing.

"The Jehovah-Rapha who heals in the Old Testament is the Lord Jesus who cures in the New Testament.

"Don't forget the importance of the wood of a tree that turned saltwater fresh. All of our problems began with a tree! The tree in the Garden of Eden. And the problem of sin was resolved because another piece of wood supported our Lord on the cross. He himself, in his body, bore our sins upon the timber so that we might kill sin and live for justice. Through his wounds you have been healed.

"Only Jesus can sweeten the bitter salt of life."

"Jesus!!!!" the people shouted, calling out to him.

Julieta listened in disbelief. From a rational point of view, the content was practically incomprehensible, but the strange conclusions he drew, which must have made little sense to anybody, inspired cheers and applause.

Before he finished, the pastor said, "Now, the orphans alone shall come unto me. Here in front."

Julieta thought, *Here's where the kid appears.*

"The orphans, the orphans!"

The crowd began to roil and shift. As some walked toward the stage on the left side of the room, others withdrew, leaving the front seats empty.

"You, the orphans of life and the world, are God's first children!"

People of all different ages filed past the stage to shake his hand. The pastor didn't just shake—he held out his hand so his followers could touch it, like a relic. Each congregant touched it then held it to their heart, and left with their hand on their chest and their head low, as if they'd just received communion.

"Orphaned boys and girls, orphaned men and women, come unto me!"

People kept moving past the stage, where the pastor was now kneeling, gazing heavenward.

Julieta joined the crowd and moved toward him. She wasn't an orphan, but she wanted to touch him to find out if he really did emanate something special. Plus get closer to the stage and take a look into the back, where the kid must be.

The people in front of her shuffled slowly forward. The hand touching lasted four seconds, she estimated. Pastor Fritz seemed to be in a trance, his eyes fixed on an enormous cross silhouetted on the ceiling. When she had almost reached him, the woman beside her began sobbing.

Then it was her turn.

She touched him without looking at him, her attention focused on one side of the dais, where several people were lifting and operating cables. She didn't see the kid, and after a moment she looked back at the pastor.

She almost fell over.

Almayer had lowered his eyes from the cross and was staring at her intensely. Less than a meter away. A laser piercing her brain.

"Why have you come to touch my hand?" Almayer asked in a booming voice.

Julieta didn't know what to say; panicking, she froze, unable to flee from his powerful gaze.

"I'm not an orphan," she told him, "but it's my greatest fear."

She almost said "for my children," but the words wouldn't come out.

The pastor removed his gaze from her.

As she started to move away, the pastor whispered something that she felt like an icy gust of wind. "Don't worry about them so much. They are with me."

The words plunged her into a strange submissiveness.

The pastor seemed to be reading what was in her mind.

When she reached the corner of the stage, she didn't dare look at him. She did see that Johana had joined the line of orphans and had almost reached him. She looked at him again. Once more the pastor's eyes turned toward her, and as their gazes met she heard the whisper again . . .

They are with me, they are with me.

She wanted to run, to get far away, but it didn't make sense. She wasn't in danger. Nothing had actually happened. She walked to the exit, and when she emerged from the warehouse into the outside world, the heat and the street noise roused her from her spell. She stepped to one side, lit a cigarette, and waited for Johana, no longer worrying about searching for the kid. Shortly after, her colleague appeared.

"How did it go?" she asked. "Did you touch his hand?"

Johana's cheeks flushed.

"You're going to say I'm an idiot, boss, but when I got close to him I saw my father's body in the river again, the wounds on his head, the car destroyed. I cried for him. And when it was my turn and I touched the pastor's hand, I was filled with a feeling of calm and . . . How can I describe it? I realized that my father's soul was at peace. I felt that he was with me, watching over me, even loving me. Did he hypnotize us?"

"Just wait till I tell you what happened to me."

They went out to the street, crossed over to the service station, and caught a taxi back to the hotel.

The prosecutor greeted Cancino in the domestic arrivals area at Bonilla Aragón Airport.

"How was the flight, boss?"

"Short and peppy," Jutsiñamuy said. "Where are we headed?"

"Kilometer 18 on the highway to the coast. Laiseca is with them. It's the family of Nadio Becerra."

"Have they said anything useful?"

"Not before I left. Since you were coming, we didn't want to alienate them."

They drove across the city from east to west, following the line of the Cali River upstream.

The house, a humble structure clinging to the hillside, was reached via a set of incredibly steep steps. A woman came over and welcomed Jutsiñamuy in. He saw that her eyes were wet. She'd been crying all day, maybe since the night before. The prosecutor politely introduced himself.

"Tell me what happened to him, sir," the woman said. "Who killed him?"

She seemed to be biting her words as she spoke.

"That's what we're trying to find out, ma'am," Jutsiñamuy said. "My condolences. I'm so sorry for your loss."

"Please sit down, sir."

The other two women, a bit younger and also in black, had also been crying, but they were now sitting stiffly, dignified and expectant.

"Something cold to drink, a cup of coffee?"

"A glass of water would be great," Jutsiñamuy said.

The house was neat as a pin, with every ceramic or porcelain tray perfectly placed. Though it wasn't fancy, it had an air of abundance, of people who are slowly prospering, though not enough to move neighborhoods. A shabby house full of showy, useless things: a supersized HD plasma TV in a small living room that still had knitted cushion covers. Objects seemed like they were about to fall, glass figurines overflowing the end tables. There were ashtrays with place names: Santa Fe de Bogotá, Belém do Pará, Quito. A statue of Saint George driving his spear into the dragon's shoulder, two porcelain sheep and a shepherd in a rustic landscape, angels with little lutes, dancers. Ceramic dogs. A sampler in a glass frame: "This house has opened its arms to the Lord." Behind the letters, in shadow, the image of Christ, with long hair and a red tunic, and beside it, a print with the face of the soccer star James Rodríguez.

The young woman reappeared with his drink on a tray. She'd folded a napkin around the glass like a paper ring.

"All right, ma'am. The first thing I'd like you to tell me is when you last saw your son," Jutsiñamuy said.

"It's been at least a month, I think?" the mother replied, confirming it with the other women.

"Yes, Mom," one said.

"He'd been working in other cities for a while. In Caquetá, the Amazon, even Brazil."

She picked up a ceramic figure from the chest of drawers. A peasant with a machete.

"See, he brought me this from there."

Jutsiñamuy took the figurine and turned it over. It was hideous. On the bottom was a maker's mark: Lavorio. Then the place: Manaus.

"He didn't tell us much, but he called every month. And he always sent a little money—that was sacred to him. Right?"

One of the women nodded. Jutsiñamuy thought she must be the widow.

"Yes, Mom. That was sacred to him. He was always really responsible with money. He supported the family to the end." She covered her face with her hands.

"Do you know what kind of work he did?" Jutsiñamuy asked.

They looked at one another as if trying to decide how to respond. Finally the mother spoke.

"Security guard at SecuNorte. That was his job the last few

years because he had military experience. You probably know he was in the army until two years ago. Then he got out and started working for private companies. That's what he did."

"And whom was he protecting lately?"

"We don't know."

The widow pulled herself together and spoke. "When he came home a little while back, he didn't say anything. He just wanted to spend time with his family. I didn't ask. Ever since he was in the army I learned not to ask. Only what he wanted to tell."

"Do you know where he'd been?"

Again they looked at one another. Their eyes seemed to agree that the widow should speak this time.

"Brazil. But he didn't tell us that; we know it from the gifts he brought. All things from there, really nice. Some delicious candy. Why do you want to know?"

Laiseca and Cancino, who were behind him near the door and hadn't sat down, were taking notes. Laiseca had surreptitiously started recording with his cell phone, leaving it on one of the tables, on top of a glass ashtray with the Colombian flag on it.

"So we can figure out what happened to Nadio, ma'am."

Jutsiñamuy tried to set his glass down on the table but couldn't find an empty spot. The young woman took it from him.

"Now I'm going to ask you to try to remember," he said. "I want you to think about names. Did he mention anyone? Last names, first names, nicknames, anything. Please think hard."

The three women nodded silently, then closed their eyes and concentrated. It was the widow who spoke.

"I heard him mention a Lucho several times, and somebody known as 'Mr. F' or 'Dr. F.'"

"Very interesting," Jutsiñamuy said. "And you never asked about him? In what context did he mention him?"

"No," the woman said. "He never said the name to me. It was things I overheard when he was talking on the phone. As I said, he never talked much about work."

"And this Mr. F—did you hear him mentioned once, twice, ten times?"

The woman shook her head. "I'd say a lot, more than twice. I don't know if it was as many as ten."

The prosecutor leaned toward the woman and continued his questioning. "Do you believe that Mr. F could refer to a man named Fabinho or Fabio? A Brazilian?"

"I don't know, sir."

"Did you ever hear the name Fabinho Henriquez?"

The woman lowered her eyes and blushed. "No, sir. I'm sorry I'm not much help."

Jutsiñamuy placed a hand on her arm. "Don't worry about it, ma'am. The important thing is for you to tell me the whole truth, just like you're doing." He continued. "Another thing. Does the name Óscar Luis Pedraza mean anything to you? Did you know him?"

"No," the widow said. "He's the other dead man, right? He could have been the Lucho who called him sometimes."

Jutsiñamuy pulled out a photo of the John Doe. Despite the mortician's efforts, it was obvious from a mile off that it was a corpse.

"I'm sorry for showing you this, but it's very important. It's the body of the third man we found with Nadio. It's not a pleasant image, but I want to ask you to study it and tell me if you recognize him."

He placed the photo on the table, between two white porcelain cats. The first one to look at it was the mother.

"No," she said. "I've never seen him."

Then the sister, who was taking an empty coffee cup from the mother. "No, he's not from around here."

They passed the photo to the widow. She looked at it and

brought it closer to her eyes. She removed her glasses and looked again. "It could be . . ."

She stared intently, turned the paper over, brought it closer to the light.

"I think I saw him once," the widow said, "but I'm not really sure. Death changes people, doesn't it? I'm thinking about a guy they called Carlitos. He came by with money and some medicine for my son that he hadn't been able to get here in Cali. That was like two years ago. Hang on, was his name Carlitos? Yes, I think so. His hair was shorter, but those eyebrows look familiar."

"Carlitos?" Jutsiñamuy repeated. "So you'd say he worked with your husband."

"Yes, sir. For him."

"A subordinate."

The widow looked at the other two women, not understanding.

The sister said to her, "Nadio was the boss."

"Oh, yes," the widow said. "Nadio was in charge, of course."

She kept looking at the photo. "It's just . . . now that I'm thinking about it, he was a driver for him or something, because another time when he came he took us for a drive downtown. And he took the kids to a lodge out in Jamundí so they could swim in the pool."

Laiseca stepped forward and, nodding to his boss, addressed the widow. "Pardon me for intruding, ma'am, but do you happen to remember what lodge that was? What was it called?"

"No, he suggested taking them there while we were doing some repairs at home. A big restaurant out in the country with a pool and games."

"It would be extremely helpful to know where that was. The name or at least the location."

Surprised by their interest, the woman told them to wait

and went over to the stairs. "Maybe my older son will remember. They had a good time, so he might."

She went upstairs and the others waited in silence. A minute later she came back down. "The Jamundí Inn," she said. "Grill, restaurant, pool."

"Thank you so much, and congratulate your son on his excellent memory," Laiseca said, jotting down the name on his notepad.

"All right," Jutsiñamuy said. "Let's leave Carlitos for now and go back to Mr. F. Ma'am, when you heard your husband talk about him, did it sound like he was talking about a boss or a coworker?"

The widow looked up at the ceiling. "Definitely a boss. They were always saying he was about to arrive, that they had to go meet him. It was all very secretive, what he was up to. That's why they called him Mr. F."

"Do you have any idea what he did?" Jutsiñamuy asked.

"No, I don't."

The prosecutor settled more comfortably in his chair and said, "If I told you Mr. F is a Christian pastor, would that seem strange?"

The widow met Jutsiñamuy's eyes, surprised again. "Well, no," she said, "because I did notice that Nadio started using words like 'saint' and 'reverence'—things he never used to say before. He would talk about the saint of martyrs, I remember that."

"Did he go to Christian churches or to the regular Catholic one?"

The mother shifted in her chair. The widow understood that she should let her speak and lowered her head.

"Nadio was raised with Catholic values," the mother said. "Baptized and confirmed, and he got married in the Church. He did everything right. If he abandoned or strayed from that education afterward, that's not my fault."

The widow shot her a look that the prosecutor felt like a pistol going off. "Well, I'm the one who married him," she said in response, "and as far as I know, he was always a good Catholic. Just because he didn't use words from the missal doesn't mean he went astray. That's why I say it was weird to hear him saying those things on the phone."

"Any Catholic would say them," the mother snapped.

"They might be nicknames or aliases, Mother, don't contradict me. 'Master,' 'Saint' . . . What do they mean? Around me he was still just as Catholic as the day we met."

The mother ate a handful of potato chips, crunching loudly. She was annoyed. "Maybe what was bothering him was other things at home, don't you think?"

The widow looked up. Her eyes were two flamethrowers. "Go on, then, say what you have to say," she challenged her mother-in-law.

"If a man's wife spends her time giggling and flirting with other men, it makes everything harder."

It was clear to Jutsiñamuy that the interrogation was over and he should leave as soon as possible. He wasn't going to get anything else from the two women, at least not for now. He said goodbye, thanked them for their time, and went outside.

"Where's the other family?" he asked Laiseca. "What's the dead guy's name?"

"Óscar Luis Pedraza, boss, but all due respect, given that it's nine at night, I'd suggest we do that questioning tomorrow."

"Tomorrow? Why?"

"Remember, today's Friday and people in Cali go out. It's like in Bogotá, but even more so," Laiseca said.

"They go out to do what?"

"To party, boss."

"Oh, hell. But a dead man's family won't be partying. Call them and tell them we're on our way over."

"Yes, sir."

Jutsiñamuy suddenly stopped and said, "You wouldn't happen to be the one wanting to party, would you, Laiseca?"

"No, boss. I don't even know how to dance."

"What about Cancino? Where is he?"

The agent had stayed behind to use the bathroom.

"Here he is, ask him yourself."

Jutsiñamuy looked at his watch again. "All right, call them and tell them eight tomorrow morning."

"Yes, sir, at your orders," Laiseca replied.

On their way back to the car, Jutsiñamuy stopped with a finger on his forehead and spoke to Laiseca. "Isn't there supposed to be a good sancocho place around here?"

"I can't confirm that, boss," Laiseca said. "I'm not familiar."

"What about you, Cancino? Any idea where the sancocho is in this neck of the woods?" Jutsiñamuy asked.

"Of course. Kilometer 18. I'll take you."

After eating, the prosecutor returned to El Peñón, a neighborhood in the west of the city. He'd reserved a room at the Dann Carlton, which had an arrangement with the prosecutor general's office for its employees.

Unbeknownst to him, he was only a few blocks from his journalist friend.

Julieta went back to the hotel with Johana and decided to extend their stay another night. Pastor Fritz's gaze had left her deeply unsettled. How had he done it? He'd known she wasn't an orphan just by touching her. And the whispering she'd heard about her sons—how could he . . . ? *They are with me,* she repeated in her mind. She thought again of Franklin. Had he actually meant his own children?

Julieta wasn't a believer—quite the opposite. She disdained anything that cast itself as "spiritual," unless it also taught valid ethics and morals. There had to be an explanation for what had happened that morning. After a rest, she sat in front of the window and began to write.

First theory: Pastor Almayer knew about her because Franklin was with him and had told him about her interest in the incident on the road. Second theory: if the information hadn't come from the kid, most likely the person who'd come into their hotel room and broken into the car worked for the pastor.

The sequence of events she wrote in her notebook was as follows:

1. Franklin spotted her in the line to enter the church.
2. He told Pastor Almayer, who had his men watch her inside the warehouse.
3. When she got up and joined the orphan line, someone let him know.
4. In a show to intimidate her, Almayer feigned that his knowledge had come at the touch of her hands.
5. The fact that he knew she wasn't an orphan meant they'd already looked into her.

It was logical—it could explain it.

The mystery was still the kid. Looking at her own summary of events, she realized that all her cards were on the table. There was no point in hiding; she should speak with the pastor directly. Would he agree? She called Johana and told her to request an appointment for the next morning.

To her surprise, the pastor agreed. He would expect her at nine thirty at the church.

Julieta felt a strange shiver. The idea of meeting him in that place suddenly seemed terrifying.

"Call back and tell him I'd prefer to meet somewhere else," she asked Johana. "In a café, a public place."

Johana called back a little while later. "The church secretary says a café isn't an option for security reasons. He can meet you in a conference room at the InterContinental Hotel, same time."

"All right," Julieta said.

"I'll confirm the appointment, then."

She had the rest of the afternoon and evening to update her notes. But first she went out for a walk along the river.

She liked that area of Cali. The majestic trees. The rain tree outside La Tertulia Museum and the sand-colored building, a smaller version of Brasília's Itamaraty Palace. Apartments with wide balconies, the hills in the distance. The Casa Obeso Mejía, on an island in the middle of the river.

She walked upstream to the historic neighborhood of Santa Teresita and was surprised to see old crumbling mansions— how could they be standing empty? Maybe because of inheritance disputes or asset forfeiture. The river had some trash in it, but the water still looked clean, and imposing stones were arrayed like sculptures along its banks.

Spotting an antique shop, she decided to go in.

A small warehouse crammed with dusty objects: yellowing plates and glasses, crooked furniture, useless things. She liked hotel ashtrays, especially the classic ones made of porcelain. She had a good number of them at home. Also bar paraphernalia with brand names like Martini, Campari, Cinzano. It was relaxing to stroll through the smell of damp wood and freshly polished copper. She saw a trunk full of canes and picked up one topped with an eagle's beak; she saw old books in French and German, leather-bound and musty; she saw music boxes and wound one up, and it played a balalaika; she wandered down a narrow passage of shelves piled with religious objects: Christs in a variety of sizes, their bodies wounded and suffering; winecups and altar candles, threadbare chasubles, robed Virgins carrying the Child, hands cupping the world, like the Infant Jesus of Prague.

She suddenly got a gut feeling and started digging in a chest until, surprised, she picked up a small wooden carving and studied it in the light.

It was an open hand, with the wound of a nail through the palm and the words "We are healed" inscribed across it. She pulled out her cell phone and found the photo of the tattoos Jutsiñamuy had sent her.

It was identical.

She went to talk to the owner.

"How much is this?"

The man pushed his glasses up his nose. "Forty thousand. It's original."

"Original? In what way?"

"From the Assembly of God in Brazil. They make these pieces. It's supposed to be the hand of Jesus. Look on the bottom—there's the stamp. Without that, it'd be worth about ten thousand."

"I'll take it."

She handed him a fifty-thousand-peso bill. The old man wrapped her purchase in newspaper.

"Do you have anything else from that church?"

"Let me see if I can get some for you. At the moment just what you can see in that trunk." He handed her a business card. "Call me in a few days. I can try to track down other things."

She walked out with her heart pounding and headed back to the hotel along the other side of the river. Now the traffic was coming toward her. That may be why, looking the other direction, she saw the motorcycle again.

Following her.

She crossed the road and stood staring at him. With the river between them, the man, in his tinted black helmet, held her gaze. Julieta raised her hand to her forehead in a salute. But he didn't respond. He just took off and turned at the first corner.

It's him. He knows where I am and what I do and where I go,
she thought. *It's him, that fucking guru.*

After much consideration, Johana decided to spend the
afternoon meeting up with a former comrade from the guerrilla who'd returned to Cali. She'd had the woman's phone
number for more than a year, so she called. Her name was
Marlene. They agreed to meet at five at Ventolini, a café in the
Unicentro shopping mall. On her way there in a taxi, Johana
thought back on a battle against paramilitaries in the Yarí that
had left Marlene injured. She'd been hit six times, but none of
the wounds were serious; the bullets had just grazed her.
Johana had helped her up the hill to safety and washed each of
the wounds. Marlene had passed out on the stretcher, and
when she came to, she started crying. Johana asked her what
was wrong.

"Nothing, comrade, I just can't believe I'm still in this hellhole after getting riddled with lead," Marlene said, battered
and with her arms and legs smeared with dried blood. "I don't
deserve to be alive, I'm such a moron."

"Easy, sister. Don't talk, save your strength. Don't waste
your energy saying silly things," Johana said.

"You don't understand," Marlene said. "With all that
shooting going on, I came out of the shelter to retrieve a chain
that had gotten pulled off my neck. I almost died because of
it."

"What chain?"

"Here," she said, and pulled it out of a fold in her uniform.
It was shiny and looked like gold, with a crucifix.

"What is it?" Johana asked.

"My father gave it to me before he was killed by the paramilitaries," Marlene said. "He was the only good man I ever
knew in my life."

Later, when peace came, Marlene had said she wanted to

leave the country. Study abroad, if she got the chance. Maybe in Cuba. But in the end she'd had to stay in Colombia.

When she saw Marlene, Johana felt a lump in her throat and a fierce nostalgia for the guerrilla camp. They hugged. Marlene had gained weight, and her limp from an old injury was more noticeable now. Johana looked at her neck and there it was: the chain with the crucifix. The same one.

They sat down to talk.

Two women with their memories, of marching through the country's high tundra, jungle, mountains, its plains and canyons; women who had fought together and shared ideals, in heroic, complicated circumstances; who had helped and hidden each other; who knew so many things about each other, and about other women who had been there. And so their conversation, once they'd caught each other up, turned to their comrades. Where was one? What was another doing? Not forgetting her reason for being in Cali, Johana asked if Marlene remembered a comrade who'd gotten together with a Nasa man near Inzá and had a son about fourteen years ago, maybe a little less.

"I remember a few women who had kids. Hmm, with a Nasa man? Do you mean Josefina?" Marlene said.

"Doesn't ring a bell," Johana said. "I wasn't in that area much. Were there a lot of women who had children with indigenous men?"

"I don't know if they were Nasa, you don't really ask about that stuff. They were rural folk. There was this one woman named Myriam who ended up getting punished because she hadn't asked permission to be with the man. Do you remember her? She had a kid. I was there when he was born."

"A son? What was his name?"

"He didn't even have a name yet when they took him away."

Johana decided to tell Marlene why she was interested. She

told her about the kid from San Andrés de Pisimbalá. Franklin. She laid out the story his grandparents had told her.

"There were several instances like that," Marlene said. "One kid was taken to Pasto. A comrade . . . what was her name? Mariela, I think. Another went to Ecuador, Carmen's kid. She was from the coast and was going around with another fighter, from Guapi."

"Was the guy from Guapi black?" Johana asked. "Or, I mean, Afro-Colombian?"

"Yes, his name was Walter."

"No, that's not him. The kid isn't Afro-Colombian. He's Nasa."

Their ice cream arrived. Marlene had ordered chocolate and vanilla. Johana, just chocolate.

"How old is he?" Marlene asked.

"We don't know exactly, but I'd guess between twelve and fourteen. He could be eleven. He's big, even though indigenous people tend to be pretty small. His face looks Nasa, but he's taller than most."

Marlene stopped eating and said, "There was another comrade from Bogotá who had a kid. I remember now. They took that baby away really early on because he cried constantly, especially at night."

"Did you know her?"

"Of course, but hang on . . . Her name was Clara, that's it. She was from San Juan del Sumapaz. Don't you remember her?"

"Now that you say it, that name does sound familiar," Johana said. "Was she the one who was with us in La Macarena, at one of the conferences?"

"Yes, her. I think I've got a photo of that conference somewhere," Marlene said. "I'll find it and send you a copy on WhatsApp."

"Thanks, it would be great to see that," Johana said. "Send

me a good high-res scan with all the detail. Did you know the father?" she added.

"Of course. He was a quiet kid who read a lot," Marlene said. "Really strong, too, pure muscle. Handsome guy. It was so sad when he was killed."

"Where did it happen?"

"In Puracé. He'd stayed behind to help fend off an attack on a commander—it wasn't even his squadron, but he stayed because of some mystical conviction. He said he knew the area. They held off the army for more than three hours till two helicopters were brought in and fired on them from above. That took out six of the ten men. Two others were badly wounded. One lost his leg. It was a heroic sacrifice, but brutal. Trying to protect that corridor came at a huge price."

Johana pulled out her notepad and wrote, *Clara, from Bogotá.* "There must be a lot of kids out there, huh?"

"Yeah," Marlene said. "You remember, we lived life to the max in the guerrilla camps."

They talked till seven in the evening.

"Do you ever see other comrades?" Johana asked.

"No," Marlene said, "Braulio a bit—remember him? He was a medic. I saw him during the first year of peace. We lost touch after that, when people started getting killed. It was dangerous here in Cali. Sometimes I see Joaquín at church. The guy who led the squadron."

Johana pretended like she didn't understand. "At church? What church?"

"The Church of Divine Justice, with Pastor Domínguez, here in Cali. They've got a really pretty church in Siloé. Joaquín is like the pastor's bodyguard or something; he always wears dark clothes, with wires coming out of his ears."

"When did you become Christian?" Johana asked.

"Everybody here is into that stuff."

"But you have to pay them."

"You have to pay for everything in this life, sister, and at least this is to spread Christ's message. It's a good cause."

"The Catholic Church is free—why not join that instead?"

"Noooo," Marlene said. "It may be free, but it's totally useless and all gibberish. Pastor Domínguez talks about everyday life: about doughnuts and the América de Cali soccer team, about the corruption of the mayor and city government, about seedy bars and brothels. He talks about husbands who beat their wives and children who get raped, about the way a person should live to be at peace with Christ and their fellow humans. The guy's on it. He knows about real life. They never talk about that stuff in the Catholic Church. It's all symbolic. That symbol bullshit is for the rich." She paused a moment. "Hey, how's your brother Carlos Duván?"

"He went to Buenaventura after the demobilization," Johana said. "He's still there, working with the people in the community—displaced people living around the port and that sort of thing."

"He was always such a sweetheart."

They stood up to leave. Marlene had to go make dinner. She lived with a taxi driver who got home at around that time. She didn't have children. She told Johana she'd look for the photo and send it as soon as she found it, but then she said, "Hang on, you should have that photo too. Remember? Javier took it, and afterward he made copies for everybody there. You must have it."

Johana didn't remember. Years ago she'd scanned her photos from her time in the guerrilla and stashed them away in a folder on her computer.

"Look for it. You'll see," Marlene insisted. "Javier gave us all copies as a gift."

"I'll look for it," Johana said, "but you look anyway in case I lost it."

They said goodbye.

Johana took a bus back to the hotel. When she arrived she found a note from Julieta: "Call my room."

"What's up, boss?"

"I have a surprise for you," Julieta said. "Our motorcyclist from Tierradentro is here and he's still watching us."

"Really? You saw him?" Johana looked surprised.

"This afternoon. It's got to be one of Pastor Fritz's men. I even waved at him."

"How did he respond?"

"He took off. But it was the same guy, and it makes sense. They know everything about me from those papers in the car."

"You think they followed us here from Popayán?" Johana said.

"Anything's possible. I'm more and more convinced they were keeping an eye on us this morning, at the church. The pastor knew we were there."

"Well," Johana said, "if they know everything already, might as well show our hand, right?"

"That's what I'm planning to do tomorrow."

They went downstairs to eat at Turk House, a restaurant next to the hotel reception area.

"But there's more," Julieta said. She opened her purse and pulled out the object from the antiques store.

Seeing the hand with the inscription, Johana was startled. "Where did you find that?"

"I went for a walk and found an antiques shop," Julieta said. "It's from a Brazilian evangelical church, the Assembly of God. The owner said it was original, and he's agreed to find me more things."

Johana studied the carving carefully, scrutinizing its surface.

"It's weird for a church to use things like this," she said. "It's so macabre. The service today was happy, but this is sad."

"Well," Julieta said, "that's how religion is: dark and funereal. I'm almost positive now there's a link between the incident in San Andrés de Pisimbalá and the evangelical churches."

"Yes," Johana said. "Everything's pointing in that direction."

They both examined the open hand again, analyzing every bump and groove.

"It's wild that this was tattooed on the dead guys, huh?" Johana said.

"Yeah. They've brainwashed half of Colombia."

"I saw an ex-comrade this afternoon, and she's in a church too," Johana said. "She talked about a lot of others. People are going crazy in this country."

"Maybe we're the crazy ones," Julieta said, "for not having noticed earlier."

"I've got another bombshell for you," Johana said. She paused dramatically.

"Go on," Julieta said.

"It's a photo, but I've got to find it on my computer."

They went up to Johana's room, and while she was looking, Julieta went to the bathroom. Before she sat down on the toilet, a strange impulse made her peek into the shower. Hanging from the knob was the thong she'd seen in the hotel in Popayán. A bolt of lightning shot down her spine. Without thinking, she grabbed it and held it to her nose.

She inhaled deeply.

Under the scent of soap was a strong smell that must be fluid and sweat. She felt an urge to touch herself, but refrained. Instead she turned on the tap and splashed her face with water.

What the hell was happening to her?

Johana opened several folders before she came across the old photo she was looking for. It had been scanned and was somewhat blurry, but it showed a group of fighters sitting in a circle in the middle of the jungle. Men and women waving to the camera, posing, as if they were on a casual hike. Johana showed Julieta the photo, and Julieta thought how young they all were. Practically children. Their cheerful affect was that of a group of teenagers who were still intrigued by the mysteries of life, but who above all wanted to live. Or maybe were pretending to live. Pretending that their small lives, despite the uniforms and the weapons slung across their backs, steered toward the same truth and the same meaning as other people's lives, other people who were not rebels fighting for their ideals. Some were smiling, others holding up two fingers in a V for victory, two were hugging. Her own children, Julieta thought, posed for this kind of photo, except they were at malls or dance clubs.

This damned country!

"That one's me. Recognize me?" Johana said.

Lost in thought, Julieta started. "Of course, you haven't changed a bit."

"All right, boss, no need to go overboard. This was my group when I was twenty. What I wanted to show you was this comrade. Look, this girl here."

She pointed to a young woman who looked a bit older. Her face was blurry, but you could tell she was smiling too. A tense smile, as if a cloud of sobriety prevented her from fully joining in the jovial scene. The smiles of the group told of hope, the certainty that the best of their lives was still ahead of them, but this woman's face said something else, an expression of something inescapable that she kept from the others behind her efforts to appear happy.

"Who is she?" Julieta asked.

"Her name is Clara," Johana said, "and she could be the kid's mom."

"Franklin's?"

Johana recounted in detail her conversation with her ex-comrade and how they'd remembered Clara's story, which had nearly been forgotten.

"Could we find her?" Julieta said.

"I'd have to talk with other comrades," Johana said, "but probably. She might not be in Bogotá anymore. If she's the one, of course. She could be."

Julieta studied the image again. An innocent face, not yet tainted. The young woman's left hand rested on the rifle barrel. And the left? She zoomed in as far as she could. It was just a shadow, but she'd swear it was holding her belly.

Julieta stared and stared, and was suddenly struck by an idea. "The kid's looking for her too," she said. "That's why he ran away. That's why he spent so much time on the internet." She knocked gently on the table. "That's my hunch," she said.

Searching for his mother. A reason to take off and travel the world—or a country smaller than the world, but just as cruel and violent, Julieta thought. Just as inhumane. She thought of her sons and felt a pang. She'd call them when she got back to her room.

"Go ahead and look into this woman, Johanita. Let's see if we can find her. This investigation is opening up all sorts of new ones—I love it. All right, I'm going to bed. See you at seven at breakfast."

Johana saluted. "Aye aye, boss."

Julieta looked at her affectionately. "You goof."

A t eight on the dot, Jutsiñamuy was at the house of the second identified corpse, Óscar Luis Pedraza. The family was waiting in the living room. As he sat down in the place of honor, an overstuffed black armchair, three children stared at him despondently. Though it was Monday, they were in their Sunday best, like the adults: dark suits, ties, long skirts.

"Is there a family gathering happening? Did I come at a bad time?" he asked.

"No, sir," said an old man who might have been the father. "We were waiting for you. We're in mourning."

He scanned the group and tried to deduce who was who. Those were his kids, that was the father, and the mother. She must be the widow over there. The brothers and sisters. When he'd finished his assessment of the room, he said, "I believe you know why I'm here."

They all nodded, but didn't say anything.

"For the investigation, I'd like to ask what work Óscar Luis was doing and what you think might have happened to him."

They exchanged glances to figure out who should respond, and their eyes turned to the father.

"All right, sir," he said. "Let me tell you."

The old man clasped the hand of the old woman who must be the mother, and began to talk, sometimes staring at his toes, sometimes studying the cracks in the ceiling. He talked for a long while, not just for Jutsiñamuy, but maybe also for his family and for himself.

Óscar was in the army, in the Fifth Brigade, up until about three years ago. You probably know this already, I imagine. He had some problems there—got involved with strange people, let himself be manipulated, and got into trouble. He was always a good guy, but he was easily influenced by others, you know how things are. We brought him up right, but in the army, instead of him learning to honor the nation and God, they changed him. This country, sir—you must know better than anyone . . . This country is being swallowed up by evil. And anything that's happening to the country will happen to the people too.

Óscar was so trusting and naïve, and they got him mixed up in some bad stuff. I never knew how serious things were. No dead bodies or "false positive" murders, just money. He liked gambling, and that was his downfall. A man with debts is screwed; the mafia will bleed him dry drop by drop. He'd been into that crap since he was a young man. Games of chance, betting. If I told you how many times I punished him . . . I burned his hand on the stove once. Because the debts always ended up landing on me. A man will do anything for his kids. I thought the army was going to straighten him out, which is why I recommended him to an old family friend.

He started at the bottom, as a third corporal. He took the exams, and they approved his military service. He entered the Third Brigade, here in Cali, as part of the infantry battalion. He moved up fast. Within a few years he was already a first sergeant, then a sergeant major. He kept himself on the straight and narrow because he had to, plus the kids were born. But it didn't cure him. Once he acquired a little bit of power and felt secure, that was it. He couldn't resist anymore. Whenever he had a day off, he would spend the afternoon at this bingo parlor on Plaza Caicedo. I figure mobsters must hang out in those places, looking to reel people in who have a problem. And he was a soldier to boot! They opened up tabs for him at the casinos and took him to higher-stakes games, where he lost even more. Who knows what else they gave him—that world is a hellhole.

It was Angelita who called one day to say Óscar was in debt again, that he was drinking too much and neglecting the family. In the battalion he came across other guys who were even worse off. The mafia had them in a vise, forced them to do things. The gambling mafia is dangerous, sir. You'll know more about that than I do. I talked to Óscar and asked him, All right, what kind of crap are you caught up in, and demanded details, how much he owed, who to, but he always said the same thing: Don't worry about me, Dad, I'll get out of this, don't torture yourself, I'm going to win enough to give my old lady a house, have faith in me, and I'd tell him, Damn it, this isn't about you, it's about your family, your children—what kind of example are you setting for them?

The years went by, and I knew that the string he was holding on to was pulled so tight it was about to snap, and then it did snap, and all hell broke loose: turned out he'd been stealing ammunition from the brigade, supposedly to sell—he would hold his fire during gunfights so he could pocket the bullets afterward. It sounded weird to me—how much can a box of ammo possibly be worth? That much? I don't know. That was what he told us, why he'd been kicked out. For stealing ammunition. I asked him, And did you steal it? And he told me, No, Dad, it wasn't me! It's the ones in charge who do the stealing, and then they blame us. So I asked, Why do they steal it? And he said, So they can sell it to the paramilitary or even the guerrilla groups. I couldn't believe that. Why would you sell bullets that could then be used against you? And he laughed: No, Dad, the people selling them never take part in combat, get it?

In the end he got off easy. I told him, Figure out what you're going to do to support your family, you hear me? And he says, All right, I'll look around, I know how to handle weapons, so I said, Be careful not to get involved in anything dirty, and right away he answered, No, Dad, don't worry about that, I'm going to work security. One day he invited us over for lunch. He had the place all fixed up, two bottles of wine, roast chicken, arepas—the works. And his mom asked, Son, what is it we're celebrating? And he answered, I got a good job, it's a firm that provides security to private individuals, with a great reputation, it's called SecuNorte; and I thought to myself, As long as he's fooling around with weapons, I'm always going to be nervous about this idiot—and I was right to be.

Later I found out he was working with a Christian church, protecting a priest, something like that, and Angelita told us he'd become really religious; and that basically cured his gambling addiction, and he started coming home after work to spend time with the kids. It was a Grace Communion International church; sometimes they transported VIPs or money, and they had to be really smart. I asked him if he'd gone back to the casinos, and he said he hadn't, that it was a sin and offended Jesus.

After about a year he started traveling, or so he said: I'm going to Barranquilla, I'm going to Armenia, I'm going to Calarcá. He would head off, and even he didn't know how long he'd be gone. That's why when this happened, we weren't worried at first. Angelita thought it was strange he hadn't called again, but he was with the church, and they'd go to these villages in the middle of nowhere with no cell service. When he stopped calling, Angelita came to me. How long since we've heard from him? About three weeks, give or take. Then you all showed up, sir.

Jutsiñamuy listened attentively. Laiseca scribbled notes in his notebook, and when the old man finished speaking, nobody dared say anything.

"Did you all realize he wasn't working for SecuNorte anymore?" the prosecutor asked, looking at the widow.

"No, sir. I didn't dare ask him. I never understood why

everything had to be such a huge secret if it wasn't anything bad, you know? I even suggested one day that we take the kids to his church, but he refused. No way. If we wanted to go to church, we should pick another one—there were plenty to choose from. It made him nervous to have the family around. But he always came through with the grocery money and the rent."

"Did you hear him mention anybody? Do you remember any names?" Jutsiñamuy asked.

"No, sir. Like I said, he didn't talk about work here at home," the widow replied.

"Or did you overhear anything when he was on the phone?" Jutsiñamuy kept pushing. "Did he ever mention a Carlitos?"

The woman scratched her head, looked first at the ceiling and then at her two younger children, who were fidgeting restlessly.

"He always went into the utility room to talk, but once, not too long ago, I overheard a bit of conversation when I was in the bathroom. I didn't pay much attention, but he said something about a man who'd be flying in from Quito and I remember he said, We need to call Carlitos, you call and give him the itinerary. That's what I heard. Why?"

Laiseca pulled out the photo of the John Doe and handed it to the woman.

"Look closely at this person," the prosecutor said. "We found him next to your husband. Do you recognize him?"

The woman sank once more into a tense silence.

"I don't think so, sir, but it's harder to recognize someone when they're dead, don't you think?"

"That's why I encourage you to take your time."

The older boy tried to sidle next to his mother to look, but she pulled the photo away.

"No, son! This is adult business. Go sit down."

She studied the photo again. Her face expressionless, she handed it back to the prosecutor. "No, sir. I don't know him."

Jutsiñamuy looked at Laiseca, giving him an order with a glance that his officer understood immediately. Laiseca took a couple of steps forward into the middle of the room and said, "Are you familiar with a restaurant in Jamundí called the Jamundí Inn?"

This time the woman looked surprised. "Of course. We've taken the kids there for the day, maybe three times. They've got a pool."

The questioning clearly made her uncomfortable.

"Did it seem like somewhere expensive?" Jutsiñamuy asked.

"Kind of," the woman said, "but I didn't know anything about Óscar's money situation, how much he had. After all the trouble he got into in the army, I tried not to think about that. If there was money, great, and if not, same difference. He was an extravagant guy, and sometimes even when he was broke he'd give us presents, buy expensive things. A real spendthrift."

"But when you went to the Jamundí Inn, did you feel comfortable there?" Jutsiñamuy asked.

"No, sir. But I never felt comfortable anywhere."

He felt bad for keeping up the pressure, but sometimes people under pressure remembered things they thought they didn't know. "Never?" he asked. "What was that like? Talk to me about that."

The woman looked around, visibly uneasy. Realizing what was going on, the prosecutor apologized to the rest of the family, offered the widow his hand, and said, "Is there somewhere we can talk in private?"

The father stood up immediately. "No need, sir. You all stay here and we'll leave." He herded the family out a side door.

Jutsiñamuy continued. "All right, now tell me, ma'am . . . Ángela?"

"Yes, Ángela Suárez Medina."

"Nice to meet you."

She stroked her cheeks with her fingertips and said, "What I wanted to say, sir, is Óscar had another woman. That's why I didn't want to talk in front of the kids. All that secrecy on the phone was partly because he didn't like us knowing about his work, sure, but it was mostly because of this woman. They'd been together about two years. When we'd go to the Jamundí Inn, he'd hide from the waiters so they wouldn't say hello to him—I noticed it. He'd make faces and shake his finger no at them. But they all knew him because he used to go there with that tramp. Her name is Luz Dary Patiño. She works at Almacenes Sí, in the school uniform department. Can you guess how they met?"

"I assume he was buying uniforms for the kids," Jutsiñamuy said, gesturing to Laiseca to take note: name and place.

"Exactly," the widow said. "Can you imagine? A young girl, and not even that pretty, actually. I don't know what she gets out of taking up with a married man who's got kids. Not even money, because what money? He was broke."

She was silent a moment.

"When Óscar disappeared I thought he was with his hussy, so I didn't worry about it. Just between the two of us, sir, I'll tell you Óscar and I hadn't done anything for at least two years. I was even sleeping in the kids' room. Lots of times when he was away for a while it wasn't because he was working—he was away with her on a trip. I knew. I'd call to ask for her at the department store, and they'd tell me she was on vacation or out sick. Always. Sometimes he'd come back with a tan, and I'd ask, Oh, did you go to the beach? And he'd say, Yes, we had to provide security for somebody in Coveñas. A couple days later I'd be at Almacenes Sí and see that tramp across the floor, her brown as a nut too."

A phone rang in a nearby house. Instinctively, Laiseca touched his jacket pocket.

"This time, since he'd been gone more than two weeks,"

the woman continued, "I went to Almacenes Sí, but there she was, standing all snooty behind the register. I wanted to go up and ask, but in the end I didn't. I thought it must be true that he was working, and look. Turns out he was dead. Go talk to her, sir. She'll know more about the bastard than I do."

With that, the prosecutor saw that the visit was over. He got up, and they went to the door. "Give my thanks to your family," Jutsiñamuy said. "And if you remember anything important, please call." He handed her his card.

He was almost out the door when he suddenly turned back. "Sorry, ma'am, one last thing. Does the phrase 'We are healed' mean anything to you? Written on an open hand?"

She thought a moment and said no, no. "Doesn't sound familiar. Why?"

"One of your husband's tattoos, on his left side, under his nipple."

"I don't know what to tell you. He liked covering himself in those tattoos—things for soldiers and losers. I don't remember that one in particular."

Jutsiñamuy met her gaze. "You told me you two hadn't had anything for at least two years," he said quietly.

"Yes, but I saw him shower and dry himself off by the window every day."

"I see."

"Go ask that other woman," the widow said. "Maybe she saw it."

Jutsiñamuy tapped his lips with his index finger. "Another thing, Doña Ángela—what about the name Mr. F? Did you ever hear it?"

"No, sir, what's that? It sounds like the name of a gym."

"That's what we're trying to find out, ma'am, to figure out what happened to your husband. What about the name Fabinho Henriquez?"

"No, like I said, I never knew anything about his work."

*

Johana and Julieta ate breakfast early, at about seven, beside a large picture window that looked out on the abandoned mansion that had once belonged to the illustrious nineteenth-century writer Jorge Isaacs, with a rusty sign announcing a shopping center that was never built.

The menu was a huge buffet with fresh orange and mango juice, sliced fruit, cheese, cereals, and scrambled eggs with onion and tomato. Plus a selection of arepas, cassava cheese bread, and croissants. Julieta was tempted to spend the whole morning there, but she was feeling restless. She glanced at her watch every two minutes, picked up her coffee cup, turned it in her hands, and put it back down without drinking.

Her appointment with the pastor was at nine thirty at the InterContinental Hotel.

"Do you want me to go with you, boss?" Johana offered.

"I don't know, I don't know," Julieta said. "Let's go together, and we'll see once we get there. I'm a little nervous."

"I can tell. Don't worry. The InterContinental is really close by."

Julieta pulled out her notebook.

"All right, Johana, let's go over it again. Why the hell did I ask for an appointment?" She answered her own question. "To see his reaction when I ask him about two things: one, the gunfight in San Andrés de Pisimbalá, and two, the kid. Other things will come up from there. Oh, and the guy on the motorcycle who's been following us."

Johana watched her write it down and said, "Ask him about his life too: how he started, that sort of thing. He probably likes talking about himself, and it'll earn his trust."

"Don't worry about the how—I've got a handle on that," Julieta said. "Men are so vain, you always ask them how they got where they are. They love that."

"So why are you so nervous?" Johana asked.

"The way he looks at me, I don't know. It's unnerving," Julieta said, irritated.

"Maybe it's best if you're not alone."

"We'll see when we get there. If he's alone, I'll go in on my own."

"When you ask about the gunfight," Johana said, "he's obviously going to deny it."

"I want to see his reaction and let him know that we know," Julieta said.

They drank a third round of coffee, then a fourth. What time was it? Almost nine. They went up to brush their teeth. At 9:27 they were in the InterContinental's vast lobby. A young man was behind the reception desk.

"We have an appointment with the pastor from New Jerusalem Church," Julieta said.

"Yes, of course." The receptionist studied a schedule. "Ms. Julieta . . . Lezama?"

"That's me," Julieta said, and gestured to Johana. "This is my assistant."

"Follow me," the receptionist said. "He's in the Belalcázar Suite, but you'll need to go through a brief security check first."

"Of course."

They went up to the second floor, where they proceeded down a corridor to an X-ray machine similar to the ones you see in airports.

"Could I have your bag? Do you have a laptop? Cell phone?"

They put everything in the trays. Julieta walked through the metal detector, which beeped. A young, muscular, good-looking guard came over with a hand-held wand. Julieta met his eyes.

"Raise your arms, miss," he said. "Great. Now turn around."

"You want me to turn around?" she said jokingly. "Without offering me a drink first?"

The guard flushed. The other officers laughed.

"Go on."

They walked down another corridor, this one lined with sets of double doors with the names of conference rooms. Finally they turned onto the last hallway and saw it in front of them: Belalcázar Suite. Three guards were standing by the door. Their bags were searched again. They walked into a room where there were three more people.

A secretary.

"Ms. Julieta Lezama?"

She stepped forward. "That's me. This is my assistant."

"Pastor Almayer would like to see you alone, miss."

"No problem," Julieta said. "Johana can wait for me here."

The young woman escorted her to the rear of the room and, with a somewhat theatrical gesture, opened a set of double doors.

When Julieta walked in, the pastor had his back to her.

She was bothered by the room's dim light and stark atmosphere. He was wearing the same black outfit he'd had on for the service. Outside of that context, it didn't look like a priest's clothing. Before she could say anything, she heard the door close.

"Good morning, Julieta," the pastor said, his back still to her. "Please, come closer." He spun in his chair. He was holding a book of classical religious paintings, opened to a page in the middle. Rather than getting up or looking at her, he kept studying the images. "It's incredible what man is capable of when he seeks transcendence, don't you think?"

Feeling awkward, she looked at the illustrations. She had no idea what to say. At last the pastor looked up at her.

"Would you like some tea?"

"I just had breakfast, thanks."

The pastor silently turned the page, looked at one more illustration, and closed the book.

"My assistant told me you're a journalist and showed me some of your articles. I appreciate your interest in me. What did you think of my talk yesterday?"

Julieta met his eyes. He had thick, very black brows.

"Effective and direct," she said. "Devoid of anything your audience might understand, but very moving."

The man rested his chin on his hand. "Moving? Effective? Explain what you mean."

"You moved people, you made them believe in your words," Julieta said.

"What about you, Julieta? Were you moved?"

"I'm not a believer."

"You don't need to believe in something to be moved," the pastor said.

"In a way you do," she said. "I can say I was struck by the staging and the way people idolize you. They really believe in you."

The pastor scratched his chin. "Staging . . . You use tough words. Theater, drama? A performance, fundamentally, is an artifice. All I do is take the words people carry inside them and put them in contact with other words, those of the Bible and those of Jesus. There's no artifice in that."

"The Bible, Jesus, his story, his words," Julieta said. "I get it. But for a nonbeliever like me, it's all unrealistic."

"Unrealistic?" the pastor repeated, more surprised than angry. "In what way?"

"It's an exciting story, full of wisdom and lovely metaphors," Julieta said, "but as far as believing it's true . . ."

Pastor Fritz's eyes widened. There was a strange gleam in them, and Julieta lowered her own.

"Interesting," he said. "And do you think that what the people feel is an artifice too?"

"Just because they believe it doesn't make it true . . ."

"Truth is merely our perception of the truth," the pastor

said. "How do you know all of this is real? This room, this hotel?"

"The same way you do," Julieta said. "But let's drop the rhetoric and metaphors, pastor. I'm here for another reason that you may be able to . . . intuit."

Pastor Fritz rubbed his chin. It was clear he was ready for a frontal assault. "I'm listening."

"There was a shoot-out on a road in Tierradentro, near San Andrés de Pisimbalá," Julieta said. "Ten days ago. Two SUVs and a black Hummer were attacked with assault weapons, and in the end a helicopter intervened. A man dressed in black and two women got out of the Hummer."

Not a muscle moved in the pastor's face.

"Exciting tale," he said. "What happened next?"

"That's what I'd like you to tell me," Julieta said.

"I'm not familiar with the story, sadly."

Julieta forced herself to meet his eyes again. "You were there."

"There? You mean . . . ? I don't understand."

"You're the man in black who got out of the Hummer," she said. "I know that much. What I haven't been able to find out is who attacked you and why. That's what I want you to tell me."

Fritz smiled faintly. Their faces weren't all that close, but if she'd wanted to touch his, she could have simply reached out her hand.

"I'm touched by your faith, Julieta. Do you really think it was me? Tell me what makes you so certain."

Julieta thought longingly of a cigarette. She was dying to smoke. She glanced around but didn't see any ashtrays. It must be prohibited in the entire hotel.

"Is something wrong?" Pastor Fritz asked.

"I'd like to smoke," she said. "I quit a while back, but I started up again a week ago."

"Don't worry," Pastor Fritz said. "Sigmund Freud quit for thirty years, and then one day he lit one and started smoking again. Know what he said? 'I couldn't concentrate.'"

Julieta smiled briefly.

"Let's go over to the window," Fritz said. "You can smoke there. I'm a former smoker myself. They won't give us any trouble."

With the first drag, she felt her soul being restored. She blew the smoke out into the sweltering air of the city.

"But don't forget your story," Fritz said. "You were about to tell me how I'm related to this gunfight."

"You must be a powerful man, pastor. The police made everything go away and covered it up with a story of an intoxicated driver firing shots into the air."

Pastor Fritz moved away from the window, paced around the small room, and returned to her.

"The problem with this conversation, Julieta, is that you already knew I'd say it wasn't me. And yet you came to ask anyway."

"Of course," she said. "It's no surprise that you'd deny it."

"So why come, then?" Fritz asked.

Julieta realized she wasn't going to get very far. "I wanted to know who you were. The bit about the orphans at the end of your talk struck me."

"You want to know who I am?"

Julieta again looked at him steadily. "Yes, that's what I'm most interested in. Knowing who you are and what kind of person does the things you do. I don't represent the law or anything. I'm interested in stories, in telling a story that is good, convincing, and true."

"If you want to know who I am and why I do this, I'll have to tell you my story," Pastor Fritz said, smiling. "I don't know if you're interested. It's called 'The Boy on the Park Bench.'"

"Let's hear it," Julieta said, lighting another cigarette.

The pastor went to sit in one of the armchairs in the corner, where it was darker. Maybe to avoid her gaze so he could choose his words better.

"The Boy on the Park Bench," that was my nickname for a while. It's a short, simple story. Listen.

The father took the boy to a bench and told him, "Wait for me here, son. I'm going to take care of some business nearby, and I'll be right back." The boy sat and watched him walk away, head down some stairs, and go down a side street until he disappeared from view. The boy didn't dare stand up, so he couldn't see which building he went into. What is he doing? the boy wondered, swinging his feet. Beside him was the bag his father had left. Curious, he opened it and found a sandwich and an apple.

By noon, he was feeling hungry, so he took out the apple and ate half, leaving the rest for later. At about five, people started coming to the park and the boy got impatient. Every time he saw someone in the distance, he'd think, He's coming, he's coming, but he never was.

Soon night fell.

Before dinnertime, the park again filled up with people from the neighborhood. He saw other children playing, but he didn't dare move from his spot, afraid that his father would come back and fail to find him. A little while later everybody returned to their homes, and the boy was left alone. He took a couple of bites of the sandwich and kept waiting. A breeze picked up, and he felt cold. He put his legs up on the bench and lay down to sleep. He was sure that while he was sleeping his father's hand would shake him awake, his voice saying, "All right, son, we can go now."

But he opened his eyes, very early in the morning, and he was still there, alone.

On the second day, a woman who lived nearby came to talk

to him: "Boy, what are you doing on this bench?" and he replied, "I'm waiting for my father, he went to take care of something on the next street over." On the third night the woman invited him to sleep at her house, but he refused. "If he comes back and doesn't see me, he won't know where I am," the boy said. On the sixth day the woman managed to persuade him and they left a note:

"Dad, I'm at the house across the street, the blue one. Come back soon."

The note stayed pinned to the back of the bench for several days until the rain washed away first the writing and then the paper.

The woman opened her door to the boy every night and made him sandwiches for while he was waiting. She didn't interfere, but clearly something weird was going on. She did ask the boy his name and where he was from. "My name is Rafael, Rafico. I'm from Florencia." What about his last name? The boy's eyes darted around, tense. He looked at her and said, "Bolívar." It wasn't his real name, but the boy figured it didn't matter since nobody knew him anyway. After a month the woman talked with a school in the neighborhood and persuaded the boy to go in the mornings. She bought him a uniform and school supplies and told him, "I'll stay by the window watching the bench, and if your dad comes, I'll tell him." The boy was reassured, and every day, coming back from school, he fantasized that his father would fling the door open and give him a hug.

And so the year came to an end.

He got good grades. The woman was named Carmen, and she had a daughter who lived in Barranquilla, married with kids. They came for Christmas, and the woman told them his story. The grandchildren eyed him with curiosity. "Do you really not have a mom or dad?" they asked. "I do, but they're not here," he said.

The boy got older. One day he decided to sit down in front of *the house that he'd figured out must have been the house his father went into, to see who came out. But no one did. It seemed unoccupied. There were no lights at night. Maybe the people who lived there had gone somewhere else and taken his father with them. But sooner or later they'd come back. All houses have mysteries, especially empty ones.*

The boy became a teenager, and then a man.

The father never came back.

I am that boy, Julieta.

One day I decided I couldn't stay with Carmen any longer. A strange voice murmured these words to me: "Go back, go back." I returned to Caquetá. Maybe my father was there. But when I got to Florencia, I didn't recognize anything. Or anybody. I walked through the town many times and finally decided to leave.

What would I do with my life?

I went to the jungle in search of solace, and there I grew up, alone, like Mowgli, like Greystoke, or even like Jesus, when he went to the Orient and northern India; I grew up the same way as certain special people in the history of the world: alone, utterly alone. Those of us who have been abandoned believe we have a mission on Earth—and do you know why? When you look up at the sky, you see stars and think they're beautiful, but when I look up I see only wounds that swarm and sparkle, burns on its face, blemishes, scars—mine and others'. Behind those wounds I hear voices, cries of pain or rage; those words plead with me, they're on their knees, they're a sigh, a sob; only those who have experienced abandonment can hear those voices, those sighs in the dark; it's the sound that rings out across the world when happy people are sleeping, an echo of lament, the pleas that nobody hears except yourself. All of that is present in the terrifying night, Julieta, while you are sleeping, dreaming about soft sounds and caresses, because the darkness of the world, to us, is a hostile territory full of pain and memories. Other people,

*happy people, see twinkling stars, a romantic, loving moon, a
night full of fragrances, of murmurs . . .*

Congratulations.

*You will be happy, and you will die happy. I won't. I was aban-
doned and will die alone. Life is a slow process of loss, a space in
time that only confuses my ideas. I don't want to be loved, just to
be understood by others. I look for the right words—can you
imagine such a task? I am too far away. I seek them in books, in
ideas.*

*I'm talking about things that exist only in memory, or in the
imagination of memory. Because the most lasting thing in this
world, Julieta, cannot be touched with the soiled fingers with
which we touch bread or the earth, with which we touch one
another. No way. Only with words, and that's why I'm here,
telling you all this. That's why I talk about Christ, about myself.
But we're not the same person, even though Christ is born and
dies over and over.*

*I talk about him because I can cause him to be born in the
people who hear me.*

*As a boy I left in order to return, because I had to learn on
my own and come of age in a vast, unpopulated realm known as
Solitude, and the best way to do it was to go live in the jungle,
surrounded by sinister trees and wild animals, cannibal fish and
terrifying noises that made me tremble with fear. Until I put
myself back together.*

That's where I get my strength.

*Wise men say: "When you gaze long at the jungle, the jungle
also gazes at you." You don't get what I'm saying, I can tell.
That's OK. My word isn't a disease that's transmitted through
the air, like Ebola, or through the gaze, like faith. It is just the
word of someone who's lived. That's enough for me. I am here to
save others. That's what I do every day. Tend the wounds that
others have on their bodies and make them my own, kiss them,
suck them, heal them. I seek to be infused with the strength that*

is born of the pain of those mutilations, of lacerated, broken, tattered bodies.

Wounded bodies that wander around, lost—do you understand that? Tell me what you understand; or no, best not tell me anything. Just contemplate it. Bodies that suffer and cannot understand why they must experience such pain. A pain that selected only a few and set so many others aside, because those who talk about Christ in this country, and even those who are oblivious to him—their hearts remain unscathed. Christ, too, was abandoned by his father. "Why have you forsaken me?" he says, looking up at the heavens, already on the cross. And what reply does he get? Silence. The same reply I've gotten for fifty years.

Silence, and the vast emptiness of the night.

The pastor took a long pause, and Julieta realized he was finished.

She was surprisingly moved, so she lit up another cigarette.

"That's a very sad story, pastor," Julieta said. "And very beautiful. Now I get why you talk about orphans."

"Why did you join the line?" he asked.

"You found me out," Julieta said. "How did you know?"

"There are some things I can't explain," Fritz said, "because they can't be put into words. If somebody asks me for those words, I have no idea what they might be. If nobody asks, they're right there."

"Don't tell me you can read minds."

"Ha, that would be torture. I just have intuitions. I'd have to call it something like clouds of electricity or hollow zones in the air. It's no use trying to verbalize it—I just come up with random metaphors. But that's what it feels like to me."

Julieta blew out a long line of smoke. "Ask your intuition what else I want to know and why."

He met her eyes again, his gaze fierce. "You're different

from when you arrived," he said. "I'd almost say that now, right this moment, you feel closer to me than you have to many of the people you've met in your life."

Julieta blushed. "You don't need superpowers to know that, pastor," she said. "You know you're charismatic. What else do I want to know about you? Because there's another important thing."

Fritz kept watching her, not saying anything. There was an uncomfortable silence. Julieta closed the window and put away her cigarettes.

"Do I need to leave now?"

The pastor moved as if to get up, then settled back in his chair. "No, of course not," he said. "You leave when you want to leave."

"There's something we haven't talked about. I imagine you'll deny this too, but I should just show you my cards. For some strange reason, I don't mistrust you."

"Go on, you'll find the words you have inside and want to bring into the light," the pastor said.

Julieta went back to her seat, looked at him coolly, and said, "But I want to ask for something first, a simple request: don't talk to me like I'm one of those people who kneel in your church and idolize you. I respect your story, and I think it's interesting, but treat me like the person I am."

"Do you consider yourself superior to them?"

"I have an education and convictions, that's all," Julieta said.

"You are strong and fragile at the same time, that's what I see. What else do you want to know?"

"Franklin Vanegas, the kid from Tierradentro. Why is he with you? Did you bring him against his will? That's a serious crime. Kidnapping a minor."

Pastor Fritz closed his eyes. He looked at the floor, then at the ceiling. Two, three seconds passed in silence, and Julieta sensed that she'd finally managed to break through his armor. She was aware that the man had a military force protecting him from his enemies and a shiver fluttered in her stomach, but she stood firm.

The pastor spoke at last. "Can you say the boy's name again?"

"Franklin Vanegas."

"You said he's from Tierradentro? How old is he?"

"He's a Nasa boy, fourteen years old max," Julieta said. "Maybe twelve, I don't know."

Pastor Fritz got up and went to the door. "Excuse me a moment, I need to consult with somebody."

He went out into the hallway. Julieta couldn't see anything, but she heard low conversation. A moment later, the pastor came back in. He remained standing in the middle of the room.

"Tell you what, Julieta," Fritz said. "Let's exchange numbers, and I'll look into the boy. As soon as I learn anything, I swear in the name of Christ I'll call you."

"So he is with you," Julieta said.

"A lot of people work around me," the pastor said, "and sometimes there are new people, people brought in temporarily, people I don't know. I can't know all of my employees' names, but I promise I'll look into it. Why are you so sure he's with me?"

"He was at your church yesterday," Julieta said. "I saw him from a distance when I was in the line. I tried to look for him, but it was impossible with all those people."

The pastor came over and placed his hand on her arm to guide her to the door. "I know you can believe me," he said in her ear, "even though you're wearing a sort of protective helmet to shield against my words. Have faith in what I'm saying. What's your number?"

Julieta recited it, and the pastor dialed and hung up once her phone had rung.

"I'll be in touch as soon as I hear anything, I promise," he said. "And if you need to talk to me about anything, text me, and I'll call you as soon as I can."

He accompanied her to the door. They said goodbye.

As she was leaving, the pastor called to her. "Thanks for this talk, Julieta. You're an exceptional person."

She looked at him again. Feline eyes, but she realized that despite everything they were full of fear. She walked into the other room, where Johana was waiting for her. She was flattered by his parting words: "An exceptional person."

Two bodyguards led them down to reception. When they reached the street, Johana looked at her eagerly.

"Tell me, boss, how did it go?"

Julieta took a deep breath. "What time is it?"

The clock on her phone said eleven.

"It's early, but I need a drink," Julieta said. "Let's go to the hotel bar, and I'll fill you in."

THE JAMUNDÍ INN

Downtown Cali is noisy, clashing, full of casinos and street stalls that block pedestrians' paths. A feral kingdom where no law seems to hold sway. Next to a civil notary's office is a steamy fried-food vendor and then a medical laboratory. There are used bookstores, corner shops, lottery ticket sellers, copy centers, cheap hotels.

Entering the maelstrom, Jutsiñamuy saw people selling cell phone covers, USB chargers, fake designer watches, CBD creams for arthritis, hair tonics, libido supplements, plus vendors hawking tools and magnifying glasses, wafer cookies, fresh-squeezed juices, peach palm fruits, lulada in plastic cups, and the pre-Hispanic drink said to be a favorite of the dead, known in Cauca as *champús*, all amid pirated copies of movies, documentaries, and concerts from all over the world. On the working-class streets of central Cali, as in Bogotá and Medellín—and all over the country, in fact—another common sight was the woeful human contingent so typical of developing countries, made up of rock-bottom addicts who sleep off their coca-paste highs under sheets of plastic; toothless, filthy glue sniffers; women near collapse who stretch out scrawny arms begging for coins; and battalions of the crippled and mutilated, especially around churches or next to café entrances.

Survivors of a silent, secret catastrophe.

Cancino and Laiseca trailed behind Jutsiñamuy, panting. It was too hot for their dark uniforms and Bogotá neckties. Over eighty-five degrees. But Jutsiñamuy, who wasn't much affected by temperature, decided they'd better go on foot rather than in the over-air-conditioned vehicles of the local prosecutor's office. With the streets crowded with traffic and people, it would take them forever to get there by car.

There it was at the end of the street: Almacenes Sí.

Kind of like Tía, Jutsiñamuy thought, recalling a Bogotá department store of yesteryear. The uniform department was on the third floor, and as they went up they had to pass through several other sections via a complicated system of unconnected escalators, evidence that the store had annexed adjacent properties as it grew.

They got lost a few times and had to ask the way. The fifth person they stopped stared at them with hostility: a group of three men dressed in dark clothing and looking for the school uniform department was a bizarre sight. At last they found the place, a huge room full of clothing racks, organized in alphabetical order by school name.

They squinted at each of the female employees in the department, trying to guess which one was Luz Dary Patiño. The lover. Given the widow's words and the hatred in her eyes, they had pictured a woman with surgically enhanced lips and a prominent bosom. When the wife said she was "not even that pretty," they pictured a voluptuous woman with a piercing gaze and a round posterior.

The prosecutor went up to one of the cashiers, a young black man with a horizontal scar on his eyebrow.

"I'm looking for Ms. Luz Dary Patiño."

The cashier asked him to wait a moment, picked up a microphone, and said, "Luz Dary to register 2, Luz Dary to register 2."

The three men, four counting the employee, stood waiting, but the customers buffeted them like a sea swell. Some standing in line, making sure nobody cut in. Others poking their heads in from the sides with questions.

"Where can I find the uniforms for the Virgin of the Consolation of Martyrs School?"

"Second row in the back," the young man replied, unfazed.

"Are the Carolus Ponciano uniforms on sale too, sir?"

"Eight percent with a Comfandi loyalty card and five percent on checked or polyester skirts in medium," he said.

"Can I help you?"

Jutsiñamuy turned to find a short woman with a round face and almond-shaped eyes, her skin discolored by vitiligo.

"Did you call me? I'm Luz Dary Patiño. What do you need?"

They'd never pictured someone like this.

She limped as she came closer, courtesy of the orthopedic apparatus on her left leg. Polio.

"Nice to meet you, I'm a prosecutor and I've come all the way from Bogotá to talk to you, miss," he said. "Is there someplace quiet? These are my agents."

Luz Dary stepped back, or rather aside, leaning on the rod of her apparatus. She looked over at her boss, somewhat nervous, and he nodded his permission. They walked to the rear of the department. The young woman opened a door, and they entered a small room with a table and three chairs. Hangers and boxes of T-shirts in various sizes were piled up in the corners.

"All right, how can I help you?" she said again, looking wary.

"We know that you were in a relationship with Mr. Óscar Luis Pedraza," Jutsiñamuy said, "and we're here because . . . well, I assume you know already."

A look of surprise appeared on the woman's face. What was going on?

The prosecutor decided to continue. "Óscar Luis Pedraza was found dead last Friday, miss, on the road to Popayán."

"What?" was all she managed to say; she supported herself

on the table with one hand and brought the other to her forehead. "Are you serious?"

"Yes," Jutsiñamuy said. "I'm sorry to have to tell you like this, out of the blue."

The woman closed her eyes, and when she opened them again they were damp and bloodshot. Two black rivulets, like watercolor paint, rolled down her cheeks to the corners of her mouth.

"What . . . happened to him?" she asked. "Are you sure it's not . . . a mistake?"

"That's what we're looking into, miss," Laiseca said. "But unfortunately it is him, no question."

Suddenly the woman stared at them in distress. "And am I a suspect or something?"

"Not at all," Jutsiñamuy said, grasping her arm. "Quite the opposite. The first thing we want to do is offer our condolences."

"Oh, it's just that your agent's tone . . ."

Jutsiñamuy looked at Laiseca sternly. "Agent, apologize to the young woman and offer her your condolences right now!"

"Please forgive me if I was inadvertently rude to you," Laiseca said. "And please accept my apology and my sincerest condolences."

Luz Dary looked at him through a haze of tears, sniffled, and said, "Thank you, there's no need to apologize. Life is life."

"As somebody once said," Jutsiñamuy added, "life isn't worth a thing."

"That's a José Alfredo Jiménez song, boss," Laiseca said, "if you'll excuse me."

"Of course I know it's a song, dumbass," the prosecutor said, irritated. "I'm trying to be friendly. Understood?"

Luz Dary kept staring at the floor as if in a trance. Abruptly, she said, "Óscar can't be dead!"

204 · SANTIAGO GAMBOA

Jutsiñamuy put his arm around her. From the other side of the glass, the store customers started eyeing them curiously.

"You don't know how much I'd like to tell you it's not true," the prosecutor said, "but unfortunately it is. We found him by the side of the road with two other bodies."

"For your information," Cancino stepped in, "he was shot three times, I'm sorry."

"Three?" She started crying again. "Who did it? Who would do that? He didn't have any enemies."

"As far as we know, he worked in security," Jutsiñamuy said. "Even if he didn't have enemies, his boss may have."

"And who are the other two bodies?" Luz Dary asked.

"One hasn't been identified yet," Jutsiñamuy said. "The other is named Nadio Becerra."

"Nadio? Oh, don't tell me that . . ." She sobbed again, covering her eyes with her hand. "They were such good friends. Was Nadio shot three times too?"

"No, miss," Cancino said. "He was shot six times."

"Six?! So he had it even worse. Poor guy."

Jutsiñamuy took her affectionately by the shoulders and said, "You can help us, Luz Dary. Please concentrate and be completely honest with us. But first I want to make it clear that nothing you say will be used against you in any way, not now or later—do you understand? You can be absolutely open." Having said that, he pulled out his identification badge from the prosecutor's office and signaled to his agents to do the same.

Luz Dary took the three badges and scrutinized them as if they'd handed her a credit card for payment at her cash register. After confirming that they belonged to each of them, she gave them back.

"All right," she said. Then, lowering her voice, she said to the prosecutor, "I'll help you, but it's kind of an intimate subject, so it makes me uncomfortable being closed up in here with three men, you know?"

Jutsiñamuy looked over at his agents.

"Whatever makes you comfortable, ma'am," Laiseca said.

"You can record me if you want," Luz Dary said, "but I can't talk in front of three men."

The agents left. Jutsiñamuy sat down across from her.

"You can already guess what I need to know," he said. "How you met Óscar, what you knew about his work, and when you last saw him. Take your time and tell me everything that comes to mind; any information, however minor, could be crucial. I'm listening."

I started working at Almacenes Sí seven years back, soon after I graduated in accounting. I don't have connections or bene-factors—I'm from a poor family, so I started at the bottom. And I'm still there, as you can see. My appearance doesn't help, of course. I've had this condition since I was a kid, and though it was a mild case, it caused muscular atrophy in one leg, and the depression messed up my skin, though that comes and goes. It's actually quite an achievement that I've made it as far as the cash register, and I imagine I'll be there till I die.

I met Óscar here.

He came in looking for uniforms for his kids and was very sweet and kind. At first I thought it was weird he was asking for so much advice about shirt sizes, since they're one-size-fits-all, but he was actually trying to chat me up. I could hardly believe it. Men haven't exactly chased after me, sir, and when I saw how attentive and interested he was, I kept talking to him. After two hours he asked what time I got off work and whether I'd have coffee with him. I said yes. He told me how to get to a little place around the corner from here and said to meet him at seven. I agreed, convinced he wouldn't show. But there he was, all romantic.

That very night, I was his.

We started seeing each other regularly, when I got off work.

I was wild with happiness. I didn't care that it had to be in secret or that he sometimes called his wife in front of me. One day I asked him what he did for work. "I'm in security, honey." That's what he said. So you go around with a gun in your pants? And he said, "Well, yeah, I do, and if things get ugly I take it out and shoot, that's my job." Whenever I got worried, he'd say, "Don't worry, honey, life expectancy in this country is improving." I thought he was going to keep me hidden, but he started taking me out with his friends, though all the other men brought their girlfriends or second wives, who obviously were much prettier and more elegant than me.

Do I remember his friends' names? Of course. Let's see, there was Nadio, Ferney, Nacho, and Colachito—he's from Antioquia. I remember Mario and a guy named Carlitos, who was the driver. And there was this one guy they called Dim Bulb, maybe his name was Germán. And the girls—there was Yeni, Estéphanny, Clara, Selmira, Cruz Marcela. Some of them were Venezuelan . . .

They all snorted that stuff and drank loads of aguardiente. I didn't like it, and luckily Óscar didn't either, so we were the squares of the group. The nerds. The men all worked together, I think. If one of them said anything about work, the others would all give him a hard time. "Shut up, man, we're here to have a good time. Or would you rather we head back to the office?"

He was working security for somebody associated with an evangelical church. He was always having to go to other cities, and sometimes he'd take me with him. The first time was to Barranquilla. I wanted to go to the church, but he said no, it stressed him out to think about having me there at his work. I understood and didn't push it. There was a problem that time, I remember, because there was a casino at the hotel where we were staying, and one night after they finished work he suggested we go down for a bit. I'd never been to a casino. We sat at the roulette table and he had me call the numbers. He made bet after bet, but he never won, and at first I thought it was funny; then he bought a huge bundle of chips and started putting piles of them on all the numbers. He just kept losing. At one point his friends said we should leave, but he said no, he was losing a lot of money and needed to stay and win it back. He kept buying chips on his credit card and betting great stacks. One time he won and they gave him a big pile back, but those didn't last long. I fell asleep in my chair, and when I woke up the sun had already risen. He was still at the table. He said he'd won some back, but he was still down. He asked me if I had money; I said I had a little and went to get it. That's what I was doing when his buddies came back and said, "Come on, man, what are you doing here still, they're calling us in," but he said no, he was losing. They dragged him out of there, and I don't know how he did it, but he worked all day. I started to worry, because in Cali he wasn't like that.

I never saw the boss. The famous pastor. They used to call him Mr. F. No idea what his real name was. It always seemed weird to me that a pastor would have bodyguards. I didn't realize they had so much money.

I'm a believer, sir, but I'm Catholic; I go to La Ermita in Cali. It's not like they're poor, but priests don't look like drug kingpins.

As for the Jamundí Inn, that was their place. It was like a resort without the ocean. We used to go a lot, though I didn't like getting in the water. With this vitiligo, I'm not supposed to get a lot of sun, but I did it anyway. I never understood the deal with that place. Always with Carlitos and Nacho. Sometimes with Nadio and a young girl he'd snagged; she was from Pasto, but she was sharp. What always struck me was how they helped themselves to anything they wanted, like they owned the place. I went maybe ten times. We'd stay in these really nice bungalows, with a living room and deck. The best ones, on the back part of the property. We'd spend the day there, me sitting at a table, listening to music or reading magazines, and them drinking and horsing around in the water or doing swim races with the girls at the pool, who preferred sunbathing and posing to show off their butts. In the afternoons the dancing would start, and Óscar would dance with me. I may be crippled, but I've got rhythm.

Almost three years went by like that, sir. The last time I saw Óscar was more than a month ago. He told me he was going on a job out of the country. He sent me several text messages with photos, but he never said anything else. That was the last I heard from him. Who knows what he was up to.

His tattoos? Of course I know them. He definitely didn't have that one with the hand and the weird phrase, "We are healed." Maybe he had it done during the time I didn't see him. He liked getting tattoos while he was on trips. He said that when he was far away he would remember something or miss somebody, and he'd go out and get a tattoo of the image or name. He had ones of his kids, Cali, things he liked. He was like a kid that way. No impulse control. If he liked something, he had to have it right away. He spent money on gifts and doodads. This is for my son, this is for my little girl, or my old man, who's a total grouch but I love him, he'd say. And that's it, sir. I don't know what else I can tell you.

He walked with her to the cash register, offered his condolences again, and thanked her. He pulled out a business card and handed it to her.

"If you remember anything else, miss, please give me a call. Could I take your number?"

The young woman wrote it down on a promotional flier for the Legionnaires of the Black Christ School in Buga. They parted ways.

"What do you think, boss?" Laiseca asked.

"She's being honest," the prosecutor said. "It's weird that

neither the widow nor the mistress knew that Mr. F's name was Fabinho Henriquez. That makes him more suspicious, don't you think? I've got the guy's name underlined three times— let's follow that up."

"Aye aye, boss," Laiseca said.

"We should start at the famous Jamundí Inn, right?" Jutsiñamuy said. "I'll see if I can find a woman to go there with me."

He thought of Wendy, but figured she must be starting the process of infiltrating the church and decided not to bother her. He called his secretary and told her he'd be staying in Cali another day.

"Anything new on that end?" he asked.

"Yes, sir, you got a call from Cafesalud, something about a mix-up with a doctor's visit payment. And the University of El Rosario called to confirm whether you'll be coming to give a talk about fighting corruption."

"Piedrahíta didn't call?"

"No, sir. But if you want, I can put him in touch."

"Don't worry about it, I'll call him in a bit. I'm heading to the hotel. Forward any calls to me there."

"Of course, sir. Have a good night."

It was getting dark now, so he hailed a cab. Before getting in, he said to his two agents, "Go hard after intel on that Brazilian pastor. I want to know everything—what brand of underwear he wears, every ache and pain, what kind of suppositories he uses, understood?"

"Understood, boss."

"I bet he wears pink Punto Blanco boxers, but I'll get back to you on that tomorrow," Cancino said.

Jutsiñamuy looked at him, his face expressionless. "Hilarious."

He climbed into the taxi.

When he got to the hotel, the prosecutor took off his black

suit jacket, shirt, and tie. He smoothed them with his hand and hung them in the closet. Then he pulled an alternative outfit out of his suitcase: sweatpants, a knockoff Lacoste polo shirt, manufactured in Paraguay and purchased in San Andresito for eighty thousand pesos, and Adidas sneakers, also from Paraguay, that matched the shirt. It was his warm-weather uniform. He lay back on the bed and lifted his legs against the wall. Seven minutes on the nose, mind empty, and he was set, feeling like new. Transformed, he grabbed his computer and went up to the roof terrace. He snagged a table with a diagonal view of the river and fired up his laptop to check his email.

"It's like she heard me," he thought when he saw the new message: from Wendy, his undercover agent, with her first report.

Confidential Report #1
Agent KWK622
Place: Cali
Operation: Holy Spirit
Date: Date of email sent

A. *Place: Pastor Fritz Almayer's New Jerusalem Church is in a prime location: on the highway between Menga and Yumbo, outside the reach of Cali municipal ordinances and under the jurisdiction of Yumbo, the headquarters for a great number of corporations and which therefore enjoys a steady stream of laborers, middle management, and service personnel. Because it's on the northern edge of the city and close to the Buenaventura highway, there's a lot of traffic, not just private vehicles but also trucks, tractor trailers, and buses, so there are a lot of vendors selling their goods on the side of the road. Because of all the traffic, there are gas stations with body shops, carwashes, and tire shops. The working-class people who provide those services are the target demographic of New*

Jerusalem Church, which has adjusted the schedule for its "lectures" (what they call their mass) to take place before and after the workers' shifts and during their breaks. Nevertheless, the massive parking lots at the church suggest that people also come from other parts of the city.

To complete the description of the highway, this report notes that, due to its proximity to the city and to a number of night-clubs with all-night permits, it also boasts many no-tell establishments, motels of every level of quality, especially midrange and high-end places, with names that are blatant about their purpose: Moonlight, Kamasutra, Motel California, Eros. They also provide lunch, either included in the room's hourly rate or as an affordable add-on, because lunchtime is when most clients manage to arrive to take advantage of those services. This report does not conclude what percentage of patrons of such establishments could be considered targets of New Jerusalem Church.

B. *Facilities: The church grounds occupy a lot of at least a hectare, next to the Terpel gas station and the driveway to the Abracadabra Motel. It has a main building with a semicircular self-supporting roof (see photos 1, 2, and 3). It looks like an airport hangar; there's a twelve-foot wall all the way around it, and watchtowers with windows made of tinted (and probably bulletproof) glass. You enter via two lines that usher attendees through three checkpoints. At the final one, men and women are separated and searched thoroughly, then subjected to wand scanners and a walk-through metal detector. The guards are armed with automatic weapons and wear VigiValle uniforms. These measures seem excessive compared to those taken by other churches. Inside the building there's an elevated stage with huge screens, professional lighting, sound equipment, and special effects that create light and shadow. Above the stage is a cross, reflected on the ceiling and side walls; the large space is full of rows of pews that rise in a semicircle around the stage. I'd estimate it can hold about five thousand people. There's an administrative area behind the stage that I was unable to access. It also has rooms along the sides that serve as chapels, where people go to talk about their problems. They are attended there by the church staff (yet to be investigated) and sometimes the pastor himself. There's a sort of office where people who need help can provide their personal information, sign up using their IDs, and present a pay stub that will determine their monthly contribution to the church.*

C. *Congregation: As I mentioned in section A, these are people from the working classes. Because I arrived on Sunday afternoon, I was too late to attend the large noon "lecture," which brings together people from all over Cali and is always the most crowded. Instead, I went to a smaller one this Monday at noon. It talked about generosity in forgiving those who have hurt us and the love we must show to those who abandon us. It emphasized that the only way not to be alone in the world is to be aware of how close we are to the "intangible."*

D. *Pastor Fritz Almayer: First impression: charismatic, strong, pleasant voice, athletic build. People laugh at his jokes, but they also listen carefully to what he says. They idolize him. One young woman fainted during Monday's noon lecture. A woman dressed in black accompanied him on stage, like a sort of priestess. She handed him the Bible and turned his pages as he read. The audience clearly knows her already, since he didn't introduce her. The pastor is an intelligent, well-educated man, difficult to sum up quickly. We will continue to assess him.*

E. *Operational Activities: After attending two of the lectures, I went to the office to talk to the people known as "companions" or "pilgrims." I said I was coming to the church because I hoped Jesus would help me overcome my (fake, obviously) drug addiction and asked if I could have a private conversation with the pastor. They told me that before getting to him I would need to pass through various "purifying" stages with other missionaries, but that I would always be under his care. Before I could begin to seek this spiritual aid, they gave me a list of the documents I'd need to sign up. I therefore submitted a request to Special Operations for a certificate of income as an aesthetician at a salon in Bogotá, which they'll send me first thing tomorrow. While I was waiting in line, I established contact with another woman who said she's been sober for two years—no drugs, alcohol, or prostitution—thanks to the voice of Jesus, which came to her via Pastor Fritz. The woman, whose name is Yeni Sepúlveda, was holding a four-year-old boy and told me she could offer me some advice if I wanted it. We left together and walked to the café at the Terpel gas station, where we consumed two beef empanadas with mango juice, followed by coffee.*

When I asked about the father of the boy (Jeison), the informant claimed not to know who he was, as she'd become pregnant during the worst part of her coca-paste addiction, when she was also consuming aguardiente and amphetamines. She said she hadn't sought an abortion because at the time she couldn't spend money on anything besides her addiction. She said that the church had started out paying for drugs and treatment at an addiction clinic, and afterward they'd told her she could pay back their investment by doing some work for them and especially by staying clean. When I asked her what kind of work, she explained that she did some cleaning at the church and visited with and assisted women who were sex workers or addicted to drugs. She wanted to know if I was in a similar situation, and I said I wasn't. I explained that I was hooked on cocaine, driven by a desire to maximize my productivity and effectiveness at work, completely unrelated to partying. I said I didn't drink alcohol or use other drugs. Weirdly, she said I was a "dry addict," a term I'll have to look into, which was why I didn't have the scruffy look of a coca-paste addict. I asked if the church had a preference for people with those problems, and she said not particularly. It was enough for a lot of them to find a new path and the desire to be good people, upstanding and respectable. She said the pastor's teachings were always about respect and love, and that it was common during the weekly lectures for a violent husband, in the middle of the event, to beg his wife for forgiveness, or an attacker his victim, or an abuser the abused—in short, the sort of ritual that ends in tears and hugs, to great applause from the audience. Then we said goodbye. She gave me her number and said she'd love to help me if I needed it, any time of day or night.

Jutsiñamuy, drinking a chamomile tea with lemon and enjoying the breeze off the mountains, read the report twice more. Then he wrote Wendy a note: "Very good. This informant offers an opportunity for access to the inner workings of the church. Perfect choice. Keep telling me how great things are going. And give lots of details—I like your reporting style." Then he pulled out his laptop. He put in his earbuds and lay down on the sofa to listen to a bit of music. But he hadn't even gotten to choose a song when his phone lit up. What time was it? After nine. If it was Laiseca, he'd better have something good. But when he looked at the screen he saw it was Julieta.

He had to answer.

After eating lunch at El Escudo del Quijote, a restaurant near her hotel that someone in Bogotá had recommended, and rounding out her meal with a gin on the rocks, Julieta went up to rest in her room. She was incredibly confused. Despite the defensive barriers she had erected against priests, gurus, and soothsayers, whom she fiercely despised, Pastor

Fritz had managed to worm his way deep into her head and, quite frankly, unsettle her. As she thought back on their conversation, the memory of his gaze evoked both revulsion and delight; she was seduced by his voice and his words, even though she knew that they were calculated, fraudulent, aimed at bending her will.

Even so, there was a suspicion, a small flame that told her: there's more to it, there's more to it. But what? She curled into the fetal position on the bed and let slip a few freeing tears, but then, imagining the boy in the park, she started crying hard, disconsolate, as if she herself had been abandoned or, worse still, it was her sons there on that lonely bench as night fell, waiting for a parent to return. She opened the minibar, took out a little bottle of gin, and poured it into the plastic cup from the bathroom, without ice or lemon.

She returned to the bed, looked at herself in the mirror, and balked in shock: her face blotchy, her hair wild, her eyes bloodshot, her shirt wrinkled. Why was she in such a state? She didn't know. Not being able to find the words made her cry even harder. She felt fragile. In some sense, abandoned. The pastor had somehow passed on his orphan's abandonment to her. And where was Fritz's mother? A boy left unprotected grows up into a cruel man. The shock of becoming an orphan taints him over the years, and someone hard emerges. She recalled a sentence from Fritz's story: "Bodies that suffer and cannot understand why they must experience such pain."

Not understanding. Not understanding. Life is a constant process of loss, she mused, a loss of purity and joy.

She was startled by a sudden vibrating.

It was her cell phone. A new message.

"You said Franklin Vanegas? I'm told there's nobody here by that name."

Her heart started beating wildly, like a washing machine in the spin cycle. It was Pastor Fritz! Had he sensed she was thinking about him? She was afraid his incredible genius had told him even from a distance that she was in bad shape. *Get a grip*, she thought. The gin must be distorting her reality.

She wrote, "That's impossible. I saw him with my own eyes at your church. Maybe he's using a different name."

After sending the message she kept staring at it: one white checkmark, two . . . She waited a bit and looked again. They were still white—why wasn't he reading her message? The wait was driving her crazy. She felt like a teenager, one of the silly girls her sons hung out with. She put her phone face down on the edge of the bed, but she couldn't calm down. She felt like she was stirring a dense liquid with an enormous spoon—all her contradictions, her perversity. Now with an additional element of unease: why wasn't Fritz reading her message and responding?

She kept sobbing until she felt something on the bed. She snatched up the phone and looked at the screen. New message. But it wasn't from Fritz—it was from a dumb group chat. The message was a moronic joke. She was tempted to hurl the phone at the wall when she felt it vibrate in her hand. This time it was the pastor.

"There are several new boys, but they come and go. Others come only on Sundays. I'll keep looking."

Julieta wrote back. "If you let me into your church, I could recognize him."

She hit Send and stared at the phone. Two white checkmarks again. She punched the mattress in a fury. It was going to happen again, and she didn't think she could take it. But then her soul thudded back into place: on the screen she saw the words "Pastor F is typing . . ."

"Should I pick you up now?"

She froze. Now? She wasn't ready, but a pleasant thrill ran through her body. She set the phone down on the bed and returned to the mirror. Now her reaction was not a recoil but a litany: her eyes were still red, but less swollen; her mascara, smeared; her hair, the disheveled mop of a broken old doll; her skin pale . . .

She was a fright!

She turned on the cold water and splashed it on her cheeks. She grabbed her brush and tried to get the wild thatch of frizzy hair under control. She felt agitated. It must be the gin. The idea of seeing him brought up conflicting emotions: panic and euphoria, attraction and revulsion.

That goddamn pastor drugged me, she thought. *He gave me burundanga or something.* How long had she been at the mirror? She leaped back toward the bed and grabbed her phone, but there were no new messages. It was her turn to reply. It was almost four in the afternoon—should she tell Johana? Of course. Should they go together? She didn't think so. This seemed to be between her and the pastor. She touched the screen of her Samsung and went to her messages.

"All right, let me know," she wrote.

The checkmarks turned blue and the reply arrived.

"Go out onto the street, then, please."

Julieta didn't understand. "Why?"

"I'm waiting for you out front in a black SUV, but take your time."

He'd come to pick her up himself? She didn't recall having told him she was at this hotel—or had she? It didn't matter now. She needed to hurry! Maybe he'd been at the InterContinental still—that was the only explanation.

She went back to the mirror and opened her toiletry bag. Foundation, eyeshadow, lightly red lips. Her heart was pounding. *It's not about looking good for that bastard, it's about taking pride in myself.* She secured her computer in the safe, an old habit acquired after an incident in Cartagena, and ran downstairs. Out on the street, she saw three parked SUVs. She went over to the black one. The door opened.

"I didn't figure I'd see you again so soon," Pastor Fritz said, holding out his hand. "This could be the start of a great friendship."

Julieta shook. "Seems unlikely, but thanks for coming. Shall we go?"

As they drove, Julieta didn't say much. He did most of the talking.

"People are excited about our work," Fritz said. "More join us all the time. I can't say no to people who come to us looking for help."

"You said you hadn't found him," Julieta said.

"The people who work with us, both volunteers and employees, are listed in a database. His name doesn't appear there. We're going to confirm that now."

"I know I saw him at your church."

"Why are you so interested in this boy?" Fritz asked.

"He's an indigenous boy, a Nasa. His father is dead and maybe his mother too—I haven't figured that out yet. I talked to him in Tierradentro. And he disappeared a week ago."

Inside, Julieta was squirming. What was she doing? She should shut her mouth and ask tough questions that would force him to confirm her theory. Regardless of the boy's fate, they both knew that Fritz *was* the survivor of the roadside shoot-out, and that event had set all of this in motion.

"I'll always try to help an orphan," Fritz said. "I'll do everything within my power."

"The kid has to turn up," Julieta said.

She thought about the man who'd been following them on the motorcycle, but she didn't dare mention it. It was best he believe she didn't know about certain things, though now that she thought about it, she figured that if the motorcyclist worked for Fritz, he'd have already told the pastor she'd spotted him and knew they were being followed.

She decided not to say anything. But she needed to keep on her toes this time.

The motorcade crossed the Cali River, drove around the far end of Jairo Varela Park, and headed up 6th to the Chipichape shopping center. It kept going, passing the La Flora neighborhood on the right, and soon reached Menga. Outside, the heat was stifling. At every traffic light, people came up to beg for money, usually carrying young children. Most were poor Venezuelan families, as well as a number of internal refugees who hadn't found a way to return to their homelands. And a third group of modern youngsters, hippie-ish and lavishly tattooed, who, after a brief tumbling act, passed their hat at the drivers' windows. Argentine acrobats.

The pastor smiled, and she again felt a flutter in her belly. Something must have changed on her face, because he said, "We'll find him, don't worry. If he's been with our church, he'll turn up. I promise I'll see to it myself that he's taken back to his grandparents."

Pastor Fritz was wearing the same clothes as that morning, but Julieta figured he must have multiple changes, because he seemed fresh and like he'd just gotten dressed. His pants were still neatly creased from ironing. He wasn't wearing cologne, but he gave off a pleasant scent.

Finally they arrived at the church. The SUVs reversed and drove through some automatic doors located at the rear of the complex. The garage was partly underground, and Julieta saw other more discreet cars. There were also several motorcycles, but she didn't spot the one that had been on her trail.

The pastor climbed out, hurried around the SUV, and opened her door. It had been ages since someone had done that for her. Actually, never. It reminded her that in a way, despite appearances, she was in a position of strength with Fritz. He was trying to charm her, to win her over.

"Let's go upstairs," the pastor said. "I asked everyone to gather in the auditorium."

They climbed a spiral staircase to some offices. Fritz offered her something to drink. Julieta looked at him indifferently and said, "No thanks. I doubt you've got any hard stuff."

The pastor looked at her with surprise. "Follow me."

He opened a set of wooden double doors and they entered a luxurious office. He led her to one of the corners, to a large cabinet. There Julieta saw dozens of bottles of liquor.

"Choose whatever you like. I'll fetch a glass and some ice."

"Won't you be joining me?"

"Not this early in the day, Julieta."

She saw bottles of Lagavulin, Knockando, and Springbank whisky, which were difficult to come by in Colombia. She pulled down a bottle of Hendrick's gin and poured herself a generous splash, more out of anger than real desire.

"I love this gin," she said. "It's the best digestive after a good lunch."

"I agree."

"I didn't know pastors had such fancy, well-stocked bars."

Fritz looked sideways at her, his eyes gleaming under his dense brows and long lashes. "Jesus turned water into wine and associated drunkenness with a desire for elevation. Liquors help us find the crack where we can peek through and see the world from another angle. They offer us the possibility, however risky, of submerging ourselves in something that gives us pleasure. Pleasure and pain in a single nerve."

Julieta took another sip of her drink. She liked his answers. He was sharp and sophisticated. "What's the worst thing you've done in life, Fritz?"

The pastor picked up a slice of lemon and raised it to his mouth. "The worst thing . . . I've believed in myself too passionately, since I'm the only thing I truly possess. But sometimes it's like a chicken skin, old and greenish—a skin full of stagnant water that I'm forced to carry around with me—or like a soldier who comes home with a dying comrade on his back."

Julieta took another sip. She felt a little dizzy, but also strong. "Where were you, Fritz, before you went to Inzá for the Alliance gathering?"

The pastor bit into the lemon slice again. "In San Agustín. I led a religious ceremony with demobilized guerrilla fighters and victims and we made a peace offering to the Magdalena River."

"Very symbolic," Julieta said.

"Believing and naming alters reality. That's how we're able to change things, don't you think? Language creates the world. You must have experienced that."

"I might have, maybe unwittingly."

"Have you ever been in love? Fully, I mean?"

A voice inside Julieta told her, *No more, get out of this conversation, walk to the door and say you want to go to the auditorium. You can't keep handing him arrows to shoot at you!*

"Of course, a few times."

"So you know what it means to talk to yourself, to yearn for something, to want reality to change."

"I guess so, though maybe not in those words," Julieta said.

"That's what we all want, Christians too: for the torrid air of this country to fill up with matter. For humanity to be the measure of human love, invoking Jesus, who came to stay by our side and show us the measure of all things."

Julieta listened somewhat haughtily. She let him finish and then said abruptly, "To travel from San Agustín to Inzá by road, you have to go through Tierradentro. Whoever tried to kill you knew the road well and decided to lie in ambush near the village of San Andrés de Pisimbalá. But they weren't counting on your bodyguards or the firepower of the men in your helicopter."

Pastor Fritz dropped onto the sofa, looking drained. Julieta kept talking.

"You had heavily armed bodyguards. You knew you might be attacked."

She moved into his eyeline, but saw that he had his eyes closed.

"My question," she continued, "is quite simple: who wants to kill you and why?"

The pastor got up from the sofa and walked to the door. He opened it and gestured for Julieta to go through. As she walked past him, he whispered, "It's a great story, very exciting, but I'm sorry to say it wasn't me. I don't know that road."

"So why do you have so many bodyguards?" she asked. "Why all the security here?"

"Don't forget, this country is unique in the world: it produces both upstanding people and their killers. A person needs protection. The real land of Cain wasn't the kingdom of Nod. It's Colombia. Of course, that doesn't mean I think I'm special."

Julieta stared back at him defiantly, but she didn't say anything. She thanked him for the gin. In the auditorium, about forty people were sitting in the first row. Pastor Fritz, Julieta, and two other collaborators settled into the armchairs onstage.

"Please, brothers and sisters," the pastor said, "let's go around in order and have everybody stand and introduce themselves. But first I'd like to introduce a friend of the church, Ms. Julieta Lezama, journalist. She's here because she wants to know if anybody has met or heard about a Nasa boy named Franklin Vanegas."

A microphone went around.

A plump young woman in a sweatsuit and flipflops spoke first. "I'm Lorena Berrío, I've been at the church seven months. I didn't meet the boy. I don't know that word—Nasa?"

The pastor explained affectionately, as if she were his daughter.

Next came a teenage boy, his cheeks still marred by acne. "I'm Wilmer Manrique. I've been here five months. I don't know the boy either."

A woman in trendily ripped and frayed jeans, with tattoos and piercings in her belly button, eyebrows, and nose: "I'm Yeni Sepúlveda, I've been here three years. That name doesn't sound familiar."

One by one, they all spoke. Nobody knew him.

Julieta had been watching a woman sitting in the back rows. She looked different from the others. She was tall, strong, and slender, even a bit masculine, with toned arms, visible muscles, and triangular tattoos with images Julieta didn't recognize. Julieta guessed she was in her early forties. She had light brown, almost blond hair. A few streaks of gray, which she carried off elegantly. A strange darkness on her eyelids, as if her eyes were staring out from two caves, and a somewhat untamed allure. When it was her turn, she said, "Egiswanda Sanders. Been here for many years. I haven't seen the boy."

Her Spanish was good, but Julieta could tell she was Brazilian.

When the introductions were over, a young man who introduced himself as Ariosto Roldán, the church's administrative director, took the microphone and said, "All of us are permanent staff. Sometimes other people come in to help, but they come and go. And there are the cleaning staff—some of them are day laborers. If we had a photo of the boy, it would help."

Pastor Fritz turned to Julieta. "So, you've met my little family, which isn't actually so little. Like I said, the boy isn't with us."

"I saw him on Sunday, I'm sure of it. Isn't there anyone else who works for you?"

"The security people are at their posts—they're private guards sent by a company. That's why I didn't call them in."

"He must be one of the day laborers."

"We would have found him by name," Fritz said, and then called to his director: "Ariosto, come here a minute."

"Yes, Father?"

"The young lady thinks the boy could have come in as a day laborer on Sunday. Do we have a list?"

"Of course, and we reviewed it already. He's not on it." Turning to Julieta, he added, "We keep track of everyone who comes. We write down their names and ID numbers."

"How much do you pay?" Julieta asked.

"Thirty thousand pesos plus lunch," the director said. "They help us clean up the auditorium and the halls. You can't imagine the state they're in after a lecture."

They went back up to the second floor.

Julieta saw that the Brazilian woman was following behind them; when they reached the management offices, she disappeared into one of them and shut the door.

"Can I give you a lift anywhere?" Pastor Fritz asked.

"Just to my hotel."

One of the pastor's men came over in response to a signal from him.

"Please give the young lady a ride."

They said goodbye.

"I hope I've cleared up your doubts, Julieta."

"Some, but not the biggest one," she said, making sure to hold his gaze.

Fritz stared at her, his face serious. Suddenly he smiled, and Julieta's stomach did a somersault. "Reality is a wild forest full of snake eyes, glittering in the darkness before they attack their prey. But most dangerous of all is love that dries up. The kind that couldn't escape its tree trunk and has coiled up on itself to sink its fangs into its own heart."

"I don't know what you mean," Julieta said. "Remember, I'm not one of your followers, it's pointless to talk to me like that. I hate symbolism."

"Just commit those words to memory. Maybe you'll come to understand them later. I appreciate your visit, and like I said, anything you need, whatever the hour, you can reach out. Consider me a friend."

"One more thing, Fritz."

"Yes?"

"You can tell your motorcycle spy to leave me alone. If you need to know something about me or what I'm doing, just ask."

The pastor looked at her in surprise. "Motorcycle spy?"

"We've laid our cards out on the table already," Julieta said. "It makes no sense to make me explain."

"Somebody's following you?"

This time the pastor's eyes changed. For a fleeting moment, Julieta saw a wild animal.

"Yes," she said. "Up from Tierradentro. Don't tell me it's not you."

The pastor called his men over and instructed them to listen closely. "You say it's a motorcycle? Did you see the person following you?"

He was very agitated. Two droplets of sweat appeared on his upper lip.

"He wears a black helmet."

"Do you know anything else? Where did you see him? Here in Cali?"

"On the west side, yesterday."

"Yesterday Sunday?"

"Yes, after I came to your lecture," Julieta said.

"Could you recognize the motorcycle?" one of the security guards asked.

"I'm not an expert. It wasn't a big motorcycle. Normal size."

"When we were on our way here, did you see it?"

"No, not since yesterday."

The pastor gripped Julieta's arm. "It's not us, believe me, but I'm going to find out what's happening. Go back to your hotel now and don't worry about this. When I figure out what's going on, I'll call you. Will you be staying in Cali long?"

"That depends. We'll see."

"In any case, you'll hear from me," Fritz said. "Go back to your hotel and rest, but avoid going out."

Now he was acting like a boss, not a pastor. Maybe the mysterious motorcycle was with Fritz's enemies.

"Why are you so concerned?" Julieta asked.

"Sometimes I'm still haunted by the jungle, but then it passes. All of this is just words. Go rest now—we'll talk soon."

He nodded at her, went into his office, and shut the door.

As she walked out through the vestibule, Julieta stared at the door the Brazilian woman had gone into.

But the door wasn't marked and it remained closed.

When she left for the hotel it was almost seven at night.

Cali's traffic wasn't quite as heavy as Bogotá's, but close. If they didn't move fast, they'd be trapped in its streets forever. The slow pace gave her time to think. She was struck by the change she'd seen in Fritz, how anxious he'd gotten when he learned she was being followed. She looked all around. The guard riding shotgun was on high alert and every once in a while he stuck his hand in his jacket pocket, fondly checking on his weapon.

Where had the kid gotten off to? Concentrating, she pictured him clearly on the steps on the side of the building. It was him. He'd figured out a way to work with the pastor without revealing himself. Without having to say he was a minor. Maybe he passed himself off as older, under another

name, so he could go in as a day laborer. Or he had a friend
who registered his name and they split the work between
them.

Anything was possible.

She watched the traffic in case the motorcycle reappeared.
What should she do if it did? The pastor was still denying that
he was the survivor, but for all intents and purposes he'd
acceded. Tenuously speaking between the lines, or so she
thought. All those metaphors! What were they intended to
achieve? The worst part was that she'd memorized them, just
like he said, or at least she had no trouble remembering them.
They were there, as if she'd written them down and was now
reading them out.

"Reality is a wild forest full of snake eyes, glittering in the
darkness before they attack their prey. But most dangerous of
all is love that dries up. The kind that couldn't escape its tree
trunk and has coiled up on itself to sink its fangs into its own
heart."

*Anyone who talks like that, like he's the new Jesus Christ, is
an arrogant dumbass,* she thought. What love had dried up?
Was he in love? *I bet he's doing the Brazilian woman.* She
would have sworn to it. The Brazilian had a nice body.
Colombian men love Brazilian women. They've got that fantasy cliché in their heads of the girl from Ipanema and round,
chocolate-colored asses. The land of the thong bikini. And
plastic surgery. Ivo Pitanguy, the Picasso of the tummy tuck
and breast implant. This woman—Egiswanda, was it? She
seemed like she was about Julieta's age, but she looked a lot
better. Better legs and a better ass. Judging by those muscles,
she probably spent half her day at the gym. Did she live with
him? Where was her house? Did she have kids? "The kind
that couldn't escape its tree trunk and has coiled up on itself,"
Fritz had said. He couldn't have been referring to the
Brazilian. Maybe he was thinking about somebody else or,

since he's a pastor, about the love we should have for God, and how some people don't feel it. Was that what he'd meant by "coiled up on itself"? Or was he talking about the person who'd attacked him on the road? They might seem friendly and polite, but his people had been involved in a bloody gunfight. The fact that it was self-defense raised even more questions about who he truly was.

Suddenly she remembered Johana. Was she at the hotel?

"Hi," she said into her phone. "Are you at the hotel?"

"Yes, boss. I've been here all afternoon, waiting in case you needed me. I was reading. Did you go out wandering?"

"I've got a bunch of stories for you. I'm almost there. Let's meet in the café."

"All right."

When Johana arrived, Julieta told her everything, writing notes about it all at the same time. It had been a rough day emotionally, so she ordered a fresh-squeezed lemonade with ice rather than her usual tonic.

Johana ordered a Fanta and said, "And you believed him about the guy on the motorcycle?"

"Yeah, it really did make him nervous. But we'll see. It was like he was linked somehow to his enemy, the guy who attacked him."

"If the pastor thinks that, he must be afraid the attacker is looking for something through us. Sounds dangerous, don't you think?"

Julieta drained half her glass in one go and said, "Dangerous for him, definitely."

"And for us. If he's an enemy spy, he must know you spent the afternoon at the church," Johana said.

"True, but what can he do?"

"Use us to get to him, take us hostage. Torture us."

"All right," Julieta said, "let's not go overboard. And to think I believed that the war was over in this country!"

"A lot of people believe that," Johana said, "but with a rightwing government trying to drag us back to the 1990s, things are going to blow up again fast."

As they talked, the brake lights of passing cars gleamed in the gentle drizzle.

Suddenly Julieta got up. "I don't know if we're in danger, but let's go up to my room to make some calls. I haven't spoken to the prosecutor in a while. What time is it?"

"After nine," Johana said.

"Not too late. Come on."

They went upstairs. As soon as they entered, Johana went over to the window to scan the street. She scrutinized the neighboring buildings to see if anyone could see them. It wasn't likely. She closed the curtains anyway.

Julieta picked up her cell phone and dialed the number.

"Prosecutor Jutsiñamuy? Sorry for calling so late."

"No problem, Julieta. Any big news?"

"Well, I wanted to tell you some things. Is this phone line secure?"

"No worries about that."

She described in detail her two meetings with Pastor Fritz. She talked about the Nasa boy, who hadn't shown up among the people working at the church, but she was sure he was there in some way she didn't yet understand. And finally about the motorcycle.

"Do you think you two could be in danger?" Jutsiñamuy asked.

"Not really," Julieta said. "If they wanted to do something to us, they've had plenty of time. Judging by the pastor's behavior, the people watching us could be his enemies, the same ones who attacked him."

"It would make sense," Jutsiñamuy said.

"What do you advise?"

"Go back to Bogotá."

"That's an option," she said, "but not right now. How did things go with identifying the bodies?"

"We're working on it. We can meet up tomorrow if you want. What hotel are you in?"

"El Peñón."

"Oh, I'm really close by. At the Dann Carlton. Come over and we can have lunch here. There's a good restaurant, and that way we can be sure nobody's watching us. Do you know the place?"

"Of course, thank you so much. See you then."

Julieta was still tipsy from the gin. She decided to have another drink to even things out and went over to her minibar. She offered one to Johana.

"Do you want anything?"

"No, boss, thanks. You know I'm a lightweight. Three sips and I'm done for. If you don't need me, I'll go to my room."

"Go ahead," Julieta said. "I'm going to put my notes in order."

Johana paused at the door on her way out. "I don't mean to butt in, but be careful with the alcohol, boss. You've been drinking a lot."

Julieta looked at her, startled. "I drink when I'm on edge, but it just means the investigation's going well, don't worry. But thanks for mentioning it."

"Good night," Johana said.

Once she was alone, Julieta took two long sips, one right after the other, and felt her soul being restored to her body. Johana was right about the drinking, but that's how she'd always been. She was compulsive—what could she do? At least she wasn't into coke or other drugs.

She went to look in the mirror. She couldn't deny that the pastor had affected her. There was something special about him. She glanced at the messages they'd exchanged, and a voice deep down made her wish he'd text her right that moment. She looked at the screen and wondered if she dared send him a message now. She imagined what she'd say: "I'm drinking gin at the hotel, alone." How would he respond? Plenty of sinister criminals have been charismatic, entertaining, intelligent people.

She needed to be careful.

She kept staring at the silent screen. Could she go to a bar for a drink? She was tempted, but she looked at her notebook and remembered that she needed to work. She peered out the window and saw the lights of the neighborhood, the lively cafés, and, higher up, the three illuminated crosses on top of the hill. She imagined all the young, strong men she could meet with just a bit of effort, but told herself no, maybe another day. Right now she was wedded to that notebook. She opened the minifridge and took out a Coca-Cola before sitting down to work.

FURTHER TESTIMONIES

The next day, Jutsiñamuy got up at 5:30 A.M. and did his morning exercises next to the bed: push-ups, running in place, sit-ups, stretching, head to the side and front, in circles, ear to shoulder, touch toes. When he finished each set, he looked in the mirror, flexing his muscles and turning to observe the silhouette of his torso. It wasn't out of vanity. Even apart from the issue of health, as he saw it, allowing himself to get out of shape would constitute an act of moral negligence. The hotel had modern gym facilities, but it seemed undignified to perform such movements in front of other people.

Later, after showering and donning a casual warm-weather outfit—leather loafers, Lacoste polo shirt, sand-colored linen pants—he went up to the poolside terrace and served himself breakfast from the plentiful buffet: fresh fruit, especially pineapple and papaya (antioxidants), a bowl of cereal, unsweetened yogurt, green tea (he should have brought his own, since all the hotel had was a blend of green tea and mint).

As he sipped his drink, he pulled out the day's edition of Cali's *El País* newspaper. He flipped through, stopping on each news item and carefully reading the summary and the first three paragraphs. He finished the cereal, but a smell wafting from the platters on the buffet distracted him. Next to the scrambled eggs was another smaller platter with fried bacon, curly and dark with a paler vein down the middle. His mouth watered: *Once a year can't hurt*, he thought.

He went back to the buffet—feeling defeated—and took a

large plate, but thought, *You can't eat the stuff on its own*, and served himself two large spoonfuls of scrambled eggs. The same platter also contained Santa Rosa sausages. He glanced over at the waiter, who was watching him, and moved down the table till he found the arepas. His mind conjured the image of an arepa with a sausage on top. *No, no*, he pleaded weakly, seeing his hand, acting of its own free will, place two arepas on his plate and crown them with the meaty zeppelins of chorizo. He told himself, without much conviction, that he could still set the plate down and leave it there, but he found himself carrying it to his table instead. He met the waiter's eyes, who immediately said, "Enjoy your breakfast, sir. Would you like more juice?" Yes, fresh-squeezed orange juice. He kept flipping through the paper until he reached the regional section, on Valle del Cauca, and saw the photo of a young man named Enciso Yepes. His family had reported him missing. Mechanically, Jutsiñamuy began to read the article:

> *Enciso Yepes, 35, from Cartago (northern Valle del Cauca), disappeared three weeks ago, according to his wife, Mrs. Estéphanny Gómez, 41, who lives in Cartago. Mrs. Gómez notified the authorities that her husband, a private security professional with VigiValle, has not reported home for several days. VigiValle claims not to have heard from its employee since the beginning of the month, as a result of which it had rescinded his contract on the grounds of unauthorized absence. Mrs. Gómez declared she was taking legal action and said that her husband had not informed her of any change in his work, instead telling her that he would be traveling to another part of the country to provide security, which he had done on numerous occasions in previous months. Accompanied at the lower court in Cartago by her lawyer, Anselmo Yepes (the missing man's brother), Mrs. Gómez stated that recently her husband had been providing security*

*services throughout Valle and Cauca for the New Jerusalem
evangelical church.*

When he read this, the prosecutor almost spilled the tea he
was holding. *Oh, shit,* he thought, *this is getting good.* He
looked over at the waiter. Seeing that he was distracted, he
ripped out the page.

Then he called Laiseca.

"Good morning, boss," the agent said when he picked up.
"At your orders."

"That's the spirit, Laiseca," Jutsiñamuy said. "Good morning. I've got a present for you this morning. Have you read the
local paper yet, *El País?*"

"Not yet, boss. I'm just finishing the *New York Times.*"

"Very funny. Get a copy and read page two of the regional
section. There's a report of a missing man that I think you'll
find interesting. They mention New Jerusalem Church. Read
it, and we'll talk. What did you learn about the Jamundí Inn?"

"I spoke with our legal office twice this morning, and
they're looking into it for me. The owner turns out to be an off-
shore company registered as R.I.N.T.R.I., based in Panama. It's
classified as three stars. No names yet. Are we going to
Panama, boss?"

"Let me guess, Laiseca, you want a trip to the Panama City
airport for some duty-free shopping," Jutsiñamuy said. "Not
for now. I'm heading to the Jamundí Inn later to take a look
around. Is Cancino with you?"

"Yes, boss, right here next to me. He says hi. Do you want
to talk to him?"

"No, no need," Jutsiñamuy said, "but I think he's going to
end up taking a little jaunt to Cartago. Look at the paper—
you'll see why. Call me once you've read the article."

His plate of eggs and bacon was empty. He felt profound
guilt and, at the same time, an old hunger to sate. Glancing

from side to side to check whether anyone was watching him, he got up and strode toward the buffet.

The entrance to the Jamundí Inn looked just like any other pretentious rural hotel in Colombia, but in a rococo Valle del Cauca style: flower-filled gardens, a fountain with three vertical jets falling in a parabola, two stone paths, birdcages hanging from the eaves, and bowls of sugar water for the hummingbirds. It was hotter there, south of the city, than in the neighborhood where he was staying, so Jutsiñamuy was glad he hadn't brought a jacket. He would have looked very odd. He went into the reception area and asked to speak to the manager.

"Manager?" A young Afro-Colombian man looked at him with bloodshot eyes; it didn't take a scientist to guess that he'd spent the morning smoking up.

The prosecutor looked at him sternly. "Yes, the manager. You understand the concept?"

"Yes, yes," the young man said, somewhat befuddled. "I'll call him."

Jutsiñamuy sat down on the sofa in a rustic waiting room. At the far end, a city councilman was on TV giving an interview. Atop a heavy wooden table was a large carafe of water with slices of lemon. It had a spigot and little plastic cups next to it. *Nice detail*, Jutsiñamuy thought, rubbing his belly. He was assessing whether a glass of lemon water might help him digest his enormous breakfast when an athletic man in a guayabera shirt came over.

"Welcome to the Jamundí Inn, sir, how can we help you?"

Jutsiñamuy looked him up and down. He was the typical manager you saw these days: about thirty, sterile-looking, with close-cropped hair and tattoos on his arms.

"Good morning," he said. "I'm looking for a venue for a family party and someone recommended this place."

"Well, they know what they're talking about. We specialize in family and business gatherings, clubs, and associations. Come on into my office. Coffee, soda, tea?"

The idea of consuming anything else made him gag.

"No thanks," he said, "I went overboard at breakfast this morning. Buffets are trouble that way."

"Are you staying at a hotel?"

"Yes," Jutsiñamuy replied, then immediately regretted providing that involuntary information.

"Let me get you a bicarbonate of soda—that'll have you feeling better in no time. And may I ask what hotel you're staying at?"

The question was a consequence of his own mistake. Now they could track him. He needed to be cautious.

"Well, I was, anyway, but I'm leaving for Bogotá today. But I will take a bicarbonate of soda." He looked out the office window at the garden.

"How many people are we talking about and what services would you like to include?" the manager continued.

"There would be four families, five people each."

"Does this include lodging?"

"Absolutely, the idea would be to spend a weekend here."

An employee came in carrying an aluminum tray. On it was a glass of water and a sachet of bicarbonate. Jutsiñamuy poured the medicine into the water and drank it down in one go. The effervescence did help.

"And a celebration on Saturday, with a special dinner," he continued.

"Is it a birthday or other family occasion?"

"Yes," Jutsiñamuy said. "My mother's eightieth. We wanted to get the kids and grandkids together."

"Lovely idea, the whole family together, as it should be. Well, listen, we can arrange everything here: a dinner with regional, international, or eclectic cuisine, traditional music, and we offer entertainment too if you want it. Lots of people love the dance performances. If you'd rather have a religious service, that's no problem. You just tell me what you want, and we'll make it happen. Come on, I'll show you the facilities."

They left the office and walked through a shady breezeway with arches over Doric and Ionic columns, all done in pink stucco, to find themselves back in the garden, where there was a full-on natural installation: wooden bridges over streams and waterfalls, a little treehouse in a mango tree, stone paths, pools stocked with goldfish and neon tetras, rose gardens, and, in the middle, the majestic central swimming pool, turquoise blue, a jewel amid the greenery and flowers, with two smaller round pools and two hot tubs under a thatched roof. Beyond that were the bungalows, which looked like huts made of brick and glass, each with its own deck furnished with seating and a grill.

This is three stars? Jutsiñamuy thought, and then, *You can smell the bleach from here.* They went in to see the bungalows. Pretty big, HD TV, fridge, cooktop, fully equipped with dishes and cutlery.

"We have bungalows for three, five, and seven people. They are Onyx, Diamond, or Sapphire, depending on the level of comfort you're looking for. Sapphire is the best, very high standard. Guests book them for honeymoons and then never want to go out!"

"Who wants to go out on their honeymoon?" Jutsiñamuy asked.

The manager laughed.

They moved on to see the performance hall, the chapel, the gym, and the rooms for something the prosecutor had never seen before called thalassotherapy, which consisted of jets of hot, salty water and whirlpool baths. Good for the circulation.

"Wow," Jutsiñamuy said, "this is something else."

"It really is. Our establishment is among the finest in the country."

They walked back to the office. Jutsiñamuy allowed himself to momentarily forget that he was on duty and drift off on the birdsong and the darting hummingbirds. The office walls were bare. Only a crucifix next to the desk, hanging in a frame, and another on one of the tables. The manager pulled out a notepad and began to write down the information for an estimate.

"Name?"

"Misael Borrego Daza," Jutsiñamuy said.

"Phone number?"

He gave one of the open (but secure and monitored) numbers for his office in Bogotá.

"Email or WhatsApp?"

He gave his office contact once more.

"I'll be sending you three separate estimates at different price points for three days with all meals, a celebration dinner, entertainment, and a religious service included. One question—does your family belong to a particular church, or are we talking about a traditional mass?"

"I have to admit I'm not much of a churchgoer. But I know my mother goes to one of those new churches in Bogotá. Let me ask her, and I'll get back to you."

Saying this clearly got the manager's attention. Behind him, in a small built-in bookcase, there was something lying among some books that had toppled over. What was it?

"That's perfect, Mr. Borrego. Is your family from Bogotá?"

"Yes, but only recently; earlier generations were from Cali. That's why we want to bring my mom back here."

As he spoke, he tried to get a better look. The object seemed like it had been hidden or disguised. He tried to distract the manager's attention, but the young man was a perfect, efficient bureaucrat. What could he do? Then he was granted a miracle: the manager's cell phone rang.

"Would you excuse me a moment?" the manager said. "It's an international call."

"Of course."

The manager got up and paced in a circle as he spoke, then discreetly left the office, not wanting to be overheard.

Finding himself alone, Jutsiñamuy rushed to the bookcase and pulled down the books. He couldn't believe it: a wooden hand with the inscription "We are healed"! He considered taking it with him, but he thought better of it, as there could be cameras. Instead, he picked up a couple of books as if his sudden curiosity had been provoked by one of the titles. He needed to do something, make a decision. He pulled out his cell phone and took several photos: front, back, top, bottom. He replaced the hand among the books.

A second later, the manager came back.

"I'm so sorry about that, Mr. Borrego, but it was an international call, some Americans who are planning to hold a company meeting here and call every five minutes asking for details."

"No worries, I know what working with Americans is like. They pay well, and it's worth it, but they're a pain in the ass!"

"Exactly," the manager laughed. "So, look, I'll probably be calling you . . . When would the event take place?"

Jutsiñamuy quickly gave a date two months away.

"Oh, great, that's plenty of time. I'll call next week or email you a detailed estimate. Sound good?"

"Absolutely."

The two men stood and headed to the door. The prosecutor sent a text from his phone, and the driver, who looked like he was from Uber but was actually from the prosecutor general's office, came to pick him up at the entrance.

They said goodbye, and as soon as Jutsiñamuy got in the car he grabbed his cell phone to review the photos. He'd missed six calls from Laiseca, but he didn't lose focus. Luckily, the images were fairly clear: the slogan "We are healed" engraved on the palm of the hand, where you could see the wound from the nail. The hand of Jesus. Then, in the photo of the bottom, another inscription: "Assembly of God, Belém do Pará, Brazil." Fabinho Henriquez's Brazilian church! The pastor that the dead men, Pedraza and Becerra, had worked for. The gold hunter. He opened WhatsApp and searched for Laiseca. He selected the photos and sent them, saying, "Look at the treasure I found at the JamInn."

Five seconds later the phone rang. It was Laiseca.

"Impressive, boss," the agent said. "We should give that place a thorough going-over, given all the information we've got, don't you think?"

"Cool your jets, Laiseca. I'm the boss here, remember?"

"But I can read your mind," Laiseca said. "Are you saying you weren't thinking that?"

"We do need to investigate the goings-on at this hotel. Call Guillermina at the technical investigation unit, the one who used to be my secretary—remember her? Ask her to pull up the calls from the Jamundí Inn, especially international ones: where they're coming in from and the ones going out too. This is getting good."

Laiseca cleared his throat. "All right. I wanted to let you know Cancino left for Cartago two hours ago in an agency car to see what he can get out of Estéphanny Gómez, remember her? From the newspaper you sent me."

"Great, Laiseca, this is great—you're in my head, making decisions."

"I've always said it's better to act than to keep your head down."

"That's a good one, who said that?"

"I did, sir, though it's similar to something Gandhi said."

"I'd heard it before, but slightly different," the prosecutor teased. "It's better to act than to direct."

"No, boss," Laiseca said, "that one was Pepe Sánchez."

"Enough with the stupid jokes. Call Guillermina and we'll

talk later. I'm going back to my hotel now to have lunch with the journalists. Report back as soon as you learn anything."

Julieta got up after nine. She'd managed to sleep like a log thanks to her hangover-prevention cocktail, downed before she turned out the light, and now she felt great. She had night-owl tendencies, a holdover from her university days, and enjoyed working when the space around her was silent and every little thing seemed to resonate more. Ideas, in those quiet hours, are sharper and more precise, as if the mind, deprived of other stimuli, can focus its energy better. Solitude makes what we carry inside us stronger. She thought about the motor-cycle spy: was he out there, waiting for her to emerge? It wasn't the first time she'd been tailed, but it was the first time that might mean she was in danger. Shit, the kids! Heading down to the breakfast buffet, she texted her eldest: "Are you in class? All good? How's your brother?" She looked at the checkmarks next to the message—white, and then blue. He'd read it. But no response. He must be in class, he'd reply later. As she pondered their safety, the image of her children came to mind—privileged and thoroughly spoiled by their dad, but hers.

She sat down at a table with an enormous cup of coffee and two croissants. *These people are dangerous.* She couldn't get her mind away from the corpses by the side of the road. There was no telling what Jutsiñamuy would discover, but deep down she wanted the case to move away from Pastor Fritz. Though he was involved in a deeply ugly world, he was a victim of this country too.

Thinking about their conversation yesterday, she remembered a dream: she was scuba diving beside a coral reef that plunged into the darkest depths of the ocean. She descended rapidly, drawn by something, and the amazing wall of coral, as intricate as the façade of a Gothic cathedral, evoked for her the possibility of other worlds. She came to a huge tunnel and ventured in, and found a hallway with myriad passageways leading off from either side; entering one of them, she swam a hundred meters until it began to narrow; above her was an opening into a second tunnel, and she swam along it into a sort of vestibule with two large thresholds. Which way should she go? There was no turning back now. She didn't have the strength to go back or remember how to get there, so she had to choose. In the dream, she knew that one of the openings would take her to the surface, to the air that was now growing scarce. And the other would lead her into the depths.

Which should she choose?

Her experience and knowledge couldn't give her an answer. Feeling fragile, she decided to stay put, waiting for something. She had just one chance. A lobster appeared, and she spoke to it in her mind: *Friend, can you tell me which way I should go? I'm in dire straits.* The lobster lifted its antennae and waved them in gentle circles like a flamenco dancer, then moved toward one of the entrances. *Thank you, dear friend. You are showing me something.* But when she began to move the lobster scurried toward the other entrance. Its offspring must be there. Julieta chose the second entrance and swam through it, swirling the sand that had settled like a carpet on the floor. The temperature of the water changed: it was colder now and, ridiculous as it sounded, somehow wetter. Finally she saw a way out, but there was no light on the other side, and she felt far removed from the world—where had she ended up? She saw strange shapes that disappeared when she touched them, pieces of wood eternally falling. Bubbles floated before her eyes. On a rock she spotted the remains of a sunken aircraft carrier; the bombs had become mounds of lichen, covered with anemones. It was at once beautiful and horrifying, a testament to the destruction of the world: a place full of empty seashells, a basket of heads where there are no fish or light or warm currents, and the wreckage of a salt-corroded aircraft carrier, with sea monsters swimming in and out of its engine rooms.

That place was the subconscious of the world.

Johana's hand shook her from her thoughts.

"How did it go last night, boss? Did you work late?"

"Yes, I was up writing till about three."

Johana went to get a mug, poured herself some coffee, and returned to the table. "I've been reaching out to former comrades about Clara, the woman who might be Franklin's mother, remember? I managed to track down Braulio in Bogotá, and he gave me the contact info for two FARC members from Bogotá who were medics and are now working in medical labs. Johnny and Ricardo, from the Manuel Cepeda Front. They both remembered her, but they hadn't heard from her in more than five years. She may have gone back to Sumapaz or left the country. Lots of people went to Cuba or Venezuela. Johnny gave me the number for Berta, a comrade who managed the ammunition and was well connected. He says Berta stayed in Bogotá and is the person who knows the most about former comrades because she's been in politics since the democracy. But whenever I call I just get her voicemail. Berta Noriega. She has records for everybody, at least from that area. As soon as we get back I'll look her up; it's hard to do it from here by telephone."

Julieta took another sip of coffee. "Awesome. We'll decide on our next steps after we talk with the prosecutor today. We're having lunch with him at his hotel. I'd like to meet with someone from the families of the bodies on the roadside. We'll see what comes up."

At noon they took a stroll through El Peñón Park and studied the pre-Columbian designs on the fountain: warriors' faces, maybe from San Agustín. A few children were playing nearby. Groups of elderly people were reading the paper or chatting on benches. And up ahead was La Sagrada Familia church, partially restored but then abandoned halfway through over some arcane dispute. They saw restaurants, clothing boutiques. At the appointed hour they headed for the Dann Carlton and went up to the rooftop. Jutsiñamuy was waiting for them at one of the tables.

"Wow, I've never seen you looking sporty before. It suits you," Julieta said.

"Thanks! This city changes your spirit. The air is such a delicious temperature . . ."

They ordered three ice-cold beers, a caprese salad, and three pasta entrees.

Jutsiñamuy wasn't one to beat around the bush. He immediately started telling them what he'd been up to: the two dead men's families, Óscar Luis Pedraza's gambling stories and the conversation with his girlfriend at Almacenes Sí, the article in *El País* reporting on the disappearance of a man from Cartago who'd worked with New Jerusalem Church, and the visit to the Jamundí Inn.

"Hang on a minute," Julieta said. "Can you tell me the name of the Cartago man who's missing?"

"His name is Enciso Yepes; it was in yesterday's *El País*. His wife reported him missing, and apparently she's going to sue the security firm, which says Yepes hadn't shown up for weeks."

Julieta pulled out a notebook and wrote down the name. "What was the church's response?"

"No, the problem isn't with the church, it's with a company called VigiValle, which provides security services to the church."

"It's weird he'd disappear like that without telling his wife anything, right?" Julieta said. "He could be the other dead man from Tierradentro."

Jutsiñamuy looked at her somewhat mischievously and said, "Remember, in this country, everything out of the ordinary turns out to be either a crime or a miracle." He went on. "But let's not get ahead of ourselves. For now, without knowing what happened to him, he's just a guy who ditched his wife. Maybe he's just gone on a bender."

"I'm going to look into it with the church anyway," Julieta said.

"Agent Cancino," the prosecutor said, "one of my finest men, is currently with Estéphanny Gómez in Cartago, trying to find out what happened and what kind of information she can provide. But I can tell you it won't be much. My professional experience has taught me that, at least around these parts, wives are the least likely to know what their husbands are up to."

"There's got to be a reason for that," Julieta said. "Hey, I have something else for you. Remember that weird tattoo on the dead bodies by the side of the road? The photo you sent me?" She opened her purse and pulled out the little wooden hand with its inscription "We are healed." She placed it in front of the prosecutor and said, "Here you go. I came across it in an antiques shop."

Jutsiñamuy stared in shock. He picked it up to examine it more closely and saw it was identical to the one he'd seen at the Jamundí Inn. On its base was carved, "Assembly of God, Belém do Pará, Brazil." It was the same size, the same wood. After turning it over in his hands, he asked, "An antiques shop around here?"

"Yes," she said, "really close by. I have their card. Hang on, I'll see if I can find it. And he offered to get me more things, said I should call back."

She stuck her hand in her purse and rummaged around till she found the little card: "El Mesón de Judea Antiquities."

"The shop owner seemed really knowledgeable," she added. "He told me it's a figurine of Jesus's hand."

Jutsiñamuy pulled out his cell phone and took a photo of

the card. "All right, it'll be added to the investigation. Just wait till I send the photo to Laiseca with a note—he'll be floored!"

He pushed his cell phone into the middle of the table and showed them the images of the hand he'd seen at the Jamundí Inn. "See? It's identical, right? What do you think? Coincidence? It's amazing we both found the same thing in a city of three million people. That means we're on the right trail." Julieta and Johana studied the photos, stunned. "And it might mean the Jamundí Inn is involved."

The prosecutor continued. "There's another story we haven't talked about yet. The two bodies that have been identified, Becerra and Pedraza, were working as bodyguards for a Brazilian evangelical pastor and gold hunter named Fabinho Henriquez. No accent. An eccentric guy who apparently comes to Colombia regularly. We don't yet have a clear indication of what his relationship to all this is, but it caught our attention that he was a pastor too, like the other guy, and the founder of a Pentecostal church that's part of the Assembly of God, which uses this hand of Christ as its symbol and this slogan. Agent Laiseca is working on the matter. The guy lives in Cayenne, the capital of French Guiana. He has a gold mine in the Amazon."

Julieta grabbed her notebook, excited. Incredulous. "Brazilian?" she said. "Oh, shit."

"Does that mean something to you?" Jutsiñamuy asked.

"It's nothing, but one of the people working for Pastor Fritz is a Brazilian woman—I've got her name right here . . . Egiswanda Sanders. Quite a character, by the way."

"How so?"

"A real hot mama, total stereotype of Brazilian women: incredible body, really fit, nice tits, tattoos, a hungry gaze, huge lips, maneater eyes."

"Maneater eyes?" Jutsiñamuy exclaimed, laughing. "I've never heard that one before! My dear friend, if I didn't know you, I'd say you sound a little . . . jealous?"

Julieta regretted having said anything. "Don't be an ass."

"Well, it may just be a coincidence," he said. "I think Brazil's got, what, more than two hundred million people? If we can assume fifty percent of each gender, that means there are a hundred million Brazilian girls and women wandering around."

"You're right, I only noticed, that's all. Does this Pastor Fabinho have a criminal record? Is his gold-mining company legal?"

"Laiseca will tell us. His ears must be burning."

"Sounds interesting. I'll look into it too," Julieta said. She set down her notebook and took a sip of coffee. "But let's get back to the subject at hand. If the bodies on the side of the road worked security at a Brazilian evangelical church, and here we've got another church, Fritz's, and we assume he's the survivor, then the picture starts getting clearer, right?"

Jutsiñamuy scratched his chin again. "A religious war? Well, shit, if that's the case it'll be worse, and deadlier, than the clash between the Catholics and the Muslims."

"What's weird isn't that they're fighting, but that they have so many weapons, and that they'd carry out that kind of attack. Assuming they did," Julieta said. "Of course, New Jerusalem does look like a bunker inside, with armed guards up in watchtowers. There are more security checkpoints than at the airport. The fact that they have so much money makes me sick, but maybe that's why they have to protect themselves."

"Money, always money," the prosecutor said. "This may all be immoral, but until something concrete can be proven, it isn't illegal. They're protected by religious freedom, which is a civil right. Do you realize they don't pay taxes or even have to present their accounts? In practice, if you look at their finances, they're money-laundering operations. But if anyone calls them out, they say it's religious persecution. They're the most efficient mafia in the country. They've got senators and representatives defending them in Congress."

"Of course, this case goes way beyond than that," Julieta said. "Can we imagine two enemy churches attacking each other with assault rifles, rocket launchers, and helicopters?"

"Well," Jutsiñamuy said, "it could be not the churches, but the pastors themselves. Maybe they're enemies for some reason. Even with the peace accord signed, this is still a very violent country."

With that, he made a note on his notepad and apologized before phoning Laiseca.

"Hello? Look, Laiseca, I'm giving you another task to keep you busy. Find out if there have been any disputes between the two churches in this investigation, New Jerusalem and the Assembly of God. Any particular problem with either one is helpful too. And see if Pastor Fabinho has a record. All right? OK. Oh, one more thing: find a contact for Fabinho—an email address, WhatsApp, Facebook. Whatever."

Jutsiñamuy stifled a laugh. He covered the mouthpiece with his hand and told Julieta, "Laiseca's asking if we want a mango lemonade while we're at it."

"Tell him I'm on a diet," she said.

The prosecutor went back to his phone call. "She says thanks but she's on a diet. What's happening with the Jamundí Inn?"

The agent's voice sounded faraway and muffled, as if it were behind a flock of carrion birds squabbling over a cow skull.

"Guillermina's already on that, boss," Laiseca said. "I'm here at the Chamber of Commerce to find out whether the property info and business name match what they sent from Bogotá."

"Very good, excellent initiative. And have we heard anything from Cancino?"

"Not yet, but I'll call him in a bit. It's impossible to hear anything here, boss. There's an air conditioner vibrating, and it's really loud."

Johana and Julieta finished their pasta and ordered two coffees. The prosecutor accompanied them with his usual tea.

"I'd like to know about this Fabinho guy," Julieta said. "As I said on the phone, somebody's been following us, and one possibility is he's working for Fritz's enemies."

Jutsiñamuy's eyes bugged out. "You're right! Shit, I'd forgotten. Tell me more about that."

"It's a guy on a motorcycle. He's been watching us since Tierradentro. We've already spotted him here in Cali. I thought he was one of Pastor Fritz's men, but when I told Fritz about it, he got so jumpy I was convinced he was being straight with me."

"So he thinks it's his attacker who's following you?"

"He didn't say anything specific, but his attitude completely changed. All of a sudden he turned into a mafia don."

The prosecutor looked across the terrace at the river. A group of women was crocheting on a bench in Gato Park. Further up, two little girls were playing with a lapdog, racing around the fountain. A pair of students were making out behind a bush. On the bridge, a group of Venezuelans held signs and wove among the cars. He saw several motorcycles, but nothing suspicious.

"What does the person following you look like?"

"He wears black, or at least dark clothing," Julieta said. "And his helmet's black. He's skinny. I've always seen him from a distance sitting on his bike. No idea whether he's tall or short."

"And the motorcycle?"

"A Kawasaki 250," Johana piped up. She'd been sending an endless stream of texts throughout lunch in an effort to track down her former comrade Berta Noriega.

"Oh, I thought the cat had your tongue," Jutsiñamuy told her.

"Sorry, I've got all these texts going back and forth to Bogotá to see if anyone can help us find the kid's mother."

"Do you have any leads?"

"Yes," Johana said. "There's a former comrade of mine who's a possibility. From San Juan del Sumapaz. I'm trying to track her down, but it isn't easy, and this is from several years ago now."

"Well, good luck with that, Johanita," Jutsiñamuy said, "because I definitely can't help you there. Anything to do with ex-guerrilla fighters sets off alarm bells at the prosecutor general's office."

"I figured," Julieta said. "We'll keep you posted."

All at once Julieta slapped her forehead and pulled out her cell phone.

"Excuse me a moment. I forgot to make a quick call to Father Francisco, who works at the San Andrés de Pisimbalá church with the boy. In case he's turned up."

She dialed a number, and after a moment the priest answered. "My dear journalist friend, how's it going?"

"Doing well, Francisco. Have we heard anything about the boy?"

"No, my friend, not a thing. I was in San Andrés on Sunday, and it was a disaster. The church covered in dust, filthy—it didn't look like a house of the Lord. It was more like a pathetic little hovel. Franklin isn't back. That's the truth. I figured I'd wait another week and then find someone else. I can't leave the church in that state."

"And you haven't talked to anybody?" Julieta asked.

"No—like who? Nobody knows the boy except here."

"Like his grandparents, for instance."

"I haven't seen them. And to be honest—well, I don't know if I feel like upsetting them. We should wait till we find out what happened, don't you think?"

"Yes, you're right. But when you hear anything, good or bad, please call me, OK?"

Where the hell was that kid? The church and Pastor Fritz

had been kind, but there were things that didn't fit. And one of them was the whereabouts of Franklin Vanegas.

Julieta sat down again. She was interested in this Pastor Fabinho business. There was something inscrutable there that matched up with Fritz's personality.

"If your agent finds a way to contact the Brazilian pastor," she said, "please pass it on to me. I'm going to look for him too. I'd like to talk to him."

"That would be great," Jutsiñamuy said. "But you'd have to go to Cayenne."

"Couldn't he be in Colombia?"

"If he really was the attacker," the prosecutor said, "I doubt he stuck around. But it would be great to talk to him, of course—we could confirm what for now is still pure speculation. Laiseca will call to check in soon. Stay close."

"How do you get to Cayenne?" Julieta said, more to herself than anything.

"No idea," Jutsiñamuy said. "By plane, I assume, because there probably aren't any roads."

Julieta started getting excited. She told Johana, "Find out what the trip involves and how much—let's see if I can get the magazine to cover it as an expense."

"All right, boss. As soon as I'm back at the hotel, I'm on it."

The check arrived, and the prosecutor, with a theatrical gesture, signed the slip. Julieta tried to give the waiter her credit card, but Jutsiñamuy rebuffed it.

"No way," he said. "You two are essential to this investigation, and I'm treating you today. I'm paying personally, of course, not my office."

"Thank you," Julieta said. "You should run for president."

"My only presidential run was at thirty, for a chess club. I lost."

"They made a big mistake."

"One more thing, Julieta," Jutsiñamuy said. "What about

that motorcycle? Do you want us to provide protection? I can't offer an official escort, because it would have to fulfill no end of requirements, but I could informally ask an agent to stick close to you."

"I don't think it's necessary," she said. "So far he just stares at me from a distance. I think his job is to report on what I'm up to."

"Maybe he's out there right now," the prosecutor said. "You don't think it could be something else? I don't know, your jealous ex-husband, maybe?

Julieta leaned back in her chair and laughed. "No way! He's been following us since Tierradentro!"

The prosecutor scratched his head and kept gazing out at the square. "Well, apparently your tail clocks out at five, because there's nobody around."

"He could be watching from a hiding place."

"You have to learn your enemy's ways," Jutsiñamuy said, "and this one doesn't seem very professional. Sure your ex isn't collecting dirt to sue for a divorce?"

"Don't be an ass, damn it."

They parted at the front door to the hotel.

Agent José Trinidad Cancino reported that when he arrived in the steamy city of Cartago, famous throughout the region for its linen shirts, he went straight to the local courthouse and identified himself as an agent from the prosecutor general's office investigating the case of missing-person Enciso Yepes. He was given the contact information for Estéphanny Gómez, the wife who'd reported Yepes missing, and a short time later he was knocking on the door of a modest two-story house with a spiral staircase coiling up the exterior. When the door opened, the agent was momentarily confused (or startled) by the appearance of the woman in question, and even thought he might have the wrong address, having mistakenly arrived at a massage parlor or brothel, since Estéphanny, unlike the other wives of missing men he'd visited over the course of his career, was wearing denim short shorts with horizontal rips through which he could see her underwear—which was, he reported in meticulous detail, made of black and pink lace—and a bikini top that covered only a third of her enormous breasts, which had been augmented with silicone implants.

According to Cancino, Estéphanny, upon learning that he'd been sent by the prosecutor general's office, took him into the living room and offered him a shot of liquor, which he rejected, opting for a glass of soda instead. The agent began asking questions about the missing Enciso Yepes, but Estéphanny, who even at barely two P.M. on a Tuesday was showing signs of inebriation, said that for that sort of thing, she'd need to call her lawyer, which she did immediately. While the lawyer was on his way over, Estéphanny excused herself to go to a bathroom located very close to the living room, thanks to which the agent was able to overhear two sharp nasal inhalations. The woman then returned to the living room, rubbing her gums with her index finger, and proceeded to play a reggaeton song on the stereo. "We don't have to be boring while we wait for my lawyer," she told Cancino. "You like this music? You like the bump and grind?" They almost didn't hear the doorbell, but when Estéphanny answered, the agent saw that it was not the lawyer but someone from next door, a dentist's office, complaining about the volume. The woman closed the door and said, "What drags!"

When the lawyer arrived, Cancino was finally able to inquire about the subject of interest. According to the lawyer, Enciso Yepes had received death threats for being a security guard and because of his political beliefs. The lawyer claimed that the threats had been from former guerrilla fighters or dissidents, and when asked what proof he had, he said all he had was cell phone conversations, since death threats don't arrive by certified mail. Everybody was certain of what had happened, so he was considering suing the national government on behalf of the wife.

Cancino reported that when he asked the lawyer—who turned out to be Anselmo Yepes, the missing man's brother and Estéphanny's brother-in-law—what political beliefs had put Enciso Yepes in danger, he responded that Enciso had supported the Democratic Middle and participated in demonstrations against the peace accords and against the negotiations to hand the country over to the terrorists. Agent Cancino asked for more details, pointing out that if such beliefs led to death threats, half the country would be receiving them, whereupon the lawyer stated that he had witnesses who'd been with Enciso Yepes on two specific occasions on which he'd been approached by people on motorcycles who told him, quote: "If you keep opposing the peace accords, we're going to break you, motherfucker." Asked about the identities of those witnesses, the lawyer replied that they would be revealed at the appropriate time. According to the agent, when he asked if the people issuing the threats were known to anyone in Cartago, the lawyer said no, but that they were local to the area.

Regarding the nature of Mr. Enciso Yepes's work, the lawyer said it consisted of providing security to the Pentecostal New Jerusalem Church, and that he'd been assigned to that post by the company VigiValle, which they were now suing, not just because VigiValle refused to accept its responsibility for Enciso Yepes but also because it had stopped paying his salary, claiming breach of contract and abandonment of duties, which was a violation of labor and human rights. This topic seemed to rouse Estéphanny, who'd come down from her high, and she said that he'd enjoyed the job at first because, like her, he was very religious, plus it paid well, so he liked it even though it required frequent travel to Cali and other cities, but that later, because of the threats and the dangerous atmosphere, he became more and more unhappy. When asked when Yepes had last been seen, the lawyer said three weeks ago.

Wrapping up his interview, Agent Cancino informed them that the prosecutor general's office was investigating another case that might involve Enciso Yepes and asked them to remain available for further statements. The lawyer asked what kind of case but was told that for now that information was being withheld. Cancino also reported that before he left, Estéphanny gave him a loud kiss on the cheek and said, "It was a pleasure to meet you, detective, but next time you should accept the drink."

Once outside, Agent Cancino reported that out of curiosity he looked in at the dentist's office next door and that as soon as she saw him, the receptionist, a woman of indeterminate age—somewhere in her mid-forties to mid-fifties—invited him in and said, "Are you from the police?" He identified himself, and she unleashed the following: "That Estéphanny woman is a tramp. She's sleeping with Anselmo, Enciso's brother. Every time Enciso went to work in Cali, Anselmo would come visit her—the moaning was unbelievable! That woman isn't right. When we neighbors complained, they started meeting at a motel, the Olafo, on the road to Pereira. I know because I saw them leaving there once in Anselmo's car." Cancino asked if she knew that Enciso Yepes was missing, and the receptionist said, "No way, I bet they killed him so they could get compensation from the government."

Given these accusations, Agent Cancino decided to go to the Olafo to confirm what the dentist's receptionist had said. It wasn't hard to find, and when he arrived in reception with his badge from the prosecutor general's office, the manager came out to speak with him. Before going in, Cancino had found two good photos of Estéphanny Gómez and her lawyer, Anselmo Yepes, on Facebook. When asked if those individuals had ever been in the establishment, the manager looked at his schedule and called the employees in. Of the eleven housekeepers, seven recognized the couple, since they were notorious among the staff, who'd dubbed them the macaws because of the raucous noise they made. When prodded for details, a young employee in a white apron and knockoff Crocs told the agent with a combination of shame and amusement that the last time the couple had stayed there, a few days earlier, she'd heard the woman shout things like "Pound me, honey, whip me good!" and "Harder, Papi, give it to me!" and "It's so good to fuck stoned, baby." At that, everybody started laughing and quoting things the couple had said: "Hurt me!" "Make it sting!"

The housekeepers said that when they made up the room they used to find empty bottles of aguardiente and rum, marijuana cigarettes in the ashtrays, and traces of cocaine. When asked about the last time, they said it had been two Wednesdays ago. An employee remembered because it had been her birthday. What time? In the afternoon. They'd arrived at noon and had stayed until nighttime. The manager looked it up in his records and confirmed that, in fact, on that date he had a payment of 408,000 pesos for a suite with a jacuzzi, two lunches, a guanabana smoothie, a tube of KY jelly, and a bottle of Viejo de Caldas rum, paid with a Bancolombia debit card in the name of Anselmo Yepes.

After this, Cancino decided to return to Cali.

On the drive, he called in to the central office and requested Anselmo Yepes's rap sheet, but they told him they didn't have anything. He was clean. It was clear, though, the agent said, these two were up to something and were looking to take advantage of the situation in some way. Maybe it doesn't have anything to do with our case, Cancino said, and instead Estéphanny and Anselmo have been planning to run away together, so Enciso's disappearance is good news for them. He emphasized that the wife hadn't displayed the least bit of sadness about her missing husband.

In sum, though the relationship with the Pentecostal church pointed to a link between Enciso Yepes's disappearance and the bodies on the San Andrés de Pisimbalá road, his trip to Cartago to interview the wife did not turn up any information to back up that theory. In any event, even if the two things were later found to be unrelated, Agent José Cancino recommended keeping an eye on this case, the unusual aspects of which roused not just his desire to establish the facts and ensure justice but also (and especially) his interest.

Agent Cancino attached a log of expenses incurred on said mission (tolls, gasoline for the car provided by the Cali prosecutor's office, coffee at Parador Rojo) and listed the mission end time as 10:32 P.M., when he arrived in Cali once more.

Upon returning to his room, Jutsiñamuy sent a message to Agent Laiseca: *Get in touch as soon as you hear anything. I'm at the hotel. Or just come straight here, but let me know first.* He then pulled out his HP Xperia laptop and connected to the wifi network and from there, using the security protocol, to his private account. He had a new report from Wendy.

Confidential Report #2
Agent KWK622
Place: Cali
Operation: Holy Spirit
Date: Date of email sent

Approaching the informant: Update on report #1, sent yesterday, on the informant Yeni Sepúlveda. This morning, when I attended the Tuesday morning service at the church, I ran into her again. She told me she'd just dropped off her son

Jeison Maluma at the neighborhood daycare center and was there to provide support to the girls battling coca-paste addictions; first she pointed them out to me and then introduced me to them. The three were very young, though looking at them they seemed older because of their parched hair and blackened or missing teeth and their sunken eyes, with a sour expression, like they no longer believed in anything. Yeni said they were the most recent arrivals, who were currently being treated and monitored via daily meetings. Then she took me to see two other girls, who were church helpers. Both had been into drugs but got out about a year and a half ago, and in fact you could see the difference: their hair looked healthy again, their skin younger, they had good teeth (they may have gotten some dental treatments, I need to find that out), and basically they looked more or less normal—I say "more or less" because all the same they still have this harsh, rigid gaze, empty of all feeling, even perverse, to the point where it seems like at the least provocation they could fall back into old habits, their miraculous healing a mere thread that could break at any moment. There those poor miracle girls were, kneeling, eyes closed, at the pastor's words, which, this morning, spoke of the goodness needed to believe in what seems unbelievable or not believable, and he said it several times: "Believing in the unbelievable, working out of an urge to give truth to all those things that lack it, but need it," he said, "the way each of us is a mote of dust in the dense, infinite air of God, but one that has weight nonetheless, we are all important to him, we all have weight in his world, so we should give thanks, not just in words, but especially in deeds, in doing all we can: only through doing shall we enter the shining path, the only one that will lead us toward those stairs, which could be made of wood or plexiglass or even sturdy traditional fibers such as cabuya—in short, stairs that must be solid, because they're taking us straight to where

*Jesus abides, where he is sitting quietly, waiting for us to arrive, and when I say stairs it's because I imagine that place is up above us, in the sky, but remember that this is only a metaphor—*above *is a human measure: he is above us because he has thought and reflected and come to conclusions that our minds cannot yet contain, and because his intelligence is divine. He is above us because of that: not because he's the son of God, which all of us are, but because he possesses a mental fury and intensity and contains life and memory and the sound of stiff, dry trees, even those that have been felled and reduced to firewood; he still hears them swaying in the wind, and so he is divine, a supreme poet, because words anchor us to the earth and allow us to scream and give meaning to our sufferings, but those are very few, very few . . ."*

That's what Pastor Fritz said that Tuesday morning as a light drizzle fell on the auditorium roof, and though hardly anyone understood what he was saying (including the author of this report), they all wept and looked up at the ceiling believing that they were gazing at heaven, as if something inside them had understood—an intelligence lodged in their bellies or in their sinews that had comprehended the meaning of the pastor's words. And so, though the lecture was brief, the audience was left dazed, motionless in their seats, and when the junior pastors, the priestesses, and everybody else came out to continue the program, they remained in a trance, and then, little by little, they began to pull themselves together and after a while trickled out, some to the bathrooms and others to the exits, and I swear, boss, nobody was the same as when they'd entered; it was like they'd been recharged, as if they'd connected to the pastor's current and their batteries were at full power.

Afterward I went with the informant Yeni Sepúlveda and saw that the young former addicts were smiling, but their smiles now corresponded to something real; they weren't the halting or frozen smiles of people in an altered, semi-unconscious state. We went for coffee and cassava cheese bread, and I heard their other stories—they talked about their children and how healing it is to be with them, take care of them, because in the past they'd left them with their mothers.

This mission's investigation will continue along these lines, since both Yeni and the other former addicts have a close, direct relationship with the pastor that seems worth pursuing.

THEORY OF LIFELESS BODIES

After lunch with the prosecutors, Julieta and Johana went in search of a pleasant terrace where they could decide what to do, whether to return to Bogotá the next day on a morning flight or wait in Cali a little longer. After a short stroll they sat down at the coffee shop El Remanso, one street over from the hotel. Julieta wasn't sure what her next move should be, but she sensed that it was here, in this steamy city, that the important elements of the story were brewing. At the same time she recognized that the information she needed wasn't actually available to her, since she had to wait for the investigations of the prosecutor and his men to bear fruit. Most fascinating to her for now was the relationship between Fritz and the Brazilian pastor. Fabinho Henriquez. Her intuition told her that was the way to go.

They ordered two berry teas and disappeared into their telephones.

At the time of the incident—3:46 P.M., to be precise—the terrace wasn't particularly full, just five tables. Some employees were taking orders at the counter, charging and handing out numbers, while others ran the food, mostly mid-afternoon platters of cassava cheese bread and oat drink or milky coffee. The Colombian palette isn't terribly varied in such things. A few patrons ordered hot chocolate instead of coffee or a plate of fresh fruit.

But that's all.

Everything happened very quickly and chaotically.

The motorcycle stopped on the street, just before the corner. The sicario was perched on the back, behind the driver. His face still hidden behind a helmet, he climbed the nine steps to the terrace and headed to the counter like he was about to place an order. Somewhere in her mind Julieta, already paranoid about motorcycles, registered him. Johana found it odd that the man hadn't removed his helmet, and perhaps for that reason she watched him. And so she saw him loop around the far end of the room and approach a man from behind who was sitting at one of the tables against the wall. Her intuition told her, *Alert, alert!* and she tensed; a moment later, the sicario pulled out his pistol and pointed it at the back of the target's head.

Johana grabbed Julieta's arm and yanked her down onto the floor as five gunshots went off. Five booms that echoed in that tranquil environment, sowing confusion, shouts. The patrons from other tables also threw themselves on the floor, terrified. There was running and the crash of breaking glasses and mugs. The victim toppled over, lying on his left arm. The first and second shots had struck him in the head. The other three, probably unnecessary, in the chest.

The killer stopped and looked around, still holding the pistol, as if to confirm something. Nobody dared meet his gaze. Johana watched him from the floor, not moving. She was just five meters from the sicario, who stepped toward them, not to threaten them but to see the dead man's head from another angle. The bullets had done the job. They'd entered from behind and gone out through the forehead, opening a hole in what had been his face.

The murdered man looked to be in his forties, Johana thought, but he seemed young and robust. If he hadn't been stopped by the man settling scores with bullets, he would have lasted several more decades. Time is elastic in moments of panic, and remembering it in words seems longer than the event itself. Such was the case with the eight or ten seconds when Johana was staring at the killer's feet, which were shod in blue Reeboks with dirty white soles. She guessed they weren't the real thing. Paraguayan knockoffs purchased in San Nicolás. She could feel people's breathing, their panic. A little knot of humanity suddenly assaulted by reality. Dense seconds. Fear of death upon seeing it close up.

Johana recognized the pistol: a nine-millimeter, fast, light.

Suddenly, as if reality had been set back into motion, the sicario strode across the terrace, leaped down the steps to the street, and climbed onto the motorcycle. The driver revved the engine and sped off going the wrong way, toward the river and Colombia Avenue.

What happens after a crime?

It depends—sometimes nothing.

Johana helped Julieta up. Everybody else gradually stood too, one by one. A few women were sobbing and saying, "Oh God, what just happened?" The terrace floor was slanted slightly so rainwater would run off, and the blood was already trickling down the drains. Death is a strange thing. Not just blood but also lumps of bread had fallen from the dead man's mouth; he'd been chewing and about to swallow. Most people left without looking at him, but two of the employees came over to see if he was alive and exclaimed, "Don Alvarito!"

They crossed themselves.

Still dazed from the gunfire and the horror, Julieta couldn't move. Johana went to talk to one of the employees.

"Who was this guy?" she asked.

"Don Álvaro Esguerra. He used to come in for breakfast or afternoon coffee."

"A friend of the owner?" Johana persisted.

In the distance, they could hear a siren, which turned out to be an ambulance. Soon a team from the prosecutor general's technical investigation unit would arrive. She didn't have much time to question the woman.

"No, Don Alvarito was a good customer," the employee said, wiping her tears. "He was a big tipper. To think he just got out of the army last year . . . He used to say the military had become a ladies club now that we were in peacetime, and now look at him!"

The body, doubled over with the arms pinned underneath, looked fragile and exposed.

Three police motorcycles arrived and six officers swarmed the terrace, cordoning it off and organizing people to record them as witnesses.

Julieta called Jutsiñamuy, but she got his voicemail. She made a second attempt, and a third. No dice. Suddenly her cell phone buzzed, and it was him.

"You'll never guess what happened!" she said.

"Oh no, Julieta, don't tell me . . ."

Julieta didn't know where to begin. "A sicario . . . shot a guy five times right in front of us, in a coffee shop . . ."

Jutsiñamuy remained ever calm, even in moments like this one. "OK, Julieta, but which murder are you talking about?"

She was silent a moment, uncomprehending. "Which one? The one right here!"

Julieta explained that she was still in El Peñón, very close to the hotel.

"The thing is," Jutsiñamuy said, "there were just several of these crimes all at the same time. Seems like there were four. I'm headed to meet Laiseca right now at one in the south part of the city, in Ciudad Jardín, which was at a café too. I'd already left when I learned about the one in El Peñón, but I had no idea you two were there! There was a third one at the Unicentro mall, and another at a no-tell motel. The sicarios were busy today!"

He paused briefly to think. "Go back to the hotel and don't

budge until we figure out what's going on, OK? I'll let you know when I'm back, and we can meet up."

The second crime had taken place in the southern part of the city, at La Suprema sandwich shop and café in the Ciudad Jardín neighborhood. According to the employees' accounts, a man with a coarse complexion and dark skin entered the room, his face hidden by the hood of a windbreaker and a pair of sunglasses. He sat at a table in the back and ordered a cold oat drink with cassava cheese rolls. The victim, Edgardo Castillejo, thirty-eight years old, arrived some ten minutes later, sat near the entrance, and ordered coffee, a Coke, and a ham-and-cheese sandwich.

Apparently the sicario drank half of his glass and ate two knots of cassava cheese bread before getting up and, looking as if he was on his way out, moved beside the victim, pulled out his gun, aimed it at his temple, and let off three shots. Then he put the pistol away and fled, bumping into a group of people as they entered. He ran to the corner and climbed on the back of a motorcycle that swiftly disappeared into traffic.

The emergency medical units from the Fundación Valle del Lili hospital arrived exactly twelve minutes later and noted that Castillejo was still alive; or rather, that he still had vital signs. He'd been bowled over by the force of the gunshots and fallen under the neighboring table, which fortunately had been unoccupied. Two of the bullets remained lodged in his body, and the third had embedded itself in the baseboard, right in an outlet where someone had plugged in a cell phone charger.

The shots had come from a nine-millimeter.

The café customers, hearing the gunshots, had flung themselves to the floor. Sixty-three-year-old Bertha Ruiz de Poveda had banged her forehead on the edge of her table, where she'd been having tea and cookies while waiting for her husband, who arrived a few minutes later and got the fright of his life when he learned what had happened and that his wife was being treated for her injury.

Edgardo Castillejo died before reaching the hospital, caught in a traffic jam on Cañasgordas Avenue.

The initial theory was that the third gunshot had punctured a lung, filling it with blood and causing him to suffocate to death. The gunshots to the head had caused major injuries, but he could have survived them. Castillejo was the owner of three casinos in the downtown area and several motels in Menga. In reviewing his criminal record, the prosecutor's office found two investigations for money laundering and an arrest for gun running in the early nineties. But he wasn't a well-known figure in Valle del Cauca's mafia world. A sleeping but not entirely invisible cell, according to Agent René Laiseca.

The third crime took place at the Condoricosas motel, located at the intersection of 8th Avenue and 24th Street; besides hosting secret trysts, it is a monument to Latin American genius, as its decor features images from the Chilean cartoonist Pepo's comic strip *Condorito*. This double murder seemed to have been premeditated as well, since the sicario entered the motel accompanied by a woman to avoid arousing suspicion. Given the discretion such places generally provide their clientele, it is likely that an employee conspired by informing the sicario which room the victim was in. This discretion would also make it more difficult to identify the killer and his companion or accomplice.

The events, according to security cameras and the few witnesses, unfolded as follows: At 3:08 P.M. a Mazda with (stolen) Cali AXY 634 plates arrived and entered the motel's front parking lot. The couple walked inside and requested a VIP suite, located on the fourth floor (next to the Presidential Suite), and there they settled in to wait; it is unknown whether they made use of any of the erotic accoutrements provided to customers in such rooms. Twenty-two minutes later the victim, Ferney Alejandro Garrido, thirty-six, arrived, accompanied by Karen Dávila, twenty-four, of Venezuelan nationality, a professional capillary reengineer; they requested the Presidential Suite and ordered a KissMe charcuterie platter for two along with a bottle of Viejo de Caldas rum and Coca-Cola Light. It is not known who informed the sicarios of Ferney Alejandro's arrival, whether an inside or outside accomplice, but eighteen minutes later they burst into the suite, armed with an Ingram M-10 and silencer. From the naked bodies' locations, it can be deduced that the victims were in the middle of sexual intercourse, in the position popularly known as doggy-style. There were a total of thirty-six gunshots, which impacted the victims at various vital points from the gluteal area up to the head. Most of the bullets passed through the man's body before hitting the Venezuelan woman, causing her death. From the large quantity of gunshots that penetrated the wall, damaging the decorative image of a naked Yayita—Condorito's girlfriend—investigators concluded that the sicario was not well trained in the use of a semiautomatic pistol, which, when fired in long bursts, tends to rise in a semicircle.

Ferney Alejandro Garrido, whose briefcase was found to contain an unlicensed Remington pistol, had priors for arms smuggling in 2011 and 2012. He had been in the army until 2009. He left with the rank of sergeant and was involved in a "false positive" murder case that, after two years in the courts, failed to result in a conviction. After that he disappeared. Ms. Karen Dávila, born in the city of Barquisimeto, had entered Colombia from Caracas in September 2017 via Bogotá's El Dorado Airport, from which she then traveled to the city of Pereira to be reunited with her father's family. Though her father was Colombian, Ms. Dávila did not have Colombian citizenship, for which the paperwork was in progress. The Venezuelan embassy has been informed of their compatriot's death.

The fourth murder victim was Víctor Herrera Garcés, thirty-six, born in Toribío. He was shot at 3:51 P.M. inside his car, a 1996 Chevrolet Sprint with Cali plate VMH 472, on 5th Avenue near Unicentro, where he'd just been shopping. Eighteen bullet holes were found in his vehicle. Herrera died from a round that entered his temple and split open his skull, like a melon struck by a hammer. He fell into the space between the two seats, and when they lifted him up, the forensics unit made two macabre discoveries: first, under the body was a dead cat, which had been struck by several bullets; it was unclear whether Herrera had flung himself on top of it to protect it, in a moving and noble, if futile, gesture toward his animal companion, or whether the sicarios had opened fire indiscriminately and the cat had been collateral damage. In light of the events, investigators agreed that the sicarios' fate was sealed, since popular wisdom leaves no doubt that killing a cat results in seven years of bad luck.

The second find, equally macabre, was that when they removed the deceased's shirt to perform a preliminary analysis of the gunshot entry wounds, they discovered that he was already healing from three additional rather large bullet wounds, two in the abdomen and one in the chest. He still had stitches and gauze bandages. What other gunfight were they from?

He had his documents with him, so they looked into his background, finding a police record of three car thefts and two arrests for the use of restricted army material, such as camouflage jackets and pants. He had been in prison twice for extortion, and his most recent rap sheet linked him to the Gaitainista Self-Defense Forces of Valle del Cauca.

"Now the good part is going to be organizing all of this," Jutsiñamuy said.

"If that's even possible," Laiseca noted.

They were at La Suprema, the café where Edgardo Castillejo had been killed. Jutsiñamuy was sipping his ever-present tea. Laiseca and Cancino, after assisting the agents from the Cali prosecutor's office in their investigations, had gotten the boss's permission to order a Poker beer.

"Goddamn it," Jutsiñamuy protested. "I'd been planning to go back to Bogotá first thing tomorrow morning. I miss watching the sunrise from my office."

"For real, boss," Laiseca said, grasping the bottle by the neck. "And those guys didn't even know we were here. They went all out today."

"The people here are taking care of it," Jutsiñamuy said, "but what I'm interested in, the reason I'm looking into the Cali guys, is in case this spate of bodies has something to do with our investigation."

"It wouldn't be a surprise," Laiseca said. "Every time I hear mention that somebody worked in private security, I prick up my ears."

"What do you think, Cancino?" the prosecutor asked. "Why so quiet?"

The agent moved his head down and up again, like a bob-blehead toy, and said, "The thing is, boss, this Ullucos River investigation is opening up still other lines of inquiry. But if you think about it, everything that happens every day in this country is suspect, and it could all be tied to a single case."

Laiseca took a swig and mused, "Well stated, Cancino. It's one massive case: we're a nation of ignorant, violent, resentful people."

"Jeez, Laiseca, tell us what you really think," Jutsiñamuy said. "Don't forget, we public servants have a constitutional obligation to love this country."

"No, I do love the country, boss," Laiseca said. "The mountains and the plains and you and my blessed mother. But everybody else who lives here is a dangerous bunch."

Jutsiñamuy set down his cup of tea on the saucer and said, "All right, the national opinion session's over. Shall we get to work?"

"The Cali prosecutor's office is already looking into the details of who these guys are and what they were up to," Laiseca said. "Let's wait till tomorrow to see what they find out. They don't know about our investigation."

"That's important," Jutsiñamuy emphasized. "It's better for now if they don't know what we're looking for. The only people we've shared this with are Julieta and Johana." The prosecutor tapped his forehead with his index finger. "By the way, Laiseca, Julieta is waiting for you to send her contact information for the Brazilian pastor, Fabinho Henriquez."

"With these murders, I haven't had the chance to tell you, boss," Laiseca said. "I've got a number of juicy tidbits."

"Is that right? Well, let's hear them."

"Hang on, let me get my notes."

This is what Agent René Nicolás Laiseca reported:

Well, boss, the Jamundí Inn hotel and restaurant is a real grab-bag of surprises. Doña Guillermina's office at headquarters gave me a rundown of the legal status of the property's business activity and ownership. It belongs to a corporation, Bethlehem Investments, which turns out to be a Panama-based mixed consortium whose primary shareholder is something called Alliance Cooperative, which in turn belongs to the gold-mining company Ouro Amazónico, from French Guiana, based in Cayenne, which is owned by Fabinho Henriquez. The other two firms that serve as shareholders have only five percent each, so we think they belong to Ouro Amazónico too.

From there we started looking into Ouro Amazónico; the

people at headquarters are on that. In the meantime, I went to visit the Jamundí Inn, pretending to be interested in arranging a honeymoon there. I explored the place and befriended one of the waiters at the terrace bar, Beilys David Moncada, an Afro-Colombian of twenty-two, who told me he always looks after the people who rent the larger bungalows.

When I asked what kind of clientele they attract, he said all sorts; when I then asked, "Foreigners too?" he said, "Yes, sir, especially Brazilians, Americans, sometimes Ecuadorians or Mexicans"; he also recalled a Chinese guest. I asked, "Do you remember the last time there was a Brazilian guest?" He looked wary and said, "Hey, mister, are these the kind of questions everybody who's about to get married asks?" So I had to show my cards. "Look, young man," I said, "I've got a proposal for you—you could earn some good money in exchange for infor-mation." Opening his eyes wide, he said, "Like how much?" And I said, "Well, you tell me, how much is the information you've got worth?" The kid thought a minute and said, "Depends what you're looking for." Well, after some negotiations we agreed to meet at the end of his shift at a place he chose, a café called La Panificadora near the road to Santander de Quilichao.

I found him there later, now out of his Jamundí Inn uniform, looking like your typical Afro-Colombian kid from the area: tank top, baseball cap, jeans, and knockoff Reeboks. He told me I could ask him whatever I wanted, but first I had to pay 600,000 pesos in cash, in advance, which I proceeded to do, taking a photo of the handover and immediately sending it to headquarters as an official record of the expense. Then he told me what he remem-bered: the last meeting of VIPs had been about two months back; a group of people had come in from Brazil, including one man who seemed to be the boss. Even the manager of the Jamundí Inn had been incredibly deferential and called him sir all the time, and the man spoke Spanish well but with a noticeable singsong Brazilian accent. He would have been about fifty, more or less, and what Beilys David noticed was it was an unusual meeting, with lots of people from here in Cali and around Colombia, men only, and he found it odd because they never requested liquor or cocaine, and not even professional female companions. For three days he served them soft drinks, and all they did was talk and look at maps, and when I asked if he remembered what kind of maps he said no, he hadn't looked because the people made him nervous, they fell silent when he entered and watched him serve each person, so he always tried to get out of there quickly, but he did notice that they were working on maps spread out on the table because he saw they'd marked them with a yellow high-lighter; I asked if any name had caught his eye and he said yes, one of the words highlighted was Popayán, and when I asked why he'd noticed that word he said something very typically ado-lescent, "I had a girl there who broke my heart, you know?" and then added, "plus the y looks like a pussy, right?" thus confirm-ing that the maps were of Cauca Department, where Tierradentro is located. I asked if he'd seen any of those people before, and he said some of them yes, that they came fairly regularly, and here comes the good part, boss, because I showed him the photos of our stiffs, Nadio Becerra and Óscar Luis Pedraza, and he recognized them immediately, said of course, they both went to the Jamundí Inn a lot, and he also recognized the third guy, the one we think might be named Carlos, and said he was there a lot too, though sometimes he didn't stay, and he worked for the other guys, and then, boss, I started putting together the theory that Beilys David's meeting might have been preparations for the Tierradentro attack, and with that in mind I asked the informant some final questions: "Would you say the Colombians with the big boss were soldiers, or looked like soldiers?" and he said, "I don't really know, sir, but they were definitely beefy and strong," so I asked, "And did you happen to see any weapons at that or any other meeting?" And he said, "No, I didn't see anything, but I knew they had them, you could tell they were packing a mile off."

That was enough for me, so I dismissed the young informant, though not before identifying myself as an agent from the prosecutor general's office, which he didn't believe at first, saying, "You're really an agent? I thought you were paramilitary."

My informant's morals and habits seem to be very disordered, so I told him that from that moment forth he would be under the monitoring and guidance of the authorities, and recommended that he not tell anyone about our chat, which he promised by making the sign of the cross ("I swear on my blessed mother," he said). He also agreed to cooperate on further identifications and promised to keep an eye out in case those people returned to the hotel or he heard anything about them from the other staff and waiters.

After that I called headquarters to analyze the calls that had gone in and out from the Jamundí Inn's offices, and what a treasure trove, boss. Just imagine, three calls from a number in Cayenne! It's pretty much certain that Pastor Fabinho is Mr. F, and that he planned the attack with his henchmen at the Jamundí Inn. And that the bodies dumped by the side of the road, with the Assembly of God tattoos, are from his group. It's the part tying Fabinho to Pastor Fritz that's the weak bit; the only link could be the Nasa boy who talked to Julieta, but we don't have an official statement from him, especially now that he's disappeared. We'll also have whatever theories come out of Wendy's undercover operation, but so far, as I understand it, she hasn't turned up concrete proof that the combat in Tierradentro was between those two pastors.

After this report, Jutsiñamuy drained his second cup of tea and told his agents, "Come on, let's go see the girls. They're freaked out—they were in the café where the sicario took out . . . what's the guy's name from El Peñón?"

"Álvaro Esguerra," Cancino said, reading from his notepad.

"That's the one," Jutsiñamuy confirmed.

"Seriously, boss? They were there when everything went

down?" Cancino asked, surprised. "So they're eyewitnesses. We could question them."

"They're working with me," the prosecutor said, "and right now I'm more interested in getting their help on the other case. I still haven't been able to figure out who's covering up or tried to cover up the combat in Tierradentro, but I know it's somebody from the police. Orders from above."

"So who's looking into that?" Laiseca asked.

"I'm doing it myself," Jutsiñamuy said. "But it's slow going because I haven't had a free moment. It would be great if Julieta reached out to the Brazilian pastor and was able to talk to him—that would be key. He wouldn't suspect anything, and she's good at wangling information out of people."

"We'd have to confirm that the person who was attacked was Pastor Fritz," Cancino said. "That would change everything."

The prosecutor scratched his chin with his index finger. "The problem here is we can't confirm anything until the attacker turns up. It's a bifurcated case: two suspects, two confirmations. We won't get one without the other."

"Two Christian pastors beating the hell out of each other," Laiseca said. "If that's what happened, what would poor Christ say?"

"He'd probably laugh," Cancino said.

The sound of a cell phone interrupted the conversation. It was the Cali prosecutor's office, calling to inform Jutsiñamuy of the day's four murders.

"I'm waiting for criminal records that will allow us to connect the dots with other ongoing investigations. But thanks for the heads-up. What's your theory?"

On the other end of the line, a prosecutor said, "Same one as always: score settling between criminal gangs. The problem is finding a connection—hopefully we pull it off. There's no way it's a coincidence, right?"

After the shooting, her nerves completely on edge, Julieta opened the minibar, took out a tiny bottle of gin, and downed it. *Bottoms up.* Feeling a warmth spreading pleasantly through her body, she lay down on the bed.

Was she really in danger?

She thought back to her motorcycle tail. Had he observed the crime? Was he involved in some way? It wasn't the first time she'd witnessed a hail of bullets. In her career she'd seen bodies wrecked by high-caliber ammunition. Skin is too fragile; the blood comes pouring out. She recalled something a farming boy had said about one massacre: "It's not the bullet that kills you, but the terrific speed it's traveling at." The shattered bones, the awful sound they make as they break inside the body. And yet she'd been unnerved by the gunfire. Nobody who hears a gunshot can shake the thought that the next bullet will fly right into their head. Fear of death? Of course. Fear of pain, of disability. Johana was probably in her room, but it was different for her. Childless people are fearless and, in some sense, freer.

They were waiting for a signal from Jutsiñamuy to go downstairs.

Johana was looking into Pastor Fabinho, but Julieta opened her computer anyway and typed his name into the search engine. She clicked from page to page and was supremely annoyed to discover a huge number of men with the same name, from car salesmen in São Paulo to doctors in Brasília and Curitiba to even a professional model in Belo Horizonte. Out of patience, she called Johana.

"Did you find anything about the Brazilian?"

"I'm working on it," Johana said. "I found the Assembly of God, but there are several contacts shared with a French Guiana corporation called Ouro Amazónico—is that the one?"

"I'm sure it is. Look for their emails so we can write to them."

"All right, boss, as soon as I've got them I'll call you."

Johana was a whiz with computers. But as she waited for the information, Julieta had an idea and started composing a message:

> Dear Mr. Henriquez,
> I am an independent journalist interested in the gold-mining industry in South America. I am writing a book on gold extraction methods, from their pre-Hispanic origins into the present day, and I have found countless references to your company that have convinced me you will be a vital source for my work. The idea would be to create a biographical profile of you that will serve as an example of someone who managed to establish and grow a major company in the Amazon, with all the challenges that entails. A person needs heroism and faith to get as far as you have. Because of that—because I see you as a true pioneer—I wish to make special mention of you in my book, and so I am hoping you will grant me an interview. I am happy to travel to Cayenne to speak to you on any date that works for you, ideally as soon as possible. I am sending you copies of some of my articles for different press organizations around the world to give you an idea of my work.
> I await your kind response.
> All my best,
>
> Julieta Lezama

The idea was simple: try to get to him through his gold-mining company to avoid rousing suspicion. It could work. Just as she finished this initial draft, her cell phone rang. It was Jutsiñamuy.

"I'm on my way to your hotel, Julieta. I'm with Cancino and Laiseca. What do you say we meet in the café in ten minutes?"

"Absolutely, I'll be here."

She reviewed the text for the thousandth time. It was fine. The important thing was to touch (or should she say: massage, kiss, lick) the egotistical fiber that every successful business-man, even one who's a pastor or priest, has inside him. The buzz of the room phone shook her out of her thoughts.

It was Johana. "Boss, I found an email address on a Facebook page with the name of that company, but I don't know if it's current. The page doesn't have any recent activity. The address is ouro.amazonicodirec@yahoo.fr, and there are some phone numbers too."

"Excellent!" Julieta exclaimed, copying the email address directly into her Gmail. "I'll send them a message right away. And get ready to go. Jutsiñamuy is on his way."

When they arrived, the agents inspected the café and then sat down near the window. Jutsiñamuy kept glancing outside. It was raining.

It was amazing how many things could happen in such a short time.

"What do you think of today's little surprises?" he asked Julieta. "Are you two all right? Are you over the scare? I imag-ine Johana must be better accustomed to it."

"No way, sir," Johana said. "You never get used to seeing someone shot right in front of you."

"This country will be the end of us," Jutsiñamuy said. "I don't know where we're going to end up."

"And yet the government claims there's no conflict here," Julieta pointed out sarcastically.

"Well, this kind of thing has always happened," Jutsiñamuy said. "Four assassinations in less than an hour!"

"Do you think they're connected?" Julieta asked.

"That's what the Cali prosecutor's office is looking into," he said. "For now there have been no arrests, and there's no clear motive. We can announce that all of the murders are settling scores or unpaid blackmail. The Cali guys are looking into the victims' records, but all they've found are vague factors that don't establish a clear link: their ages, for example. They're all between thirty-five and forty, and they all have some kind of military training from the army. But that's something they have in common with most of the criminals in this country."

"Why do you say that's vague?" Julieta asked. "It sounds pretty specific to me."

Jutsiñamuy took the beer he'd ordered and poured it into his glass. Laiseca and Cancino drank from the bottle.

"All Colombian men from the middle and working classes," Jutsiñamuy said, "have done military service. The rich pay to get out of it, but for everybody else it was obligatory. I went through it. I know what I'm talking about. Save a very few exceptions, you don't see rich kids in the army. When the 38th Battalion was still around, a few joined up from bilingual schools, but not many; most were sent to the Sinai as a gesture of international cooperation. Julieta, you know there's nothing more shameful than being poor, but being poor in Colombia is the worst."

"Well," she said, "being poor in Africa is up there too. Anyway, what else do we know about the Brazilian, Fabinho Henriquez?"

At a signal from Jutsiñamuy, Laiseca brought them up to date on everything, especially the suspicion, practically confirmed, that Henriquez had held a meeting at the Jamundí Inn to plan the ambush in Tierradentro. The three roadside corpses had worked for him.

"At any rate," Laiseca said, "this is all a house of cards that depends on confirmation that it was those two shooting at each other at the Ullucos River. By which I mean Pastor Fritz and the Brazilian. Otherwise, all we'd have is the bodies from the roadside identified by a hotel employee."

"That's why it's so important to talk to Henriquez," Jutsiñamuy said. "But you understand, Julieta, that the prosecutor general's office can't interfere or call for an investigation until we have something concrete. Which is practically impossible from here."

"I'm interested, too, for my feature," she said. "The problem is tracking him down. I wrote to an email address Johana found, but we don't know if it's current; the page looks old and it doesn't have a date."

"Did you find anything, Laiseca?" the prosecutor asked his agent.

"I have the phone numbers," Laiseca said, pursing his lips. "But you can't get an email address from that. I failed there, boss, I forgot that detail. Hang on a second and I'll call Bogotá and have them look."

Laiseca walked over to the window, holding his cell phone to his ear.

Julieta felt her own phone vibrate. She read the message. "There's no need to look anymore," she said.

She handed her phone to Jutsiñamuy, who read on the screen,

Dear journalist, thank you much for your interest on our company and our boss's testimony. Monsieur Fabinho Henriquez will be delighted to receive you any day in the afternoon next week. Thank you for confirm the date that works best for you once you have arranged your travel and your stay in the city.

Amicably,
Thérèse Denticat
Sécretaire PDG
Ouro Amazónico, Inc., Trade.
Cayenne, Guyane

"It's like he heard us," Jutsiñamuy said. "Though this secretary could use a couple of Spanish lessons."

"They speak French there, boss," Laiseca said, "and judging by her last name, I'd guess she's from Haiti."

Jutsiñamuy looked at him with surprise. "Damn, so now we're Haiti experts too? Don't be a tease, Laiseca—how many PhDs have you got?"

"Only the ones life gave me, boss," the agent replied. "A divorce with no kids, the public library, and an impoverished childhood."

The prosecutor slapped him on the shoulder. "Well, hell, don't get glum on me," he said. "That's the best PhD this country offers, and the one most of us have." Then he looked at Julieta. "So, you're going to French Guiana?"

"I have to look at schedules, get a few things in order," Julieta said. "But yes. I'll go immediately. Johana? Get me a ticket for the first flight out." She pondered a moment. "How the hell do you get there, anyway? It's on the other side of Venezuela, right? Do you go through Brazil?"

"Maybe via the Caribbean," Laiseca said, "possibly Aruba or Curaçao."

Johana opened several browser pages and searched for a while. "There aren't any direct flights," she said eventually, "not even ones with just one layover. Or, well, there is one, actually: you fly to Paris first and then come back from there. That's the only one I see."

"Julieta," Jutsiñamuy said, "if I can help in any way, let me know. And go back to Bogotá as soon as possible. With everything that went down today, this city makes me a little nervous."

"Don't worry, I'm on the first flight tomorrow."

They said goodbye. The prosecutor said he'd be going back to Bogotá tomorrow too, leaving Laiseca and Cancino in Cali to take care of things.

They'd be in touch.

Once she was alone, Julieta sent a quick message to Zamarripa, her editor: "Daniel, there were just four more assassinations in Cali, one right in front of my nose, in a coffee shop. All related to the evangelical churches here and maybe in Brazil. To untangle all this, I'm going to have to travel to French Guiana; there's a pastor there who may have the key."

Response from Zamarripa: "Sounds exciting. How much are we talking, more or less?"

Julieta: "I figure about a thousand dollars. If it's more, I'll cover it myself."

Zamarripa: "All right, go ahead, but now it really does have to be something big. Incendiary. Front-page material. Save your receipts. And don't get shot, please."

MEN ON MOTORCYCLES

At eight in the morning, Julieta was waiting for her bill at the reception desk at the El Peñón Hotel. Johana still hadn't managed to find a reasonable air route to Cayenne, but she'd find one over the course of the day. The employee drew up the room charges, taking a particularly long time tallying the minibar; she reviewed the number of bottles of gin several times and surreptitiously shot Julieta a look, though she didn't say anything. Lucky thing, too, because Julieta was ready to eat her alive if she made some stupid comment. Then they left. Their Uber was waiting on 3rd Avenue. They loaded their suitcases in the back and climbed in, glancing at their smart phones.

First: to go to Cayenne, she needed to extend her children's stay with their father. With great reluctance, she called him.

"What's up, Joaquín, how are the boys?"

"Hi, babe, I'm great, thanks for asking," he replied.

"Haha, silly," she said, without a trace of humor in her voice. "Are they doing OK?"

"Well, what do you think? They're happy to be with their dad!"

"Can I talk to Jerónimo?"

"He's in the shower."

"Samuel, then."

"OK, but only if I can get him to take his nose out of my iPad."

"Tell him it's me . . ."

"I'd already planned on that," Joaquín said. "You underestimate my intelligence. But he may not find that argument terribly persuasive."

"Just let me talk to him."

"Hang on, I'm heading to his room."

"It's not like you live at Versailles. Hurry it up."

She spoke to her son less than two minutes. He responded in monosyllables. Julieta had the impression that he was still playing as they talked.

"Sam, pass me to your brother."

". . ."

"Sam, do you hear me?"

"Yes, Mom."

"Pass me to your brother."

"In a minute."

"Please just walk into the bathroom and pass me to him."

"Hang on, I can't right now."

"Why not?"

"I'm finishing a race, hang on . . . Can you call back in ten minutes?"

"Pass me to your father, damn it."

There was a silence. The boy didn't even say goodbye.

"Look, Joaquín, I hate to ask you this, but I need to extend the favor. I have to travel to French Guiana for work. I'll be leaving today if possible. Can you keep them a little longer?"

"Of course, baby, happy to."

"If you call me *baby* again . . . So that's OK? I'm leaving for Bogotá now and might come by tonight to see them. If I can't travel this afternoon I'll take them out for dinner, OK?"

"Does that include me?"

"Obviously not. We agreed we weren't going to say stupid things."

"It's not stupid. The boys like going out with their parents. Both of them."

"Anyway, I'll let you know if I'm coming by, OK?"

Before Joaquín had finished responding, out of the corner of her eye Julieta spotted a motorcycle approaching the taxi.

Then everything happened in slow motion: the man in black, her staunch pursuer, was about to reach her window. He had his hand outstretched, possibly intending to knock on the glass and get her attention. A moment before he could, a white SUV accelerated and struck the motorcycle from behind, making it slide into the left lane of 6th Avenue, near the La 14 supermarket. The man rolled down the sidewalk, crashed into one of the store's pillars, and tried to flee, but the men from the SUV trapped him against the front entrance. A store guard, seeing the commotion, deactivated the automatic door.

Joaquín, on the other end of the line, heard his ex-wife's scream and the squealing of brakes.

"Baby, what's going on? Are you OK?"

"Don't call me *baby*, damn it. I'll call you later."

She hung up and climbed out of the taxi, feeling something between fright and confusion. She figured the men in the SUV must be bodyguards from the prosecutor general's office and thought of Jutsiñamuy. But when she saw them dragging the motorcyclist away, she knew they weren't agents. So who were they?

"They aren't law enforcement," Johana murmured. "Stay calm."

The men forced the motorcyclist into the back seat of the SUV. Another picked up the motorcycle and started it. The one who seemed to be the boss came toward the women and handed Julieta a cell phone. "Talk," he said. "It's for you."

Julieta put the phone to her ear.

"It's Pastor Fritz, Julieta. I want to ask you to stay calm. Get into my bodyguards' SUV and come to my church. I'll explain what's going on once you're here. That motorcyclist won't bother you again."

Julieta was bewildered. "Were you following me?"

"No," Pastor Fritz said. "I was protecting you. Please come. We'll talk here."

A second SUV pulled up next to her. The back door opened. A man took their suitcases out of the taxi, handed the driver some money, and ushered the two women into the SUV. They headed off.

When they reached the church parking lot, Pastor Fritz was waiting with several other men. They got out of the SUV and he walked toward them.

"Everything's under control, Julieta. You can leave very soon—I imagine you're on your way to the airport, right?"

"Yes, back to Bogotá." Julieta stared at him, unsure what to say or do. "How long have you been . . . protecting me?"

"Since you left here," Pastor Fritz said. "You said you were being followed, and I wanted to make sure nothing happened to you. That's all."

The motorcyclist was manhandled out of the second SUV.

"Bring him here," Fritz told his men.

Standing in front of Julieta, he looked harmless.

"Let go of him," the pastor said, and then, addressing the motorcyclist, instructed him, "Take off your helmet and tell us who you are."

The man looked from side to side as if calculating whether there was any possibility of escape. He raised his hands to the edge of his helmet and pushed up, revealing his face. Julieta couldn't believe it.

"Franklin!"

The kid.

The two women stood still in shock. They couldn't believe their eyes. How was it possible that he was riding a motorcycle? And was in Cali following them? How had he come here? Why?

"What are you doing here?" Julieta managed to ask.

He seemed bigger now, but he was still a scared little boy. Refusing to answer, he lowered his head and sunk into the characteristic silence of the Nasa.

The man who seemed to be the head bodyguard grabbed him roughly by the arm and said, "Answer the question." Then he looked at Pastor Fritz and added, "We searched him good, boss. No weapons. We don't know what he wanted with the ladies."

"He's scared," Julieta said. "Let him go."

She kept staring at him, stunned. He was a child, a child! But also . . . He was at a confusing age: sometimes a child, sometimes a young man. His appearance made him look ready for the world, maybe readier than he actually was. She thought of her younger son. He was still a boy, but he was already shaving and could get a girlfriend pregnant. She tried to imagine him on a motorcycle, traveling to Cali and sleeping—where? Why was he following her? She felt anguish, anxiety, despair.

When things calmed down, she thought, she'd give the kid the third degree. All of a sudden everything seemed incomprehensible, absurd.

They went up to one of the offices in the church.

Upstairs, Julieta saw the Brazilian woman. She waved, but the woman didn't recognize her at first. *Look at her*, she thought, *in her skimpy miniskirt and bare feet.* She had gorgeous tanned legs, an ass that probably caused heart attacks, a face like Batgirl, and lips that seemed to say, "If you come closer, I'll suck you off." Julieta couldn't believe she was having these ridiculous thoughts in the middle of such a tense situation, but as they climbed, with the boy walking in front, her arm brushed against Pastor Fritz and she felt a powerful jolt.

What the hell was happening to her?

The pastor was wearing a black Lacoste T-shirt that showed off his strong, toned physique. His hair was pulled back with a purple band, like an Italian soccer player. She was a bit obsessed, but with good reason.

When they entered one of the offices, the boy went over to a corner and stared at the floor. Julieta and Johana asked the church people to leave them alone with him.

"Why were you following me?" Julieta asked.

The boy didn't look up. Nor did he say a word.

"Did you want to tell me something?" she persisted.

They sat next to him a while. Then Johana said, "We talked to your grandparents. They told us the story of your mom and dad. I was in the FARC too."

The boy's upper lip trembled slightly. He raised his eyes and looked at Johana. They were the saddest, most beautiful eyes she'd seen in her life.

"You knew them?" Franklin said, his voice frightened.

"I think so," Johana said.

The boy's face lit up.

"They were in the Sixth Front," Johana continued, "which was active around Belalcázar and the Nevado del Huila. I used to come from Caquetá in a mobile column, but we occasionally climbed up into the highlands. I never met your dad, but I think I did meet your mom. If it's the woman I'm thinking of, I saw her a couple of times. Was her name María Clara?"

The boy looked sad again. "I don't know her name," he said.

Julieta put her arm around his shoulders and found that he was still shaking. "Ever since your grandparents told us the story," she said, "we've been looking for her. And we've been looking for you. Why did you leave?"

He shook his head, not knowing what to say. Suddenly he asked if he could sit down and said, "I've been looking for her too, for two years. I've been searching on the internet for people who were in the FARC. But it's hard without knowing her name. When I saw you two in San Andrés I thought you could help me. That's what I wanted to tell you."

"That's why you followed us?"

"Yes."

"And why didn't you tell me that first day?"

"Because . . . you were asking about what happened on the river, the gunfight." The boy slumped and looked down at the floor again. "I just want to know if she's alive."

Julieta made a decision. She stood up from the sofa and said, "Franklin, you're coming with us to Bogotá."

She strode out of the office and found Pastor Fritz. "I'm taking the boy. He's the one I've been looking for."

The pastor looked at her in surprise. "Are you sure? Why was he following you?"

"He wanted our help; he's looking for his mother, if you can believe it."

"He's an orphan?" Fritz asked.

"Yes, or at least he doesn't have a father. His parents were in the FARC. They left him with his paternal grandparents and the father died in combat. He doesn't know his mom."

They went to the office where the boy was waiting. The pastor looked him up and down. "They tell me you're looking for your mom," he said, squatting down so his face was level with the boy's.

"Yes, sir."

"Give me your hands."

The boy held them out toward him. The pastor took them and placed them on his chest. He closed his eyes and prayed.

"I can hear inside of you the voice that's calling to her," he said, "and I see that she's there, waiting for you, sitting near a cross. Christ wants you to find her. Close your eyes and pray with me."

The boy closed his eyes.

"Our Father who art in heaven, hallowed be thy name; thy kingdom come . . ."

Halfway through the prayer, the boy's eyes lit up like lanterns. The pastor kept speaking and pressing his hands.

Julieta watched in disbelief, but she felt that she shouldn't be judging: it was a private, intimate moment, and incomprehensible to her. She touched her cheek and noted something wet. Tears. Furtively, she pulled out a handkerchief. They finished the prayer, and the boy stood up.

"Go to Bogotá with them and look for your mom," Pastor Fritz said. "I'll keep your motorcycle here. Is it yours?"

The boy looked shamefaced again.

"Sort of."

"I won't ask," the pastor said, "unless you want us to send it to somebody."

"Keep it here," the boy said. "I'll come back for it."

Julieta pulled herself together. She glanced over at Johana, who was also moved. Fritz was a con artist, but she had to admit he was very good.

Suddenly, the pastor caught her arm and pulled her aside.

"I apologize for following you," he said, "but this is a dangerous city. You saw what happened yesterday."

Does he know I was close to one of the murders? Julieta wondered. If he'd been tailing her, he had to know, but she chose not to ask. She assumed he did.

"You should go back to Bogotá and see your kids," Fritz continued. "I would just ask that we keep in touch, and when you find the boy's mother, let me know. I'll pray for him in the meantime."

He looked at her intently as he spoke, as if waiting for her approval.

"Of course, pastor, I'll tell you as soon as we find her," Julieta said. "What about Tierradentro? You still don't want to tell me what happened?"

"All I can tell you, dear friend, is that we must celebrate life. That's the only thing that makes it worth being here, on this side of the world."

"And what's the other side?" Julieta asked.

"That of death and memory."

"Do you believe in that, pastor?"

"Let me tell you a secret," Fritz said, lowering his voice again. "Sometimes I feel my faith slipping away from me. There's so much suffering. Every day, all over the world, Christ suffers and is bombarded, tortured, spat on, and humiliated. Faith eludes me. But even so, I am able to help it to be born in others."

"I understand," she said. "Like those diseases a person can transmit without suffering from them."

"I snap out of it in the end," he said. "Faith returns, slipping in through the window like everything else from the world outside."

Julieta grabbed her bag and went over to the boy, who was waiting for her with Johana. "Let's go," she said.

"Can someone from my team take you to the airport?" Pastor Fritz asked. "It isn't far, but I don't want any more surprises."

"Do you think something might happen to me?" she asked.

"You might miss the plane. That would be terrible."

Julieta laughed. "I haven't even bought tickets yet."

"Let my men take you, out of courtesy."

They shook hands and said goodbye.

In the parking lot the same driver was waiting for them. Crowds were entering and leaving the building. It seemed less like a church than it did the headquarters of a massive corporation.

At the airport, they bought tickets on the next flight to Bogotá. She had to ask the kid for his ID card. She did some quick math. *Damn!* she thought. *He's only fourteen.*

It was noon.

They boarded the plane. Franklin seemed more excited than nervous. It was his first time flying. Before sitting down, Julieta leaned in close and said, "When did you learn to ride a motorcycle?"

"Like two years ago, the owners of a farm gave it to me to bring them milk and things from town. I planned to return it."

"And how have you been getting by all this time?"

"I saved a little money for gas, miss. I've been sleeping in an abandoned shack I found near Yumbo, next to a dirt road."

"Well, you're very brave, damn it."

The boy blushed. Then she whispered to him again. "What about Pastor Fritz—is he the man you saw get out of the Hummer at the Ullucos River?"

The boy looked her in the eye, unfazed. "It looks like him, ma'am. I saw him from a distance, and I'm not sure, but it could be. He looks like him more than he doesn't."

They settled Franklin in the office, and Johana offered to stay with him. Julieta was supposed to travel to Panama that afternoon, to carry on from there to Curaçao and then to Paramaribo. She went to pick up her sons from Joaquín's apartment for a brief visit. Whenever she went to that building, she felt a knot in her throat. It was his bachelor apartment, where they'd spent their first nights together. The initial dream had started there. Even the same doormen were still around. The boys came running down the stairs, and when she saw them she felt a vague sense of guilt. It was two in the afternoon, and she was supposed to be at the airport at five. They had just over an hour. They walked to an ice-cream shop. The boys told her a little about school, but she could tell they weren't really present. Damn electronic devices. As she tried to engage them she could see they were somewhere else, immersed in their interminable games.

"What are you playing right now, Samuel?"

The boy actually responded to the question. "Look, it's called Minecraft. You build these planets and islands and then . . ."

She reassured herself by thinking that as they grew up, life itself would drag them away from childish games. In the end, the boys' childhoods would inevitably draw to a close, unlike Franklin's. The Nasa boy's childhood had been abruptly snatched from him. By what? By reality, Colombia, two hundred years of a perverse republic that abandons its most vulnerable people. Everyone, including her, was guilty of doing nothing to change it.

She spent the hour pretending to be interested in their games and then hailed a taxi to go by her apartment again. And then to the airport. Johanna had arranged everything for her trip.

To go to Cayenne from Bogotá, there were just three options: via Brazil, going first to Rio de Janeiro, to Brasília, and finally to Macapá, a jungle city at the mouth of the Amazon, and then twelve hours by road to Cayenne; the other option was to cross the Caribbean: from Panama to Curaçao, from there to Paramaribo, Suriname, and then by road to Cayenne, crossing the Maroni River. The third option was the fastest, but also the most absurd: fly to Paris and return to Cayenne on Air France, on a domestic flight, but that would mean crossing the Atlantic twice on the way there and twice on the way back. Naturally, she had chosen the Panama-Paramaribo route.

It would take two days to reach Cayenne.

Part III

Travel Diary to French Guiana

Wednesday

Boarding at El Dorado Airport and leaving for Panama on an uncomfortable Copa flight. Seat 26D. I had to fight for them to give me an aisle seat. I can't stand sitting in the middle. The woman next to me has doused herself with half a bottle of an absolutely foul scent, probably a gift from her husband—one of those perfumes purchased in San Andresito where the bottle says Paco Rabanne but they're actually made in Paraguay. Paraguayan Paco Rabanne.

What is Fabinho like? Is he really the attacker from the Ullucos River? And if so, what does he have against Fritz? I have my notes from the entire investigation. I'm going to type them into my laptop in case I lose them.

Panama. So hot. The air conditioning in the airport is on the fritz. They say the place is "being remodeled." Obese police officers. With such unappealing physiques, how can they expect to inspire respect for order? They look like gringo cops. I stopped to look at the Crocs store, but the prices were sky-high. The dollar is up at the moment. Then I went to the VIP lounge and had three glasses of gin. I ate too many peanuts and a nasty sandwich. I got distracted and ended up having to race to catch my connection to Curaçao, which was leaving at 6:30 P.M. A Caribbean Airlines plane. I got a better seat. The flight was three hours.

We arrive in Curaçao. It's nighttime; the air is warm and

humid, but pleasant. The people on the plane are already in bathing suits. It seems like nobody comes to Willemstad to do anything besides swim, drink piña coladas, and surf. There are lots of Italians, the suntan kings. *L'abbronzatura*, they call it. I go to my hotel, next to the airport. It's ten P.M. I drop off my suitcase and go out for a walk. It's a small Dutch city in the tropics. Colorful houses, some made of wood. Others with metal roofs, Caribbean-style. I find a bar that looks nice. I go in with my notes and my laptop. I order a gin with lots of ice and two slices of lemon. The guy behind the bar looks like Morgan Freeman; I like him.

My theories on the Ullucos River case:

Fabinho attacks Fritz because they're rivals in the sinister world of Pentecostal and evangelical churches. They are peers, and they hate each other; they're fighting for the same thing, and they both want to come out on top, crushing the other. Human vanity—is there any limit to it? However much he talks about God, Fritz is a vain man who knows the effect he produces and enjoys it. Maybe this is over the top—do churches have armies? It would be a return to the Middle Ages, but everything about churches is a regression to the Middle Ages anyway. All due respect to the poor Middle Ages, which we always use as a metaphor for a savage world.

Another theory: Fabinho attacks Fritz and tries to kill him over an old vendetta. Money? Some buried crime? You'd have to list out a person's motives for offing someone, especially given they're both pastors and are therefore strictly prohibited from doing so. Whatever motivates them is so powerful, it overrides the religion they profess and represent. Did Fritz kill someone close to him? Did he do injury to a family member? Where? Given that one of them is Brazilian and the other Colombian, where could they have forged a bond so tense it impels them toward annihilation?

My third gin just arrived, and as I take the first sip, I see that Italian again who's been smiling at me for a while now from the other end of the bar. The dumbass sure is good-looking. My guess is he's Italian, but he could be Argentine. Same difference. He must be about ten years younger than me. I just remembered that I claimed to be interested in Amazonian gold mining in order to finagle this interview. Shit! I'd better do some internet reading so I know something about the topic.

Back at the hotel. All is well. The Italian idiot got bored and went off to pursue some other woman, who right now, as I go to sleep alone, will be doing acrobatics in a bed somewhere.

Both of them can go fuck themselves.

Thursday

Willemstad in daylight. Suffocating heat, lovely city. A town, really. Just tourists. Was anyone here actually born in Curaçao? I wonder that as I sit on the hotel terrace, looking out on a street next to the sea. All I see is foreigners in bathing suits, Bermuda shorts, sarongs. There's a Chinese minimarket nearby. I'll go buy some water. My plane to Paramaribo leaves at ten and arrives at noon. Everything's close here; it's a Dutch village lost in the Caribbean.

Another Caribbean Airlines flight. I have a window seat and stare out at the sea, the shadows of the boats on the coral reefs. It's beautiful, of course—tourists know how to spend their money. The plane lifts up into the air. Hardly any clouds. Soon a huge island appears below, and the pilot announces that it's Trinidad and Tobago. What a world this is, the Caribbean. I don't know much about it. I was in Guadeloupe once. And of course in Cuba, the Dominican Republic, and Puerto Rico. But these islands or forward islands (Antilles) pique my curiosity. What do the people born in these places think? It's like being born inside a permanent vacation, a

Cartagena resort. Living surrounded by people smeared with suntan creams and lotions, stuffing themselves with ceviche, fried snapper, rum, beer, and piña coladas.

We arrive in Paramaribo.

I look out the window. Sheet metal roofs, colorful houses. There's a yellow cathedral. The airport is small and chaotic. What happened to Holland? They built and created this, but then left. Today Suriname is independent.

When I leave the terminal I see people offering transport to a place called Moengotapoe and Albina, on the Maroni River. It's the border with French Guiana, so I'll be going with one of them. A nine-seater Hyundai minibus. I'm lucky and get to sit up front, next to the driver. The air conditioning is on full blast, and I'm freezing. The driver's name is Tito. I tell him in English that I'm going to Cayenne, and he says, "Once you cross the river, at the border, there's transport. It's easy."

I figured it would be.

A flat four-lane highway. On either side, a landscape of seemingly impassible mangrove swamps that are definitely infested with animals. Especially snakes. I take photos with my cell phone, but the sun is perpetually in my face. I'm tempted to lower the window and stick my arm out, but when I try it Tito says no and turns the AC up another notch. One of the vents is right next to my foot. My toes are going to crack off with frostbite.

The Maroni River. It's huge—you can't even see the other side. Is this what the Amazon is like? I've never been. We get out at the ferry terminal and show our passports. I almost forget that Guiana is French territory. Among the people traveling with me are two gorgeous black women. Early twenties. Tall, with pretty faces and absolutely spectacular bodies. A gust of wind blows up the skirt of one of them and I spy a beautiful ass. Yellow panties on a black bottom—perfection. The people here look different from the Caribbeans. They're tall, stronger. Incredibly elegant. The men, oddly, seem cultured and less sexist. The women are sophisticated.

I don't know why I think that.

These ferry boats have always scared me a little. The river seems calm at the shore, but the boat shakes as it hits the current. At last we reach the other side. It's called Saint Laurent de Maroni. We get our passports stamped in a wooden hut that says, "Port de'Ouest, gare fluviale." What a desolate place. A concrete pad and a metal walkway that leads to the dock. Three drooping palms and a post with two reflectors. Maybe for them that's what civilization means: an expanse of concrete with nothing left of the jungle.

There are several minibuses waiting. It's three in the afternoon. We head off through an identical landscape: mangroves, palms, coconut trees, jungle. It's hot as hell, and the bus is freezing. I should have brought a parka. We pass through a place called Iracoubo and then through Kourou, the French spaceport for the Ariane rockets.

It's almost five when we reach an area that's been cleared of trees. The road draws close to the sea and instead of mangrove swamps there are beaches and lovely houses. It looks just like France: the same signs, all in French. Of course, what else should I expect? I'm in France. I recall the young women in Guadeloupe once upon a time who told me they weren't Latin American, they were Euro-Caribbean. Colonial legacies are weird.

At last I reach Cayenne.

It's 6:30 P.M. local time.

The lodging Johana reserved for me is called Ker Alberte, a tidily kept and almost certainly refurbished mansion of yesteryear. It doesn't have many rooms, a sort of boutique hotel. They give me a room on the second floor, at the far end of the garden. It's small and cozy. The internet works perfectly. As soon as I log on I see a message from Thérèse Denticat,

Sécretaire PDG, Ouro Amazónico, Inc., Trade. "Mr. Henriquez will be busy today and tomorrow, but the day after tomorrow he would like to invite you to lunch at Les Palmistes at 1:15 P.M."

All right, that gives me time to get better prepared and explore a little of this strange, so far incomprehensible city. A sort of Amazonian village with signs in French, FNAC, Carrefour, and Darty. They use the euro, and I see that things are incredibly expensive. That was to be expected. Everything's brought in by plane from France. It's like Guadeloupe, but without sugarcane and, therefore, without rum. We'll see. There's got to be something.

Cayenne—what a mysterious, lonely city.

There aren't many people around—is it the heat? It's stifling out, and humid. I go for a walk and can't figure out where I am. They say this is downtown, but it looks like a suburb. There are hardly any businesses. A French woman (the hotel owner?) pointed out the central square, and on my way there I walked down a street full of Chinese minimarkets, Rue de Rémire. Orient Shopping. I went in to buy the thing I always forget: toothpaste. And a bottle of Perrier, as expensive as in Colombia. How did the Chinese end up here? It's weird. As I walk, question after question occurs to me. Finally I reach the square, which is very pretty. Lots of coconut palms. The Place des Palmistes. A huge lawn full of palms. On one side is a statue of someone whose name is illegible. The humidity has erased the plaque, but it's probably a national hero, the first Frenchman to colonize Guiana.

What's that in the distance?

Of course, it's the ocean. I walk toward it. There's a narrow, crumbling alleyway. I turn the first corner and suddenly the waves appear, lapping against a pile of trash. How odd. The place is next to the city's main square, but it is charmless, even somewhat unpleasant. It stinks of rotting garbage. There are the ruins of an ancient wall. I walk to a wide beach, remaining alert. Sometimes, unwittingly, you wind up wandering into the lion's den. I come across a young couple, probably high school age. He kisses her and she responds passionately, lying beside him. He strokes her knee and moves his hand up, but when he gets to the edge of her skirt she pushes his hand away. And he starts over: kiss, knee, thigh . . . Off! Kiss, knee, thigh . . . An old man appears beside the wall; though they see him, they remain unfazed. The defiance of youth. As the man walks past them, the young woman lets her beau go a little further up, but as soon as the man's out of the picture, she pushes the hand away again.

Cayenne resembles the port cities in the Caribbean.

The houses have wooden shutters and whitewashed walls that let the breezes through. Metal roofs. I walk down a sandy path next to the water to a park with a viewpoint. The Atlantic Ocean. The beach is full of dry, stripped trunks carried in by the sea, the great devastator of trees. Where do they come from? There are piles of wood drying in the sun. The houses are made of wood. It's the traditional architecture. The water is brown; the surf stirs up the clay on the bottom.

I buy a book about gold mining, which in French is called *orpaillage*, and go sit in the café next to the square. It's called Les Palmistes, the same place where Fabinho arranged to meet the day after tomorrow. It offers a variety of services: hotel, bar, restaurant. Founded in 1908. I sit down on the terrace. What do they have? I order a Guianese punch. They bring a glass with slices of lemon, sugar syrup, ice, and a cup of rum of a sort they call "agricultural," which is strong like cachaça. La Belle Cabresse. Rhum agricole de Guyane. I should drink slowly—I can't get drunk here. I'm alone. I ask them to mix it for me and take a sip; it's delicious.

I start reading about gold mining, the subject I'm supposed to be an expert on. The book offers a historical overview. It talks about how mining began in the Amazon after the arrival of the Brazilian *garimpeiros*, who came from Minas Gerais, where mining started in the sixteenth century.

Damn, this punch is delicious, but it packs a wallop. I'm going to order another—how many does that make? I think three. The sugar makes it go down easy, and what a flavor. This terrace is gorgeous. There are people at every table, mostly French. It seems to be the city's major meeting spot. Some people are working on their laptops or staring at their phones. The music isn't blasting. There's a stage and a sign announcing live music later on. Jazz. I think this place is going to be my office in Cayenne.

Yes, that's decided, Les Palmistes.

As night falls, the square empties out. What time is it? In the darkness, the streets, especially the poorly lit ones, look scary. I memorized the way back: I go out through here till it ends and then three blocks to the left. As far as I know, there's no crime here. They didn't say anything about being careful at the hotel, but maybe they don't want to scare people. We'll see.

Shit, I finished my damn punch again right as I figured out what I want to write in this notebook. Let's see if the waiter spots me—will this be my fourth or my fifth one now? I don't remember, but I'm feeling good on this delicious tidal wave: a soothing jacuzzi of rum and lemon. Hopefully it's not too pricey. I didn't even look at the price—a rich-kid habit I haven't managed to break. Ideas are buzzing in my head. Is that the La Belle Cabresse?

Focus, damn it! Fabinho, gold miners, the Amazon, Pentecostal and evangelical churches. Fritz is fucking the Brazilian woman. That's for sure. Those guys might be pastors, but they still get horny. Plus they can. Sultry bitch. Next thing you know she'll be howling at the moon and running on all fours.

Fabinho, gold miners. Pentecostal churches. On one side of

the room, the jazz band is tuning their instruments and the sound techs are hooking up the amps. In ten minutes it won't be possible to think, at least not about anything except music. This is wonderful. I've ordered some empanadas and a fish steak, plus another punch. If I don't eat something I'm going to end up drunk. At the next table is a young couple. She is staring raptly at her man—they're French. And like all French people, they travel the world with those little green books, the *Guide du Routard*. Is it true the French invented oral sex? The young woman looks a little mousy, but she's probably pure fire when her man turns her on. They look like they're on their honeymoon. In Spain, they call a blowjob a "Frenchie." The music is amazing. The jazz group is made up of two guys and two girls.

I think I'm tipsy now. I'm going back to the hotel before some *guyanais* makes a move and I end up practicing my French in the bathroom.

Good night, notebook. Bisous.

Hope I don't get lost on the way back to that fucking hotel—what's it called . . . ?

. . . . . .
. . . . . .

Friday

What time is it? 9:22 A.M. This headache is killing me. That punch is delicious but deadly. I'm going to venture out into the world slowly and a little at a time. The poolside breakfast is still being served. I'll get in the water for a bit.

It's nice to have the day free, so I can pull myself together and continue preparing for the interview. This coffee is fantastic, as is the bread. A baguette just like the ones in France. I'm in France!

About the interview: I'll need to find a way to shift from the subject of gold to the churches. It will be interesting to see his reaction when I mention Fritz's New Jerusalem Church.

. . . . . .

. . . . . .

Today's a hangover day.

I knew it even as I ordered those damn drinks. I hate myself for that. I can go without drinking for weeks, but once I start it's hard to stop. A certain melancholy tone in this notebook is the product of an excess of alcohols derived from cane sugar.

A walk after lunch, in the stifling heat. I went down to the ocean and pictured how, traveling in a straight line, you'd run into Saint Helena, the island where Napoleon was exiled. Does it look like this, with the beach full of tree trunks polished by the surf? I imagined the prisoners escaping, like Papillon, and disappearing into the jungle. The heat and the vast swarms of mosquitoes. I'm more scared of the mosquitoes than I am of snakes or jungle beasts. After my walk I went back to the hotel and spent the rest of the afternoon in the pool. I just ordered some grilled fish and zero alcohol. Early to bed.

Tomorrow's the big day, the reason I've come all this way.

Saturday

The day could be summed up as "Meetings with Remarkable Men," like that legendary book by Gurdjieff, guru of subjectivity and the power of the spirit. But in my case, it's spiritual charlatans. Spiritual scum and tinkerers. Recyclers of spiritual rubbish. The first tinkerer, of course, was Fritz, and the second one is this guy. The famous Mr. F.

Let's start at the beginning.

I met up with Fabinho Henriquez at a table at Les Palmistes.

My first impression, walking toward him and observing him from a distance, was contradictory: I'd never seen anyone like him, but at the same time he was the most ordinary-looking person you could imagine.

This would be my description:

A sturdy man, not fat, Caucasian, balding, with deep black eyes. The kind of bald that's finished off in the barbershop, a look I can't stand. He was wearing a somewhat faded indigo T-shirt with the letters *NYC* across the chest. A leather vest on top of that. Very strong, tanned arms, tattoos of the face of Christ and the cross. On both wrists, woven and leather bracelets, cuffs made of copper and little shells. I thought, *His arms are a showroom of local artisanry.*

"My dear friend, welcome."

He greeted me solemnly. He caught my hand between his, like a priest would to a member of his congregation, and looked me up and down. An indifferent look, without a speck of desire, though there was no hint of rejection or scorn either.

"Please have a seat. Would you like a soda, a punch, something warm to drink?"

I ordered sparkling water with lemon.

"You are from my beloved Colombia, the loveliest country in South America."

"Thank you," I said. "And the most problematic."

"Oh, yes, problems, of course," Fabinho said. "God bless that beautiful country. May Jesus place it on his highest seat, and may it prosper."

As he spoke, he crossed himself quickly several times, kissing his fingers and looking heavenward.

"Problems are human; only God resolves them in the end. Ah, divine love." He crossed himself again. "You're an interesting person. I read some of your articles."

"As I told your secretary, I'm interested in gold extraction in the jungle. As you're no doubt aware, illegal mining is a serious problem in Colombia. That's why I want to tell the story of somebody like you, who works on the side of the law and respects nature."

"God put gold there for us to find and, seeing it gleam in our hands, be closer to his word and his works. Nature was conceived by him, and gold is part of that work, maybe his masterpiece. It's good to take it out and look at it. It's part of divine love."

As he said this, he glanced at the next table, where two men sat. One of them furrowed his brow in a sign of agreement. They were with him. Someone on the sidewalk came to the edge of the terrace to beg for money, and the men at the table stood up, their hands at their waists. Bodyguards.

"Relax," Fabinho said, waggling his hands, "it's just a poor man. *Viens içi, comment tu t'appelles?*"

The man was Haitian. Lots of destitute immigrants were arriving from the Caribbean.

"*Tiens,*" Fabinho said, giving him some euro coins, "*et remercie Dieu pour ça.*"

The man went off toward the Chinese minimarket. I figured he was going to buy a carton of cheap wine.

"Christ was always on the side of the poor," he said, sitting back down. "And though I know that man is going to spend the money I gave him on alcohol, it will bring him some relief. Who am I to judge . . ."

We engaged in small talk and asked polite questions for a while. He made a few jokes; I laughed obligingly. The awkwardness gradually eased. When I thought the time had come, I asked his permission to record.

"What do you say we get started? As I said, I'm interested in writing a professional profile, but above all a human one. In any business venture, it's people who make the difference. So I'd like to start with this: How do you introduce yourself? Who are you?"

Fabinho cleared his throat, took a sip of water, and said these words, which I recorded.

(Transcript without corrections or omissions and some comments)

You ask me who I am?

That's the hardest and most terrifying question, or the most human—or maybe the most unlikely in a world crammed with empty words.

Miss Julieta, who am I? Do you know who you really are? Before telling a story that might be mine, I'm going to tell you how I feel about life and God and the life questions that are our daily bread. This whole incredible world is made of words, and that's the only way our minds can understand. It's part of divine love. Oh, yes.

Oh, divine love.

You see me as a successful man who runs a large company in the Amazon, but who also has a clean conscience. And yes, that's true. But it wasn't always the case—I come from a place far away from here. I come from below. From the darkness. Maybe that's why I like mines and gold hidden in the earth.

If I could, if I were strong and not worn out, I'd like to triumph in a world of creatures who dwell underground and light their ways with mineral sparks; creatures who walk hunched through long tunnels that connect to other tunnels, and still others, and the triumph would consist of sneaking up to the surface from time to time without anybody spotting me . . .

Why? So I can't be betrayed, my dear. So I don't have to see mankind offending the Lord and failing to abide by his word. I'd rather be an underground animal or a solitary treetop bird whose only task is the silent work of living my life.

Because the most inhuman thing is a longing to resemble the men who go around the streets and squares with their minds locked on fornication or violence or wealth, in a way that can

only be offensive to God. Most of what they think is just garbage, crudeness, pornography. Or even worse: selfishness, vanity, envy, resentment. And what is in the heads of young people, who are the future? Not much. They think about drinking, fornicating, and becoming numb. Loneliness makes us vain. The word of Christ is the only thing that tames the ego. It is in our minds, our hearts. The two go together. His word and each of us.
    It is part of divine love.

    Life—what value does it have? Long ago, in the mines or in the fields, you used to see the garimpeiros, *weather-beaten people. The men had wrinkled faces and clothes torn from labor. They had scars from fighting, sometimes with jungle animals and sometimes with each other. Each scar told a story. Everything you saw in them recalled something, and that was their portrait. Things have changed now. Clothing is sold already torn, and since people don't have scars they get tattoos, wanting stories they haven't suffered inscribed on their skin. How can they suffer when they don't savor life? That's the big question I wonder about. The people who work in the mines are greedy. So am I, because it's my business, and most of all because it's what I've always known how to do, since I was a kid. Maybe you've heard of a dowser, which is someone who can detect water beneath the ground. I can do something similar. I sink my hands into the rocks, touch the soil. I smell the manganese. I soak it in and rub it into me. And suddenly I see it. Something tells me,* It's over there, *and the machines go looking for it—can you imagine how much it would cost to do it blind? You have to wring out the earth and break it in half like a cookie, and the metals pour forth. You have to drag it out with dredges and buckets. It can take days. Gold is the last metal to become solid, and its veins meander without any logic. When you find it, you have to know where it's coming from and where it's going. I know how to see that. Thanks to my ability, I survived in Minas Gerais.*

That's who I am: the man who knows where the gold is going.

"And you don't think," I said, "that gold increases man's greed? Aren't you afraid of destroying everything because of that greed?"

Fabinho finished his mineral water with lemon and called the waiter over. He ordered a Coke with ice.

"It's all part of the same thing, which is divine love," he said, taking a long sip. "We shouldn't worry about things that don't worry nature. The earth contorts and cracks. When the continents formed and Africa separated from the Americas, the soil layer cracked and the two parts moved away from each other. That's nature, and we are part of it. People say we're destroying it, but you can't really say that. The history of the planet is the history of its fractures and holes and its infinite chasms and the collisions of its tectonic plates. When this happened for the first time, where was man? Running away in fright. Man is part of nature and will die in it. You have to understand creation. To build a church, you have to topple trees, just as you do to erect cities, hospitals, schools. Should we stop doing that? Now man, who used to be naked, has machinery and dynamite and can bore deep into the surface. It's not the end. A fly can't topple a wall by flapping its wings faster."

I broke in, trying again. "But the same scientists who made machines to perforate the earth and do fracking say it too: today the planet is small and fragile; we're on the verge of damaging it irretrievably."

"Those are just words," he said, waving away the air in front of his nose as if an insect were buzzing there, "and that's just because the apocalypse has such cachet. If we don't talk about the end of the world, nobody listens to us. They also said the sun revolved around Earth and condemned Galileo, and today they say there's no other life in the universe but us—can you imagine that? Or they claim God doesn't exist because science made him obsolete. Do you believe them? Scientists are the quacks of the twenty-first century. That's a fact, miss."

"And yet you use machines invented by those scientists," I persisted, needling him. "And you understand the order of the layers of Earth's crust because of the knowledge they've granted."

Fabinho stared off at the end of the street, which I found unsettling. Was there a new danger? Nothing was there.

"What I know doesn't come from speculations I've read," he said, "but from knowledge of these jungles and God's work. I inherited it from having been born close to the soil, smelling firewood burning in the stove or the clay pot. The indigenous people didn't study at Harvard, nor do they need to, to know what a plant has inside it.

"It's knowledge accumulated over generations; indigenous children don't start over from scratch. Just like our science, it gets stored. There's a pedagogy.

"Intimate familiarity with the earth is more important, I'm telling you. Believe me. You're good with words—it's your job. For me, I know the things I know. In my bones. If I can't explain them any better, it's not because the ideas are weak, but because my powers of expression are limited."

I nodded in agreement, but thought, *This guy is totally nuts; he's even more tangled-up and mystical than Fritz. They must know each other. They're exactly the same.*

"We're living through the days before the Lord's coming," Fabinho continued. "And it's not me saying that—it's the Bible. That's why we need to be in harmony with nature and the Creator's work. People who keep throwing their lives away will not be able to receive grace. That's why I created a church in the jungle, and that's why I work here. Is there anything in the world closer to God's work than the jungle?"

He was wearing a heavy gold chain with a medallion that he

suddenly stroked. It was the hand of Jesus with the phrase "We are healed."

"Are mining gold and building Pentecostal churches part of the same concept?" I asked.

He smiled, pleased by the question. "Of course, it's all part of divine love. I told you that already. The end is coming, and it's better to be close to the Lord's work. That's why I use the gold I mine to establish churches. It isn't for my own personal enrichment."

I was tempted to really get into that, but I held back. "Do you have any relationship with Colombian mining?"

He looked me in the eye, and I felt a sudden pang in my belly.

"I worked in your country for a while, near the border. But the people's hearts were shattered, and I didn't stay. I did what anyone would have done: work and keep my mouth shut. That jungle still dwells in my heart, one of the toughest places I've been. The trees block out the sky. The loneliness of the world is more intense, like the parking lot of an abandoned shopping mall, or a ghost town where all the people have fled or died of the plague; a universe without any life but one's own is the most terrifying notion a person can conceive, and it is precisely there that the figure of Christ comes down and penetrates your heart and leads you by the hand to a boat or shepherds you into a drone for humans and lifts you above the world, close to the only source of heat that can console the spirit, which is God himself, he who is about to arrive. I am waiting for him—are you not?"

I was startled by the question. I told him I wasn't a believer, that I didn't have a religious background. My spirituality followed a different course.

"And what course is that?" he asked.

"Art, music, books," I replied awkwardly.

"Oh, of course," he said, leaning back in his chair, "but

those, too, are manifestations of God, so in the end we agree. Receive my blessing. Everything is part of divine love." He looked at me cheerfully and said, "Would you like to see the mine where I'm working now?"

I said I would.

He said he'd send someone to pick me up tomorrow at six A.M. Then he got up and, with a comical bow, we said good-bye. He turned to one of the waiters and made a circle in the air with his finger. I understood that he was saying, *Put it all on my tab*. He went down to the street, accompanied by two men, and as he turned right along the park the people at four other tables got up and hurried out. More security.

Sunday

At 6:11, as I was having breakfast, someone asked for me at reception. An Afro-Guianese woman, no older than thirty, with natural hair. She said her name was Thérèse Denticat and I remembered her emails. Fabinho's secretary at Ouro Amazónico. I finished my (delicious) coffee, went upstairs to brush my teeth, and came back down.

"Mr. Henriquez is waiting for you at the mine," she told me.

A fancy Peugeot 4x4 was waiting outside, its air conditioning hardly noticeable. Wonderful.

"How long is the drive?" I asked.

"Five hours," Thérèse said. "The first three hours are on a good road; you'll be able to rest and relax."

Rest and relax? As soon as we left Cayenne, Thérèse turned onto a very rudimentary road (not even two lanes, let alone a proper highway) and immediately sped up to 160 kilometers an hour, which sent me into an unbearable panic. I was consumed by thoughts of imminent death. Why were we going so fast? I didn't dare ask her to slow down, but if a dog ran into the road or we hit a pothole—and I saw several—we'd go flying. We'd crash into the trees in the jungle. Every so often the chassis of an abandoned car appeared.

Palms, towering trees, lush vegetation, and sometimes, when we got nearer the ocean, mangrove swamps. The same landscape I saw on my way from Suriname.

I almost wept when we turned off onto a smaller road that cut through the trees. We were slowing down! Containing my fear had given my abs a workout equivalent to an hour at the gym. As if that weren't enough, every so often the idiot would ask me if I wanted to listen to anything in particular and would let go of the steering wheel to dig for a CD in the driver's side door. I almost screamed.

Now that I'm writing it all down, my stomach's hurting again. The road is striking. The treetops cover the sky. Sunlight doesn't enter directly, and there's a greenish light, like those low-wattage bulbs. The road becomes a track, and the dirt is the color of clay. There are prehistoric plants. I don't know the names—they look like ferns or bromeliads. If a dinosaur lumbered out from behind them, I wouldn't be surprised. Moisture drips off the leaves, as if they were sweating; a carpet of crushed branches covers the ground.

The Peugeot had amazing suspension, which my kidneys appreciated, since the ineffable Thérèse stepped on it again. Finally we reached a hill, and to the right a wooden tower appeared. Thérèse just honked, and the guards waved and signaled for her to drive through. At the third tower, tents appeared along with a wooden hut with a corrugated metal roof.

There, wearing rubber boots and with a pistol at his waist, Fabinho was waiting for me.

"Welcome to Ouro Amazónico," he said. "First I should note that for security reasons, we don't allow photos. If you need some for your article, there's an archive of recent and stock images that guarantee us protection and maximum security."

The men in the towers had machine guns and, it looked like, assault rifles.

"I see it's a dangerous job," I said.

"I'd love not to have these armed guards, which make the operation look . . . I can't think of the word . . ."

"Illegal?"

He looked at me, amused. "Well, no . . . You have quite a sense of humor. The company is completely legal; it's fully registered and . . . what is it they say? Compliant, that's it. As you know. But since it's in the jungle and has guards, it looks like a guerrilla camp. There's nothing we can do about that. Come this way. Shall I show you around?"

We went to the gold deposits. The light was different there. The sun poured in through the hole left by felled trees. A machine similar to the ones used for oil drilling was punching into the earth to break the crust and access the deeper layers. Fabinho explained that those drills, with their steel heads, crushed fifteen tons of rock every twelve hours and extracted them with suction tubes into an enormous bucket, where the stone was washed and smashed. There were about fifteen grams of gold in each ton.

"Ever since I was very young, I've worked in underground mines, and it was there that I started to get to know the seam. We looked for what's known as the vein, which technically is an inclined mass of exquisite auric chloride, mixed with quartz. It seems incomprehensible, right? Gold is in something known as ferruginous pyrites, impregnated with arsenic. There are other minerals too: white, needle-like crystals and impure aluminum sulfate, embedded in the walls."

He waved his hand in the air, as if to erase what he'd said, and added, "These words seem like gibberish to you, but they are a miner's psalms. Each occupation has its own language. I was born hearing them, and through them I came to know the world. God made language for that purpose. A dog or a chimpanzee can express rage or fear, but they can't wonder about the meaning of life, right? And because they can't, they don't think about it. What came first? I'm a creationist, so I believe the Bible when it says that the first thing was the Word. Everything is explained by that. Look around—you won't see anything but foliage and bushes. And do you know why? Because you don't know the name of each plant. Whereas the indigenous people go into the jungle and read. To you it's just landscape."

Next to the water wheels and barracks was a lean-to sheltering something that looked like a catafalque. We walked over. I saw a painting with the image of Christ, a tree trunk made into a cross, and a carving of a hand with tendrils of vines and insects.

"This is our chapel," he said. "We have services here with the workers twice a day."

"Including the guards?"

"Sadly, no," he said. "Since we've been here, bandits have attacked us four times. Satan is with them."

"Thieves?"

"Yes, people looking to take advantage of other people's labor."

"What do the police say?"

"The officers come, make their report, take names, and leave. Nothing ever happens."

"They don't protect you?"

"Our contract says it's our company's responsibility. Anyway, we don't want to make too much of a fuss because, you know, plenty of people don't want us around. If we become a problem, they'll end up shutting us down, and only the bandits will win, the people engaged in illegal mining."

We went back to a wooden bungalow where an office was set up. He offered me coffee. We sat in director's chairs.

"Tell me about your work as a pastor."

"Miss, the most important thing to me is to communicate Jesus's word to many people. To reach as many souls as possible. That's my aim."

I looked him in the eye. "Why?"

He was a little taken aback. "Why? Well, because . . . it's the right thing to do. It's what must be done to glorify God's word and his work on Earth."

He sat in silence and, for the first time, looked down.

"I understand that, but why do you do it?" I persisted.

"Because . . . Like I said, because it's the right thing to do . . ."

From outside, jungle sounds drifted in: birds taking flight, animals running, branches rubbing in the wind, amphibians croaking somewhere. And above it all a deafening noise: the crash of the drills striking the subsoil and the steady rhythm of the water wheels, like the sound of the sea on rocks.

"Maybe I should tell you a little more about my life. Sometimes I get theoretical and forget that the substance that people are made of is memory. If you would, please join me in an exercise in memory."

With that, he closed his eyes and lifted his arms for a few seconds, as if invoking some jungle spirit. It was moving and a little ridiculous. Then he looked at me and began to speak.

What I transcribe here, again without corrections or cuts, is his direct narrative:

First of all, you should know that I'm your typical socially embittered person. Why hide it? It's part of me. I walk down the street and see other people, I watch the way most of them laugh and talk, busily coming and going. For them life is a piece of warm toast that they load up with delicious things: butter and then a bit of ham, cheese, gherkins, slices of tomato. Other people spread dulce de leche or jam for a sweet flavor, and from there they start taking bites of it, if you get what I'm saying. Nibble, nibble, nibble.

That gives their life meaning and makes it something to savor, because the task of living is to endure, even to thrive in this long span of time that was granted to us for our existence. It can be sad and bitter, or it can be sweet. That's why those who triumph smile.

Seeing those people, I used to feel sadness. That's what my life was like for many years.

I had pain in my stomach, a burning sensation akin to an ulcer that ruined my digestion. The symptomology of resentment. Other people's smiles were a dagger in my belly. Why?

Throughout my life I've experienced lack of love, humiliation, fear, loneliness; I have been pushed out for no reason from places where I was comfortable and happy; I have endured the indifference of people I loved; I have felt jealousy and pain when I saw others receiving the love I craved, the attention I needed; I begged a thousand times, but always in vain.

Nobody listened to me.

I've been lucky to experience all those things, which now have converted into an enormous fortune. Time is a stream of water. It gradually heals everything, washes everything. The cruelest and most painful things fade away. Memory is there to prevent complete healing. That's why some addicts flee from memory, a well-honed knife that reminds you: this is how it was, this is how you felt, it was there and now it's gone, you lost it for ever, you loved something and it went away, you used to be so happy, they died because of you, they left without a word, you were a kid, they humiliated you, you want to go back and it's not possible, the door is closed, you want a smile, just one, they're gone, left for good, they're buried, mother, friend, brother, father, I'm alone, I'm scared.

Fabinho wiped away a couple of tears and looked up at the

heavens again, as if expecting to be refreshed by a nonexistent drizzle.

He pulled himself back together and kept talking.

I scream and scream, Where are you? *And sometimes that scream is the scream of someone calling down the tunnel of a mine, toward the darkest, deepest center—can you imagine?* C'est dure. *The only reply is its own echo. When a person screams into the darkness, what reply is possible? None. When a person screams into soil that has been partially pried open, who replies? Nobody. When a person is at the seashore and is dragged off by a tsunami and gnawed by salt, who listens to him? The sea? The wind?*

We are irremediably alone.

You're the only one who'll listen to you. An enormous silence that means being alone and never getting a response to what you say. Like the loneliness of Christ, who suffered and was abandoned by his father. That is where ignorant man's understanding breaks down. It is the vastest silence.

Why do you do it? *you ask me.*

After much suffering, I found words inside me. Tattered though many of them were, they were still useful. Until I learned those words, I could not look at myself. I understood their meaning. Like a tremendous author who writes the book of the life of all humans and all animals and minerals and fire and water.

Can you imagine writing the story of water?

I do that.

Can you imagine writing the story of the wind and the trees that murmur when the wind moves them?

I write that story every day.

Can you imagine writing the story of fire and of the wood that transforms into fire?

Or writing the story of the birds, even those that are already dead?

I write it.

Every story that's told is the story of a fall, because nobody tells happy lives. Just living them is enough.

And so my story is the story of my fall.

My parents sold me when I was a boy.

They sold me to a mine in Minas Gerais. I was seven years old. And so I grew up in a world of tough, unrefined men. My games were solitary races between the barracks. My toys were old, broken tools from the equipment storeroom. To a kid, a toy is not a passing fancy, it's a need. I made believe as best I could, with empty hands. I always wondered how much my parents got for me. What my price had been. I once asked the old mine foreman, but he didn't remember.

I concluded it couldn't have been much. They purchased my sense for navigating seams of gold, which is like navigating air or water.

When I was twelve a priest taught me to read and told me I wasn't an orphan. That we were all children of God. He is your father, he told me, forget everything else. Pray to him every day, you know the prayer. And every day I did; even today I still do. My other father was a poor man, ignorant and without malice. That's the way life is when things are tough. You have to understand where a man's coming from, and forgive. It took me a long time to be ready for forgiveness, but in the end it swelled inside me. It's like love: nobody can force us to love or to forgive. Sometimes you can and sometimes you can't. But it's better to forgive because unforgiveness *is resentment, it perforates the colon and inhibits protein absorption. I read that somewhere, I can't remember where. I like mixing science with life, excuse me.*

I'll continue.

I see photos of the mines I worked in and I feel dizzy. I hear the name Congonhas, where I lived, and I am seized by a great bewilderment; being an adult means no longer being afraid. Or being afraid of other things. I wanted to go unnoticed, to stop being the kid everybody felt sorry for, and I decided to make up another life.

I made up that my parents had died in an epidemic of the Spanish flu, that they'd emigrated to Ouro Preto or Belo Horizonte, and that, when I was older, they'd come looking for me.

And so I became part of a different group of kids. Not the abandoned ones now, but the ones who had someone who'd "come looking for them." In that group there was hope, and the kids were fragile. I was strong. We drank together, got high. We thought life was going to give us a second chance, you know? Like a gambler, you're convinced you can recover what's been lost.

I filled up with rage and often went out looking for fights as a way to let off steam. I always found them, and afterward, once I'd broken somebody's nose and was being hauled off in hand-cuffs to the police station, people would glare at me and call me scum or thug. It was true, though it wasn't my fault. Nobody said, He was sold as a child, he raised himself. *There was no way for them to know. And I took some hard blows. Because of one fight, I lost my sense of taste. It's a pity. I lost the flavors of food. And I love food.*

I pause Fabinho's account here only to note that with that last sentence, a deafening rainstorm opened up on the jungle. I don't remember ever hearing rain fall so hard in my life. Maybe it's always like that here. The branches bend, forming aqueducts that create even more torrential streams, and when they hit the ground they seem to break it open, pierce it like mining drills. The fiber cement and corrugated metal roofs writhe. It smells like wet earth. That incredible smell drives into your nostrils with the force of the water falling from the sky. The workers continue on, unflustered, accustomed to these incredible storms.

A vegetal vision of the apocalypse.

That's how I grew up, until something happened. In every life there's an incident that changes things, don't you think? If I'd known, I would have just sat down calmly and waited, but, not knowing, every day was like being in a race I had to win. One afternoon, coming out of the barracks where the miners had their bunks, I saw a man in city clothes. He looked like he was from another world. He was sitting in the mine cafeteria and talking to the foremen. I was headed toward the library, where I used to study on my own, when one of them pointed at me. I noticed they were scrutinizing me carefully. A whistle and then my name.

"Hey, Fabio, come here."

I was nineteen. I'd been living there more than twelve years. Three days later I was leaving in a car for Belo Horizonte. The man was Colonel Wagner Cardoso, mining tycoon, who had an operation in the Amazon. He needed somebody like me and paid my way out. He bought me. I got the equivalent of a thousand dollars, and he told me he'd pay me every month.

It was my chance; I took it. Somebody up there had finally seen me.

In Belo Horizonte I got on a plane for the first time and flew to Brasília. I'd never seen the world from above. It seemed to me I was lucky to have been born in it, though I didn't really know why. We arrived in Brasília, but I didn't leave the airport. We waited a couple of hours, and I entertained myself by studying a map. I traced the route we'd flown with my finger. At bottom I was still a kid, a little boy. Later we left on a small prop plane, heading for Macapá. Through the window I saw the Amazon River. Dark, wide, ancient. Intimidating. We landed and went to sleep at a hotel. Mr. Cardoso was nice and paid for a room for me, plus dinner and breakfast. The next day we headed out really early, and I soon saw the jungle for the first time. The

town where we would be staying was Água Branca do Amapari.
A good place.

With what he'd be paying me, Mr. Cardoso said, I'd be able
to rent a room. Or live in the mining barracks, if I'd prefer that.
I said that for now I'd stay at the mine, while I got to know
the place and made a few friends. Cardoso thought it was a good
idea.

And so my Amazonian life began.

Again I pause F's story.

After lunch at the barracks that served as the dining hall
and a walk down a trail to a river that frightened me with how
beautiful and incredibly wild it was, we decided to go back to
Cayenne. The rain stopped suddenly, but for more than half an
hour water continued to drip from the trees, and the jungle
gradually woke up from the deluge. Like a city putting itself
back together after a violent bombing.

Fabinho grabbed the keys to a 4x4 and gestured for me to
hop in. Thérèse Denticat came along with us. I was glad she
wasn't at the wheel. We left the camp at around four. We drove
the unpaved track, and only when we reached the main road
did Fabinho resume his tale. Before he continued, he asked if
Ms. Denticat's presence posed any problem. I said it didn't.

In the Amazon I was reborn. The sun was different. Different
food. When you eat new things, your body changes. It is
renewed. Every seven years our cells die and are replaced by oth-
ers that retain our DNA; that's why we age. Our fears, our para-
noias remain. And the malaises concealed in our memory. The
things we have suffered are a source of wealth. Ah, oui. Human
beings are well made; they're perfect machines. Look at our
hands, able to beat something to death or gently stroke the grass.
God is a marvelous corporal engineer, miss. Sometimes I picture
him assembling his finest creation: man.

What incredible work!

It was an open mine, not like the ones in Congonhas. We were on the surface. There's nothing a miner longs for more than air. Though at times, I admit, there's also a desire to be deep in the earth, which is like being close to a wild heart. The old clock of the world with its tick-tock, over and over. The desire to be buried, the return to the womb. Do I sound like a psychologist? Not even close. Pas du tout! I'm a person who observes life, in silence, and draws his conclusions.

Small, unimportant . . . No doubt. But mine. I am an incomplete human, but that did not cause me grief; rather, it gave me strength. It's a contradiction, but so am I. You know what? If contradiction were a product, I'd be its most loyal customer. If it were a drug, I'd be the biggest addict. My drug of choice is contradiction. Sorry, I get carried away . . . Like I said earlier, I'm a chatterbox. Did I say that? I don't remember.

We understand each other, you and I.

The years passed, and one day I realized I'd become a man. I was living in a small house. Mr. Cardoso's wages went up over time—he was a fair, generous boss, and I was able to improve my station. The mine, the house. On my days off, I would go to Macapá to stare at the Amazon. A man staring at a river. Nobody can stare at a river without wondering about the meaning of things, and it was there that I started thinking about Christ.

A river doesn't just lead to the sea; it also leads to the darkest places of the universe, to the idea of an origin. After spending one Saturday afternoon at the port watching people and boats go by, I decided to visit a chapel for the first time. I tiptoed in and was soon filled with a strange feeling. As if that place had been waiting for me, or something even more intimate: as if the dim light and the air that smelled of melted candle wax knew me. There was nobody there at that hour of day, just a young man sweeping in the back. I sat down on one of the pews and looked around at the figures on the walls. I felt intimidated, but as the light grew dimmer, I understood that it was my place.

My place in the world.

Soon I heard voices. A very loud one said, Fabio, once a boy and now a man, why did you take so long in coming? I went up to the front of the church, where the voice seemed to be coming from. And I heard, It doesn't matter, don't bother answering. You have come, and now you will never leave. I felt all sorts of things—ah, oui, things I wouldn't be able to describe, miss, because I swiftly convinced myself of something: it was the voice of my father, the ignorant man who abandoned me and whom I had forgiven. It was my pain. Maybe those voices were at the end of the road, waiting for me.

I had to go to them.

I returned to Água Branca do Amapari and went to sleep in the mine barracks. Now I needed to be close to the jungle. At night in the midst of all those trees, there is great peace, great calm. The animals have hunted and mated; the quiet is vast. It's what I needed: that silence that rises from the earth. The jungle keeps going when we're not in it; everything we don't see is breathing. Do you understand? There's only one other thing like it: the bottom of the ocean. There is life there, and something moves in that instant—there's a murmur of undersea currents and a blind fluttering and jaws that yawn open to devour something. That is happening now, miss—can you imagine it?

Where we are not present, something is happening that is mysterious and unsettling. The jungle taught me that.

There I found the figure of Jesus; I studied him, loved him, and most of all embodied him. You can't love the son of God without transforming into him, and that's what I did. The first church I built was there, at the mine. One Saturday morning I collected some materials and set up a little altar at the far end of the barracks. When Mr. Cardoso saw it, he told me, "That's great, Fabio, that way we can gather ourselves for a moment and ask forgiveness for our sins."

"Thank you, sir," I said, "but I don't have any sins. My life here is exemplary for God. He knows I have nothing to hide from him."

"It's a manner of speaking, Fabio," he said. "It's a good idea. When you finish it, you can give a lecture about your experience with religion to the other men."

And so the second Fabio was born. The Fabinho who would later build six churches for the Lord Redeemer. Talking to those rough men, who seemed to have the devil in their eyes, transformed me. People started knowing who I was in Água Branca do Amapari and the nearby villages—Serra do Navio, Cupixi, Pedro Branca—and at the other mines. People came to hear me, and gradually a tradition was born of giving a late-Saturday-morning lecture and another on Sunday. I started reading more; it was useful to be more educated. The thirst for knowledge comes from outside us—you know that—and it reels in the listener's energy and intention.

Within a year Mr. Cardoso agreed to build a wooden chapel. He asked people to contribute, and everybody did, so we were able to complete it. We used it to hold weddings, children's parties, baptisms. For the first time, I was happy; I would open my eyes in the morning and remember that I was someone whom others were eager to hear. I was twenty-three. After about two years, another important thing appeared: woman. A jungle woman, but not indigenous. Her parents were from the coast; they'd come from Rio. They tried their luck with the mines and built a site, but they never found gold (sometimes it hides; sometimes it refuses), so they were forced to find jobs instead. They were well educated and did administrative work. Her name was Clarice, and she was a beautiful young woman with a strong personality. She came to my talks on her own; she never missed a single one. As I was leaving the chapel one day, she asked if she could talk to me alone. She was very open, said I was the only person in the entire jungle who was able to find beauty in words, and she wanted to know if I'd be interested in having a relationship of affection or love—that's how she put it, "of affection or love." I looked at her, surprised, and said, "Of course, I love everybody the same," but Clarice wagged her finger no and said, "I'm not talking about that kind of love. The other kind, the kind that men and women have, do you understand?" I told her I did, but for some strange reason I felt as if I should step back. "I'm not ready, Clarice," I told her. "Give me a little time."

From that day on, when the weekend came, my heart would pound like one of those drills over there; I wanted to see her, I didn't want to see her. She was always there. When I entered the chapel through the rear door, Bible in hand, I'd see her in the front pew. I thought about Christ. Did I love her? I didn't know yet. Sometimes she'd stay to the end with one of the community groups, but she never spoke of her feelings again. She was very generous. She would bring food from home for everybody: a basket of tasty cowpea and shrimp fritters; or chicken croquettes, delicious. She'd come over and place one in my hand, and I'd tell her, "Clarice, you're the best cook in the jungle," and her cheeks would flush—she was very shy. Her eyes seemed to be telling me, I'm waiting for you, I'm waiting for you. Almost two months passed. One Sunday afternoon I was fishing in the ravine alone when I heard a noise. I turned to look and saw Clarice walking toward me. I let her come, and as soon as she was close enough, I reached out and pulled her to me and licked her face the way an animal that's been thirsty for days would lap at a puddle of water; my lips clung to her neck as if I was trying to extract something. And love began, miss. Please excuse this strange story; as I tell it now, I am reliving it. Christ, the power of words!

Clarice became part of my life. She started helping me during my lectures by reading texts—she had a pretty voice and read *well. She would bring me lunch at work during the week and tidy my little house. She'd get me flowers. One day she announced she was coming to live with me. Just like that.*

"From now on I want to live here with you," she told me. "If you don't want that, tell me and I'll go."

"I do want it," I said.

I helped her organize her clothing on the board-and-brick shelves. I asked her what side she preferred to sleep on and made the bed larger with a few planks. I worked hard, wore myself out. Whenever I woke up and saw her beside me, I understood the meaning of companionship between people. When someone looks at you and recognizes themselves. You smell their scent, and that burrows deep inside you, into your soul. You say to yourself: I am fragile now, I depend on someone who is not me. Have I made a mistake?

No, because I'm happy.

Months passed, a year.

It was Clarice who said it one day: "We should open our own mine. That's enough working to make other people rich."

I told her that Mr. Cardoso was a good man, that I owed everything to him, but she insisted: "Of course he's a good man, but he's someone else. He's not you or me. He has his own desires and pursues them and achieves them. Does he pursue yours? No, of course not. Yours are yours. His are his. But now yours are mine too. They're ours. Right? Why can't we pursue them now?"

I told her it was risky; we had nothing, and the jungle was foreign and sometimes unjust. What if we lost the job and the house?

"No," she told me, "no."

We had that discussion in complete darkness, very late at night, which is when words have value, as if they've been silently stamped by a notary, and she kept saying, "You're not going to lose, you're only going to gain, and you'll gain a lot, and so will

I along with you, we'll both gain, that's what I see when I close my eyes and think about time stalking us; here in the jungle we're surrounded by eyes. Something is always watching you. Especially at night. All we see is little eyes shining, signs on a map. And the anxious gaze of hidden animals is them waiting. As if to say: When are you going to own a mining operation? When are you going to be the one who collects what the earth conceals?"

She said I knew the soil and how to find gold, and that was the most important thing. The rest could be achieved with effort. Knowing is the most valuable thing, and you have that, she said.

I listened to her as I lay in bed, under the mosquito net, naked on a clean sheet that Clarice changed every day. Even though we were alone, we were whispering. It was hot, and our words expanded in the air. From time to time the sound of a manatee drifted in through the window.

You know, and together we can.

With that sentence ringing in my head, I went to work the next day, and the rest of the week. "Did you talk to Mr. Cardoso?" she'd ask when I came home, and I'd say, "No, not yet. I'll find the right moment."

Until the day came. I went to Mr. Cardoso's office and asked to talk to him. He invited me in. I explained that I wanted to start a family and open my own operation, further upriver, deeper into the jungle.

"Is there something you'd like to have that you don't have here?" he asked, understanding, but I told him no. "It's not my idea, it's Clarice's. She thinks we might get lucky. We have a little money saved, and with what I make selling some of my belongings I'll be able to buy a boat to go upriver, to the Upper Pará. I've been thinking about exploring the Araquã region. I can hire Indians. I know I owe you my life, Mr. Cardoso, don't think I'm not grateful."

The man came over and said, "I understand. I didn't inherit

*this either. In my youth I felt the same way, and if that's the case,
you should go. Upriver. You'll find something. And if you don't,
you can come back. No hard feelings. Only friendship and help.
I'll come to your aid if you have any problems. You can take
some old gear. Pickaxes and hammers and shovels. Borrow some
baskets. Go with God, my friend."*

*He shook my hand, and I left his office and went home.
Clarice looked at me, worried that I was back so early. "I talked
to him, we're free," I said. She flung herself at me.*

At this point in the story we reached Cayenne. As we drove
into the city, he suggested we go to Les Palmistes. It was after
six in the evening. It was starting to get dark, and I wondered,
Why am I doing all this? I assumed that his journey must, at
some point, intersect with Fritz's.

I no longer disliked him. That evaporated as I listened to
his life story. Is this sensitive, Christian man really capable of
an attack like the one the kid described?

We'll see.

*I went to Araquá on my own and started searching near the
rivers and streams, near the waterways. Wide beaches where you
could set up a small base from which to travel into the jungle. I
touched the earth, sucked the stones I pulled out, smeared myself
with mud. I found a place and marked it, then returned for
Clarice and the Indians. We worked for five months, and when
I next went to town again I was carrying two kilos of gold, well
concealed in my backpack. Mr. Cardoso accompanied me to
Macapá to open a bank account. We celebrated. And so my life
as an* orpailleur, *a gold miner, began, following the currents of
the rivers. It was a different kind of work from in a big mine.
The veins I worked were small and close to the surface. They ran
out faster.*

Two years later I went to live in Manaus and opened an office to arrange expeditions in the area. It was hard work, but I was young and strong. There was a lot of mining there.

One day I met someone who, like me, led expeditions. He was a Colombian guy named Arturo.

We went out together twice and were successful. He was a good organizer—he knew how to handle the Indians and spoke good Portuguese. He'd escaped from the violence in your country—just think, when he arrived in Manaus, the guerrilla had issued two orders for him to be killed. He told me the story one night while we were drinking cachaça in the middle of the jungle. He'd learned river mining in the Putumayo, but after a few months the FARC demanded a cut of his earnings. He refused to give them money—big mistake. They came back and told him it was the last time they'd come in peace. Arturo was aggressive and told them, "Come after it if you want, my labor is my own labor." They came back and burned the hut where he kept his gear. He wasn't there—it was a miracle he escaped. He saw it burning from a distance.

He fled to another area, near the Ecuadorian border, and the same thing happened. After seven months the FARC showed up at his camp. This time he didn't even wait to talk to them. He jumped in his boat and fled downriver. That's how he arrived in Brazil. He'd been in a mine for three years, but he wanted to open his own operation. That night, with the heat of the cachaça in our spirits, we decided to become partners. We returned to Manaus the next day and started making plans. He had a good idea, though it wasn't very legal, to mine in the Tarapacá region, in Colombia, a hundred and fifty kilometers from Leticia, on the Cotuhé and Putumayo Rivers. He knew the area well and had experience; we wouldn't need much: a boat, a hydraulic dredge, good hoses, and diving suits.

What else do we need? I asked, and Arturo pondered a moment and said, "About four divers. You have to be underwater a lot, and one person can't handle it longer than three hours.

Plus some guys to run the machine and keep an eye on what's coming out of the hose. And that's it—easy, right?"

I asked how illegal it was. He told me that in Colombia, like in Brazil, you needed to apply for a license. "So why don't we apply for one?" I asked, and he said, "That's the problem, it's an indigenous reservation, and it's prohibited without the local government's permission, and they'll never agree to it. That's the bad part, but there's a good part too," he said. "Because it's a reservation, there's not much security, and it's easy to disguise yourself as a fishing boat; the indigenous communities don't like people coming into their rivers, but they aren't violent."

And he told me, "I know how to deal with them."

I told Clarice, and she said, "All right, if it's good money, maybe it's worth the risk once, to see how it goes."

Clarice was intrepid. I wasn't. I grew up terrified of losing the little I had. I was always insecure, but she would push me, "Go on, you have to take risks to get ahead, it's worth it." I told her I loved her, I felt her strength in me. That's what she meant for me: the world, life. I agreed, and we started the strange business. The first time we traveled upriver with Arturo and the men we'd hired, I was uneasy. Nobody talked—it was late, and all you could hear was the murmur of the bow cleaving the water. We smoked, looked at the stars and the unsettling blackness of the jungle on either side of the river. The jungle makes whatever you have inside you more intense, whether that's ambition, cowardice, or just fear. Did I say just? My God, if you're fearful, in the jungle you tremble down to your marrow.

That's what I felt that night.

But it went well. We stopped the boat, and a diver plunged into the black water, a hose tied to his waist. After a bit he gave it two hard yanks, and we connected it to the dredge. The motorized pump started up. It seemed like the noise must be audible for hundreds of kilometers, but nobody came. We dredged up rocks and silt, and then gold started to appear, little by little.

Arturo was right. It was easy. We kept going back for more than a year until we were able to open a small office in Tabatinga, across the Brazilian border from Leticia. Have you been? Then, in time, we got better organized and started sending groups of Indians with dredges to other rivers. We got mercury so we could burn the ore and extract more gold. Once an army boat searched us, but when they saw we didn't have any weapons they kept going.

They were looking for guerrilla fighters.

But a problem arose: Clarice didn't like Arturo. She tried to get along with him, but when she met him she said he was dark, strange, bad; that we needed to be careful. She managed the accounting books, convinced that sooner or later the Colombian—and pardon me for saying so, miss—was going to swindle us and bring us trouble. I would say, "Don't be like that, why do you think that? He's quiet and reserved, but he's a good guy."

The business thrived, but after a while we started having problems. One night a diver died when he got tangled in some weeds in the river. He couldn't get free; it was a tragedy. It took hours to pull him out. Another time the army came again in a boat and seized everything. The indigenous community started complaining because the mining process stirred up the water and scared off the fish. Diesel fuel and mercury polluted the river, and they cooked with its water, drank from it. God forgive me! Ah, oui. Life is hard, and a person has the right to survive, no matter what it takes, but it was too much.

The Indians were right, so we arranged with Arturo to give them a percentage of what we brought in. That really pissed off Clarice, who didn't see why they should profit from our labor.

"It's their land, calm down," I'd say.

"They're lazy savages," she'd say, "they don't live any better with our money or buy things for the community; they just drink and visit hookers."

"They're simple people," I'd say, "don't talk about them like that."

Over the years, Clarice became a bitter person. I loved her, but day by day she was changing. She was obsessed with money and the accounts. Once she made a mistake in her calculations and came to me claiming that Arturo was stealing from us. I was on the terrace, smoking a cigarette. She was in a towering rage, with a revolver in her hand.

"Where did you get that?" I asked.

"When I find that thieving Colombian, I swear I'll kill him," she said furiously.

We looked again and saw that she'd been mistaken. She apologized, and I said there was no need for a gun, our life was going great, why invent problems? Seeking a bit of calm, I renewed my passion for Jesus and built a church, which I made part of the international congregation of the Assembly of God. It took several months, and she was excited about it. When I was finished, we invited the neighbors. I restarted my lectures on Saturdays and Sundays and found, to my delight, that that universe remained intact. My words still worked, they resonated with people. I became a Pentecostal pastor. I studied the New Testament.

Arturo used to come to hear me too, though he never participated. He'd sit in one of the rear pews and, as I spoke, peel an orange very slowly or whittle a piece of wood with his knife. Like any good loner, Arturo was methodical. He didn't like having a house, so he lived in rented rooms. I visited him only once, and asked, "How can you live like this? You earn good money, you could buy a house, have a wife."

"I have what I need," he said. And then silence.

He used to come over to eat with us often. I hoped that if Clarice got to know him, she'd stop harassing me with her ideas about embezzlement and scams. For Christmas and New Year's, we'd have a party at the office with the indigenous people and the boat people, and he was always very generous. He gave the *employees incredible gifts. He once gave Clarice a beautiful watch, but she said, "He bought it with the money he's stealing from us."*

One day I got home and found Clarice in bed, her eyes red from crying. "What's going on?" I thought something was wrong, but she told me she was happy.

"I'm pregnant," she said.

A huge wave of heat, like a nuclear warhead going off, ran down my spine. I was going to have a baby? Reality shattered into a thousand pieces; I felt that this tiny being was coming to save me. The past might contain only sadness, but the future was hope. That's how I saw it, and I started crying too. She was three months along, and she was supposed to rest at least until the fifth month to prevent complications.

Pregnancy changes women, miss, maybe you know that already. And she got worse, ah, oui! Anything that happened in our daily life could turn into a problem. Or even into rage. I was afraid for the baby in her belly—would her fury harm it? Sometimes at night she'd calm down, and I'd press my ear to her belly. I wanted to hear the heartbeat, and sometimes I thought I did. At other times, Clarice would cry, sleepless, in the middle of the night. "What's wrong?" I'd ask, and she'd just stare into the darkness and say, "I don't know, Fabio, I don't know," and keep sobbing. I went to talk to the doctor, and he told me not to worry, that it was normal for pregnant women, but I was convinced there was no way such a happy event to come could be the cause of so much anguish, of the immense desolation I saw in Clarice; if I said anything, she'd find a way to turn it around and vent at me, hurling awful insults. Then she'd start crying, throw her arms around me, and apologize.

I said to her that it was normal in her condition. "Your body is flooded with progesterone and estrogens," I'd explain. "Hormones affect your neurotransmitters, the messengers between neurons, plus there are all the changes happening in your body: your belly swells, your breasts are getting ready for the infant," and she kept asking, "Do you think I'm ugly?" And there was no way to placate her. Once she accused me of sleeping with a woman from work, but it was all in her head. She had my child inside her. After the ultrasound, the doctor said it was a boy.

At around that time, a letter arrived from Macapá with sad news. Mr. Cardoso was very sick; he'd had a heart attack, and because of the complications with transport had ended up in a coma. I started calling the hospital or his house every few days. His wife told me he could die at any moment. I thought I should visit him. The fourth time we spoke, I made up my mind. We owed him our life, and it was my duty to see him before he died.

So I arranged the trip. There's a flight that goes from Tabatinga to Manaus, and from there another goes to Macapá, with a layover in Belém. It's a long trip. I would be gone a week, so I asked the Marian Sisters to come keep Clarice company. Two came and stayed at the house, and I felt OK leaving. Clarice saw me off at the airfield. She was very calm—she'd relaxed, and her body was still growing. She asked me to bring her flour and other ingredients, since she wanted to cook her favorite dishes. She handed me a gift for her sister and another for her mother, and we agreed to invite them to our son's birth. I flew over the Amazon, looked down from above at the ocean of green, and mused that my life would always take place there. It was my home. There was nothing for me in Minas Gerais, but there was in Macapá.

When I arrived, I went straight to the hospital. The family greeted me like one of their own and put me up at their house. I sat by Mr. Cardoso's bedside for three days, telling him about my life and my dreams. He was connected to various tubes and was breathing. The nurse said he might be able to hear, that listening helped.

I talked and talked.

I told him about my business operation, about my partnership with Arturo, about Clarice and her anger, about the Putumayo and Cotuhé Rivers, about the barges with dredges, about the hideous noise of the motorized pumps and the darkness at the bottom of the rivers. The only light is from gold, I said, and told him that I'd gradually built a business. We had an office with several employees. We had a future.

On another day Clarice's mother and sister came to the hospital. I met them in a small waiting room, and they asked me to give Mr. Cardoso's family their best wishes. I gave them the gifts, showed them photos. "Is it a boy?" the mother asked. I said yes, we hadn't chosen a name yet. They'd brought a basket of things for Clarice and the baby. We took a couple of photos, and they left in good spirits. I said that we'd send tickets so they could be with Clarice at the birth and for the first few weeks. They were delighted by that.

The last night I asked Mrs. Cardoso to let me sleep at the hospital, keeping her husband company. I slept by his side, except I didn't really sleep. I told him about my childhood just the way I'm telling you about it now. That was the first time; I hadn't even told Clarice. At dawn I embraced Mr. Cardoso, kissed his forehead, and left. I took a taxi to the airfield, now eager to return home. Return trips are always longer because you're impatient to be back, don't you think?

When I arrived, my life changed.

Clarice wasn't at the airfield, so I went to the house and found the door open. Nobody was there, and the rooms were in shambles, with things strewn everywhere. What had happened? I called to her and went out to the courtyard, but nothing. I figured she'd gone out. I was worried to discover that her things were no longer in our bedroom. I opened the dresser drawers, and they were empty. I went to talk to the neighbors. They said they didn't know anything, hadn't seen her for a couple of days. Neither had the nuns. I went to the Marian community, and they told me Clarice had asked the women keeping her company to leave. Was something wrong? My heart pounded in my chest. She was the one who'd told them to leave? "Yes, Clarice drove us back here, saying she was fine, saying you'd be returning soon. She thanked us profusely and gave us some money for the congregation. She's a kind person."

I raced to the office, which was on the second floor of a small four-story building. But before I could go up, a candy seller on the street, Joãozinho, called me over and said, "Mr. Fabio, it's great to see you! Please be careful, they're looking for you. The police came and confiscated things. I saw them come down with boxes of books and folders." Then the neighbors told me they'd sealed off the office and had men guarding it.

I couldn't understand what was happening and didn't know what to do. I called Arturo, but the woman who was renting him a room said he'd left. "When?" I asked. "A couple of days ago."

Everything was upside down. What had happened in my absence? I went home, frightened. Where had Clarice gone? How could I reach her? Maybe she was in hiding. What crime had I committed? I thought about the rivers on indigenous lands. It was illegal, but it didn't seem like a big deal. Arturo had arranged everything. Had he been arrested? I called Joaquim, one of the employees. By some miracle, I found him at home. When I heard his voice, I felt relieved and asked what was going on, but he said we shouldn't discuss it over the phone. We arranged to meet at a café on the outskirts of Tabatinga, on the highway; he said it was dangerous. When? In an hour, the sooner the better.

I took precautions. I arrived early and sat at the darkest table, at the rear of a room that looked out on the tributary of the river. I waited about fifteen minutes until I saw him come in. I waved to him. He sat down at the table, looking scared. "What's going on, Joaquim?"

"Somebody reported what we're doing on the rivers, and the federal police showed up. They seized everything, asked me to open the files. And the thing is, sir. The business account—it was

completely empty! Did you pull out the money? Since you were traveling, we thought you'd taken everything."

"No," I said. "I was visiting a dying friend in Macapá. My wife, Clarice, knew that. What about Arturo?"

"He wasn't there when the police came, sir. It seems like he got away in time."

"I have to find him. Have you heard from my wife?"

"No, sir," Joaquim said, getting more and more nervous.

I saw that sweat was beading on his upper lip. His right eye was twitching.

Suddenly he got up and went to the bathroom, and a second later a dozen police officers came in, weapons drawn. One of them said my full name, told me I was under arrest, and read a very long list of charges. They took me out to the road, where two police vans were waiting. When I walked out I saw Joaquim talking to one of the police officers. "I'm sorry, sir. I had to do it," he said. Poor man, I thought, he believed I'd betrayed them. My head started spinning. What had happened to my life? Suddenly everything was topsy-turvy. I assumed Clarice must have gone into hiding after pulling the money out of the company. But why hadn't she warned me in Macapá? It was an urgent situation—she could have sent a telegram or called her mother to warn me. Where was Arturo? He must have gone back to Colombia.

They took me to jail. They interrogated me. I figured Clarice would show up with a lawyer at any moment. Presumably she knew I'd been arrested. But days went by, and I didn't hear from her. I tried to call her mother in Macapá, with no luck. Was that where Clarice had gone? Why had she fled? She wasn't responsible for what we'd been doing at the company, and she was pregnant.

After two weeks, a young legal intern took my case. He was my contact with the outside world, and he could do me a few favors. I still hadn't heard anything—I was desperate. I asked him to go to my house and talk to the neighbors and tell them I'd been arrested, hoping she'd get in touch. Everybody had disappeared! You can't imagine what every second of the day was like in that cell, in prison alongside drug traffickers from the Familia del Norte, which controls the drugs on the three countries' borders. Rough, dangerous people with no humanity. A month passed, and I thought about death. I imagined stealing a knife and cutting my veins, or a faster method: a gun. I remembered Clarice's pistol. I was alone and abandoned, obsessing about a woman I loved and who was carrying a child who was my son—can you imagine?

Finally a message arrived via the community of Marian nuns. One of the nuns brought it to me. A small envelope with a Colombian postmark. I opened it, shaking with emotion and fear. The letter was just a few lines, very short, that said basically this:

The child isn't yours, Fabio. I ran off with the father and now we're far away. I don't expect you to forgive me, only that one day you will understand and try to forget. Please don't look for me. Pretend it was all a long dream. Clarice

I went into my cell and cried for several days. But as I was deciding to end it all, the truth struck me like a bolt of lightning: Arturo!

She'd run off with him. They'd been having an affair all along, and when Clarice got pregnant things snowballed. They took the money, and he reported me to the police. He'd provided detailed evidence: mining routes, sales networks, everything. Only he and Clarice knew the business inside and out. The ongoing theft that she'd complained about could have been setting the stage for them to run away. And you know what, miss? The hatred I felt in that moment was one of the purest and most uncontaminated feelings I've had in my life. I no longer wanted to commit suicide.

Soon I was sentenced to seven years in prison. The jungle gave me a life, then took it away. But from outside, on the nights I was most in torment, the jungle itself seemed to answer: Wait, be patient. *I slept on a shabby, filthy cot. I lived with vicious men. I sank down into my sorrows, and the only thing that came to me was Christ's name. This time I rebuked him. One night, clutching the bars and listening to three men beat an indigenous boy, a drug dealer, in the next cell, I said, "Christ, you abandoned me in the most difficult moment of my life. Why didn't you warn me what was going to happen? Why did you put that man in my path?"*

Silence, nothing but silence.

Gold, the intense green of the jungle, the heat.

Images of the placid rivers that I ravaged with my pumps and dredges seemed to be telling me: It's your fault, you're a convict, now you're going to pay. *I was burning up with fever. Sweating. I repented and acknowledged my guilt. I waited. Those seven years were the worst, but I endured them in silence, observing humanity and learning from every uncivilized gesture, every grunt. Animals and men, in captivity, are quite similar. I prefer animals. Animals don't need a father, and we do. I didn't have one. And so I was a fragile, incomplete man walking a cliff's edge. Vertigo, and then the fall. Icarus disobeyed and fell, but disobedience requires that somebody restrict us and protect us in the first place. Somebody to fend off the serpent or the jaguar stalking us. But we orphans are alone in the jungle. Our only fathers are the gods. The distant gods . . .*

At that point I interrupted him and asked, "All these things you're telling me happened a long time ago. Have you heard from them since? Have you looked for them?" I knew I was showing my hand, but it was impossible not to ask. Fabinho stared at the table for so long and so intently that someone might have thought he was trying to move the ashtray with his mind. Inside him, his thoughts must have been on fire. The memories were giving him goosebumps. He was clearly fumbling for words.

I never heard anything else. But I did think about them all the time. Especially around the supposed birthday of the little boy, for whom, luckily, we never chose a name. Afterward, when I got out, I returned to Macapá, but soon emigrated north and began a new life here in French Guiana. Things went well for me, and I started up again founding missionary churches in Brazil, since the only security in my life had been Christ.

I gave myself over to him and became one of his most faithful pastors. Every time I struck gold, I would build a new church in the jungle where I was living, which is why today lots of good people have a place to pray in Macapá, Araquã, Pedro Branca, Água Branca do Amapari, Cupixi, and Serra do Navio. Places equivalent to Bethlehem or Nazareth for me. The jungle gave me everything, so I give back to the jungle. I expanded the Assembly of God all over northeastern Brazil, and about once a month I go to give my word to the people. I also travel to other countries and meet with Assembly pastors. I'm taking notes for a book on initiation into faith through my own life. I read a lot, seeking knowledge, but over time I've realized that the only book that still gives me answers is the Good Book. Every day I read it and underline its lessons.

I don't want to appear arrogant, but I think I'm the best Pentecostal preacher in this whole region, and do you know why? Because my word is born not out of study, but out of my untarnished contemplation of the world. That's what divine love did inside me. It crushed me, transformed me. It gave to me and then took away, but it allowed me to survive. Today I've got fourteen churches in the region, built from what I pull from the earth. I don't ask for money from the people who come to listen to me, no. Other preachers do, but not me. And people love me more every day. If I wanted to get involved in politics, people would vote for me. If I wanted to be mayor, governor, even legislator. But I'm not after power, just the power I feel when something speaks through me and the people hear it and fall to their knees. Transforming people's lives—that is my power. If I wanted, I could go far, but I no longer want that. And you know what? As a result, I was able to forgive them.

You might think it unbelievable, or impossible, but I forgave them. And that freed me—I recovered my will to live. I exchanged hatred for something more tenuous: mercy. I felt mercy toward them; I imagined they must be haunted by a sense of guilt. You can flee justice, but not guilt. It always catches up to us. It's an eye looking at us, watching us, tormenting us. I suffered from the enormous damage I did to nature. Today I am glad to have paid my dues to justice.

It was he who fell silent this time, as if to suggest that his story had ended, but I wasn't done yet.

"Do you have a relationship with other Pentecostal churches?" I asked, to see his reaction. "Any in Colombia?"

He thought about it for a minute and took a sip of water. I sensed he was exhausted from his confession, but it was my last chance to fully understand this long tale.

"Yes, we have relationships with sibling and associated churches throughout the continent. Some in Colombia too, but very superficial and never there in the country—only at conferences and international events. You'll understand why I never visit your country."

Before we parted ways, I asked him to show me a photo of Clarice. He opened his billfold, rifled through some cards, and found it. I thought it was odd he still carried it with him. It was a very old and somewhat faded image of a couple beside a river, in the jungle.

I didn't recognize her at first, but it was her. Egiswanda,

Fritz's girlfriend. There was a silence—I didn't know what to say. She's very beautiful, I said. I'm really sorry.

He tucked the picture back into his wallet. He drank down the rest of his sparkling water and said, "All right, miss, you know my life story now; all that's left is to wish you a good life. Telling you all this brought back painful memories, but it's a great relief to dig them out and see that they fit together by unexpected principles. *C'est la vie!* You know how to listen because you know how to write—I didn't mention I've read some of your articles. Or did I? Congratulations. I enjoyed them. I'll be off now. Thank you for your interest and attention. I don't know what I'll do in the future—I might stay here, or I might not. The only thing I possess is my love for Jesus. My hands are empty." Gazing upward once more as if praying, he added, "I'm not young, I'm not old. I have lived. It's time to think seriously about death."

He got up and signaled to the waiter to put the check on his tab. He went down the steps to the street, surrounded by his bodyguards. Just as he was about to climb into the vehicle, I called from the terrace, "What was Arturo's last name?"

He hesitated a moment. "Silva," he said. "Arturo Silva Amador. But please don't mention him."

"Don't worry," I said.

"Goodbye again."

His SUV pulled away, followed by two others. I raced to the hotel to transcribe everything in my notebook. *So that was that,* I thought.

I pictured him returning home, alone. A man broken inside, shattered into mismatching pieces of unequal value, like the subsoil from which gold is extracted.

There was no longer any doubt: Fabinho had organized the attack in Tierradentro, seeking revenge on Arturo (Fritz), who'd run off with his pregnant wife, stolen his company's money, and framed him for the authorities. I felt an overwhelming desire to be in Cali and see Fritz. The end of this story pointed straight to the traitor. What would he say? What would his version of events be? Where was Clarice's son? How had he known that Fabio had found him and was setting up the ambush?

The next day, before beginning the long trip back to Bogotá, I sent a message to Jutsiñamuy that said, "I have everything now—I'm heading back there. I'll arrive tomorrow or the day after. We can confirm Mr. F's identity. Please look into a Colombian by the name of Arturo Silva Amador."

Hours later, when I arrived at the Suriname airport, I had a message from Jutsiñamuy: "That's great. I'll be expecting you. We've got some surprises here too."

PART IV

WILD ANIMALS

W hen he reached Bogotá, the prosecutor went straight to his office. It was six in the evening. One of his favorite hours of the day, out of the many he spent in that oblong, messy office that had ended up becoming home. More than that: the perfect container for his soul. He liked to gaze out at the spine of the mountains in the fading light and the pinkish glow on the rooftops and terraces. They looked like they were alive: like a giant breathing as he sleeps, believing himself innocent. Houses helpless in the face of the orphaned state that takes hold of the city just before night falls. He made himself a cup of green tea with water from the urn and opened his laptop. He lay down on the sofa, lifted his feet against the wall, and waited. Seven minutes. Then he turned on the computer. He smiled to see that one of the messages was from Wendy.

Confidential Report #3
Agent KWK622
Place: Cali
Operation: Holy Spirit
Date: Date of email sent

A. *In this report I will elaborate on certain activities already alluded to in previous communications, ones related to the nighttime movements of Pastor Fritz and some of his follow-ers—namely, certain women who, having been addicted to drugs or caught up in other vices, must have been easy marks for the practices I will detail below, just as they were described to me by the participants.*

B. *The testimonies were obtained during nighttime social interactions with a group of these women, who, under the influence of shots of unsweetened Blanco del Valle aguardiente, became quite chatty. To this writer's surprise, despite some of them being former drug addicts, they had no problem drinking aguardiente, and when I asked whether it jeopardized their sobriety, they all said that hard drugs were one thing, especially coca paste, whereas having a drink with friends was wholesome entertainment, something that Jesus himself would have approved of—after all, there was the story of that famous party where he turned water into wine, a miracle that only a real party animal would have thought to pull off, since it's every drinker's fondest dream. Another woman argued that since the liquor was unsweetened, it wasn't a problem. Once they'd ordered their second bottle from the Estrellita de Oriente shop on the corner of 38th Street and 6th Avenue, the confessions began.*

C. *What most struck this writer was the sexualized, lascivious tenor of these nighttime gatherings, especially given that they were linked to the pastor of a church that, while evangelical, purports to observe a set of virtuous or at least more prudent behaviors. But according to these women, it's quite the opposite, and on the weekends the pastor makes use of an apartment of his near Menga to bring in women, of the highly skilled variety, and invite friends or acquaintances to partake in vices of all sorts, involving these women with no real agency. Their testimonies include standard accounts of not just harassment but also rape through coercion and exploitation of power dynamics, since it is the church itself, when the time comes, that will be responsible for assessing culpability. In addition, the apartment is generally overflowing with all* sorts of liquor and drugs, though only the men consume the latter. The parties involve music, dancing, and playing games that inevitably end up in explicit situations, such as a woman being forced to perform oral sex on one of the men in front of everybody, or even several men, since that's how the game penalties are set up, until each woman ends up engaging in the act with one of the men present and sometimes more than one, depending how long the party lasts.

D. One of the young women, a devotee of the pastor named Cindy Raquel, told me the following. I'll transcribe it here: "The guy picked me up and carried me to a little room in the back that's really more like a suite in a fancy hotel, a brothel, you know? There the pastor became a man, a male, with spittle on his lips, his eyes green with dilated pupils, probably because of the coke, and kind of by force he threw me on the bed, and I say 'kind of' because I knew where things were going anyway, though I would have preferred being treated less like a blow-up doll, some kind of cheesy little kiss or caress, but anyway, the guy was really horny, his cock standing straight up, you know, with the artillery ready and aimed at the enemy, and without any further preamble he yanked off my jeans and underwear and splayed me on the mattress. He straddled over me, me with my legs wide open and expectant. I saw him undo his pants with his right hand, the same one he crosses himself with, and pull out his massive prick— it was huge, like a boxer's arm, dark and veiny—and then he pushed my knees farther apart, and I said to myself, So we're going with the roast chicken, and before I knew it he was embedded in my tonsils, shoving my head up and down, grabbing my hair kind of rough. I tried to pull away, but the guy grabbed me harder. Then I pressed my teeth into him so it would hurt, but the pastor glared at me and said in a sweet voice, 'Open that fucking mouth a little wider, little girl' and I didn't dare continue that strategy. Finally he got tired and

*stuck it in the usual place, and I was able to catch my breath.
I let him go to town, splayed out like a chicken on a spit, but
suddenly a thought struck me like a lightning bolt, and I said
to myself,* Oh, fuck, this bastard better not come inside me,
*I remembered it was a bad time of month for that kind of
input, bunny in heat, baby, watch out, the factory is running
full blast! So I pushed and tensed up to see if he would notice,
but no, the guy kept doing his thing. Then he turned me over
and put me on all fours, and I thought,* I should encourage
him from behind, *and I used my hand to guide him, inviting
him but not saying anything, and the pastor, who's supposed
to represent God here in this earthly shithole but turns out to
be a horny male like all the rest, took the bait and, to my
relief, plunged into the little alleyway, through the back door,
as they say, and I was able to relax. When he finished and I
saw him get up I felt bad, real guilty.* 'We aren't going to be
punished for this up there, are we, pastor?' *I asked, and he
looked at me very tenderly and said,* 'Don't worry, Cindy.
Every time you pull down your panties, an angel is born in
heaven.'"

E. *I also include here the story of Yismeny Laura, who emigrated to Cali from Corozal, Sucre:* "Oh, yeah, that guy took
me into the bathroom and flattened me over the sink. I was
wearing a miniskirt, which is your best bet at those parties, so
the man stuck his hand in, pulled my thong to one side, and
started really plowing me, massive cock he had, and I was
watching him in the mirror, like in the rearview: he popped
in a little blue pill and chewed it like a mint or a Coffee
Delight, then sprinkled a line of coke across my ass, and I
think the stuff ended up getting me too, with all the writhing
and rubbing, because after the pastor finished, I was shrieking and hopping around until six in the morning with the
other guys—not the security guys, I know them, but real
fancy dudes, sophisticated and totally loaded—they looked*

like business partners." I asked for some details about those "partners," and Yismeny said, "They're almost always staff from other churches, pastors or people who work for them, in marketing or accounting; there are also government officials or people from the mayor's office or even the police, who help them resolve problems, because the churches bring in a lot of money and they're closely watched. The pastor knows those people like a bit of debauchery. And you know what I found out?" the informant asked, her tone changing, becoming almost fearful. "But you have to swear you won't tell anyone about this, because if the pastor finds out he'll send them after me, OK? You won't say anything? The other night we were with these bigshot guys, and I walked in the wrong door looking for the bathroom, and instead of the bathroom there was a dark room with a guy in front of these screens that showed the living room and bedrooms, and the man told me, 'Scram unless you're looking for trouble, cunt, bathroom's through the other door,' and when I stumbled out, pretending like I was wasted, the guy locked it behind me, but I'd caught a glimpse of what they were doing in there, you know? The pastor films the VIPs while they're screwing the girls, how about that?" This account of presumable blackmail, however, could not be pinned down further, as the informant did not recall the professions, much less the names, of the people in attendance that night. As a result, there is suspicion of a second set of crimes.

F. *The other stories are very similar and can be reduced to three activities: drinking, doing drugs, and having sex with people whose close association or collaboration could serve the church's interests. It is strange that on the one hand they help women get off drugs through the word of Christ, and on the other they invite them (though not all of them, only a select few) to those kinds of parties. The third testimony is of additional interest, as it describes Pastor Fritz's relationship with one of his so-called priestesses, the Brazilian Egiswanda Sanders, whom everybody describes as the pastor's life partner, wife, or something along those lines. The woman who provided this testimony is a thirty-four-year-old Afro-Colombian known as Piriqueta, a former prostitute who's never had a drug problem: "The night I was there, the most bizarre part was something really weird and twisted—look, picture like four of us girls there, ready for whatever. He's there with his bodyguard, and then, ding-dong, the doorbell rings; I thought he was going to shush us in case it was somebody important, but no, he opened the door without checking who it was. I flushed when I saw Wanda coming in, and since we'd already downed two boxes of sugar-cane liquor, plus I'd sneaked three fat lines of blow, I was high as a kite, you know. I thought Wanda was going to blow a gasket and we'd have to take off running down the stairs, but no. I was surprised to see her sit down with the rest of us, not the least bit upset, pour herself a shot of cane liquor, and set up a couple of lines for herself, like she was alone with her husband after a day at work."*

At this point Jutsiñamuy grabbed his phone and called Laiseca.

"What's up, boss?" the agent said.

"I want to ask your advice. There are some new suspicions, serious ones, based on Wendy's reports, so I'm going to request a tail on Pastor Fritz and have people keep an eye on New Jerusalem."

"So what's the advice you're looking for?" Laiseca asked.

"I want to know what you think of that, dumbass. Why else would I be telling you?"

"I think it's totally the right call, boss," Laiseca said hastily. "The pastor seems like real piece of work."

"Thanks, officer," the prosecutor said, "but there's something else: Wendy's report says the guy throws these incredible parties where he invites the authorities—people from town hall, the regional government, and even the police, so we need to tread carefully."

There was silence on the line.

"There's no problem as far as investigating goes, boss—we can request that from Bogotá," Laiseca said. "What we can do, at least for now, is put me and Cancino on his tail this weekend. That way we keep it quiet till we have more information."

"All right," Jutsiñamuy said. "Do it. And I want reports every hour."

"Overnight too?" Cancino asked.

"Until two A.M., and then starting up again at six."

"Understood, boss. Over and out."

That Saturday, Jutsiñamuy spent some time getting on top of the postal mail and other things that had arrived at his office. He had two large piles and treated it all the same, even the junk mail. His theory: everything a person sees generates hunches, questions, hypotheses. Wielding a letter opener shaped like a Toledo sword, he opened and sorted, but he found nothing of interest. The only upside was making it to lunchtime with the illusion of doing something useful. A little while later he saw that a cycling race was on TV in the waiting room. A huddle of agents was yelling at the front riders. Was Nairo Quintana in there? Why wasn't he making a move?

Before going down to lunch, he called Wendy.

"Afternoon, boss. What can I do for you?" she asked.

"Sorry for calling, Wendy. I don't usually do this when we've got an undercover operation. Are you OK to talk?"

"Of course, boss, otherwise I wouldn't have answered, or I'd have said something so you understood."

"Look, Wendicita, first of all, I want to congratulate you on your reports. As I said, they're excellent. Second, thanks to your information we've decided to place the pastor and his church under surveillance and investigation. Crimes were committed in Cali, and we want to see if there's any relationship between all of this, which just keeps getting bigger and bigger, and anything we've already got."

"I'll keep an even closer eye on what goes on in there, boss," she said.

"One more thing," the prosecutor said. "For now I've only got two of my agents on this. In your report you say that the authorities attend the pastor's parties, right? So I'd rather not ask the Cali police for anything at the moment, not until I've identified his friend at the top, the one who's blocking the investigations. How have things been for you?"

"Good, boss. The women trust me, and since I'm there every day, nobody's suspicious."

"Fantastic. Take care of yourself and we'll be in touch."

"Bye, boss, thanks for the call."

He left his office, went down to the street, and walked to the Corferias convention center. None of his usual lunch spots struck his fancy, so he hailed a taxi and went to the Gran Estación mall instead. He enjoyed being surrounded by families, couples, packs of teenagers, and single-minded youngsters looking to hook up. He wandered into several shops selling things he didn't need and studied the displays carefully. He bought a box of Chiclets to freshen his breath. A young woman in a bodysuit and skates invited him to buy a raffle ticket to win a Chevrolet, so he patiently filled out a little form with all of his information. He tried several eyeglasses frames at Lafam Optical. He recalled his old fantasy of going to the gym when he walked past the Adidas sales, but when he saw that a discounted T-shirt cost 250,000 pesos, he kept going. He looked at pens, entered two computer shops and an appliance store. How much is that washing machine? He examined it seriously and requested all the specifications. Then he decided to go into the grocery store and do a lap of the aisles. He liked looking at how much things cost. Onions, broccoli, condensed milk . . . Chocoramo cakes and Poker beer were on sale.

Finally he decided to have a hamburger. He wouldn't be caught dead in a McDonald's, so he went to Corral Gourmet and requested an Argentine sandwich with chimichurri. That's where he was when the phone rang.

It was Wendy.

"Hey, boss, real quick, I wanted to tell you Pastor Fritz just suggested I go to one of his parties tonight. According to his assistant, they had some spots to fill and called me, since some of the girls are out of town this weekend."

"Oh, hell," the prosecutor said. "That's your call to make, honey. Given his record, I don't want to expose you to anything ugly."

"I'm an agent in the prosecutor's office, boss. Don't forget that. I may be a woman, but I'm an officer too. One of the guys we're trying to identify might come tonight. I'm letting you know I'll be there; make sure the guys tailing Fritz are aware. We're supposed to meet at the church at eight tonight, and they'll transport us from there."

"Where is the party going to be?"

"It's not in Menga as usual, it's at his private apartment," Wendy said. "That's why I think somebody important is going to be there. I don't know where it is, but if our guys have been following him, they're probably already familiar."

"Right, right," Jutsiñamuy said. "OK, get ready. I'll tell them to look sharp in case something happens."

"I'm fully trained, boss, don't panic. It's not like the pastor's a dangerous murderer, is he?"

"That's what we're trying to figure out, Wendy. I hope not."

He hung up and immediately dialed Laiseca.

"Hello? Everything's quiet here, boss. The man is shut up in his office."

"And where are you?" the prosecutor asked.

"I'm watching him from a service station a little ways up the street. There's a café area on the second floor with a clear view."

The prosecutor told him about the party that night. He said he was worried and told them to keep a sharp eye out.

"I hadn't heard about this, boss," Laiseca said. "He hasn't mentioned it on the phone, or I would have been told about it. But don't worry. Cancino is watching from another spot, so we've got it all under control. It's great about the party, that way we can get close to him."

Jutsiñamuy kept walking around the mall, faster now to stimulate his digestion. He needed to take at least a thousand steps. It was the rule for a healthy life. Mall walking for exercise was popular in the United States, where they'd even mark routes on the floor tile with information about distance and water fountains. It wasn't like that in Colombia, but he tried to keep up a fast pace, which was unusual here.

He was anxious—what time was it? Past four in the afternoon. During his third loop around the mall, feeling impatient, he realized he needed to do something to distract himself. He decided to go to the movies; that would kill some time. He bought a ticket for a Norwegian film, thinking, *How strange, a Norwegian film here?* At the concession stand he bought a medium popcorn and a Coca-Cola Light, more out of habit, since he'd just had lunch. When he walked into the theater, he was startled to discover he was the only one there. Of course—who else would go to a Norwegian film at the Gran Estación shopping center in Bogotá? Then something occurred to him: he would like to live in a country where lots of people went to see Norwegian films at the mall. The lights went out, and he lolled back in his chair. He ate a piece of popcorn and thought it had too much butter. He took a sip of his Coke, which struck him as cold and watery.

He was getting old.

First was a short by a Colombian director that was all about fishermen on the Pacific coast and how their shrimp boats pulled the plump crustaceans out of the sea. Then the film started.

A young piano teacher was giving private lessons to two little girls in a town. The girls' father was dead. The mother was a middle-aged woman who, while the young man was teaching her daughters, would go out to a roadside bar to pick up men. Jutsiñamuy figured it must be a thriller; maybe the woman was seducing them and then murdering them. But no, she just chatted with them while she drank gin and then returned home, all amid an unsettling darkness. But there was something else: a persistent silence. A silence that the prosecutor deemed "very Norwegian." The movie had no music, or very little, which sometimes made it feel long and tedious.

One afternoon the young man has to cancel the music lesson since his girlfriend has left him for another man (his best friend), and he decides to go to a bar for a few beers to try to forget her. Jutsiñamuy figured he'd go to his piano students' mother's bar, and they'd see each other and something beautiful would blossom between them despite the age difference, but no. The bar turned out to be even dimmer and more sordid. There was nobody around, just an old man with a long beard and a red nose at the end of the bar. He drank three beers waiting for something to happen. Since the young man hadn't been to the bar before, he sat down in the far corner, near the TV. That's where he was when he saw his own father come in, holding another man's hand. Then more people started arriving, all men, as if work had just let out, which in fact it had. He spotted his father and saw that he was talking and laughing, leaning in close to his drinking buddy. Everybody else was doing the same, and the young man swiftly realized that it was a gay bar. He considered leaving, but he was afraid his father would see him and things would get awkward. He had no idea what his father was doing at a gay bar. He started thinking back on his life. His parents had gotten divorced when he was a teenager, and their relationship had grown chilly after that. In fact, he hadn't seen his father since Christmas, more than three months ago. Was this why his father had left his mother? Because he was gay? He timidly ordered another beer, to give himself strength, and when he looked over again after that moment of distraction, he discovered that his father was staring straight at him. He'd seen him. Finally a bit of music played in the movie as the father started walking toward his son. At that point, the prosecutor couldn't keep his eyes open any longer.

He was exhausted.

When he opened them again, a young man in a movie theater uniform was saying, "Sir, sir, you need to leave now." The movie was over, and the theater lights were up. What had happened between father and son at the gay bar? He'd have to watch the film again to find out. He got up from his chair, aching and somewhat shamefaced. Christ, how long had he slept? He checked the time on his phone: seven thirty. He figured Wendy must be leaving for the church. He took a taxi back to his office, ready for any eventuality.

This was Wendy's account of the events that Saturday night:

Statement by undercover agent KWK622:

I arrived at the entrance of New Jerusalem Church at five to eight. Because of the kind of party I was going to, I was wearing a short skirt and ripped fishnet stockings, something you don't see much of in Cali because it's so hot, but everybody knew I was from Bogotá. I opted for a goth look for self-protection at least at first. The other women started arriving, all in miniskirts and ridiculously high heels. Piriqueta, Yismena, Cindy Raquel, and two others I didn't know, Lorena and Dorotea. I smoked a cigarette with them, waiting for eight o'clock, but our ride didn't show up on time. Piriqueta pulled

*a carton of Del Valle aguardiente out of her purse and said,
"Look, girls, let's get some drinks in since these guys are late,"
and everybody took a swig. It tasted like shit to me. Finally, at
about eight thirty, a Nissan Discovery showed up, and we got
in. The girls were pretty hammered and were singing and
telling dirty jokes, so much so that when we got to the apartment, in a fancy building in Juanambú, the drivers asked us to
be quiet and not cause a scene. The SUV drove straight into
the garage, and the area has lots of trees, so I didn't manage to
see where we were. We went up in the elevator to the fourteenth floor, and when the doors slid open I saw the living
room of the apartment and several men on the sofas.*

*"The Marías are here," one of them said, and they got up
to say hi. We filed in. Each of us said her name and shook
hands with the four guests.*

*Pastor Fritz was dressed in black from head to toe. He
looked like a member of the Indian government, not an evangelical minister. When I saw him, I felt embarrassed about
my vulgar outfit. It seemed like this party was going to be different from the ones I'd heard about, which was a relief.
Somebody important must be coming. The Brazilian woman,
Egiswanda, greeted us in an adjoining living room after we'd
all said hello. She told us we could put down our purses there
and have something to drink. There was a bar and trays with
typical local foods: pork-stuffed fried green plantain, fried
ripe plantain, plantain cheese fritters, empanadas with guacamole, pork rinds, rice stew. It was after nine, so I served
myself a large plate and a glass of lulo juice, which looked
delicious. Doña Egiswanda was very kind and treated us as if
we were the wives of the men who were in the living room
with the pastor, so I started feeling curious. I couldn't imagine
how such a serious, formal dinner could turn into what the
women had described. I quietly asked Cindy Raquel about it,
and she said, "Just wait, they all start out like this."*

At around midnight, they called us in. The men were a little drunk now, and Egiswanda put on some music. I looked at them closely and tried to assess them. The oldest one was named Pedro, and he looked like your typical man from Cali: light-colored linen pants, yellow shirt, and white loafers without socks. The next one, Samuel, looked like he'd come straight from the office. Then Horacio, who was younger, around forty, with an athletic build and a blue striped shirt, and finally Abdón, very young, in a collarless shirt and jeans. I didn't know who was who or what they did, but I observed them all carefully.

As far as I could figure out, they had called us in once they'd finished talking. Sometimes one of them would say something. They mentioned some lots in Menga, near the church, that Pastor Fritz would be interested in buying. It was the pastor himself who first invited me to dance. I agreed shyly, of course—he was the great guru, and Egiswanda was in the room. We danced, and he asked me how I felt, what I planned to do in the future, whether I'd found peace in the word of Christ. I replied enthusiastically that I had, and I even asked if the other people were pastors.

Not all of them, just him, he said, pointing to the youngest. He's from Barranquilla. We're going to build a branch of New Jerusalem there; that's why he's here.

After a little while, the party started heating up. Through dancing with the guests a bit and asking them questions, I was able to figure out that Samuel was from the legal team at the mayor's office, a respectable-looking civil servant who spent his Saturday afternoons at work; Horacio, though, was in banking, and I figured he must be there for the financial aspects of the pastor's real estate projects. Pedro, in the white loafers, remained a mystery, though my guess is he was police.

It was around then that the doorbell rang and Egiswanda opened the door. A short man with a clumsy, crooked tie that made him look like a low-level bureaucrat was there. When they saw him, the pastor and Pedro walked over and greeted him, but instead of inviting him into the living room they led him down one of the hallways farther into the apartment. Seeing that Egiswanda had gone to the women's lounge, I decided to take my chances. I left Abdón, the young man from Barranquilla, saying I had to use the bathroom, and went down the same hallway. There were several doors, and one was the bathroom, but I kept going a little farther and saw another one ajar. They were inside; it was an office. Pastor Fritz was talking. "Are we sure everybody made it out?" he asked, and the newcomer said, "Yes, pastor, they're all across the border. We'll look after some of them in Quito and some in Cuenca until things calm down here." The man in loafers broke in, patting the newcomer on the back. "I told you, Fritz, Gustavo's a trustworthy guy. Plus he helped us shut down the police investigation into the Valle del Cauca incident. Let's go back to the party. Everything's good." I managed to leap into the bathroom before they emerged, pulled out my cell phone, and sent my first message requesting identification of the person they were calling Gustavo.

When he got Wendy's message, the prosecutor alerted Laiseca, who was hiding near the building entrance. He'd already made a note of and photographed the man's arrival. But it wasn't possible to identify him since he arrived in an SUV with tinted windows and was surrounded by a throng of bodyguards when he climbed out. The photos didn't capture him clearly. All they had was his name. Jutsiñamuy texted his undercover agent, asking her to try to get a better photo there inside the house.

Agent KWK622's account continues:

Feeling my phone buzz, I went out onto the balcony and

read the boss's message. There were bodyguards on either side of me, which made things a little difficult, but I managed to place my cell phone against the glass and take several photos without them noticing. I sent the photos and went back to the party, but soon another text arrived. "They can't really make out the face of the man named Gustavo. Try to figure out his identity."

In the living room, aguardiente was flowing freely. I had to have several glasses, though I watered them down. At one point the newcomer, sweating profusely, removed his jacket and hung it on the back of a dining-room chair. Here was my chance. I approached slowly, dancing, and patted it as I moved past. His wallet was there. I used Abdón, the pastor from Barranquilla, as a cover to move close to the jacket again, and I managed to pull the wallet out with two fingers and stick it under my skirt. Then I went to the bathroom, took photos of his ID card and driver's license, and sent those, keeping an eye on the bodyguards on the balcony. When I returned to the living room, I saw a terrifying sight: at the other end of the room, mid-dance, the man called Gustavo was patting his pants pockets and then looking over at his jacket. He walked toward it, but I was closer. I pretended to trip on the chair and knock it over; the jacket fell to the floor, and I managed to slip the wallet into it. He reached me just a moment later and offered me his hand. "Did you hurt yourself, baby?" He helped me up and gathered his things. He stuck his wallet in his pocket and poured himself another whisky (there was whisky for the men).

A little while later I got the message from headquarters saying I should inform them of the number of bodyguards and their locations.

And leave the house immediately.

When he received Wendy's photo of the ID card the man

was carrying, Jutsiñamuy sent it to the technical office and a few minutes later had received a full identification. The ID, which was clearly a fake, claimed he was Alfredo Varela Hernández from Tuluá, but they were nevertheless able to identify him as Gustavo "The Umbrella" Manrique, from Buga, a former paramilitary fighter and army lieutenant, with two outstanding arrest warrants for "false positive" murders. Jutsiñamuy immediately called Laiseca.

"We've got to get Wendy out of there," the prosecutor said. "The guy who showed up is paramilitary with arrest warrants from seven years ago. His name is Gustavo 'The Umbrella' Manrique. This pastor's buddies are something else, huh?"

"Well, boss, all those people are really into Christ—or do you think Carlos Castaño was Muslim? No way."

"All right, Laiseca," the prosecutor said, "tell me what you think. Do I call for backup and we do this thing, or do we wait till tomorrow?"

"The problem I see right now, boss, is that the place is probably full of bodyguards, and we could end up in a real bitch of a gun battle, with who knows what outcome. But if we leave it till tomorrow, they'll disappear. If the man's been on the run for seven years, he must know how to get around. I don't know, I can't decide."

They let a few seconds pass in silence.

"Let's wait till they've had a few drinks," Laiseca said, "and we'll catch them when they've got their pants down. Or we can get them on their way out."

"Yes, that's great, once Wendy's left," Jutsiñamuy said. "Listen, it's likely someone will take her home—I doubt they're going to call her an Uber, for security reasons. So we can grab them at that point and return to the building in their vehicle. A Trojan 4x4 SUV with tinted windows."

"That seems like the best plan, boss," Laiseca said. "Legally speaking, are we covered?"

"Absolutely," the prosecutor said. "I'll get everything set up and request backup for the raid. It would be worth it just to bring Gustavo in. If we can nab the pastor too, that's a bonus."

"You're a Napoleon, boss."

"Stop fawning, damn it," the prosecutor said. "Get to work!"

Jutsiñamuy called one of his colleagues at the Cali prosecutor's office, brought him up to speed, and explained the situation and described the occupants of the apartment. He noted that there were people from the mayor's office and maybe from the police, so the operation needed to be executed with great care. Highly trusted agents only.

Half an hour later, the Cali prosecutor called back.

"I've got it all set up," he said, "a dozen trustworthy, highly professional men. We got the blueprints for the building. Should we put in for a helicopter?"

"These people are tough, well armed. You can't be too careful," Jutsiñamuy said.

Special Agent KWK622's account continues:

The men started getting really drunk. The first couple to pair up was the pastor from Barranquilla, Abdón, with Piriqueta. They writhed against each other as they danced, then grabbed a couple of glasses of aguardiente and a baggie of coke and snuck off down one of the hallways. I wondered, What do I do? Dredging up my training, I opted for the tried-and-true fainting technique.

In preparation, I wiped all recent information from my cell phone. There's no real mystery or science to this move. Basically, you do something bizarre in front of everyone and then pass out. So I did. I picked up a glass of aguardiente, which was actually less than a quarter liquor because I'd added a bunch of water, and started dancing with Don Pedro. Halfway through the song I rested my head on his shoulder

and slumped to the floor, careful not to hit my head on any-
thing.

From there it was a breeze. I heard someone calling my
name, sensed someone kneeling beside me; I was picked up
and carried to a bedroom; there I opened my eyes and said I
felt sick, with a terrible headache and nausea. "Do you want
someone to take you home?" Egiswanda asked, and I said
yes. "You're not used to this, poor thing," she said.

She got up and called two drivers.

I didn't go back through the living room, I went out
through the kitchen door to a service elevator. They helped
me into an SUV, I gave them my address, and we took off. A
few blocks later, two SUVs blocked our path. They were full
of agents from the prosecutor's office.

Seven agents returned to the building in Juanambú
crammed into a single SUV. This allowed them to enter the
parking deck without having to identify themselves.
Suspecting nothing, the doorman and three bodyguards in the
lobby waved them through.

Jutsiñamuy's Trojan horse was inside. Two agents headed to
the elevator; the rest, having located the cameras, avoided
them by weaving between the cars. They all went up together
and got off a floor early, on the thirteenth. Stealthily, they
climbed up to the fourteenth floor via the stairs. The bodyguards out in the hall put up some resistance, but they'd been
drinking and were slow to react. They were disarmed before
they had the chance to go for their weapons.

The agents entered the apartment.

The music was pounding, and it was as dark as a nightclub,
so they were able to spread out along the sides of the room
before anybody noticed them. The bodyguards on the balcony
were nodding off and easily neutralized. At an order, the
agents turned on the lights and stopped the music. Nobody

resisted; instead there was laughter and an angry face or two. Gustavo the Umbrella put up his hands and looked around, but seeing that his people were in cuffs, he moved his hands, calling for calm. The bodyguards from the lobby took off running, maybe on instinct, and additional agents swarmed into the building.

Laiseca and Cancino were with them.

They called Jutsiñamuy.

"We're in the man's apartment, boss," Laiseca said.

"Everybody rounded up?" Jutsiñamuy asked.

"I'm counting and there are two missing," Laiseca said. "I don't see the hosts, the pastor and the Brazilian woman."

They searched the hallways, went up to the roof, went down floor by floor to the parking area. The doorman, who was with an agent, hadn't seen anybody on the security monitors.

How had they gotten out?

They couldn't evacuate every apartment in the building. They rewound the cameras and saw only themselves entering.

They searched thoroughly. Not a trace. Pastor Fritz and Egiswanda had disappeared.

If they'd been arrested, Pastor Fritz and Egiswanda would have been held a couple of days at most. All they would have had to do was show they didn't know about Gustavo the Umbrella's record, and they would have been released. Same with everybody else. By running, they'd incriminated themselves, justifying the subsequent actions taken. The women were luckier, and were released as soon as they'd been booked.

The arrest warrant was transmitted to the police. At six A.M. on Sunday, twenty-four agents raided the headquarters of New Jerusalem Church and confiscated everything, down to the last notebook. The prosecutor's office was hoping to prove the connection between Gustavo the Umbrella and Pastor Fritz. Based on Wendy's testimony, it seemed clear that Gustavo was a secret head of security for the pastor, probably the one who'd led his defense in the combat by the Ullucos River.

Jutsiñamuy was eager to hear from his friend Julieta with confirmation from the Brazilian side. The idea provoked some uneasiness, since despite all the progress they'd made in the investigation, much of it was still only a theory. A house of cards.

On Monday, he got to the office at 6:05 A.M. He was impatient. He knew that at such an early hour it was unlikely he'd get any news that would bolster the weekend's events. He was walking down the hall to make a cup of tea with water from the urn when he felt his cell phone vibrate in his pocket.

A message from Julieta—just what he'd been hoping for!

I have everything now—I'm heading your way. I'll arrive tomorrow or the day after. We can confirm Mr. F's identity. Please investigate a Colombian by the name of Arturo Silva Amador.

Despite his excitement, he kept it under wraps. He merely responded, *Great. I'll be expecting you. We've got some surprises here too.*

Immediately he called the technical unit.

"Is Guillermina in yet?" he asked the secretary, who was probably finishing her night shift.

"Of course, sir, I'll put you through."

There was a silence.

"Hello? Good morning."

Jutsiñamuy recognized the voice and said, "My dear, you and I must be the only ones working at this time of day, ready for action."

"Oh, boss," his former secretary said, "that's because to fix all the messes in this country, you have to get an early start. What can I do for you?"

"I've got a name for you. Write this down: Arturo Silva Amador."

"Anything in particular?"

"All of it, from his very first baby bottle."

"Count on me, boss. I'll start digging."

He hung up, wondering why the hell Guillermina was no longer his secretary. But he knew: a promotion. If he ever became prosecutor general, he'd hire her to his staff.

It was only 6:27 A.M. Maybe he should go to Cali, he thought. They'd be doing the initial interrogations of Gustavo the Umbrella, and would bring him to Bogotá in the afternoon. Maybe even by lunchtime.

His phone rang again. It was Laiseca.

"Good morning, boss. I've got good news for you."

"Oh, shit, what's up?"

"Do you remember Beilys David, the Afro-Colombian kid from the Jamundí Inn?"

"Of course, who could forget him?" Jutsiñamuy said.

"He called me a little while ago to say he had information to sell. I'm here with him, because his shift starts in ten minutes. He's holding a page from *El País* with photos of the people killed in the cafés, and you know what he says? He recognized them all. They were some of the guys who used to come with the Brazilian."

"Oh, great. Tell him he won't be able to work today. I'm leaving for Cali now. Hold him there for me; I want to talk to him."

"All right, boss," Laiseca said, dubious. "But remember I made an agreement and gave him my word nothing would happen to him."

"Tell him he has to stay with you on my orders."

Jutsiñamuy heard muffled conversation.

"All right, boss. No problem. I'll take him to pick you up at the airport."

"Well done, the law comes first," Jutsiñamuy said. "Tell him I applaud him for doing the right thing."

"As if, boss. The first thing he did was ask me for more money. This guy's a real piece of work."

At 8:45 A.M. the prosecutor landed at Bonilla Aragón Airport on an Avianca flight that, for once, hadn't been delayed or overbooked. Laiseca and Cancino were waiting for him with the witness.

"You're sure you saw them?" Jutsiñamuy asked Beilys once they were in the car.

"Sir, look, a man does change when he gets shot in the head," Beilys said, "but not that much. I saw those men at the Jamundí Inn, and I remember them. They were with the Brazilian and the other guy, the one your partner showed me . . . The one who showed up on the side of the road."

"Óscar Luis Pedraza or Nadio Becerra?" Cancino asked.

"No, I don't know his name," Beilys said. "The guy from before. The one who was the boss."

Cancino pulled out the photos again. Beilys pointed to Óscar Luis Pedraza.

"That's the guy who brought them in. I took them to the bungalows, and there was a screw-up because one of the reservations was wrong and they got a room with a double bed by mistake; the men made jokes and ribbed each other, you know? The boss told them, all right, well, you're stuck with sharing a bed, decide which one's going to wear the pink pajamas. They joked around for a while, and I had to go back to reception and get them a room with separate beds—there aren't many because the inn mostly gets couples."

The traffic was heavy heading into the city, lots of trucks. They passed the Poker beer plant and the Colombina candy factory. The Rey del Mundo Hotel.

Jutsiñamuy, staring intently at Beilys, said, "I'm going to explain something, kid. The Brazilian you met is an evangelical pastor who came to your hotel to organize an attack against a Colombian pastor. That's why we've got all these dead bodies.

But the Colombian got away, and now he's striking back, wiping out the enemies who survived the attack one by one. He removed the dead bodies from the scene himself, and now he's dumping them a few at a time."

The young man stared at him in horror. Behind the baseball cap and strutting attitude was a frightened little boy.

The prosecutor continued. "That's why I need you, as a brave, patriotic young man who loves his country, to give an official statement on everything you just told me. Colombia will owe you a debt of gratitude."

The young man recovered his composure. "And how much do you pay for that?"

The prosecutor glared at him. "We don't pay anything, damn it. Charging the justice system for the truth is a crime. Whose side do you want to be on, the country's or the criminals'?"

The young man regarded the prosecutor, unfazed.

"I'd rather be on the side of the people who got a million pesos for telling the truth, if you catch my drift."

The prosecutor looked at Laiseca, who shrugged. It was illegal; it couldn't be done.

"That's not an option, young man. Is that how you repay your country?"

Beilys met his eyes and said, "My old lady was a servant her whole life, and today she doesn't have a pension. Of my seven siblings, two died working as sicarios and my oldest sister has been a hooker since she was fifteen and right now is in drug rehab. I don't owe the country a thing."

Jutsiñamuy looked at Laiseca. "All right, fine," he said. "Let's take pity on this delinquent; as far as I can tell he's not to blame here."

But it was early still. He wanted to talk to Julieta before building the case with all of the pieces. Her information on Fabinho would cement things.

Men arrived from the prosecutor's office, and Jutsiñamuy

asked to talk to Gustavo the Umbrella, who was being held in a cell. After some paperwork, he was led to one of the small rooms used for questioning.

Seeing Gustavo, Jutsiñamuy recognized signs of the criminality found in the middle classes, related to the government or the army. The kind found in people with profound discontent and longstanding unrest.

He introduced himself.

The man looked him up and down and said he wasn't going to open his mouth without his lawyer present.

"That's understandable, but I'm going to ask a few questions. It's up to you whether to answer or not."

Gustavo scowled.

"I give you my word that nobody is listening to us or recording," Jutsiñamuy said, "and I won't pretend my situation isn't pretty complicated. What I'm interested in, quite apart from your issues with the law, is your relationship with Pastor Fritz Almayer. We have evidence that you provided security for him."

Far in the distance, an excavator could be heard digging. The Umbrella looked at the prosecutor with a frown, but said nothing.

"That's what I really care about," Jutsiñamuy continued. "You know the pastor and his Brazilian lady friend disappeared, right? Don't ask me how, but even though the operation went down in his own home, the man got away. What do you say to that! And the worst part is he had no reason to run. There's no evidence against him. It's weird, right?"

Gustavo the Umbrella rubbed his eyes as if rubbing away sleep.

"Doesn't seem so weird to me," he said, his voice tired. "The man's got God protecting him. Must be nice."

"But you worked for him," Jutsiñamuy said. "Doesn't it seem unfair that he isn't protecting you?"

Gustavo shrugged. "God knows what he's doing."

"Well, in that case you've ended up playing Barabbas, but without the pardon."

"We don't know that yet," the Umbrella said.

"In every story there's one who gets saved and another who is doomed. The key is to make sure you end up on the right side of the bars."

"And which is the right side?" the Umbrella asked.

"The outside, of course. Which do you think?"

"Are you making an offer?"

"I'm asking about your relationship with Pastor Fritz, but let me tell you a few things I know: You lead his clandestine security team. With a group of former soldiers, you saved him from an attack a couple of weeks ago in Tierradentro, on the road to San Andrés de Pisimbalá, on the bridge over the Ullucos River. It was a brutal attack, but you held your own and got him out of there by helicopter. Later you cleaned up all traces of the battle, including the dead bodies. And things didn't stop there. You found out which of the attackers had survived and then had them killed, all at the same time on the same day, because that's what your friend Pastor Fritz requested. Why did he request it? He knew that in the face of the evidence of his far-reaching power, his enemies would buckle in fear and wouldn't try anything again for a long time. You complied, and now your men, the ones who carried out the 'executions,' are gone, taken a powder—am I right?"

Gustavo the Umbrella sat stiff and still, but his upper lip trembled a bit.

"And see here," Jutsiñamuy continued, "you've got a long list of charges now, plus these new ones coming down, which are pretty serious—meaning, on the low end, some thirty years in the slammer, let's say twenty with good behavior—but since you're sixty-two, that's basically a full retirement, while the pastor and his spicy Brazilian are probably already on a beach somewhere, having a great time, sunbathing with a tequila sunrise in hand, waiting for enough time to pass that they can slip back in unharassed. Since you were such good buddies, no doubt the pastor will come visit you in prison and bring you food. But afterward he'll go home, to his warm bed with the Brazilian and the other girls he's enjoying, while you, behind bars, will have to endure prison life, which you already know too well. Life's a bitch, don't you think?"

Again there was a loud noise in the distance, as if a truck had just dumped a load of rocks. Gustavo the Umbrella looked Jutsiñamuy in the eyes.

"You really don't have anything on him?" he asked.

"Not a thing, like I said," Jutsiñamuy confirmed. "If we picked him up now, all he'd have to do is explain why he ran and why you were at his house, but a good lawyer could take care of that easily. We really want to nab this guy—he's a criminal. He might have even set you up as a scapegoat to be arrested."

"And if I tell you about him, do I get something?"

"Of course," the prosecutor said. "If we confirm that he was the mastermind behind the restaurant murders in Cali, that lets you off the hook, since at that point you'd just be the one who did the deed. It would be a 'principle of opportunity'—it would be in your best interest."

"I never said I did it."

"I know," Jutsiñamuy said, "but it'll be proven at trial. Just between us, we've got everything already. What we need to know is why. And the why is the pastor. Now, I admire you if you still want to cover for him."

Gustavo the Umbrella stammered a bit and said, "And if I ultimately did say something, how much would I get?"

"Oh, that would be negotiated between your lawyers and us. I can't really say at the moment because what we're talking about here, like I said, is between you and me. Nobody's recording, and there are no consequences. If you tell us the truth, I promise you'll be better off."

"You swear?" the Umbrella asked. "Are you saying you'll let me go if I rat on the pastor?"

"Now you're getting carried away. I'm not saying you'd be released," Jutsiñamuy clarified. "But if you turn state's evidence, it'll be good for you and for us too. I can't promise the value of the recompense, but I can tell you it's in your interest. Think about it."

The prosecutor stood up from his metal chair, and Gustavo the Umbrella looked at him in surprise.

"You're leaving?" Gustavo asked.

"I've said what I had to say."

"I'm going to talk to my lawyer and have him negotiate with you, because the pastor is involved. He hired me. I saved his life in Tierradentro. The restaurant killings, like you say, were his orders; all I did was make the contacts."

Jutsiñamuy tugged at the knot of his tie. Then he said, "We already knew all that, what matters is that you've said it. That's the only thing you can negotiate. Good luck."

They went out onto the street. It was hot.

"Now what?" Laiseca asked.

Jutsiñamuy, his neck stretched upright like a giraffe's, replied. "Now we wait for this guy to break completely, but we know the important stuff. Any news of the pastor?"

"Nothing for now, boss," Laiseca said. "He vanished."

"Look for him under this name too—write it down: Arturo Silva Amador. I asked Guillermina to look for priors and she should be calling back soon."

Three hours later he was back in Bogotá. Hearing a polite knock at his door, he recognized his former secretary. "Come on in, Guillermina."

She entered, holding a folder. "I have several things for you," she said hurriedly, barely looking at him, "and I'll start from the beginning. To kick off, Arturo Silva was born in Florencia, Caquetá, on December 30, 1965 . . ."

"Weird date to have been born," Jutsiñamuy said, taking a sip of his tea.

"He got his ID in Florencia and came to Bogotá as a Piarist priest in 1984. That didn't last long. The next year he appears as a student at the Pontifical Xavierian University. Then he enrolled in an agronomy program at the National University, but he didn't graduate. He also took classes in philosophy and anthropology. Afterward he seems to have returned to Caquetá, because in 1992 there's an application for a teaching job at a public school, which he didn't get. He worked a private school in Florencia as a teacher's assistant. That's what the caption says. He was involved in forming a teacher's union in Caquetá. He's named in press clippings as its spokesperson and treasurer. I've got copies for you here. Then, in 1998, he claimed to have been threatened by the FARC. During that period, there are records of the only two times he left the country. And then, boss, the big surprise. He turns up dead on November 9, 2002. Here's his death certificate from the local hospital in Florencia. And check this out: it says the body was hit by six nine-millimeter bullets, in the head and torso, and one at the base of the skull, execution-style. It indicates that he had signs of torture such as cigarette burns, four missing fingers, stab wounds to both eyes, and nine pulled and broken teeth; in his throat they found his testicles and penis, which had been chopped up; the forensic report adds that there were also seven deep bites from a lancehead, one of the Amazon's most poisonous snakes, on his neck, cheeks, and legs; that venom alone would have caused his death. And one final detail: his body was found in three bags, dismembered. Absolutely horrific. He's buried in the local cemetery."

"Jesus," Jutsiñamuy said, "that's a lot of violence against just one man. And we never found out who did that to him?"

"No charges have been filed, and the investigation isn't active." Guillermina opened another folder. "But boss, the interesting thing is that the other man you asked me to investigate a few days ago, Pastor Fritz Almayer, was also born on December 30, 1965. That's the date he gave the first time he registered in Florencia, on January 18, 1984, but it's weird because there's nothing on him until about 2003, when he starts as a pastor at a church called New Nazareth there in Florencia. Doesn't it seem odd to you that he didn't leave a paper trail for all that time? Like he was on ice. And that's it. I requested verification of the documents, but since they're so old, it's slow going."

The prosecutor set down his mug, now empty, on the table. "Well, what that indicates to me is that Arturo Silva Amador and Fritz Almayer are the same person, right? It makes sense. The life of Arturo Silva, with his experiences with different religious orders, philosophy, and anthropology, served as a foundation for constructing a religious discourse, which he now offers his followers. And the description of his appalling death turns out to be pure fiction."

That must be what Julieta is coming to tell me—she'll be here tomorrow, Jutsiñamuy thought, but he didn't say it to loyal Guillermina.

"That's what I think, boss."

From the airport in Panama City, the final layover on her way back to Colombia, Julieta texted Jutsiñamuy: *I'll be at El Dorado in two hours.*

And Jutsiñamuy replied: *I'll meet you there. I need to talk to you.*

The prosecutor waited for her at the gate and they headed to a police room in the airport, where they drank coffee and talked. Julieta recounted at length what she'd learned from her conversations with Fabinho Henriquez. Then Jutsiñamuy gave her a detailed report on the operation against Pastor Fritz, his escape, and what they'd managed to find out about the gun

battle on the Ullucos River. Finally, he said, "We also verified
Arturo Silva Amador's identity, and it corroborates what you
found. He and the pastor are the same guy."

"All right," Julieta said. "That means we've got the whole
story, right? I don't know if you'll have an easy time chasing
them down and arresting them. But as far as I'm concerned,
the information's all there."

"Using Gustavo the Umbrella's statement," Jutsiñamuy
said, "we'll be able to indict Pastor Fritz, but as I said, that will
depend on his negotiations with his lawyer, so it'll be a while.
As for Fabinho Henriquez, we could issue an extradition order
to France, to be sent to Cayenne. The statement from young
Beilys David at the Jamundí Inn, identifying Henriquez as the
brains behind the attack, will be key. We could use that to
explain those dead bodies."

"There are too many of those, as usual," Julieta said.

"Sadly, you get used to it in this country," the prosecutor
said. "One more thing: did Johana manage to track down the
boy's mother?"

"I'm supposed to go see her now. She said she's got news."

"That girl is a gem," Jutsiñamuy said. "You don't know
how lucky you are to work with her."

"I know. I've got to go. Hey, are you going to hold a press
conference about the case?"

"Maybe," the prosecutor said, "but not everything. We'll
have to provide updates on the murders in Cali. We'll say it
was score settling, which happens to be true: it was an exten-
sion of the fighting in Tierradentro, which was an attempt to
settle a score. Later, once we've captured the pastor, we'll be
able to tell the rest. For now the story is exclusively yours, as
we agreed at the start."

"Thanks for holding up your end," Julieta said. "Talking to
you gives me hope."

"I'd love to talk about more pleasant topics, but this

country makes that impossible, with these horrible things that happen. You always have to put off the good stuff till later."

"But this is the country we've got," she said. "What can you do."

Julieta arrived at her office a little while later in an airport taxi. Johana was on her computer, working, and Franklin was surfing the internet on the tablet. They said hi. Immediately Julieta could tell that something was wrong. Johana looked like she was about to fall apart. Maybe she simply hadn't gotten much sleep, but her appearance was alarming.

What was going on?

Johana started to speak but couldn't as she struggled to hold back tears.

"What's wrong?" Julieta asked, grasping her colleague's shoulders.

"While you were away, boss, I got a call . . ." Again she contained herself. "My brother Carlos Duván—do you remember him? He was a social activist in Buenaventura, in the El Cristal neighborhood. He'd been there a year, working with displaced people . . ."

"What happened to him?" Julieta asked, feeling distressed.

"He was taken by these guys on motorcycles . . . It's been four days. His wife called to tell me. They have a three-year-old son . . ."

She started crying again. Franklin, at the computer, seemed to sense it and looked at them, but immediately looked back at the screen.

"And nobody's called to make any demands? It's not a kidnapping?" Julieta asked.

"No, nothing. They're taking people who used to be members of the FARC."

"Oh, God. I'm so sorry. We'll have to wait, Johanita. Did you tell Jutsiñamuy?"

"I didn't want to—I'm afraid they'll find out, and if he's still alive, they'll do something to him. Though there isn't much hope. Four days . . . They'll have killed him by now."

Julieta hugged her. "Hold on. I'm going to call Jutsiñamuy and ask him to help. I just saw him at the airport."

She dialed her phone and explained what had happened, giving all the facts: Carlos Duván Triviño, thirty-four years old, El Cristal in Buenaventura, four days ago, social activist.

"Social activist?" Jutsiñamuy exclaimed. "Oh, crap, those folks are getting chopped down like sugarcane. Sorry. In that region there's not much hope, but don't tell her that. I'll see what I can find out."

"Thanks. You can imagine how important this is."

"Of course, you can count on me. Give Johanita my best. What a business."

Julieta hung up and hugged Johana. "He's going to help us. Hopefully he can do something."

"Thanks, boss. It's rough . . . He surrenders his weapons and ends up disappeared."

Julieta said hi to Franklin, heated up some coffee, and offered Johana a cup. Reluctantly she accepted it.

The boy looked over at them from time to time, avoiding meeting their eyes.

"Does he know?" Julieta asked.

"No," Johana said. "I'm trying not to make things even more complicated for him. Now we're both waiting."

They had another cup of coffee. Finally Johana seemed to feel a little better.

"So you've got news about the kid?"

"I followed several leads," Johana said, "and I'm waiting

for a reply from a former FARC fighter who went to live in the States, in Houston."

Julieta started pulling things out of her briefcase and organizing them on her desk. The boy looked at her shyly, smiled, and focused again on his screen. What was he looking at?

"What are you looking at?"

"Photos," the boy said.

"Photos of anyone in particular?"

"No, ma'am, of a city."

"Which one, if I may ask?"

"Houston," the boy said, flushing.

She turned to Johana. "All right, tell me how it all happened."

"In the end, after a lot of digging," Johana said, "I managed to track down the famous Berta Noriega, the comrade who now works in Congress, with the party. I went to talk to her, and when I told her about the kid and showed her that old photo from the La Macarena conference, she consulted her file of former combatants. She found a Clara who went to Houston two years ago, full name Clara Martínez Neira, but no other information. We don't know if she's from San Juan del Sumapaz. Since there are so many security protocols with this stuff, she asked me to leave the information and a couple of photos of the boy. She said she'd look into it and that I should just wait, since Clara has to respond first and authorize Berta to give us the information. You can imagine, boss, with everything that's going on, everybody's really paranoid. So we took some nice photos to see if she'll reply, and we're waiting—right, Franklin? If this isn't her, we'll try someone else. Until we find her."

Julieta poured herself a massive cup of coffee and started telling Johana what she'd learned on her trip. The boy remained glued to the screen.

"How has he been doing?" Julieta asked in a low voice.

"Good. He's a really cool kid, sensible and determined. We've been supporting each other through this."

Franklin lifted his head and looked at them. His black eyes expressed an undefined something that could have been hope or resignation.

"We're going to find her. We just have to give things time to develop," Johana said.

Julieta finished organizing her things and glanced at the clock. To her surprise, it was almost nine at night and she hadn't called her sons yet. She picked up her cell phone and dialed, punching the buttons hard.

"Hi, let me talk to Jerónimo, please. I just got back to Bogotá."

"What's up!" her ex said, surprised. "Thanks for the warm greeting. I'm thrilled your trip went so well."

"Stop screwing around, Joaquín. I'm tired. Let me talk to Jerónimo."

"He's not back yet. He went to the movies with some friends."

"The movies? Goddamn it, he has school tomorrow."

"As soon as he gets in, I'll tell him you called to say hi."

"Let me talk to Samuel."

"Hang on, he might be asleep already . . . Sammy, your mom is on the phone!"

A long silence.

"He's asleep, Juli, do you want me to wake him up?"

"No, let him sleep. We'll talk tomorrow."

The rest of the week passed uneventfully: Julieta transcribing her notes, Johana waiting for news of her brother, and the boy stuck to the computer screen.

Soon after returning, she wrote to Zamarripa: "I've got everything, Daniel. I confirmed the story in French Guiana. There's enough material for a longform article just like you wanted: evangelical churches, pastors, crimes, illegal mining, jealousy, gunfire. I'm writing. Give me a deadline."

Zamarripa: "Sounds fantastic. Write at your own pace and send it to me at the end of the month. I'll read it and we'll schedule publication."

While Julieta was away, Johana reached out to Francisco, the priest at the church in San Andrés de Pisimbalá, telling him that the boy had been found safe and sound and was with them in Bogotá. He'd return home soon. She asked Francisco to let Franklin's grandparents know.

One afternoon, Johana called Jutsiñamuy to ask about Carlos Duván. He told her they'd opened a file for disappearance and kidnapping, and that it was pending.

"I'm terrified he's been killed," she said. "So many have died already."

"You know it's a dangerous region, honey," he said, "with the Úsugas and other paramilitary groups all over the place. It's awful to think that they've got your brother, but we can't throw in the towel till we find out what happened. Maybe it was the guerrillas that came for him instead, right? Until we find a body, we can't say he's dead."

"That's the problem, sir. We're not going to learn anything; we'll just be left hanging. But thanks for your help."

"You've got to have faith, Johanita."

"I try, sir, but I don't really believe in anything anymore."

Downcast, they said goodbye.

Three days later, the women were still waiting. Until . . .

It must have been after ten at night. Suddenly Julieta felt her phone vibrate and saw a message come in from an unknown number: *I need to talk to you. Please trust me.*

Who was it? The question was a rhetorical one, since from the start she knew it was from Pastor Fritz, or Arturo Silva—what should she be calling him now? She thought about how a person has several different selves, sometimes contradictory ones, over the course of a lifetime. She'd experienced it herself. Looking at her phone's screen, she felt her heart start pounding.

What's going on, friend?
Please walk to the gas station at the corner of 67th Street and 7th Avenue.
Right now?
Yes.

Julieta grabbed her purse and told Johana, "I'm going out to meet up with the pastor. He just sent me a message."

"Pastor Fritz?!" Johana stared at her, her expression a mix of curiosity and concern.

"Yes, but don't worry."

"Should I let Jutsiñamuy know?"

Julieta pondered a moment. "No," she said. "No. Not for now. Not a word."

"Be careful, boss."

"I need the end of this story, and he has it. Don't do anything."

"But if you don't come back or get in touch within an hour, I'm letting him know."

"All right, deal," Julieta said.

She went out.

The streets of Bogotá, always cold and lonely at that time of night.

The air was damp, and she had the sense that something very serious and irretrievable was about to happen. Julieta walked to 7th Avenue. The grass in the front gardens was wet from a recent shower. She felt dizzy, as if she were going to a secret tryst with an old lover. She was filled with a vague erotic tremble, and an intense fear. Reality so often takes us straight back to adolescence. The age of desires. Life's engine room. She crossed 5th Avenue—why was everything so deserted?

Suddenly, a black Suburban stopped next to her. The door opened.

"Get in, Julieta, it's me."

There he was, Pastor Fritz, or Arturo Silva. The intelligent, charismatic man, the boy abandoned on a park bench, the enamored adventurer who betrayed his business partner, the murderer who had his enemies killed in cold blood. With which of those selves was she about to have a conversation? Which one had said "It's me"? The pastor was in the back seat. An anonymous driver was at the wheel. She saw his deep, cavernous eyes. He was wearing black, like he did for his lectures. He smelled pleasantly of pine cologne.

"Where to, sir?" the driver asked.

"Head back down the ring road to 58th."

Julieta didn't dare ask questions. She just waited for him to talk, but Fritz kept quiet. Finally they parked in front of a house in the Chapinero neighborhood. A park was visible in the distance.

The pastor pointed out the window.

"That's the house my father went into. That's where he disappeared." It was a dark brick building with a tile roof.

"Did you ever find out what happened?" Julieta asked.

"The theory is that he was going to a secret meeting," he said, "because he was a member of the Communist Party. The police had sniffed them out, so as soon as he walked in, he was arrested and then disappeared. They probably tortured and executed him while he was thinking about how he'd left his young son all alone. Such suffering. His bones must be somewhere. I always imagine that his body was foully abused, chopped into several pieces, tossed to the dogs."

"And the snakes," Julieta said.

Fritz looked at her quizzically.

"You sketched those ghosts to describe your own death— by which I mean Arturo Silva Amador's."

The pastor's expression turned to surprise. "I see you're a good investigator; you know me somewhat better than other people."

"I have certain resources," Julieta said.

"I haven't stopped searching for my father my whole life," Fritz said. "Even today, forty years later, I'm still that little boy waiting on a park bench. Waiting tirelessly for his father—it's known as the 'Telemachus complex.' A few years back I bought the house across the street, and whenever I come to Bogotá I spend hours at the window, imagining that the door is going to open and I'll see him come out. You know? He left me a sandwich and an apple. I think about that every day. A simple chicken sandwich and an apple. The search for Christ is an attempt to alleviate sorrows, but especially to find the missing father. It's because this country is full of orphans that so many people fall to their knees at altars, in sacristies, and in churches. All of them longing for a father. If you aren't able to understand that, Julieta, you know nothing about the country you're living in."

"Everybody has their own grief scale," she said. "Mine is different. What about your mother? Did she die too?"

"She died when I was born," he said, "in childbirth."

There was an uncomfortable silence.

"And what are you going to do now?" Julieta asked.

"Egiswanda is waiting for me somewhere safe. It's not the first time we've had to run."

The pastor instructed the driver to start moving.

"Where to?" the driver asked.

"Head north on the ring road."

Julieta looked at him, uncertain what to do. She wanted to keep being there, to stay with the mysterious man a little while longer. She remembered Johana—had it been an hour yet?

"Sorry, Fritz, I need to send a message to my colleague. Trust me."

She pulled out a cell phone and texted Johana. "Don't do anything, everything's fine." Fritz didn't stop her.

The Suburban moved through the dark night to 94th Street, then took 7th Avenue to Usaquén, in northern Bogotá.

It paused for a moment, but the pastor said, "Keep going, don't stop. Head toward the highway."

The SUV drove down 127th, leaving the Bella Suiza neighborhood behind. The streets seemed lonelier even than the sleepwalking Suburban splashing through puddles and speeding past streets and avenues. On the northern highway, near the eighteenth-century Common Bridge, the driver stopped again.

"Don't stop. Turn around and head back into the city center," the voice said.

Seen from the dark Bogotá sky, the SUV's movements were tracing strange signs, but nobody was up there to decipher them.

They went back to the Monument of Heroes and drove up Chile Avenue to 7th Avenue; when they reached 26th Street, they turned off onto the road toward the airport.

"Don't stop, keep going," the voice said.

The SUV turned back north on 30th Avenue and drove down 94th Street to 7th Avenue. Then it kept going to 5th. Finally the voice spoke again.

"Can I take you home?" Fritz asked. "It's late."

"Of course you can, nothing's going to happen."

They pulled up in front of her building.

"What should I do to see you again?" Julieta asked.

"Don't do anything, friend. Just wait. When I'm sure of who I truly am, I'll call and let you know."

She felt sorry for him, longed to help him. He noticed.

"Don't worry about me," Fritz said. "I belong to another world where these things no longer cause pain. You stay in your world. One day I'll come look for you. I'm the running-away type, maybe so I can be alone, so I can scream. At the heavens, at the universe, hoping to one day receive an answer. I have to go now."

Julieta got out of the Suburban. Before walking to her front steps, she moved close to his window and said, "I was with Fabio in French Guiana. He told me his story."

Pastor Fritz didn't look surprised. Maybe he'd sensed it, or thought the meeting was inevitable.

"What happened to Clarice's son?" Julieta asked.

"He was stillborn," the pastor said. "We buried him on the banks of the Putumayo River." Then he added, "How's Fabio?"

"Good," Julieta said. "He's a wealthy businessman, but he's very lonely."

"He's tried to kill me three times now," Fritz said, "but I still miss him. He's the only real friend I ever had."

"Maybe the two of you are the same person," Julieta said. "That's why Clarice . . ." She decided not to finish the sentence, saying instead, "Go on. You've got a long trip ahead of you, and the sun's about to come up."

The pastor looked up at the sky, which was dense and dark.

"I don't think the sun will be coming up yet. Today the night will be long."

They hugged.

Then the Suburban disappeared into the misty, dismal nothingness that swaths the mountains.

EPILOGUE

A few days later, Julieta ran across an article in *El Espectador* about the restaurant murders in Cali. Gustavo the Umbrella was accused of carrying out the crimes, and there was speculation about the brains behind them. The article made no mention of Fritz Almayer or Fabio Henriquez.

She decided to call Jutsiñamuy.

"My dear friend," he said, "it's a pleasure to hear from you."

"I just saw your press conference in the papers."

"Yes," Jutsiñamuy said. "The negotiations with the Umbrella's lawyers are finished, but we're nailing down a few last things before revealing the full story."

Julieta felt bad not telling him about her meeting with the pastor, but she'd given her word. "I'll be on the lookout. Any word on Johana's brother?"

"Not a thing, and what's worse, just between us, I don't think that's going to change. How many community activists have been killed or disappeared this year alone? More than two hundred! But in any case I'm keeping my eyes peeled."

She'd barely hung up the phone when she heard Johana shriek on the other side of the office. "There's news, boss."

Berta, the FARC party administrator in Congress, had just called to report that they'd gotten a response from the comrade in Houston. For security reasons Berta was not authorized to provide that information over the phone. Johana asked if they could go to her office that same day, and the woman said yes. "In fact," she said, "it's very important that you come today." They decided they both should go, and brought the kid with them.

Johana had never been in the congressional offices in the capitol building, and she was amazed by the bustling corridors. Berta Noriega came down to meet them at the security checkpoint and helped them with the complicated entry process. Franklin was dressed in a blue sweater and white dress shirt, and his eyes swept over everything as though they were touching every detail.

"Is this the boy? So handsome! Hello, young man," Berta Noriega said.

Franklin smiled faintly.

"Come to my office, sweethearts, I've got something to show you."

They went to the end of a hallway, then up some stairs and down another hallway. They entered a large office full of people working. Berta showed them to her interior office and closed the door.

"As I told you, I sent all the information you gave me and the photos of the boy last week, and look. Here's the reply." She turned the computer monitor.

They read:

My name is Clara Martínez Neira. I was a fighter in the FARC's Manuel Cepeda Front. I had a son fourteen years ago who was born in a camp near Puracé; we gave him to his grandparents because of the challenges of the armed struggle. I never knew where he ended up. The father was the one who had the information, but he was killed in combat so I didn't know where to look for him. You say that the father's name was Justino Vanegas, but as you know, real names were forbidden, so I never knew it. When peacetime came, I searched for the boy, but I couldn't find the trail, so I started a new life.

I have now lived in Houston for a year and a half. I am married and have a daughter. I believe that the boy in the photo could be my son. I'd like to see him. I am arriving in Bogotá tomorrow at 4:30 P.M. on the American Airlines flight from Miami. I am attaching a recent photo. You can let the people who have him know, to facilitate the meeting. I will await information on the secure lodging you mentioned.

Sincerely, CMN

The next day, the three of them went to wait for her at El Dorado Airport. Before they left, Julieta selected a tasteful outfit from her younger son's wardrobe to dress the kid. She wanted him to look nice to meet his mother.

And there they were, expectant, outside the international arrivals area, watching anonymous crowds pass through in the ritual of greetings, tears, welcomes.

Suddenly, in the distance, they saw a woman nervously approaching the automatic doors. She was pushing a small suitcase.

Johana thought she recognized her and said, "That could be her over there."

Julieta peered at her. She was young, in good shape. She was dressed simply, in sneakers and jeans. She was still several meters from the doors. Franklin anxiously clutched the railing separating the people waiting from the arrivals area.

"That's her?" he asked, blinking rapidly, like wings beating. A tic that had shown up recently.

"Yes," Johana said. "That's her." She wiped away a tear with one finger and thought that at least the boy's story would have an ending. Not like the story of her and her brother, which was still an open wound.

The boy looked down, then back at the woman. He moved one leg from side to side. Saint Vitus's dance.

"Are you happy?" Julieta asked.

"I'm scared," he answered.

The boy gripped the railing. He seemed to want to leap. Julieta placed a hand on his shoulder. His eyes were two moons.

"Relax," she said. "She hasn't seen you yet."

Through the glass they saw her walk toward the automatic doors, which opened a little early as another group walked through.

Just then, Franklin jumped backward and bolted away through the crowd toward the airport exit.

"Franklin!" Johana shouted.

Julieta didn't know whether to run after him or wait.

The woman, hearing her son's name, craned her neck to see over the people. Maybe she managed to catch a brief glimpse of him, agile and strong. But she would have seen only the shape of him from behind, in the distance, charging through the crowd. Just a shadow racing out of the waiting area and fleeing toward the boulevard.